Even in Death
Professor Stokes, ME Book One

I0553983

Max Burger

Published by Rogue Phoenix Press, LLP
Copyright © 2023

ISBN: 978-1-62420-752-5

Credits
Cover Artist: Designs by Ms G

Editor: Christie L. Kraemer

Special thanks to the Office of the Coroner's Court, Dublin Ireland for the photo used on the cover

Printed in the United States of America

Dedication

To my Patient Wife, Christine, and the 1976 Class of the Royal College of Surgeons in Ireland.

Prologue

The car bombing in Dublin in 1974 was on a mild Friday afternoon in May. The bus drivers were on strike. The streets were packed with cars and crowded with people walking home from work. One bomb went off on Parnell Street, followed by another on Talbot Street, and the last on South Leinster Street. Twenty-six people died: men, women, and children. One person was decapitated, others had their body parts strewn on the streets and sidewalk, and a full-term pregnant woman and her unborn child were killed. Over 300 were injured. Another seven people were killed soon after when a bomb went off in the town of Monaghan.

Prologue

Chapter One

"Even in death, we are more than the sum of our parts." Professor Harold Stokes, State Pathologist for the City of Dublin stood over this last corpse after the terrible hectic few days, looking down at the examination table through the yellow, fluorescent light that made everything more hideous. He had argued bitterly with the administration that the old lights were more efficient. He could point them better, but the fluorescent tubes were cheaper, so end of story.

His new assistant, Samantha Monaghan, was hanging on every word. Younger than his daughter Aisling would have been, Samantha's almost identical long red hair might be a problem in the autopsy room, but he demurred for now.

"Here are the remains. Our job is to make a sum of these awful parts, God rest his soul, or not," he paused, staring at the body, then looking to Samantha.

"First, what do you see?" he asked.

Samantha hesitated. She was not unsure, but cautious. She had graduated with highest honors and had been encouraged at her young age to continue as a clinical registrar, but Professor Stokes' lectures had lured her into a fascination for causes of death and forensics. She did not want to disappoint the master.

Even the lowliest of the uniformed Garda could tell that the man in front of her was about 35, 168 cm, and 70 kg. He was dark-complexioned, with short dark curly hair, unusual for a Dubliner or even a farmer from the west or south, unlikely a descendant of the apocryphal survivors of the wreck of the Spanish Armada. Yet, he was decorated with a black rose on his right forearm, a symbol of the Irish resistance.

"He is not Irish," she said.

"You say that because he does not look like your average Paddy, but that doesn't necessarily mean he is less of one. Foreigners have been known to settle here. Think of Leopold Bloom, or did Irish prejudice deprive you of that painful experience of reading *Ulysses*?" He, like many Irish, including his own Anglo-Irish, felt that James Joyce was "up himself," more pretentious than he needed to be, but he had read it to form his own opinion.

"How do you know he is not Irish?"

She hesitated, now some uncertainty in her voice: "I can't be sure that he isn't, but I don't understand the black rose. Who would want to identify themselves so easily if they were in the IRA?"

"Have you used the magnifier on the tattoo?" he asked.

She pulled over the illuminated overhead magnifying glass and looked at it closer.

"It's smudged," she said, looking surprised at her own observation.

"Precisely." Stokes smiled. "Get the rubbing alcohol, but we need to photograph the evidence first." He pulled out the Polaroid camera, an acquisition that he accepted as part of new technology that would help his inquiries. He took several photos at several angles to make sure he would not miss anything or fail to document his observations.

They rubbed only a portion of the tattoo away with the alcohol, to demonstrate its temporary nature. Stokes carefully placed the photos into a folder marked with the case number since no name had been obtained on the decedent.

"Maybe he was not IRA, or Irish for that matter," Samantha said, defending her observation.

"We will know in due time."

Professor Stokes dictated his observations through the overhead microphone that was conveniently triggered by a foot switch, another innovation that he quite embraced, although he still appreciated the value of handwritten notes that could be amended after careful thought and retrospection.

Nevertheless, he did not have to write it twice since that saved time with all the pressure on him from the police to process more cases.

There were simply more homicides and suspicious deaths in Dublin these days. He could remember when this job was only part-time. He could work as a pathologist in the basement of St. Laurence's Hospital and instruct medical students on how to observe. His wife was still alive then, as was Aisling.

"How are you going to describe the wounds?" Samantha asked when he paused. He always paused on the dictation to make sure that he did not miss anything in the descriptions, to avoid extra work or make any mistakes that he would have to correct. Still, it was also an opportunity to let his mind wander, always a danger, losing focus.

"That will be difficult since he had so much exploratory surgery. You should get the surgical records so I can make some sense out of what they saw and did to compare."

"First, we should finish the superficial and external exam."

He pulled the sheet off the body and raised an eyebrow. This was not missed by Samantha. He was staring at the groin. She had avoided that until now.

"He's circumcised," she said, looking embarrassed. Stokes ignored the blush, gentleman that he was.

"Precisely. Another detail in support of your first hypothesis. Not a common practice here, so what next?"

"He's tanned, very tanned. Even if he was an outside worker, it is not the tan of an Irishman."

"Even if he were, it's more of a tan from a trip to Majorca than Kerry, especially at this time of the year."

Samantha stared at the body again, looking for more clues. The only identification the dead man had was destroyed or misplaced during his hospital stay, short that it was. Samantha opened up the file with the copies of the hospital reports. It was only a few pages, mostly the operative report since he died on the table. She read from the operative report:

"Exploratory laparotomy by vertical incision initially at the site of the open wound to remove probable shrapnel and determine the site of bleeding, extended from the upper abdomen at the level of the epigastrium to the symphysis pubis to allow for better examination and access. The abdominal aorta was clamped…"

"Just the details, Dr. Monaghan," Stokes interrupted. "Let's see what the incisions on the body tell us."

"There is a long, closed midline incision with a small wound lateral to it, still covered by surgical dressing," she said.

"Pretty amateur closure, don't you think?"

"I'd say he got one of the students to do the closure," she said, looking at the irregular and awkward knots.

"You have to learn sometime. Correct me if I'm wrong—was it Mr. Clary who attempted the surgery? I don't see many of his patients down here. He is a damn good surgeon. Not good enough for this poor soul."

Samantha looked at the first page. Clary's name was at the top. He was good, but brutal to females. She knew that firsthand, having been one of his students. He got his BTA (Been To America) but his conservative Irish attitudes had not lessened there; he was a little more arrogant since he got a consultant surgeon position at one of the best hospitals in Dublin.

"Yes, it was Clary," she said, not bothering to call him 'Mr.', the title surgeons received in the British Isles.

Stokes noted the disdain with which she mentioned his name but did not belabor the point.

"Time to turn the body over before we go any further in the internal examination. Are you ready?"

She was not. She thought she would have an assistant help, but it was already half four and most of the staff were gone for the day except for Johnston, the Diener, who was still cleaning up. She realized how dark it was outside when she looked at the low windows and felt slightly chilled at the prospect of being in the drafty old exam room with a corpse. This was what she had signed up for, so she nodded in agreement.

"I will push the back up and you can cross the legs over so he will turn on his own weight."

That was easier said than done. She had to flex his hips as well as his legs. She gave a small grunt, and he was turned over with a thump. The exam table was wide enough that there were no disastrous slides or falls. There had been, before Stokes, complaining about the lengthening and widening of the autopsied population, had insisted on new and bigger tables.

There was a larger surgical dressing on the lower posterior trunk than on the anterior which, depending on the kind of projectile, could have been the path of entry or exit.

"I'll remove the bandage but check the operative report. Was there any shrapnel removed?"

Samantha scanned the report. She shook her head and, realizing that Stokes was still carefully examining the wound with a light and magnifying lens, said "No, sir." He did not respond. Since she was not sure he heard her, she said again, more loudly, "No, sir."

"You needn't shout. I heard you the first time," he said, still examining the edges and the depth and irregularity.

"Curious," he murmured.

Samantha did not respond. She thought the comment was for himself and not her, and patiently waited for him to finish. She glanced down at the operative report and reviewed it quickly again, to make sure she did not overlook anything, still keeping one eye on Stokes, knowing he could suddenly demand her attention and comments.

"This is an exit wound, not an entry wound," Stokes said. "Samantha, come here," he motioned with one hand as he held the magnifying light in place. "You see how the tissue is bulging out, and the inner layers are closer together, and the outer layers more irregular and wider. This man was shot with a high-powered gun. He was not a victim of a car bomb. Did they find any debris in the body?"

Samantha reviewed the report again. "No, there was no shrapnel."

"How could there be no shrapnel in a car bomb casualty?" he asked himself aloud. Samantha knew enough not to answer, since he would often direct questions to himself, a long-ingrained vestige of the Socratic inquiry learned at Kilkenny College.

The silence was broken by a knock on the door, followed by the entry of Garda Detective Seamus Lanigan, who had not bothered to listen for an invitation to enter. He was a small man with a large voice, no functional manners, and a sense of superiority, especially over those with more education since he esteemed street smarts and common sense more than "book learning," as he called it. Stokes and Lanigan did not get along very well, but they were often forced to work together, as in this case.

Lanigan was eager to close this case and get his name in the papers. ~~As a result of the car~~ There was pressure from the government to come to some conclusions quickly as to the source of the car bombs that had gone off in the center of Dublin Friday last.

The other casualties had been accounted for by Stokes and his team of part-time pathologist assistants dragooned into taking on the job. The other victim's identities and circumstances were easy to explain and the preferred prompt burial, out of respect for the bereaved, had been accomplished. This last case was a John Doe, a strange cipher, even stranger with the discordance of this examination.

"Well Dr. Dracula, how is the digging going?" Lanigan asked. He associated Stokes with Bram Stoker, the Irish writer of the famous book, which only irritated Stokes, perhaps more of the confusion with Stokes and Stoker than the Dracula allusion. Lanigan did not like the Anglo-Irish, a pretentious lot in his estimation.

"We've got a problem here, Lanigan," replied Stokes, who did not address him by his official title, responding to his disrespect in kind. "Have you any more information about how this man was found?"

"How do you mean?" Lanigan cocked his head to the side, barely able to look at the body, his squeamishness poorly masked by his bravado.

"Were any fragments found near the body?" Stokes asked.

"There were plenty of fragments. It was a bloody car bomb."

"None near the body or in his clothes? According to the operative report, there were none in him," Stokes said.

"There was total pandemonium at the scene, with no one concerned with an investigation when casualties were carted away by any able-bodied citizens and the rescue departments. We combed the area and tried to catalog and place everything at the site as best we could. It was a bloody mess. There were no pieces found near him specifically. What are you getting at?"

"I can't say with any certainty now, but this man was shot, and if you check the debris again, you might find a spent bullet or at least a bullet hole in the car."

"Well, we haven't found any gelignite or any other explosives; not at that spot, at least."

"Yet, you found it in the other exploded cars?"

"Yes, we did, Sir," Lanigan responded in a more respectful and professional manner. It was a reflex when he was doing real police work.

"Was there more burning with this car?"

"Yes, that part was strange. According to the reports, he was pulled away before the car burst into flames, and then it exploded. A few brave souls pulled him away, God bless them," Lanigan said.

"Then get to the gas tank and find the bullet hole. You might even find the bullet," said Stokes, trying to move the investigation in the right direction, which was somewhat difficult with Lanigan eager to have his own solution.

"I'll get on it. Anything else you can tell me about your man?"

"Check any recent immigration reports since I don't think he is Irish. From his looks, especially the tan, he looks Mediterranean. No one gets that brown this time of the year in Dublin."

"I'll get back to you on that. Just keep diggin' " Lanigan smiled with a clever grin, nodded to Samantha in gracious acknowledgment of her existence, turned, and left.

"He isn't a very pleasant man," sniffed Samantha, who had not had much to do with the Gardai or detectives before this. She was more likely to use the word "pigs" to describe them if she were with her student protest friends. She was too cautious to use the term around Professor Stokes.

"A bit rough around the edges, despite his position, but one gets used to that, having to deal with the police," Stokes said. "We better get on with the exam tomorrow. This will be complicated, and it will be detailed. It is getting too late to be focused on properly," Stokes said.

It was dark outside. His housemaid would berate him if he came late for tea. He was a bit peckish. He was old enough to be more sensitive to his limitations and needs and, despite the police and the press, the dead can wait.

"This room will have to be locked. We can leave the body in the cooler, and I will put a lock on its door as well. None of this can be tampered with and, of course, there can be no word spoken of what we have observed here. You have been officially deputized as a representative of the local constabulary. Impressive on your first month," he smiled.

Samantha helped him roll the body into the compartment. The door was closed and locked. Stokes looked around to check for any loose notes or papers, removed the tape from the dictation machine, locked it and the surgical files in a drawer in his desk, and put out the lights. He pulled the door shut and locked it with his key. No one else had keys but Samantha and the Diener, Mr. Johnston, known as 'old Jack' (but never to his face). He was trustworthy, having worked there longer than Stokes; in fact, old Jack had warned him about confidentiality when he had first arrived as a medical student.

Stokes escorted Samantha down the dark corridors, past the watchman's vacant post, and out into the rainy street.

"Get plenty of rest tonight. We will have a busy day tomorrow and, once we start, we will not finish until the task is done."

"Good night, Professor," Samantha replied, eager to be cagey about the case with her friends at the pub before going home. She knew enough to say nothing revealing but could not stop herself boasting about her new job, and the awesome responsibility she had. Her old classmates, now Junior doctors at various hospitals, would 'rag' her about "caring for the dead" and describe their grueling days. She would put up with her friends' chiding and respond with matching crocodile tears for their vicissitudes.

Stokes took the bus to Terenure Road, thankful that the rain was only a fine mist in the cold as he got off nearly in front of his house, a townhouse with a short flight of steep steps to the door. As he struggled with the key while holding his briefcase, Mrs. Kelly, his housemaid, pulled the door open. He almost fell in, muttering loudly that he was almost there, as he had done countless times before and, as she had, scolding him for not ringing the bell.

"I didn't want to wait," he said.

"Tea is ready when you are," she informed him brusquely, turned, and left him standing there in his 'Mac' and with his briefcase. He hung up his hat and coat, put down his briefcase, and washed up, looking around the empty house quickly, reminded of the quiet only disturbed by Mrs. Kelly listening to the Angelus and then the Irish language news on the wireless. He tolerated the noise because it was only ten minutes. She, mercifully, turned the wireless off afterward.

The quiet of the dining room was interrupted only by the soft clatter of the knife and fork on the plate. Stokes could hear his own chewing, which was not loud. He did not notice the food as he ate, a slice of ham and some mashed potatoes with a portion of overcooked broccoli. He was suddenly aware of the food when he chewed on the limp stalks and reminded himself that he had spoken to Mrs. Kelly several times about overcooking vegetables. He finished his meal in contemplation. He would not often think about his work when he came home, preferred reading and doing some research on ancient diseases that may have beset Ireland, the Irish descriptions of the maladies lost in ignorance and obscurity and confounded by translations...

Chapter Two

There was no more a conundrum than the body lying in the morgue, thought Stokes. Who was this person who, injured in chaos and confusion, was not in the wrong place at the wrong time, but in the right place at the right time to obscure the circumstances of his death? Had he presented as a single victim of a gunshot wound instead of a casualty in a crowd of casualties, there would have been a proper inquiry. Detective Lanigan was an unlikely delegate to the case—he usually handled crime-related homicides and despite his pretensions, usually agreed with Stokes' assessments without hesitation, being basically lazy but always hypercritical. Who had assigned him to this particular casualty since he had not shown his face at the other victims' examinations?

Stokes got up quickly and announced, "I am going out," to Mrs. Kelly, who was barely within earshot, but not unaccustomed to sudden changes in schedules, and responded with

"Heavier rain tonight, Professor. Don't forget your umbrella," as she barely caught him closing the door behind him. She gathered the dishes to finish her cleaning up.

It was raining harder as Stokes hurried down the stairs to the new bus shelter on the road. There was no chance of a cab on Terenure Road, so he waited for the next bus, which would take longer since most buses were on their way out of town rather than back in. They were always slower in the rain. With this, he was patient, as he was with most Irish systems, characterizing the Irish preference for a slower and easier life than the urgency of London or New York. He liked neither, having visited both places at conferences and would never consider them for pleasure, and now was afraid to travel anywhere outside of Dublin.

He waited 10 minutes. There was no sign of a bus. It gave him time to think, but the urgency that had prompted him to get up from his dining room table made him more anxious. Perhaps, he did need to get back to the morgue quicker. He was concerned about Johnston leaving early, the front door watchman not at his post, and more suspicious of the unexpected visit of Lanigan. He was about to run back to his house and call for a cab when the bus pulled up. It was not crowded. He took a seat and watched as the rain came down heavier. He would have preferred to be at home, but all these loose ends niggled at him. He felt a little guilty that he had not asked Samantha to stay so she could experience the pleasure of the hunt, but he was already feeling solicitous about his new apprentice. He would just review the documents first, and then examine the body only if he needed to, since he knew that once he started, he would not stop until the job was done.

He rushed in the rain to the door of the office. It was still unguarded but locked. He fumbled for the key and pulled it out. The lock opened with a little jiggle like it had been loosened. That was curious since he had just left. It felt tighter then. He looked around. There was still no sign of the watchman. He was relatively new, but there was no excuse for him to be away from his post for so long. Stokes made a note to complain to his supervisor in the morning. He pushed the button on the light timer which would allow him to get down the stairs in ample time before it turned off, all in the interest of saving money. Commendable, but inconvenient, thought Stokes.

As he got to the bottom of the stairs, he noted that the door to the morgue was open, the very door that more than an hour or so before he had locked himself. The locked compartment that held John Doe's body was wide open. The compartment was empty.

"Hello, is anyone there?" he called, switching on the light, and waiting for the fluorescents to flicker on. He heard a thumping noise down the hall and switched those lights on as well at the bank of switches that had been inconveniently placed just down from the door, so you couldn't see to put on the lights without knowing where they were. Lazy planning or none at all, he thought. As he got closer to the cleaner's closet, the thumping got louder.

"Hello," he called, louder this time. The thump at the cleaner's closet was more regular. He pulled at the knob. It opened easily. There was the watchman, trussed up like a Christmas goose. Stokes pulled his gag off.

"Get me bloody out of here," he said.

Stokes pulled out his penknife and cut the duct tape that bound him.

"Who did this?" Stokes asked, as the watchman rubbed his wrists to get the circulation back and stretch his fingers.

"Dunno," he answered in his thick North Dublin accent. "They wore Balaclavas and didn't say much. They had some kind of accent like, couldn't make out, not English or Irish anyways."

"What did they want?"

"They didn't say. They just got me from behind and bound me up. At least they didn't hit me or threaten me. I think they knew what they were coming for and where to find it."

"Could you hear any more sounds?" Stokes asked.

"Yah, it sounded like they used the morgue cart and pushed it down the hall to the back door. I heard the door slam, and then there was no sound at all until you came. Thanks be to God for that."

Stokes walked to the back entrance door and had to push it open with some force. The morgue cart rolled down the back alley in the rain. He heard muffled sounds over the sound of cars swishing on the wet road, looked towards the back wall, and saw a dark blob moving. He ran over and discovered old Jack bound and gagged like the watchman, soaked through like he had been there for a while. He pulled the gag off. Jack could barely talk for the chattering of his teeth.

Stokes undid the ropes and helped him up as he was shivering with the effort to stand.

"Take it easy, Mr. Johnston, you're a bit hypothermic, so go slow," Stokes cautioned, holding the door open as he guided old Jack in with the help of the watchman.

"That cart is soaked and needs to come in," old Jack said slowly, still taking his responsibilities very seriously, Stokes noted.

"Get the cart, lock that door, and call the Gardai," Stokes commanded the watchman, who, whether he was still suffering from being bound up or was just generally slow, was not contributing much spontaneously. Stokes let Mr. Johnston slump to the floor with his own weight as the automatic light in the hallway went annoyingly off. Stokes had to feel his way down the dark corridor to the switch at the door to turn it back on.

Damn stingy bureaucrat, he thought of the Minister of Justice, cutting costs since it was only the dead that lived here. Stokes hit the button hard.

"Did you see any more than the watchman?" he asked Johnston.

"No, sir, they grabbed me as I was leaving down the back way, not a word as they held me and grabbed my keys, and then left me to freeze in the rain."

"Did you see their faces?"

"No, sir, heads covered in Balaclavas they were, and they were silent, like commandos, just pointing and waiting in the hallway in the dark until you left, sir, like real military."

"You mean they were here while we were still here?"

"I believe so, sir. They knew exactly what they wanted and passed me right by when they rolled the cart out to the van parked at the back entrance after I heard you leave."

The Gardai arrived just then, Lanigan with them.

The quiet inquiry that had been conducted by Stokes was destroyed by the pandemonium of multiple policemen scouring the area for clues and evidence, badgering the assaulted victims with questions they had already answered.

"Can you just have your men calm down for a moment or two while we have a word?" Stokes demanded of Lanigan, pulling him aside.

"What brought you back here, Dr. Stokes?" asked Lanigan, preempting Stokes' tirade.

Stokes took a deep breath to establish a medically authoritative equanimity. He could not bite the bait this fool was dangling, he warned himself.

"There were some questions I had about the records that I needed to review before I started the autopsy tomorrow."

"Well, we have a lot more questions now, haven't we, Professor?" asked Lanigan.

"Well, you can ask Mr. Johnston and the watchman again. I think this was a professional attack. Whoever they were, they didn't want us to know who John Doe was and how he died. I will bet there was at least another bullet in that body that was not found, and that he had something to do with the bombing, but not what we think," Stokes said, trying to make it as clear to Lanigan that this murder was out of his scope and Lanigan would need help.

"You need to contact G2 (Irish Secret Service division) since these men were not Irish or British or paramilitaries. They had foreign accents and were interested in getting rid of the body and the evidence and not wreaking revenge. Have your men do their forensics, see to it that Johnston gets warmed up, then meet me here tomorrow with the G2 men," Stokes said, glancing over at his still locked drawer. He did not discuss that with Lanigan as yet, perhaps never at all.

"I expect to see your full report tomorrow since the office of the Medical Examiner is my domain. You report to me in this instance," Stokes said, put his hat and coat on, and left the office after leaving a kind word of encouragement and support for Mr. Johnston who was still shivering but sipping a cup of tea.

When he got home, Stokes rang Samantha and advised her to come into the office earlier, about half seven. She did not groan out loud, but made a face and agreed, of course, though she had hoped for a late night with friends. Stokes hung up the phone. He pulled out a yellow legal pad and began to write some notes of what had transpired, and what he could recall of the initial findings on autopsy. This was all unofficial, more of a way to organize his thoughts and plan for the next day. It allowed him to better recall the details he had only casually observed with a focus on salient aspects of the case:

1. He had observed there were two entry wounds, very close together, probably made by a marksman's rifle, rare outside of military groups in Ireland. The bullet wounds were too close for a poor shooter.

2. The body was facing away from the car and down the street. From the angle of entry of the shots their exit was straight.

3. There were no burns on the body, so the car exploded at some time after the shots, enough time for the body to be dragged away

4. The fake tattoo was part of a disguise to the IRA, probably Provos, the violently radical faction. Was John Doe working against them rather than for them? His tan and circumcision probably made him Mediterranean, perhaps Arab, or Israeli.

Stokes mulled over these details for a brief while, then looked out the window of his bedroom which faced the street. He expected to see, precisely at this time of the night, the sudden opening of the door to the house directly across the street and the exit of the Orthodox Jews in black hats and long black coats to do their evening trip in their van to wherever they went each night, except on Fridays.

He was told by Mrs. Kelly, who knew about everything on the street, that they were dealers in kosher meat, and they made deliveries each night for the local butchers and shipped some of the meat to Israel and other places in Europe. But they did not appear that night and the van was gone. It was not Friday. He washed and brushed his teeth and changed into his bedclothes. He went to bed and read a bit of a treatise on Blefed, the Yellow Plague of 543 AD in Ireland, which put him right to sleep.

Chapter Three

It was a clear morning although it was still dark when Stokes took the bus to work, early enough that he avoided the rush hour and could get a seat. The night watchman was still at his post at the entrance to the Medical Examiner's offices and he reported nothing suspicious, having been alerted. A Garda stood outside, a pretty useless waste of manpower, Stokes thought, but now that this was a crime scene itself, he accepted the precautions taken. Stokes identified himself as the Medical Examiner, corroborated by the watchman. He went through the already open doors to his office. Samantha was already in the morgue, looking over the papers she had retrieved from the drawer which she had unlocked with her own key. There had to be some trust, Stokes thought to himself, hoping that no one else knew about the vital papers she was reviewing, even Lanigan.

"Go make two copies of all these records now and, as best as you can, of the Polaroids, and bring them all back. We need to review these before Lanigan gets here."

He quickly checked around the room to see if there was anything else out of place. As far as he noted, there wasn't.

Samantha was back quickly with the copies. He took the originals and reviewed them again, especially the photos. There was nothing he could see that showed anything distinctive, but because they were black and white, the contrasts were more prominent. One of the Polaroids stood out. In the mid-chest, there was a faint outline he had not noticed on the color photos or when he had been examining the corpse. There was a vague outline of a pale Star of David in the otherwise lightly tanned skin.

"Samantha, come here. Do you see what I see?" He asked, waving the Polaroid copy in front of her.

She stared at it and then smiled. "It is a Star of David. So, he is

Israeli."

"Perhaps, or an Arab, even Palestinian, posing as an Irishman today and an Israeli yesterday. What is an Israeli or Palestinian doing on Talbot Street with a bullet or two in the gut?"

"The Provos have been talking with the PLO. Some say there have been some guns and training exchanged," Samantha said, just having heard some speculation from her friends at the pub the other night. There was a fierce debate about who had placed the bombs and some people even speculated the Provos did it to stop the Sunningdale agreement from being approved, by provoking more Irish resentment for a shared government between the Republic and Ulster. There was equal resentment by some Ulster Unionists and other Northern Irish paramilitary factions like the Ulster Volunteer Force (UVF) that this agreement would be a capitulation to the IRA.

"Let's go with Israeli for now," Stokes proposed, an admirer of Occam's razor, even when using a scalpel. "We need to put away the Polaroid chest views and hold these in confidence until we can get more information," he said, locking the pictures away in his drawer.

"Isn't that withholding evidence?" Samantha asked.

"Whoever snatched the body is withholding the evidence. We need to find the culprits. No one is to be trusted, especially the investigators," Stokes said.

Samantha nodded and was going to ask a question, but held her breath as Lanigan and his men, accompanied by a tall, serious-looking man in a tan raincoat, a la the US Secret Service, entered the exam room unannounced. Lanigan did his boisterous "Hello Dr. Dracula" which caused a little snigger from his colleagues, but no response from the "G2" man, who carefully looked around and waited for Lanigan to get serious and introduce him. Stokes waited patiently, ignoring the jibe.

"This is Detective Sergeant Niall Curran, from the Secret Service, Professor Stokes, and he will be helping with the investigation. I expect he will be asking more questions on the same evidence you have already presented to me," said Lanigan, now conducting himself seriously.

"Dr. Monaghan prepared these Xerox copies of the records and the Polaroids for you, so at least you have something to go on," he said, motioning to Samantha who handed out the two packets to Lanigan and Curran.

Lanigan barely glanced at the copies, but Curran looked at them, carefully reading rather than just gleaning the salient points. Stokes watched the two, the Gardai just stood around, some looking uncomfortably at their surroundings, squeamish.

Lanigan broke the silence: "Would you ever make yourselves useful and check the area for any more evidence of who broke in here?" he commanded the Gardai, who had respectfully been waiting for more orders so they wouldn't disturb the detectives.

"Just like bloody children they are," Lanigan waved his arms as a weak apology for his temper.

"They were merely waiting for direction since you are supposed to be their leader," Stokes said.

"Well then, do we have any more information about the John Doe?" Lanigan asked, waving his Xerox copies, waiting for answers rather than providing any insight into the documents he was holding.

"The operative report, which I reviewed again, as well as the Polaroids, reveals he had two wounds that ultimately killed him, both gunshots, close to each other and at some distance, since there were no powder marks on him. The surgery was unsuccessful, as far as I can surmise, the bullets had nicked the aorta and the celiac artery, causing profuse and fatal bleeding," Stokes answered, repeating much of what was obvious, if Lanigan had read the report.

Curran barely raised an eyebrow during this recitation, then asked in his Ulster accent, "Do you have the original Polaroids?"

"Yes, here they are, Detective Sergeant Curran," offered Samantha, startled by the thick Ulster accent in a Dublin policeman.

"Thank you, sometimes color helps," he said, looking over the Polaroids one by one.

"Awfully dark, isn't he?" he said, looking up at Stokes.

"Yes, even with the post-mortem pallor and bleeding, he doesn't look very Irish," Stokes agreed, not offering any more information.

"Did anyone discern the accent of these intruders?" Detective Sergeant Curran asked.

"No," Lanigan piped in. "The watchman and the morgue assistant could not make it out since the culprits did not say much. The two were terrified that they were in mortal danger."

"As well they were. We are treating this removal of the body as part of a terrorist act. We think it was the PLO. They have been working with the Provos. This swarthy fella looks like an Arab to me," Curran advised anyone who was listening, waving the Polaroids around as proof.

Stokes was not sure which of these two were the greater fools. He was suspicious of both of them. Lanigan had arrived too quickly after the body had been transferred to the morgue to have been assigned this as a routine homicide, especially from his previous and usual slothful and sloppy habits. Curran had already jumped to some conclusions which fit nicely into a convenient explanation—it would take the pressure off the government in preparation for an inquiry that would be punctuated with blame and accusation between the political and warring parties. Stokes wanted to recover the body, make his report, and otherwise stay out of it, but he could not ignore the possibility that these same bombers might be involved in his wife and daughter's death in the bombings in Dublin two years before.

"And what have you boys found in the way of clues?" Lanigan shouted at the uniformed men who had returned with some plastic bags of what must have been "evidence."

"Not much, Detective Sergeant," replied the senior Garda, holding up some pieces of rope left in the back alley, shoe covers, as well as balaclavas found disposed of in the trash.

"Let's take them back to the lab for prints and see if we can find anything else about this that makes sense," Lanigan said. The Gardai dutifully left with their evidence in custody.

"Why would anyone want to steal the body?" Lanigan asked himself out loud.

"He was not an innocent bystander. There was information there that someone did not want others to know. We need to know who the thieves were so we can find out what they are covering up. This is a state affair until otherwise informed. Can you all get that?" said Curran, exasperated at Lanigan's thickness, worried that he was going to say more than he should to the wrong people.

Stokes did not need to say anything. Between Lanigan and Curran, there was enough friction and confusion that all he needed was to make some inquiries in the right quarters and he might get the answers he needed. It was an opportunity for him to identify or connect the suspects in his own family's murders. He would use these officers of the law first, letting them uncover the answers that he had been searching for over the past two years, since they had access, and he did not. He had tried to ask Irish authorities about any leads in the November 26, 1972 Film Centre Cinema bombing and the others that followed in December and January 1973. He had gotten replies that ranged from true ignorance to defensiveness, or obfuscation. British authorities were worse, questioning the effrontery of an Irishman, Protestant or not, to meddle in the affairs of the crown, especially Loyalists in Ulster. But even among the scant reports he could get, it was unusual that the Cinema bombing where his wife and daughter died was ascribed to an IRA attack and that the others were by paramilitary loyalists, either the UDA (Ulster Defense Association) or the more extreme UVF.

"Are you going to take these Polaroids to compare with your mugshots?" Stokes asked Lanigan.

"We will, a tedious job, but one of the staff who is good at faces will look through the possible culprits. You did say he had a Black Rose tattoo?"

"Yes," replied Stokes, pointing to the photo in his hand, but did not offer the information that the tattoo was fake. Lanigan looked at his copy, as did Curran.

"That would point to IRA suspects and narrow down the search," Lanigan said.

"But not if he was a swarthy foreigner, as he looks in these photos," Curran countered.

"Perhaps I can come down to your offices to help. I saw him from more angles than this one photo I gave you but did not expect to have him snatched from further investigation," Stokes said.

"That would be above my security level, but this is a high-priority case, so I will contact my chief," Curran said.

"I can do the same with my chief," Lanigan said, invoking a sense of cooperation which was probably not necessary since Stokes could have gotten permission directly, being the Medical Examiner.

"Thanks to the both of you. Anything I can do to help," he said, not breaching the ulterior motive he had of closure in the deaths of his family. He turned to Samantha.

"Please complete the report as much as you can so that we can file something as soon as possible. You can review and summarize the operative reports to correlate our findings and the Polaroids. I will review the report when I return from the police station with Detective Lanigan," he said.

"When do you think you can get that clearance for me, Detective Curran?" asked Stokes.

"Probably tomorrow," Curran answered. "I will have to look at these photos myself to compare them to our rogue's gallery which I'm sure will take the better part of a day. I will ring your office when you can come."

"Could you be so kind as to review the files of the Cinema bombing two years ago to see if any of the suspects could be involved with this case as well, especially any photos of suspects?" asked Stokes.

"I can, but this was unlikely to be IRA as opposed to the UVF," said Curran with a raised eyebrow, surprised at the suggestion of a possible link.

"Humor me. There are too many things about this case that don't fit," Stokes said, escorting Curran to the door as Lanigan tagged along.

It was a short ride to the police station with Lanigan driving. Lanigan ignored most of the traffic lights and used his siren frequently, skirting the edge of the traffic, as he did most of the law. Stokes was surprised at his willingness to cooperate, but accepted the help. He would have to see if he could reciprocate somewhere along the way.

When they got to the station, Lanigan took Stokes down to the basement where the mug shots were stored. It was less a matter of more security than of use since they weren't needed as often and took up too much active workspace upstairs. Stokes was used to dwelling in poorly lit spaces, the morgue being another dark venue of crime investigation.

He resolutely looked through a pile of albums of possible UVF and IRA culprits, but of course, these were the ones who were caught. Since it was a short list and had to be contemporaneous, it did not take long to rule out that none of the suspects resembled his corpse.

"Do you have any shots of any suspects from the 1972 bombings in Dublin?" Stokes asked.

"What do you think we are, bloody Interpol? They would come from another pile that's stored at the annex, since we rarely get involved in that stuff—too much politics." He was referring to the frequent suspicions that many of the people who ran the country, or wished to, still had strong ties with the IRA, although they disclaimed and condemned violence. There was one loud minister, O'Neill, in the opposition party, Fianna Fail, who in 1970 had been accused of obtaining guns for the IRA in the North with the help of associates in the government. He had not been caught with enough evidence or witnesses, so was relegated to the back benches. He still had powerful friends in the party.

If Lanigan was involved in this cover-up on John Doe, he was either very cagey or very ignorant of the details. Stokes followed Lanigan down some back passageways and out the back door to a smaller building that looked even more overlooked than the basement. The small windows had grates on them, and it looked more like a jail than an administrative office. Lanigan pulled out a ring of keys. He opened the door that may have had cobwebs on them, though it was too dark to see, even in the gray daylight. Lanigan fished around for the chain on the one bare overhead light which revealed a table full of cardboard files and more old metal file cabinets against the wall with pale labels in the little slots below the handles. Nothing was locked beyond that front door.

"This is where bad clerks and cops go to die. No one would notice for a few days. All the better since they would already be in purgatory," Lanigan quipped. He went over to another table with a relatively new set of files that were labeled "IRA suspects."

"Here you are, Professor, you can peruse these to your heart's content, but I would just try the ones filed in the last 5 years. The rest are either dead, in jail, or exonerated, or worse, emigrated."

"Thank you, Detective, I will try to make myself comfortable," Stokes said, pulling up a chair that was dusty and creaked as he sat down after dusting it off.

He was not the least bit comfortable, and it was not the chair. It had taken him more than two years to get to a point to even consider looking for his family's killers; the Dublin bombers at the Irish Film Centre on Burgh Quay in 1972, a fluke because the bombs were on timers. They were set to go off, according to the forensics, after the film was over, but the reel had broken, and it took at least half an hour to get a replacement. Stokes's daughter called when the film was interrupted, to say they would be late back since the late-night movie was later still, but not to worry. That was the last that he heard from his daughter.

There were dead and injured as a result of those leaving the theater that late night in November. There were other bombings around that time, and all were intended to affect the voting on more restrictions and security in relation to the IRA. The awful vision of his dead daughter and wife amidst the rubble had disturbed his sleep every night since then.

It was good that the room was cool since he was sweating and slightly tremulous. He was sad and angry and almost overwhelmed. His outward coolness in circumstances of blood and gore came from years of experience of other person's tragedies. He had often waited until after he was out of the autopsy room to get the background stories of the casualties so that his objectivity would not be lost at the examination and his emotions would not be loosed again. He would commonly review his notes and only then return to the autopsy room and review the details with the perspective of the full story. When all the parts of bodies had come in that day of the last bombings, his anger and sorrow came back. He had muddled through somehow, pressed on with the job at hand, even overseeing the autopsies on the pregnant mother and the babies, but it had been hard.

He had not been able to do this with his wife and daughter and he had forced himself to recuse himself from any judgments or observations at the time. They were examined right on the exam tables in Dublin, which was quite appropriate. He knew the competence of the coroner-appointed pathologist in his stead, whom he had worked with before, which was slight consolation.

He took some deep breaths and his sweats and tremors decreased. He needed to focus on these details which finally, under these circumstances, at a time where the pain was decreased, he could probe for facts that could help him know who the killer or killers might be.

He was looking at files that were clearly labeled and well organized despite the poor lighting. It seemed that the last subordinate "offender" who had been exiled here to sort the photos had taken the job to heart and tried to make the best of it. He opened each Manila folder, flipped through the identifying pages, and quickly placed them in a pile. Lanigan smoked a cigarette despite the obvious fire danger and poor ventilation. Stokes did not try to stop him. This encouraged him to work faster so he could get out of there quicker, his occasional coughing episodes ignored by Lanigan.

Stokes sat up when he came across a file labeled PLO. There were shots of people who had known associations with Libya's Qaddafi and Palestine's Arafat. Some were Irish and some were clearly Middle Eastern, but none looked anything like John Doe. As he opened one of the folders, a loose photograph fell onto the floor. Most of the photos were copies of the copies that were there in the file, but this photo had been stuck on the page with a poor glue that did not stick as well onto the glossy copier page. The information on the page described a Palestinian who had not been captured but had some strong connections with the IRA. Lanigan, who had been looking over Stokes's shoulder when he wasn't smoking another cigarette, picked the photo up from the floor and handed it back to Stokes. He looked at the face of the man that was labeled Suleiman bin Daoud and it was nothing like John Doe.

"Someone has not been doing their job properly to have the photo unglued and loose. I will have to talk to them," said Lanigan. He had not said a word until he saw Stokes sit up when he opened and read the PLO file.

"Most of them have not been captured or seen again," he explained. "It's as if they were told to go dark since they were almost caught when the guns they smuggled were found up North. Someone tipped them off, even though we had someone on the inside who let us know who they were. No one has seen that one since he was spotted trading guns in 1970."

"What about the Dublin Film Centre bombing? Was that here too?" Stokes coughed, irritated by the dusty piles of folders and the cigarettes.

"No. We were involved with that, but no one ever caught them. It may have been the IRA or the UVF, but none of them was found in the Republic. Some say the Brits had their hand in it as well with the Littlejohn brothers —they said they were MI6 double agents with the IRA, but we couldn't pursue it up North. We respect the border, for whatever that is worth," he sniffed.

"Were any of the smugglers marksmen?" Stokes asked, picking up the PLO file again, looking carefully at each photo to make sure that John Doe was not one of them with their picture taken at a bad angle. These shots were mostly amateur or newspaper photos and four or more years old.

"Not that we know of, but we can check if you think they may have had something to do with your man," offered Lanigan. He walked over to a cabinet that had more files and pulled out the IRA file to crosscheck the names with the pictures. This was harder than it looked because nothing was organized. Lanigan did a mental note to "punish" someone to get the job done, at least for the past five years. Stokes went through the files which were mostly alphabetized. He found a few that described the member's background which might indicate military training.

"So, you think it was one of these Gobshites that did him in?" Lanigan asked, fanning out the folders like a pack of cards in a magic trick.

"Perhaps, since that was a sharpshooter who did the damage, unless he was incredibly lucky, the two wounds being so close together," Stokes replied.

"But why did he shoot him in the stomach instead of the head, and why did he do it?"

"He may have been trying to stop the bombing and shooting him in the abdomen would have obscured an assassination when most of the car bomb victims were being taken to Casualties in the confusion. He was facing away from the cars, not at them, possibly looking down the street at his killer."

Stokes looked at the other photos in the IRA folder and did not see his victim, but some of the descriptions indicated they may have been involved in the 1972 Dublin bombings, despite Lanigan's ignorance or laziness, and if they were IRA from the North, his possible "neutrality." Since there was no value of this file to Lanigan except to focus on possible subjects in this case, he ignored much of the detail, but was curious as to why Stokes was so interested in sifting through the Film Theatre files.

"Weren't your wife and daughter killed at the Cinema bombing in Dublin?" Lanigan asked, already knowing the answer.

"Yes, they were, and no one has found the culprits," replied Stokes, as coldly as he could, stifling any emotion, even resentment at the personal and impertinent query. Everyone who knew him was aware.

"Please give me a moment to review these documents. I never finished the inquiry and the two could be related," Stokes continued, attempting to remain cool.

Lanigan knew when to back off and gave Stokes a little space as he lit another cigarette. He watched in silence as Stokes looked through the pictures and the descriptions, put a few of the papers in two piles, one of IRA members possibly associated with the 1972 bombings and the other of UVF members who were more likely to have been involved in the 1972 and the 1974 Dublin bombings. Lanigan was on the clock, so it didn't matter to him. If Stokes made his job a little easier, that was fine, as long as he got some leads.

"Are you about done yet?" Lanigan finally asked.

"Yes, I think so. Can we get more on these people?" He asked, pointing to the piles he had collected. "Have they been sighted recently? Have they been in the Republic?"

"Unless they have committed a crime or been consorting with known criminals recently, probably not, but your man Curran might be able to give you more answers," Lanigan replied.

"Well, give it a try and keep these out for quick reference if you can. I will be back, but I have a lecture to give to some medical students. I am running late, so if you could be so kind as to give me a lift back to the morgue, I would appreciate it," Stokes asked politely.

"Of course, I need to get back that way to ask the watchman and the Diener Johnston, as you call him, some more questions since we still don't have a clue as to who these people were who absconded with the corpse," said Lanigan, smiling because he used the word 'absconded' and a new word, 'Diener,' a morgue attendant.

With the help of Lanigan's complete lack of concern with the traffic laws, Stokes was quickly back at the morgue where a gaggle of students in white coats was sitting in the auditorium, patiently waiting for his to arrival. Stokes glanced at his pocket watch which he pulled from his waistcoat and saw he had some time to check in with Samantha, so he quickly walked past the room and down the stairs to the morgue.

Lanigan found Mr. Johnston. They sat down to clear up and obtain more details.

"Has Curran returned to follow up with you?" Stokes asked Samantha.

"No, Professor, but the Gardai got every scrap of evidence they thought was relevant, but I only gave them Xeroxes of any of the documents we have. She looked around then whispered, "I did not tell them about the dictation." She smiled.

"Good girl. I will testify to your loyalty when you are questioned about withholding evidence," replied Stokes with a stern face.

Samantha frowned.

"No fear. Just joking. You are serving the truth which is very shrouded at this point," he smiled reassuringly. "I am off to give the lecture so be prepared for the "white cloud" of students afterward. Be kind. You were once a student."

As he stood at the podium, he looked at the fresh young faces and thought again about his daughter, her enthusiasm for learning and her plans, before she died, to start Medical School that fall. All blown away that late night in the theatre in Dublin. He gave his lecture as an introduction to the students on the need for them to learn everything they could about anatomy, physiology, and chemistry, which were the tools they would need to get to forensic pathology. He gave them some examples of cases he had reported. He never considered he was an investigator since he merely observed and reported, but there was enough of the morbid thrill of crimes and detection in the details that encouraged, if not titillated, the students, like the curious case of the girl in the bathtub or the accidental suicide, which always got their attention. He was well beyond titillation. It was a job he considered with respect and gravitas.

"Never consider your position as a physician in this or any field you choose without remembering that these are people whose lives meant something to them and their loved ones," he always concluded at the end of the lecture. They all streamed out, except for one sad-looking student who, he expected, would need to talk.

"I was there in the operating theater when they brought one of the casualties in. I was wondering if you knew how he died," the young man asked.

"What year are you in?"

"First clinicals, sir, I was assigned to St. Laurence."

"Tell me the history so that I can try to determine whom you are speaking about."

The student paused for a moment and then began, nervous in front of the Professor and anxious to tell the story. He seemed afraid he might miss some essential detail.

"When the bombs went off, some of us were napping, waiting for tea. Then we heard the thumps, like heavy boots being dropped on the floor above. No one had thought what they might be. Some didn't even hear.

But we all heard the sirens. They didn't take long in coming. Soon the sirens were around us and we ran to Casualty to see. We could hardly get in for all the ambulances crowded at the door. Inside was a shambles—there were people lying all around, some on stretchers, some on the floor, some screaming, some quietly moaning. All the doctors were there, trying desperately with the nurses to make some order. The Chief Surgical Registrar was going from bed to bed, triaging. He barked commands like a Captain. He had been a surgeon with the British in Aden.

One nursing student, short and fat, ran back-and-forth—she didn't know what to do and she was crying. The Registrar sat her down and said shut up. She did.

We helped with the man whose heart stopped. He must have been about 30—looked like a worker, big and strong. His heart had stopped, but they got it going again. We took him to the operating theater. He had lost a lot of blood. Some of us stood at his head, others at his stomach, others at his feet.

Mr. Clary opened his belly to find the site of the bleeding and look for fragments of shrapnel from the car. There were none, but there was a hole in his aorta, a nick in the celiac artery, and his bowel. He kept on bleeding —he'd taken 10 pints of blood when someone said, "turn him over, for bloody sake." There was a gaping hole in his backside – with still more bleeding. They had him on his side long enough to clamp and tie the bleeding vessels. Then they turned him back to keep fixing his bowel. His heart stopped again and Grayson, the senior registrar, announced it loudly. He yelled for them to start pumping, but Clary yelled back that he had his bloody heart in his bloody fist and that he was pumping from under the diaphragm. Again, the man's heart worked.

No one knew who he was. He had a black rose tattooed on his right arm. His wounds were from the front and not the back, as if he had not been running away. I said out loud what we all thought. Maybe he was the car bomber—the one who had left the bombs. Maybe he had been caught himself. We all stopped. Everyone looked at each other over their masks, eyes glaring down. How would you treat a killer? We were angry. We had seen what a bomb could do. Who was this man? We never found out. He died."

Stokes stood there for a moment and then put his arm on the student. He was young and this was probably the first casualty he had ever seen. There was no easy way to comfort him, but with the facts.

"I know exactly who you described. He died of gunshot wounds. The investigation is ongoing, so I can't say more, but there was nothing in the world that anyone could have done. The damage was extensive, and the wounds were fatal, but your description of the events may be helpful in the investigation. Remember what you saw. Use it to learn from and try to help others more fortunate in the future," Stokes said. He placed his hand on his shoulder.

"Thank you, sir," the student replied and turned to go. Stokes just stood there for a moment, recalling his own first experience of the death of a patient and how helpless and overwhelmed he had felt by the loss and his sympathy for the patient. Stokes had listened and explained so that this young man would not blame himself; he was only a passing participant. Stokes hoped that his encouragement of the student's testimony and his sympathy could help the student's future career.

Even after all these years, Stokes still felt guilty that he had not done enough when he left the bed or the examination of a deceased patient. He would go home to study the circumstances and causes of the condition that had killed him to give that death more purpose and teach him some lesson. It was like seeing a horrible movie and then reading the book, the words now illustrated more graphically. He would always remember the case. We always remember best by feeling, he noted. That student will recall that incident for the rest of his life, he predicted.

Chapter Four

Stokes returned to the morgue and saw Lanigan speaking with Samantha. The detective was doing his job, doggedly trying to make sense of what had happened, trying to get more clues from Samantha who was as good at protecting confidences as her training had been, which was excellent.

"So, you sure you saw nothing unusual when you left?" he asked again.

"No, I left just before the Professor and, yes, the watchman was at the front and Mr. Johnston was in his office," she reiterated. It was not unusual for a detective to make sure the same story happened the same way, so it might not be an inside job, the story changing each time because it was just a story.

"Thank you, Miss, I mean Dr. Monaghan," he said, but still had difficulty conceiving how such a pretty girl could be around such a ghoulish place. Must have a touch of vampire, he thought, but he was prudent enough not to say such a thing out loud. "So, I would say they were watching the coming and going before they did anything under the cover of dark. Did you see any parked white vans when you were leaving?"

"No, I didn't," she answered patiently to the same question she had answered the day before.

"To make your life less difficult, or repetitive, Detective, neither did I," Stokes said entering the autopsy room, interested in getting on with his work and freeing up Samantha to do the same.

"I won't hold you much longer, but the watchman noticed one of these men had a limp. Have you seen anyone lurking around with a limp?"

"No one lurks around here, Mr. Lanigan, they quickly hurry by," he answered, smiling.

"Well then, I'll be on my way, and let me know what your man Curran has to say when you see him, since G2 are not a great lot for sharing," said Lanigan.

"I will. Thanks again for the lift," Stokes said, escorting him to the door.

"You're welcome. I will try to follow up on those photos, but it might take a few days," Lanigan said, looking around once more before he left.

Stokes decided to ask the watchman what he saw, so he walked to the front of the building and peeked into his little cubicle. The watchman shoved his playing cards under the visitors' register and looked up, slightly embarrassed at being caught, but not much.

"Did you have any idea what kind of van you might have seen?" Stokes asked, unperturbed by the awkward sleight of hand with the cards.

"I think it might have been a small Vauxhall, big enough to carry a body I would say, almost like a butcher delivery truck," he said. "That would be a laugh, wouldn't it, Professor?" he said smiling.

"A bit ironic, but useful," said Stokes. "You gave that information to Lanigan, I assume?"

"Yes sir, as I did to Detective Sergeant Curran and the Gardai as well, trying to do my duty so they can get the bastards. Do you think they had something to do with the bombing?"

"Indirectly, perhaps, but we will need more evidence. All of this is confidential, you realize."

"Of course, Professor, Mum's the word."

Stokes went over to Mr. Johnston's office. It was a cramped windowless little cubicle near the dissecting room that was even smaller considering Mr. Johnston's size of 6'6". Still, he was caught napping in his chair in the middle of the morning, startled awake when Stokes knocked on the open door, out of courtesy and respect. Not a fan of busywork and recognizing Mr. Johnston's efficiencies, Stokes did not upbraid him for sleeping on the job.

"Sorry to disturb you," Stokes said, "but were you able to recall any more about the body snatchers?"

"I noticed a limp."

"Did any one of them speak with an accent?"

"None of them said much, Professor, but they did sound foreign, like not from the North or Britain, but the accent was more like French, singsong like."

"Did you see the van?"

"It might have been a small white Vauxhall, with Irish plates, nothing special and no writing on the sides," he said.

"Anything else?" Stokes asked.

Johnston paused for a while, really trying to recall and help.

"They wore those surgical booties, which I thought was strange since the only other people I seen wear them are those men who work cutting meat at the abattoir down the street. It didn't look like their lorries, which are usually bigger."

"Thanks, Mr. Johnston, that might be of some help," Stokes said, returning to his office.

As he walked down the hall, he thought of the curious bits that needed to be put together. A sudden image of the Jews in the night crossed his mind, and he recalled their unscheduled absence the night he had returned to find the body gone. Coincidence?

The rumination ended as he turned the corner and found Curran in his office, staring at the books on the shelves and the diplomas on the wall. Curran was an investigator, and he was sure his curiosity was part of the job of determining whether Stokes' involvement in the disappearance of the body was more than circumstantial.

"You have an impressive wall of sheepskins, Professor," Curran smiled weakly.

"Thanks for the appreciation," Stokes replied. "I'm sure you have an array of citations as well."

"Enough, Professor, but we only are as good as our next challenge, eh?" said Curran, sitting down in the chair opposite the Professor's desk which was piled with notes, documents, and pending reports. It had been a busy few days for Stokes since the bombing, having to process much of the information so that the bodies could be buried in a timely fashion. Samantha had been a great help.

"I suppose so. Have you made any progress in your inquiries?"

asked Stokes.

"Not enough to make sense out of this. You're sure you can't recall any more features of this fella?"

It seemed obvious from his question that Curran had not come up with any more background intelligence. But Stokes wanted to go to his office and see his notes for himself to glean any more information. He could not help but think the Cinema bombing and this bombing were more related than was obvious. The IRA and the UVF could not be more diametrically opposed, but they were both terrorist groups with agendas that used violence for lack of political power. The PLO was in the same category and there had been discussions with them and the IRA as well as arms exchanged. If the PLO was involved, the Mossad could very well have wanted to know who they were, how much they had cooperated, and where they were now. Although the government was ostensibly opposed to any violence, especially against its own people, it was still sympathetic to any movement of unification with Ulster. More than one of the politicians and ministers were from the North and it chafed that they had family and relations on both sides of the border that felt hopeless and helpless on the impasse. They pointed to the Dublin bombing as an example of the viciousness of the Protestants.

"Have you been able to get permission for me to see your files on the Dublin bombings in 1972?" asked Stokes.

"Better than that," Curran answered. "The files are in my office. I will take you down there if you don't have anything better to do."

"Now is fine. It should not take long since there are only a few details I want to clarify," Stokes said, putting on his mac since it was raining again.

Curran's driving was slower and more cautious than Lanigan's. Even in Dublin's chaotic traffic, he was courteous and patient, but it did not take long to get to the Special Branch office at Harcourt Square. There were multiple flashings of security badges and Stokes received a visitor's badge after signing in under Detective Sergeant Curran's auspices. They walked down some narrow dark halls to Curran's office. Unlike the offices of Stokes and Lanigan, there was nothing on Curran's desk except his nameplate and a pen and pencil set impaling a piece of polished wood with a clock in its center. Curran went to a series of locked files marked classified and opened one with his key.

"This is what I think you have been looking for," said Curran, placing the file on his desk and sitting down in his chair. Stokes sat down in the chair opposite, pulling it over slowly to give the impression that he was just making himself more comfortable and belie any eagerness or anxiety. Stokes was not sure what he would find in the thick folder, but first he wanted to focus on the mug shots of suspects, since they were known members of the IRA and were being hunted in the North. The Republic was cooperating with the Ulster government as much as it could.

The files were much better organized, not like the Xeroxes he had seen at the Gardai station. None of the pictures looked like Stokes' John Doe, which he had expected, but they were real photos or clippings pasted onto the page. There were a few who were described as sharpshooters rather than bombers. He asked Curran for copies of these to compare with Lanigan's files. While Curran went down the hall to Xerox the copies, Stokes glanced at the wall to look at the citations and certificates that Curran had earned over the years. He looked younger than the certifications attested, but he did not smoke, and he was thinner and more fit than Lanigan. Stokes noticed that there was an Irish Army citation for sharpshooting on the wall, below it a photo with a rifle that was reminiscent of the infamous Lee Harvey Oswald photo holding his Mannlicher-Carcano. The certificate was almost like a schoolchild certification compared to the other seemingly more important memorabilia on the wall, like a picture of him shaking hands with the previous *Taoiseach* (Prime Minister) of the Fianna Fail party or another standing next to one of the other cabinet Ministers of the Fianna Fail. The opposition Fianna Gael party was in power now. Despite his supposedly impartial government service, Curran most certainly had some predilections, Stokes thought.

Stokes continued to review the files and memorized the names of the suspects in the 1972 Dublin bombings and their faces, looking through the suspected crimes and associations as well as through their past histories and origins. Every one of them came from Belfast or thereabouts and were associated with bombings and none had formal military training or experience as such.

Curran returned with the copies and interrupted Stokes who was looking at the wall again.

"Do you have any questions about any of these people?" Curran asked.

"I assume you have many of the same files the Gardai have," Stokes inquired because there was not much in these files that he did not know already from looking at Lanigan's files.

"All the local characters are from the Gardai files. Why are you interested in the Cinema lot? It is not likely they had anything to do with bombing their countrymen in Dublin. And your swarthy fella wouldn't have been among that crew."

"The man who was shot had a black rose tattoo and was the only "civilian" victim who could not be identified. There were a lot of difficult identifications that were lost in the chaos of that day and the days after, but this man is a cipher and probably not a member of the IRA. Who killed him and why? Are you not interested?"

"Of course, I am. That's why I got permission for you to be here today. This probably was a cross-border incident. That's why I am involved, but what is the point of your reliving your tragedy? You have done your job with the other casualties, and you can't complete this one since you don't have the 'material' to work with. Give it up, for fuck's sake, and let us do our job." He had finally gotten annoyed, which Stokes had intended, hoping to get a glimmer of information beyond what he saw on the table.

Curran dug in, regained his composure. Was he annoyed because Stokes was playing detective or did he ask too many questions that Curran did not want or could not answer? Stokes used logic for his involvement. He would not be caught up in the emotion.

"I needed to know for myself that the IRA Cinema bombing suspects in 1972 looked nothing like and had nothing to do with the John Doe. How many of these lot are still fugitives?" Stokes asked pointing to the Cinema dossier.

"Most. The British and the Loyalists keep asking us if one or another has been sighted, but none have been captured or killed or identified as out of the country."

"Who outside of the country have come in to help them?" asked Stokes.

"There are rumors that the PLO might be supplying them with arms or training, but nothing has been confirmed. We are looking into it, but we can only do so much with the Troubles and new twists like this bombing. We have limited facilities and the British and Americans are more interested since the Munich massacre, so we have left it to them. At least the Yanks are willing to share some of their intelligence, although they have doubts about our loyalties since there are enough Republicans roaming around the States to annoy them as well. That could certainly explain his color, but there have not been any reports we can get that clearly link any foreigners in Dublin conspiring anything."

"Do you have any of those files of suspected PLO or other collaborators with the IRA?" Stokes pressed.

"We do," he said, going to the file cabinet again, pulling out a smaller file, placing it on the desk. Stokes flipped through the pages and saw the same originals with the organized photos attached and tried to find the page for Suleiman bin Daoud, but there was none. Stokes did not comment on that.

"These are all the originals, the ones you gave copies of to the Gardai, is that correct?" Stokes asked.

"Yes, they are," said Curran.

"What about foreign residents working here or students coming here? Surely there is a shortlist for that."

"Again, we do not have the time or the resources to go over the lists or the photos. Do you?"

"I only have one assistant and she is new, which, by the grace of God, was a great help in the past two weeks."

"So do you think there is a link between your man and the 1972 Dublin bombings?" asked Curran, still more suspicious of Stokes' hunches than convinced.

"I don't know. But I will let you know if I find out anything."

"Don't be getting yourself too involved. You're a doctor, not a cop."

"In this case, I am the State Pathologist and I need the same answers as a cop."

"So, you do. So do we. I will let you know."

Curran stood up. This was the end of the discussion. He handed Stokes the copies he had made and led him out the door of his office and out of the building. Stokes took a bus back to his office since the cost of a cab would have come out of his pocket —his expense account was miniscule and a torture to justify.

On the ride back to the office, Stokes reviewed his interview with Curran. He had received no real information, or as Lanigan would say, 'Sweet Feck All.' It was more an interrogation of him and a warning rather than a discussion about the case. That would have been expected considering he was a G-man and didn't want his turf to be trodden upon. He also was too defensive about his limitations. He could understand Lanigan's skin in the game, a cop who was hoping to make a name for himself, getting up and out of the petty thieves and unintended murderers to real cases which would show his investigative skills for a promotion or two.

But Curran was keeping all his cards to himself. He was a Detective Sergeant, bound to protect the State and its secrets, including the workings of the division of "spooks" and, perhaps, the intentions of the opposition party. His Fianna Fail photos might just be pictures of congratulatory handshakes, but those "photo opportunities" had gotten onto his office wall. Stokes was resigned about not getting any more information from Curran and felt justified about not sharing any more information without assuring allegiances.

When he got back to the office there was a Garda standing at the front door and the watchman sitting inside. After the fact, more security than was needed, Stokes thought. Such is human nature, to be more worried when all the reason for worry has passed. Samantha was nowhere to be found. She had completed her assigned duties for the day, but he had expected her to be there to discuss any other cases and report them. He walked down the hall to Mr. Johnston's office. The door was half-open, and he was there, "resting" his eyes. It had been a hectic few weeks, above and beyond the usual activity. Old Jack had done his part. Stokes politely knocked on the door and Old Jack opened his eyes.

"Where is Dr. Monaghan?" Stokes asked.

"She said she would be back soon and that she was going on an errand related to a case."

"Anyone else been here?"

"No, it's been pretty quiet today, not even Lanigan has been around," said Old Jack, with enough disdain in his voice and disrespect in dropping the detective's title to clearly demonstrate his opinion.

"Give him some respect. We still need the help of Dublin's finest," Stokes said.

"Tell that to the pieces of meat they had me put together after the bombing," sneered Johnston, not often upset in his job, despite the many years of gore and grief.

"It upset me as well, Mr. Johnston. But the police are not to blame. They are victims too. We all are. . ." said Stokes, walking off as much from his own sadness as the anger from the old man.

Samantha walked into Stokes' office about an hour after, breathless and eager to report her investigation. Stokes did not chastise her about leaving without permission or approval of investigations out of what he considered their purview, which he fully suspected she had done. How could he chastise her when he was wasting time with G-men? He did not ask her what she had found out. That came without invitation.

"Remember those booties that they found in the dumpster?" she asked.

"Yes," Stokes responded calmly, countering her excitement.

"Well, there are only 3 suppliers of those boots in Dublin, and two of them don't make the boots in that shade of blue," she said, holding up a packet of booties for him to inspect.

"So where were the booties from?" asked Stokes.

"There are suppliers just down the road. They sell scores of packs to a local butcher. He says they are for the Kosher slaughterers who work in a small section of the abattoir in Terenure. I haven't gone there yet, but we can go there together. They are more likely to discuss this with you," she said, deferring to his authority.

"This a police matter?"

"They haven't been doing feck all."

"I appreciate your enthusiasm, but not the language. If you can't control your emotions or your objectivity, and above all, civil language, you are not suited for this position."

Samantha contorted her face and almost broke into tears. It was not what Stokes had intended, but he needed her to control her impulses and curb her good intentions. She would be reprimanded by the police and the coroner if they found out she was gathering clues on evidence that was formally confidential. He could not abide the tears and looked at her, standing slumped and motionless after so much enthusiasm.

"That was a great bit of detective work, but you have to be discreet. There are too many people involved in this already. We have no jurisdiction except to observe and report," he cautioned and paused for a moment.

"Where is the abattoir?" he asked.

"They say down near Terenure Road, close to the Kosher Butcher's," she answered.

There were only two kosher butchers in Dublin these days. The Jewish population had shrunk from its peak in the '40s. He recalled the Jews emerging from the house on Terenure road. It made sense that they were close to the abattoir. As Mrs. Kelly had reported, they probably were exporting kosher Irish beef to other markets, but what else were they doing? The growing threat of the PLO was worldwide. This was a good cover for observation, especially with reports of PLO cooperation with the IRA. The body with the shadow of the Star of David had disappeared within a day of his death and rapid burial was part of Jewish law. Removing the evidence would be part of removing any associations with these men on Terenure Road.

"Let's take a visit to the abattoir, then," said Stokes, getting up from his chair and grabbing his coat and hat. It was a warm spring day, but it took him a while to get used to unbundling from the long winter. He called for a taxi, and they went on the short ride from Store Street to Terenure. The abattoir was off the main road and down a narrower lane where there were other small shops and factories to supply the local population. Not the most convenient for large trucks but adequate for small vans, especially small white ones. They did not expect to see the van there today, but there was more than one parked and waiting to be loaded, many with signs painted on the side identifying the various butchers in the vicinity.

Stokes and Samantha got out of the cab and dodged one of the vans as it was leaving for its deliveries from the side doors near the loading docks. This was a small operation, but adequate enough for its clientele, the reputation for its quality meant enough that Dubliners would buy the meat, kosher or not, to keep the business going. They went to the front office and asked for the manager, who, it just so happened was the owner. If he was Jewish, his thick Dublin accent belied the fact. His bloodied apron showed he was an active participant in his work.

"I am Dr. Stokes, the State Pathologist and this is Dr. Monaghan, my assistant. We need your help in an investigation," he explained.

"I'm certainly guilty of murder, your honor, but no Irishmen as far as I know," he smiled.

"I can testify on your behalf since we have ways of detecting human from calf and chicken blood, even Irishmen," Stokes smiled.

"What can I do you for?" the butcher asked.

"Are you exporting any of the meat?"

"Yes, yes, we are, to England and even to Israel. It keeps the business going since it is getting harder and harder to make the ends meet with just the Jewish clientele. Our little Irish Jerusalem is shrinking," he said, taking a slight breath in, a typically Dublin expression, expressing the sadness of a disappearing time.

"How many exporters do you deal with?" Stokes asked.

"Oh, just the one. They are from Israel, and they are very strict about who they deal with, so I have cornered their market and they do like your Irish beef," he said.

"Do they come in often?"

"Yeah, every day, but you just missed them. They are off for another shipment to Israel. The only day they don't show is Saturday. Friday, they arrive earlier, to avoid working the Sabbath, don't you know," he said, making sure they both understood that this was not just an abattoir, but a religious establishment that observed rules and traditions.

Stokes looked down at the blue booties the butcher was wearing. They looked exactly like the kind found in the dumpster. He did not bother asking him if the Israelis wore those boots.

"What is this all about anyways?" the butcher asked.

"A body has disappeared from our morgue, and we have reason to believe the deceased may have been Jewish," Stokes answered. He wanted as much information as he could get this Dubliner to give as his civic duty.

"It wasn't from the bombing, was it? We would have known right away. This is a small community, don't you know? We are loyal Republicans, and we were horrified by this awful tragedy. Do you know who did this?"

"Did what?"

"The bombing. Wasn't it the UVF? It wasn't our boys and what does a Jew have to do with this? Oy vay, we have enough trouble that we don't have to mix in with Protestants and Catholics, sure we don't."

"We don't think your community had anything to do with it, but we don't know who this man was, and we thought you might know him," said Stokes, showing him the Polaroid photo of the dead man.

"No, never saw him in my life, even when he was alive, poor fella," he replied, discomfited by the picture of a dead man, despite his own profession.

"Do you have the name and address of the Israelis? It will be kept confidential. Please don't let them know we have been asking. I don't want to cause any upset since they and your community are not part of any investigation, certainly not the bombing," said Stokes.

The butcher, Wolfe was his name, went back around to his desk and pulled out a business card that proclaimed, "Masada Import and Export, Pty Ltd, Kosher products imports and exports, Terenure Road, Dublin, Ireland." Stokes was not surprised at the address but was irritated with himself that his interest in his neighborhood did not extend past his doorstep.

"Thank you very much for your help," said Stokes.

"You're very welcome. Anything I can do to solve a crime," replied Wolfe, nodding to Samantha and Stokes.

"May I use your phone? We need to call a cab to get back to the office," asked Stokes.

"Of course," Mr. Wolfe pointed to the small stand next to the counter where the clerk would write down the orders, names, phone numbers, and addresses with the times called in and times that vans were taken out and returned. Mr. Wolfe waved goodbye and walked back into the back of the building to make sure the work was being done while he had been away and distracted. There were some shouting and exchanges, but no fear or anger in any of the voices, just communication above the noise of the machines. Stokes called the taxi service. He looked down at the books and saw the night the body had disappeared; a van had been signed out at 5 PM but did not return until midnight. The order had been for delivery to the port which was only a half-hour's drive away.

The taxi took less time than Stokes expected, so he did not have more time to peruse the log. Samantha did not say much on the way back to the office, but she had not been aware there was such a large Jewish community in Dublin. She knew of some Jewish classmates in school. She had not had much to do with them since she had nothing in common with them except for the school. She did not want to say anything about the case in the presence of the driver, but she was sure there was more to this. She was more cautious, however, since she did not want to overstep her boundaries again, although it gave her a thrill to follow the hunch and prove she was right.

As soon as they were back in the office, she followed Stokes into his office, nearly bursting with the excitement.

"What are we going to do about this?" she said enthusiastically, ready for the hunt.

"Nothing. Let's hope that Lanigan or Curran will follow through with this in due time."

"Shouldn't we tell them?"

"I gave you the benefit of the doubt and you were right, but it is not our job to interfere other than to find the identity of the man and complete our report."

"Aren't you afraid when the Jews get wind of it, they will scarper?"

"They are Israelis. Not all Jews are Israelis as you found with your Dublin butcher. I think he is a loyal Irishman and will keep our secret since he is not part of a grand conspiracy, as an anti-Semite might charge," he said with a little reproach in his voice. He had some close Jewish friends and had sympathy with others who were a minority in this country, even though many might be privileged. Ignorance and envy were the real villains.

"I'm sorry, I didn't mean it that way."

"It's all right, we all have our prejudices, but knowing people and seeing their places in the world makes it easier to accept and tolerate, as we do in medicine, as much as we can or are capable," he said, hoping he was not pontificating too much.

"But if the Israelis leave, the case might not be solved," said Samantha.

"I think they are here for the long term, at least that is my impression. A quick espionage adventure would not have them establish a front business years before if they were going away tomorrow," he said. "No, this is something that has been going on for some time. Why, I am not sure."

"So, we are not telling Lanigan or Curran?" she asked again, looking for guidance as to what they were going to do next.

"No, we will hold fast and let some more details come to us when they are ready to share. They have all the other pieces of evidence to do their job and I trust neither of them to give us all the answers, through negligence or suppression."

"I think Lanigan is a bit thick, and Curran is a bit creepy," she said.

"Well put, but let's not make any more judgments. Let time play this out," he said, worried that her youthful enthusiasm would get her into more trouble than she could handle. He had hoped for a dumber assistant who would carry out his or her duties efficiently without interference, but he appreciated the intelligence even if it was "without form" as yet. At least she could be guided.

"Let's get back to our work since it will take at least a few days to see any progress, the wheels of justice grinding slow," he said.

Samantha left the office and Stokes looked at the stack of papers that had quickly accumulated while he was gallivanting around the city. He had gotten nothing from visiting Curran and suspected it was more that Curran was investigating him than he cooperating with Curran. He regretted his weakness in wanting to know the facts of his family's death and seeing that the perpetrators would be caught. Curran seemed not as interested in cold cases as much as he was intrigued that a possible IRA operative had been a victim in the bombing, not from a bomb, but a bullet, or at least his interest was what he portrayed to Stokes.

Stokes could not concentrate on the forms and reports he had to review and sign. He had not been very sanguine about getting more information about the Cinema bombing but why had he been enticed to help in the investigation? What did Curran want to know or why did Curran go along with the charade that he cared? Frustrated by the thought, Stokes started sifting through the papers and resolved to complete them one by one until the job was done, so the mindless busywork could distract him for the rest of the day.

Samantha worked in her small office and did the same. Her stack was a lot smaller, but needed to be completed, nevertheless. She sorted through the documents to be signed and the reports to be reviewed. Most were after the fact of the bombing and completed retroactively since the processing of the deaths had been so hectic. The papers were just bureaucratic drivel that had to be filed. Pity these papers could not be buried with the poor souls that they documented, she thought. Still, she was aware what she was in for when she took the job, just as charting patients' status and outcomes was part of any other clinician's work in any other specialty. "Ah, the drudgery," she sighed.

As Stokes was getting through the papers, many generated by the other part-time pathologists who had been dragooned into the awful job of sorting out the body parts and quickly affirming the cause of death of each person, it had been a hectic few days. A good amount of detail might have been lost or misplaced in the pandemonium. He began to organize the papers into piles that were urgent and others that were less so. He would ask the coroner's secretary to help since this was more legal than medical, but he had to sign off on it all. As he sifted through the piles, he noticed the report of the poor French woman who had been caught in the melee, a student who had been scheduled to return to France the next day. Coincidentally, she was Jewish, and she and her family had survived the Holocaust. This all came out in the newspapers, trying to humanize the tragedy when they were not selling more papers by describing the decapitated body or the dead children. The form he had just put down triggered his recall of the day her body had been received.

He had not seen her. Samantha was in charge of making sure that all the bodies were properly identified before the autopsies and then their release after they had been completed. She was subjected to moans and screams and a few faints.

In the case of the French woman, Samantha was almost attacked, she had reported to Stokes later that same day. The person who demanded her release was a younger man with a thick accent and he wore a skullcap and a black suit with a white shirt and no tie. He said he was her cousin, and he was with another man dressed similarly who was silent. They demanded her body be released without an autopsy because it was against their beliefs. Samantha had done her homework since she had attended an autopsy of some other Jewish person, so she knew the law. In that case, they had released the body because her doctor had confirmed, at the last minute, that this probably was a natural death and that no autopsy was needed, but not after an argument with the family and the Rabbi and three calls to their GP who had been lax in filling out the death certificate or responding to the coroner's calls.

Samantha responded to these very angry men by emphasizing that since this was a criminal event, that it was necessary to get the details before the body was released and that, even according to Jewish law, if it was a matter of interest to the state, that it was necessary. She assured them that the body would be treated with the utmost respect. They relented, but it was a most unsavory incident since these two had burst into the autopsy room and saw other bodies at the time. Fortunately, the bulk of the work had already been done and there had only been a few bodies left.

Stokes, recalling her story, put Samantha's report down and rushed into her office.

"When the relatives of the French woman came into the autopsy room, what did they see?"

"They saw her body and the bodies of three other victims," she replied. "They made a bloody awful row and Johnston did not have a chance to stop them."

"Did they see John Doe?"

"I don't know. I thought they were all covered, but there was so much chaos, they may have had a glimpse of him. It was funny, though, how the quiet one did not say anything and just stared blankly ahead, looking pale. I thought he was going to faint," she said, now recalling more about the incident.

"Did either of them limp?"

"I didn't notice. They were causing such a row," she answered, still upset at the commotion but pausing. "You think they were the body snatchers?"

"They might very well have been since no one else, but the staff had seen the man before he had been delivered here. No one had asked for him while he was in surgery, according to the hospital staff. Do you think you could identify them if you saw them again?"

"Of course, but shouldn't we tell the Gardai?"

"No, not yet. That might scare them off. We still don't know who shot him. I don't think it was them. There are too many loose ends, there are too many other people involved. Just keep in mind what you told me. I will make other inquiries, not you, all right?"

"Yes, I suppose so," she answered reluctantly since she was eager to be involved in the mystery.

He did not know where to start. Stokes was interested in finding the body, but was also interested in finding the shooter, the bombers, and now, since the bombing was so similar, the identity of the bombers who had murdered his wife and daughter. His first responsibility was to find the body, if he could, and then the snatchers, which might lead him to the bombers. The Jewish butcher was a good source for clues, but he felt he was innocent of any other involvement. That was a good piece of detective work by Samantha, he thought, but he did not want to encourage her since that might be dangerous.

Chapter Five

The afternoon mail came and in it was a fancy RSVP invitation from the College to the Alumni dinner party. In the past, Stokes had looked forward to going to the parties with his wife, who loved to dress up for the occasions and mingle with the medical aristocracy. She tried to avoid the politicians but loved the literary luminaries and the actors and TV and radio personalities who appeared and made generous contributions to the College.

He loathed the meetings now. There was no buffer to questions about suspicious deaths that had been splashed about in the newspapers. There were solicitous queries about how he was doing, as if he had to be reminded. It would be worse with the ghouls that would appear asking about the bombings and likely, reporters who were hungry to sniff out yet another tabloid story. He wanted to decline but he had already committed to going before the bombing. Those who knew him would not accept that he was too busy, since homicides had drastically decreased since the disastrous day. There were too many police being especially vigilant in the aftermath, which was inconvenient for bad goings-on. He signed the RSVP and added Samantha. This would be a great opportunity for her to meet important people and, selfishly for him, for her to act as a diversion to avoid uncomfortable encounters. It would reassure her that he was not discounting her completely since he had warned her off any more dangerous inquiries.

He walked into her little office where she was intently looking over all the documents about the bombing.

"Pardon me," he said, startling her from her concentrations.

"I have an invitation from the College for the alumni dinner. Would you like to join me?" he asked. "It would be a great opportunity to meet some important people."

It took no more than a second for her to respond.

"I would be delighted," she answered, smiling broadly. "But I need to find a gown to wear," she said.

"Don't dress up too much. It is only an alumni meeting full of many pompous people who will criticize whatever you wear."

"I suppose I could wear my graduation dress; no one will notice that I have worn it before," she said. She knew on her salary she would not be able to wear something new to suit the occasion. She did not want to put her mother out, borrowing from her to buy a new dress.

"You are the same size as my daughter. I would be delighted if you could wear one of her dresses. I have not had the courage to give them away. They were quite expensive," he said, pausing, unsure if he should have offered.

"That is very nice of you, but I am not sure if I can just take one,.."

"Please," he paused, "Just consider it a loan. You could stop by and let Mrs. Kelly help you. She has gone to the trouble of keeping everything as it was without a complaint. The least I could do was offer you the opportunity before I give them all away or sell them on consignment."

"That is very kind of you," she replied. She was not sure what to say next. In all their dealings, he certainly did not come on to her in any way, shape, or form. She trusted his intentions were good. "I appreciate the offer, but wouldn't it put you in a position of offering more than what you should for an employee?"

"It was merely an offer, as was the invitation. I assure you there are no strings attached. You are my subordinate and an employee. I just thought this would be a good opportunity for you since I hope that I am a mentor, of sorts," he said.

"You are, of course, and I would be delighted to see the dresses and go to the reception. You are being very kind."

"Fine, then," he said, relieved. "I will let Mrs. Kelly know. I won't be around to influence you in any way, one way or another, on the dresses I mean. I need to be at another meeting tomorrow evening, so you should drop by then."

"Grand, and thanks again," she smiled.

"Back to the grind," he said, staring at her pile of papers. "I will call Mrs. Kelly now," he nodded and left her office to get back to his.

Chapter Six

It was raining the night Samantha took the bus to Terenure. She would have ridden her bike but did not want to get wet and ruin her clothes or the gowns she might borrow. It was already fairly late when she arrived since work had taken longer than expected. She had grabbed something at the local chips shop so she would not put anyone out offering to feed her.

As she knocked on the door, she noticed the activity across the street and the men going into the white van that was not unlike the small van Mr. Johnston had described. She was tempted to follow them, but she had already promised Professor Stokes she would look at the dresses and, more importantly, not get herself more involved. She stood at the door and looked across the street for another few moments before Mrs. Kelly answered the door. As she watched them move in and out of the house, she noticed one of them had a limp, again as Mr. Johnston had described.

"Come in out of the rain," Mrs. Kelly urged as she opened the door, smiling.

"Thanks, I'm Samantha," she said, extending her hand.

"Of course, you are," said Mrs. Kelly and shook her hand lightly. "The Professor told me about you. I have arranged the gowns in the sitting room for you to inspect. They are beautiful and I have to agree with the Professor that you are just about the same size and shape as his daughter, God rest her soul," she said, a slight tear in her eye.

Samantha looked at the clothes and was impressed with the colors and styles. She was tempted to say she would take all of them but chose two more conservative gowns and asked to try them on.

"You can use the library and just leave your things there. It has a beautiful old long mirror that will give you a good idea. No one else but me is here. The Professor will be back late. He hates these committee meetings, so he says, but he 'volunteered' himself. The man can't say no," she whispered, "and now he is stuck with attending them," she said, shaking her head.

The meetings were in support of the maintenance of some of the old buildings in Dublin that were scheduled for demolition and needed lobbying to the government and fundraising from the moneyed private citizens for their rehabilitation. Many of the Republicans in the government were all for their being torn down. They felt they were representatives of the old Georgian buildings and the British aristocracy and authority. Some were allegedly sites of torture and interrogations before and during the war of independence. Others were dilapidated buildings left by the Anglo Irish who had owned them and saw no profit in their upkeep and were in arrears of taxes, the real estate market still being depressed, so they wrote them off at a loss. Stokes detested soliciting funds from people with money and he barely tolerated the wrangling with politicians, but he had many connections with the old rich and the politicos since he was, technically, a governmental official himself.

Though quiet, the library faced the street, and the curtains were still open, so Samantha went to the window to pull the sashes closed. She was almost at street level and saw the men in black coats going in and out of the building. None seemed to be carrying any carcasses into or out of the white van. Instead, they seemed to be carrying boxes and small file cabinets into it, trying to cover what looked like papers from the rain. She saw a man with a limp doing the job, sometimes shouting orders to the others. She closed the curtains, not wanting to be too nosy, trying to follow the orders of the Professor who had warned her not to do any more snooping on her own. She tried to distract herself with what was going on just across the street by trying on the gowns, chose the long green satin gown, although she loved the bright yellow organdy one, but thought it would be too flashy for a medical meeting.

"What do you think?" she asked Mrs. Kelly, coming out of the library, smiling.

Mrs. Kelly just looked at her for a moment, almost shocked at how much she resembled Aisling in the dress, and recalled how the Professor's daughter always chose that dress for special occasions. She had mixed feelings about telling Samantha about the green gown and was worried that seeing her in that dress would upset the Professor. But she contained herself.

"You look beautiful. It suits you. Turn around," she motioned. "You will not need anything done to fix it for you. It's perfect," she said, forcing a smile. "Take it off and I will fold it for you. I still have the box it came in, from Brown Thomas," Mrs. Kelly said. This was an expensive department store just on Grafton Street that Samantha passed by regularly to get a special coffee from Bewley's when she was in the mood or had the time to meet with friends.

Samantha went back into the library and marveled at all the books along the high shelves and the old carved oak desk in the corner opposite the fireplace. Samantha was aware that the Professor had inherited the old house but was impressed at the luxury. She quickly took off the dress, put her own clothes back on, and quickly glanced out the window. The van was still being loaded.

"Would you like a cup of tea?" Mrs. Kelly offered, taking the pot down and the tea canister from the cupboard, not hesitating more than a second with the mechanics of that regularity.

"You're very kind, but I better be off. I have a long day tomorrow," she demurred. She did not want to miss the van leaving.

"I understand. But enjoy the gown and drop by any time you wish. The Professor is often out and I enjoy a chat," Mrs. Kelly offered, folding the gown carefully into the box, tying it firmly with a string. She peered out the window.

"It is lashing rain out there. I'll call a cab. It won't take too long. I would hate for you and the gown to get soaked," Mrs. Kelly said.

"Yes, thanks. It's not a long ride to Rathmines, but it does look wet," said Samantha, peering out the window, still seeing the van across the street.

Samantha thanked Mrs. Kelly, rushed down the front stairs and got in the cab. Just as she did, the van across the street started moving.

The driver turned around and asked, "Where to, Miss?"

On an impulse, Samantha said, "quick, follow that white van, but stay some distance."

"Who do you think you are, bloody Dick Tracy?" asked the driver, slightly anxious.

"It's all right, I just need to see where it is going. I am working with the Gardai. It is part of an ongoing investigation. Don't worry, I'm not getting out, I just want to know the destination, then it's to home and a cup of tea for me."

"All right then, but I won't be chasing all over Dublin and I won't be talking with the Gardai either," he said.

"It's all right, I just need a location, then you're free and there will be a few extra bob in it for you."

"I can't afford to risk too much time with this," he said, pulling out after the van, leaving a few good yards distance. The rain was still hard, and the visibility was poor in the dark, but the driver followed within sight. The van suddenly stopped a few doors down from a shop with a Kosher Butcher sign. The man with the limp opened the garage door of a nondescript building that may have been a house or a workshop.

"Drive past slowly so I can get a closer look and then keep on going," Samantha ordered. The driver did as she said and she saw the sign which displayed "Masada Import and Export, Pty Ltd." The men were just opening the back door of the van and getting in as the taxi drove by, but all Samantha could see as the taxi lights flashed forward was them unloading the same boxes she saw being loaded.

"Good enough," said Samantha, "keep going, please."

"Where to now, shall I take you straight to headquarters?"

"No, you can take me home to 32 Rathmines Road."

She said nothing more to the driver during the ride, although he seemed bursting with questions. She gave him an extra pound for his trouble, and he smiled broadly.

"Have a good night, Miss, but mind yourself," he said and drove off.

Samantha opened the door of her flat and put the boxed gown carefully on the sofa. She sat down and stared at the box for a minute. She was so excited and intrigued by her observations of these mysterious men that she wanted to ring the Professor and let him know what she had seen, but she knew he wouldn't be back until late.

What were they up to? she asked herself. She was afraid she would get an earful if she told the Professor, but if she didn't do anything, they might be gone soon. She didn't want to tell Lanigan or Curran because she didn't trust either of them. And besides, the workmen hadn't broken any laws as far as she knew.

She put the kettle on for a cup of tea. That's what her mother always did for a moment of peace and contemplation. Besides, she was hungry after only a bag of chips and would have accepted any offer from Mrs. Kelly, but the sight out the window had distracted her. She went into the fridge and pulled out some cheese, cut two slices of bread and made herself a sandwich while the tea brewed. The process took her mind off the problem for a moment, distraction enough for her to concentrate on her hunger. She realized as she chewed that she had not eaten much since breakfast, having worked through lunch to process some paperwork and had completely forgotten to eat. The cheese was just some Kerrygold cheddar, but it satisfied. She got up, poured the milk, and stirred some sugar into the cup since she still felt slightly hypoglycemic and slowly chewed more of the sandwich. You have to eat more regularly, she reminded herself as the slight shaking slowly diminished. She resolved to make a shopping list and keep to a better diet and have a proper tea in the evening.

The dinner is tomorrow. I will tell him then. He won't be able to fuss if he is among all his colleagues; then we can decide what to do, she resolved, staring at the half-eaten sandwich which she had not realized she had eaten. She finished the sandwich and the tea and tried to read but fell asleep on the sofa.

Chapter Seven

Samantha woke with a start, in a sweat. Her neck was stiff from lying on the arm of the sofa. As she moved her arm to look at the clock, she felt a twinge and realized it was only 2 AM. She had wakened because of the dream she had of watching the man with the limp running away and she had not been able to catch him, no matter how fast she had been running. She looked outside. It was pitch black save for the solitary orange streetlight that diffused in the fog. It was not raining. She got up and washed her face and noted how convenient it was she had not gotten undressed. She put on her raincoat, just in case, and went out into the night with a torch she grabbed. It was not that far from Rathmines to Terenure, so she walked to the building that she had seen the men go into. She looked through the dirty window to see if there was anyone there. It was the dead of night, you twit, she reminded herself, and tried the doorknob. It was locked. She walked around to the narrow alleyway behind the building and tried the back door. It was locked as well, but the small window next to it was open just a crack. She levered it open with a board she found lying against the wall. Fine spies these are that they can't keep their perimeters secure, she chuckled to herself and climbed in. It seemed merely like a small warehouse with empty boxes strewn about. She walked to the front of the building and saw the boxes she thought had been unloaded. They were piled next to a desk with a telephone, a copying machine, and a teletype. She looked at the printer— there were letters in Hebrew, so she could not make heads or tails of it, but there were some invoices on the desk in a pile in English and some in French that made it look like a legitimate import and export business.

Not convinced, she opened one of the boxes and saw folders with names labeled on the edges. She opened one of the folders labeled in English and saw a description of some IRA operative in the North complete with addresses, references, clippings, and a photo. She pulled out an adjacent folder with a Muslim name on it. It was a dossier on a Libyan with a Belfast address. It said this person was linked with the Irishman of the previous dossier. It also showed manifests from a ship that had arrived in Belfast six months before and though the description of goods was "oriental rugs," there was a notation in Hebrew with numbers in the hundreds next to the words in a list on the margin. She made copies of the two dossiers and the manifests, put the dossiers back, and closed the boxes.

"Are they for us or agin' us?" she asked softly.

She hurried to the back window, climbed out, and closed it. She looked around to make sure she hadn't been seen, although the fog was thick, and the streetlights were barely visible. Only someone who had expected her to be there would have noticed her coming and going, she was that quiet. She walked back to Rathmines, the copied papers folded carefully in the inner pocket of her slicker, lest they get wet. Occasional cars whished past her in the foggy night, but none stopped.

She did not sleep well the rest of the night, her mind racing over what she saw and what she should do, and how to tell the Professor. Could it wait or not? Why were they loading all this into the warehouse and what were they going to do with it? Were they going to disappear suddenly and the secrets they were protecting disappear with them? Was it anything with which she should concern herself or the Professor? She tried to pull herself together and finally got to sleep.

Chapter Eight

The office was busy the next morning. Stokes seemed to be in a terrible mood, having put up with the pompous posturing of the members of the historical committee and their inability to reach a conclusion as to what to do about an old building that was scheduled for demolition in four weeks. This could only mean another meeting and a repeat of the waffling and vacillation. He preferred medicine, where the facts were presented and a decision that mattered was made, either about the living or the dead, that mattered. Only one or two personalities needed to be satisfied, the patient and the practitioner.

He was still sitting amidst the pile of paperwork on his desk that was the aftermath of the great disaster of the bombing, with the necessity to complete the same documents for multiple ministries, including the coroner, who was notorious for avoiding decisions and sidestepping administrative forms in favor of dumping them on him as the Medical Examiner.

They had a working understanding about their jobs, he, doing the medical examinations and determinations of death and Murphy, the coroner, to report and record and discuss those findings with whomever necessary. But there was much that was not clear, so the coroner always took the prerogative as his co-worker under the same Ministry, to avoid the work. Murphy had graduated from medical school before Stokes and then read for the law, so he had the privilege of deferring as much of the "medical" work to him, whether they were medical documents or not. Stokes did not confront him often, since politically the coroner always had the upper hand because he cared to. To be fair, Murphy had been kind and understanding in promptly organizing other pathologists to stand in for him on the deaths of his daughter and wife and had marshaled all his administrative skill to help when the department was overwhelmed with bodies and pieces of bodies in the latest bombing. Still, Stokes was not looking forward to another meeting with Murphy, which only blackened his mood further.

Samantha was aware of his mood and stayed clear. She had tried to do as much work as possible in the past few days and had even offered to "triage" the many documents that required Stokes' signature, so he was not overwhelmed. They had not had an autopsy for several weeks since the bombing, the terror having chilled the hearts of even the most evil or insane of murderers. Stokes always seemed to appreciate her help, so she took the advantage of still being in his good graces and went into his office despite the visage of the black cloud. She hoped to ingratiate herself in preparation for what she was going to tell him later. She looked at him, nearly fuming at another piece of paper that rightly should have been done by the coroner.

"Murphy is pushing his luck with this unmitigated rubbish," he grumbled, as Samantha walked in. Samantha just smiled and he looked up at her, slightly softening.

"I will take on some of this if you need. Most of my stuff can be delegated to the secretary anyways. She will complain, but I'll make it up to her—I have some tickets to a rock concert that I really don't want to go to—too much noise!" she said, covering her ears.

"All right then, take this pile and get it done quickly since it is still more of the same trash, they all want yesterday," he said, pointing to a large pile to his left. It was enough of a pile when removed to allow him to see the door without straining his neck or getting up.

Samantha got a cart from outside the door and quickly piled on the papers. "Are you still up for going to the reception tonight?"

"Yes, must go. That is just the way it is, but I will leave work early to get ready. You are free to do so as well. Does the gown fit?" he asked.

"Yes, it is wonderful, and Mrs. Kelly helped me to pick it out. She was very kind," Samantha smiled.

"Yes, she is. I don't know what I would do without her, a lot of common sense. Bad life she has had with her drunk of a husband leaving her with four children to raise on her own. Strong woman," he said.

Chapter Nine

With a lighter load, or at least the promise of a lighter load, Stokes worked quickly through the papers. He was sure that Murphy would chide him about the unfinished work since there was nothing more exciting to him than an empty desktop, even if it was at the expense of others barely able to see past their own desks. Stokes was afraid he would have to deal with some politicians as well, not that Murphy wasn't a quasi-politician himself, his constituency, the other bureaucrats above and below him. He was a strong Fianna Fail man and let everyone know it, even if the party in power was Fianna Gael. Most people didn't care. There was some talk about not holding or postponing the reception out of respect for the people who were killed in the bombing. The government had not declared a National Day of Mourning. He was sure he was going to hear from Murphy about the disrespect for the dead, although that would not prevent Murphy from being there.

The reception was held in the main hall of the Royal College of Surgeons in Ireland. Tradition, history, and status superseded the fact that Ireland was now a Republic —most people just called it the College of Surgeons. All the professors and esteemed graduates of the College were there, milling around with their drinks and occasionally grabbing an hors-d'oeuvre since the reception was not for eating but for being there. If Stokes had disliked the Historical Building Committee meeting the night before, he was more uncomfortable with this meeting. He had rushed home to put on his dinner suit and took a cab to pick up Samantha at her home. When she opened the door in her gown, the sight struck him with pleasure and grief. She was stunning in the dress and so resembled Aisling that he almost called her by that name, but he caught his breath and himself with a tear of sorrow.

"Is there anything wrong, Professor?" Samantha asked.

"No, no, just irritated by the formalities and the rush. It has been a long day," he said wiping the tear and reminding himself to be a gentleman. "You look stunning," he said, his attempt at a compliment, sincere and understated. He was simply overwhelmed.

"You do remind me of my daughter, which is still a bit difficult," he said.

"I can change the dress," she said.

"No, no, it was meant for you. You must wear and keep it. We can't afford to be late. The cab is waiting."

It was a conveniently clear evening so there would be no soaking of costumes. They silently rode to the College of Surgeons, she feeling awkward at his discomfort and he feeling awkward escorting a beautiful young lady in his dead daughter's gown. They arrived at the grand entrance off St. Stephen's Green and entered through the old front doors that were usually locked but were open and staffed by the assistant Porters who stood in their traditional uniforms.

Stokes and Samantha had rushed to the College so as not to be late, but he knew he needn't have hurried because the more important of the assembly arrived fashionably late. Murphy walked in with James O'Neill, the ex-Minister of the Department of Justice and Equality, his former boss, and a member of the opposition party, all smiles. A strange couple considering O'Neill had been accused of gunrunning for the IRA in the past and was investigated, but never implicated. He was from Ulster, close to the Northern Ireland border, and still had a thick country accent which belied his education and caginess. Murphy glanced around for any other influential people he had to acknowledge. There being none as yet, he headed straight for Stokes who had tried to make himself inconspicuous but failed with Samantha at his side.

"How are you, Harold and Samantha? I hardly have had time to see you since we both have been so busy in the aftermath of this awful tragedy," said Murphy. He oozed sympathy as he gripped Stokes' hand and then Samantha's.

"You, of course, know the ex-Minister of Justice, the honorable Mr. O'Neill," said Murphy.

"I am very pleased to see you both here, considering the

tremendous and onerous duties you have been assigned," said O'Neill.

"You both have done a great job, considering the circumstances," Murphy said.

"Any progress on the missing body?" Murphy asked.

Stokes did not miss a beat, "No, sir, I am leaving that up to the Gardai and Special Branch," clarifying his position, denying any extracurricular activities, which Samantha did not dare contradict. She did not know how much of this Murphy was following but hoped that the ex-Minister of Justice did not know much more.

"You are well off this bit of mystery," said the ex-Minister. "I know they have our best men on the case, and they are dumbfounded and still overwhelmed in investigating the bombing itself. The people are demanding answers and swift justice," he said.

Stokes did not say it but thought that the ex-Minister had just said he knew nothing, which was fine with Stokes.

"We are all united, Fine Fail and Fine Gael, in finding out the truth," Murphy said.

Stokes did not say anything, knowing that proclamation was for the benefit of O'Neill since Murphy was now working for the opposition party.

"Still, we could stand with a day of mourning," O'Neill said.

"Too risky right now—what if the bastards decided to bomb the crowds at a mourning ceremony?" Murphy said. "We will just have to give support to the loved ones left behind for now and pursue these villains, whoever they are."

"Are you serious? You know who they are. They haven't come out with their statements yet, but this was a Unionist outrage," O'Neill said.

"We can't be sure until we get all the facts. It is bad enough that there have been atrocities on both sides, that we don't have to take sides now," Murphy said.

"There are many others who feel differently," replied O'Neill.

Stokes and Samantha stood quietly, looking uncomfortable. There was no point in putting more oil on the fire.

"We are here to celebrate the College and its accomplishments, let's remember that and enjoy ourselves," Stokes said.

"Yes, well, you are right, it should be a lovely evening," Murphy said, sighing with relief that it was Stokes applying the caution. The whims of political change could make O'Neill Murphy's boss again.

O'Neill nodded but did not smile and turned his head for a moment.

"I must do my duty as well," said O'Neill, nodding to the two, as he spotted the President of the College out of the corner of his eye. "You need to keep up the good work, however. I hope your investigations will succeed. I have been following closely," O'Neill said.

Stokes did not know why he needed to be talking to them or why he was even here, but he reminded himself that O'Neill was a donor to the College. Stokes watched as O'Neill nearly vaulted over to the President.

"Well, I too must mingle with the others. Have a good evening," Murphy said. He nodded in concession and moved into the crowd of people, holding his drink in one hand and shaking many hands with the other, moving to another group of schoolmates, talking and laughing, and Stokes could hear him loudly recalling old school days rather than politics.

The reception room was representative of Georgian architecture with intricate scrolling along the borders of the panels of the walls and the ceiling. The massive chandeliers hung gloriously, reflecting the electric light through its Waterford glass crystal. Opulence was the suggestion. People meeting that evening in the room were reflecting their own vision of prosperity, real or imagined. Where monied people were gathered, so money was made. This was as much a fundraiser as it was a celebratory reunion. Somewhere along the course of the evening, Stokes would be asked to contribute a share of prosperity to the College. He would pledge what he thought he should afford on his civil servant salary. It was early in the evening. The purse strings would be loosened for many by more alcohol and good cheer. Stokes looked around for someone he might like to talk to. He spotted Devlin, the radiologist who had been a drinking companion and commiserator during the rough student years, those first years of housemanship, and then up through the

Registrar days when their paths diverged. He was an astute observer of characters, and some quipped his eyes were as penetrating as his X-rays.

"Devlin, how are you?" Stokes asked. He gave him a broad smile and firm shake.

"Well, and yourself? I see you have a lovely escort with you. I suspect this is the young novice you have taken under your wing," Devlin said. He smiled and shook Stoke's hand but was looking at Samantha.

"Yes, this is Dr. Samantha Monaghan. She has been very helpful in the past few weeks, methodical and expeditious, I might say," Stokes said.

"High praise indeed from this curmudgeon, Dr. Monaghan, pleased to meet you," Devlin said. He smiled again, extending his hand.

"Thank you, Dr. Devlin, I have tried my best. It has been difficult, but I have muddled through," she said.

"Well, you have a good teacher, and he has a sense of humor when he wants to use it, but this has been more a sanguinary than a sanguine task. Sad and tragic—don't let it get you down."

"I have tried not to, but it has been horrible, all those poor souls," she said.

"It is easier to hide in the shadows at arm's length, illuminated by an artificial light, I would say," Devlin said. "Still, keep up the work, solve the mysteries," he said.

Samantha was not sure what he meant by this. She had assumed that no one knew about the missing body. She did not reveal any more than she thought he knew but recalled the room with the boxes and her need to tell the Professor before more clues disappeared. This was not the best venue, but she did not want to wait. For the moment, she smiled appreciatively at Devlin for his compliments and encouragements instead.

"You must come over some time for dinner. My older son is reading for the law and is interested in forensics. You might have some common interests to share."

Samantha blushed, appreciating the invitation, but not sure she wanted to chat casually about her job. Some considered it ghoulish. She had put off a good number of prospective boyfriends when she had told them what she did.

"Thank you, Dr. Devlin, perhaps when all the paperwork has lessened. I often have to work late to keep up."

"Of course, of course. "Stokes needs your time for now, but one needs a social life as well. Just ask his permission for an early night and he can ring me up. Well, I must mingle—I see the President of the College has arrived and I need to make obeisance," he smiled. "Let's get together for some golf soon, Harold. You don't work Sundays, do you?" and left without an answer.

Stokes and Samantha continued to "work the room." Both felt more relaxed after two cocktails. He was about to introduce Samantha to the Medical Director of the newest hospital when a large woman with an angry red face barreled towards them.

"Why haven't you gotten the bastards? Aren't you the one with all the answers? You put all the pieces together, didn't you? Who did this? Who did this?" she demanded shouting amidst tears and stuttering out the words like bullets from a Thompson machine gun.

The musicians playing pleasant background music stopped. The low murmurings punctuated by occasional laughter stopped. There was silence and stares at the distraught woman and the astounded Stokes. He was speechless. Samantha was stunned. Out of the motionless crowd came a man who grabbed her by one of her flailing arms. He was not a porter or other security man, but her mortified husband, a pompous proctologist. He gently guided her away as he might his instruments, turning her towards the door, apologizing.

"She lost her niece on Parnell Street. Please forgive her," he said, escorting her to the door. The crowd cleared his path.

Samantha bit her lip and clenched her jaw. She did not break into tears. The Professor saw she was not to be consoled or calmed. Samantha had lost her cousin Fergal St. John in the Monaghan bombing and was still angry enough to snap at anyone who accused her of not caring about what happened that day. Stokes feared they both would not be able to control themselves, the crowd staring at them. It was the first time that both of them had felt the full emotional impact of what had happened to others in the past few weeks. Neither felt like staying with this crowd or responding to any more questions or accusations.

"Let's get out of here," he said, moving her to the door. All eyes were upon them, but no one knew what to say, so they gave them both a wide berth and let them pass.

One of the porters came up to them at the door. "Shall I call you a cab, Sir?"

"No, we will walk. It is not far. The night is mild. She needs a bit of air and so do I, thanks" Stokes replied, leading Samantha down the few steps to the street where the traffic had diminished to an occasional whoosh of a car. It was a warm evening, still clear. More people were strolling down from the Green to Harcourt Road. Stokes and Samantha both walked slowly, an occasional passerby noting the fancy dress, but not commenting. It would take a half-hour or so to get Samantha back to her flat in Rathmines, but they were both walking with more energy the further they got from the College.

"Well, that was one way to get out of that awful room," Stokes said, seeing that Samantha's upset had decreased as she walked.

"I appreciate your taking me home, but I feel much better now, so you can go back if you wish," she said.

"I did mean that it was an awful room. When I was not all dressed up like this, I sat exams there every year without the chandeliers shining and the noise and the booze and the pompous people, and I was still uncomfortable" he said. "Besides, we must get you and your gown home."

"Oh, you can be sure I will take care of it for you. It was lovely for you to have lent it to me."

"No, no, I meant for you to have it. I have no use for it, and you wear it well. It is yours."

"Thank you, you have been very kind to me, but I have to confess something," she said, stopping as they were about to cross the Portobello Bridge over the Grand Canal that nearly surrounded the inner part of south Dublin. The waters were calm, the moon reflected through the trees that lined it.

"Confess what? I hope it has nothing to do with the dress, since I don't mind what you do with it. Don't think I was coerced into giving it to you."

"No. It's not that. I understand your good intentions. It is more important than that."

"If it is almost breaking down in front of that poor woman, don't feel guilty. You have done all you can to help the case, and more. It has been very stressful for all of us."

"I followed the white van last night."

"You did what? said Stokes, stopping to look at her. "After all my warnings? It is bad enough that I have jumped down the rabbit hole, but Alice did not have anyone following her. This is dangerous and disobedient. You were given a direct order."

"I just had to. The van was right there, across the street and they were loading boxes into it," she said, not caring about her interruption, hurriedly moving along now down the canal to its intersection with Rathmines Road. "I will show you what I had found. It is safe at home."

"What do you mean, 'what you have found'?" Stokes said, hurrying after her as she had picked up her speed, his anger dissipating in his exertion.

They got to her flat. She opened the door, not thinking a second about what the neighbors would say with her in her gown and he in his dinner suit rushing into this lower-middle-class block of flats that had no pretensions. Some children were playing outside and did not much care, but one of the old spinsters took note, as she did of anything that looked suspicious or out of the ordinary.

Samantha rushed to the closet and pulled out the laundry bag, empty but for the papers she had hidden there.

"Look," she said proudly, throwing them down on the table that served as her work desk and kitchen table in the cramped bedsitter. Stokes was taken aback by her triumphant enthusiasm and distracted by how stunning she was in his daughter's dress. He thought she could find better accommodations than this.

He looked at the copies. There at the top was the copy of Suleiman bin Daoud's file, with a photo that was the face of his missing corpse.

"How did you get this?" he said, picking up the copy, looking at her.

"I found the warehouse where the van unloaded the boxes and went back last night and got in through an open window in the back along the alley."

"Are you sure no one saw you?" he asked.

"No, it was the middle of the night, and it was really foggy. There was not much light around. No one saw me coming or going and I closed up everything and left the same way I got in," she said.

"That was quite foolhardy of you. These are people, whoever they are, used to commando operations and body snatching. Now that we know who this is, we have more of a problem—we don't know who to trust. I am not very comfortable with Curran since he hid the file from me, for whatever reason. I'm afraid Lanigan will blab to anyone."

"So, you think Curran knows more than he is letting on?" asked Samantha.

"Far more, and I think he is in league with more people than we would care to know. He did not discuss Curran's photo with the rifle.

"So, what are you going to do?"

"We still don't know what has happened to the body and why. But now we know that the Israelis are deeply involved in this, and they are staying around for some reason. If they had killed this person, Suleiman, they would have left already. I think he is one of theirs," said Stokes. "Do we still have the files on the dead French Israeli girl? She may be connected with the Israelis."

"Yes, we should, in the stack of all the other papers of the victims. There is a whole bunch of inquiries the French authorities have made for us to respond to and more forms to fill out."

"Change out of the gown and put on some work clothes. We'll go back to the office and review those papers."

"Now?" she asked. She couldn't conceal her excitement that they were on the hunt for more clues.

"Yes, while the tracks are still fresh. I am afraid these bits and pieces will be disappearing soon enough."

"Are you going to change?"

"No, we don't have the time to get to Terenure and back to the office. We must go now," Stokes said, loosening his bowtie and collar.

Chapter Ten

Samantha changed out of her gown, carefully folding it and putting it back in its box. Stokes waited patiently. Then he thought of the copies she had made.

"These cannot stay here. They must not know that you know. Give them to me. We need to lock them in the office," he said, folding them carefully into his jacket pocket.

Samantha called a taxi, and they were back at the office in a few minutes, but Stokes looked back during the drive to see if any cars followed. There seemed to be none. They greeted the policeman and then Rory, the night watchman, who both were surprised at him in his dinner jacket, and he just smiled "Urgent late-night details," he said, unlocking his office, "I shan't be long."

He went to his locked drawer and placed the copied papers in it. This would be the safest place for now, he thought. He walked over to Samantha's office. She was rummaging through the piles that were sorted in levels of urgency and difficulty.

"Here it is," she said, pulling out the file from the cabinet and the papers in French on the desk that requested all the extra details that she had put off until she could get someone to help with the translations. They had also sent some more biographical information which she had barely read. Her French was awful, and she did not want to make any errors when she finally responded to all the questions.

"Our stuff is sketchy, but it gives us an idea. The other stuff is in French," she said.

"What do we know so far?" Stokes asked, not having conducted the autopsy himself, so he had not yet signed off on the report.

"She was thirty-one, unmarried, lived in Paris, but had come here for six months on a student visa to learn English. She was a teacher, and she was Jewish. Remember the row her friends made about burying her body quickly? They were an obnoxious bunch," she said, shaking her head.

"Yes, I do recall that now. Unusually raucous for mourners. I have had to do autopsies on other Jewish people, and this did seem different," he said. "Let me see the French papers. Perhaps I can make head or tails of them."

He read the papers carefully. His French was rusty, but he had done some study there many years before, learning some of the forensic techniques the French had mastered but were too disinterested in translating. As it was, there was little that was said in the papers that they didn't know. She had lived in Israel for a few years and even served in the army during the '67 war before she and her mother moved to France. It did not specify what she had done in the war, but it was likely she was in support since there were very few women who were in active combat. It was a complicated life she had had, surviving the Holocaust, then another war, and then ending up dead in the Troubles. According to the papers, she had no relatives in Dublin, but did have some friends. She lived with an old Jewish couple while she was studying here. He made a note of their names and address since this was listed as her residence.

"We will need to visit this couple first thing in the morning. Maybe they will know something more about her," Stokes said. "There does not seem to be any more in the French papers, but we should contact the French embassy and see if they have any more about her. We will just say we are completing the final report."

Stokes put the file and the papers into his locked drawer and looked at Samantha. "No more skulking!" he said. "Have a good night's sleep. You will join me tomorrow."

It was late when he got home, but he glanced across the street and the white van was still parked in front of the house. There was no activity at this time in the evening. This was curious since there was a regularity to their pickups and deliveries that he thought was part of their "cover" for their import and export business. Having been so open previously, he had expected that this lack of normal activity must mean they were done and were preparing to close their operations. There was no more activity beyond the moving of the files that Samantha had noticed. They must have had some more unfinished business—did they need to find their comrade's killer? Did they plan on revenge? Nothing indicated what was going on from the lights in their building and the plain white van. He was torn about pursuing them as opposed to leaving it up to Lanigan or Curran, neither of whom he trusted. He didn't know how much they knew but didn't want to find out.

He went to bed and read a few more pages of dry Irish history speculating on the plagues and their origins and how that may have affected the history of the Irish people, their relationship with their economy, and relations with other peoples, but the story was muddled, like a game of telephone separated by not just perception, but time. The confusions entered his dreams, and he did not sleep well.

Chapter Eleven

Stokes went to the office as usual, dealt with immediate office details and thanked his luck that there were no more autopsies to perform that day. He prepared for the visit to the Jewish couple by having Samantha call to make sure they were available. They were pensioners and cooperative on the phone, if hard of hearing, but more than willing to help with any investigations although they were curious as to why another visit was necessary. They had already given information to the police. No one had indicated that they needed to know more. Samantha reassured them the visit would be brief, just to make sure no details had been missed for the final report. Samantha was not quite sure what other questions would be asked and to what end but knew that Stokes had his reasons.

Samantha called the French Embassy. The secretary there was curt and circumspect since this involved a French citizen. Samantha was told they needed to get clearance from any and all concerned departments before they could visit. Stokes expected as much and did not press Samantha to do any more for now.

"Let's get going. This should not take long. We will have to tackle the French Embassy later, if at all," he said, grabbing his hat and motioning Samantha to come along.

They took a taxi to the address in Terenure, not far from where Stokes lived, down a quiet street of small single-family houses with wrought iron fences and gates and neat front gardens. The houses looked no different, one from the other, or from any other Dublin houses but were part of the Jewish middle-class community that had prospered between the wars. The group was aging, seeing their families, as with other Irish people, move on for better opportunities. Samantha knocked on the door and a small, neatly dressed woman in her seventies opened the door. She led them into the sitting room, the bay window blinds open to the quiet street and sat them down on the sofa with a pot of tea, pastries, and biscuits already laid out. She called her husband, who hurriedly sat down in his soft armchair, out of habit, and then caught himself as his wife frowned. He stood and shook hands politely.

"I am Joseph Schwartz," he said, his Dublin accent soft and well educated. "I hope we can help you, but I am not sure what more we can tell you that we have not told the other police and detectives," he said.

"We wanted to know more about what Ana LeBow did here in Dublin and if she had any acquaintances here," Stokes asked.

"Would you like some tea?" Mrs. Schwartz offered.

"Of course, thank you," Stokes replied politely, not wanting any tea at all.

"Yes, please," Samantha replied, feeling thirsty and intrigued by the homemade pastries.

"Ana was a very pleasant, polite young lady, kept to herself but tried to practice her English at any opportunity, but with her accent and limitations, she was only just learning, so she did not say much," the husband said.

"She told us about her mother and how she had lived through the Holocaust which was so terrible for her as such a little girl. She told us she was in the Army in 1967, another terrifying time, and then this," said Mrs. Schwartz, barely holding back her tears. "Such a nice girl," she said.

"I am sorry for your tragic loss, as we all are," Stokes said.

"Did she have any friends or visitors?" Samantha asked.

"Yes, she did. He might have been her boyfriend, someone she said she met in the Army, but he did not come more than once and only when she was sick with the flu and could not get out of bed for days. He seemed very concerned. He insisted that the doctor make a house call since she refused to go to the hospital. She was terrified by doctors. It must have been the war. They spoke in Hebrew, not French. When she got better, we never saw him again" Mrs. Schwartz said. "He barely spoke to us, but he was polite."

"He was in the import/export business and was very busy most days. In fact, he seemed to work more night than day, according to the butcher," said Mrs. Schwartz.

"No other acquaintances, as far as you know?" Samantha asked.

"No, besides the French students she was learning English with. She talked about going out with them and practicing English in a café or pub, sometimes with amusing results for everyone, since a thick Irish accent is hard for an Irish person to understand, let alone a foreigner," she said.

"Do you recall her boyfriend's name?" Stokes asked.

"It may have been Solomon," Mr. Schwartz joined, "Solomon ben David, if I am not mistaken, very biblical. He gave us his name and a number to call in case she was ill again, but I have lost the paper. I was rummaging around for it to call him, but I am sure he knew she died since her name was in all the papers," he said.

"Was it this man?" asked Stokes, pulling out the photocopy of Suleiman bin Daoud, the Arabic equivalent of the Hebrew Solomon ben David.

"Yes, that was him. It was strange that he did not come to the memorial service. All her friends were there who were still in Dublin. She was supposed to have gone back to France with them all the next day. How unfortunate, how sad," Mr. Schwartz said.

"Well, you have been a great help. Please do not discuss this with anyone else without calling me," Stokes said. "This is still an investigation. You haven't told anyone else, have you?"

"No, sir, just the local Gardai and a detective. We answered questions about Ana and her mother to help them contact her with the awful news," Mr. Schwartz said. "No one asked about friends or acquaintances, or Mr. David, since it was pretty obvious she was a victim. She was, wasn't she?" Mr. Schwartz asked.

"Yes," said Stokes. "I'm afraid so."

"Well, then, I hope you find him since he seemed concerned enough when she was ill," Mr. Schwartz said.

"We must be going and thanks for the help," Stokes said, standing to shake his hand.

"And thanks for the tea and the wonderful little pastries. Are they Jewish?" asked Samantha.

"Yes, they are called *rogelach* and they are from Eastern Europe" Mrs. Schwartz said.

"Lovely, and thanks again," Samantha replied politely, trying to leave on a pleasant note. She tried to contain herself before she burst out with questions and theories to the Professor about what this all meant.

Before she could say a word, Stokes warned her: "This has gotten much more complicated than I would like, and you need to be circumspect. We do not need to visit the French Embassy. That will draw more suspicion and we certainly don't want to draw the French into Irish affairs. Their bureaucracy is awful. They invented the word."

"What are we going to do now?" Samantha asked.

"We are going to contact Lanigan and get a proper search warrant for the warehouse you burgled," Stokes said, stopping at the closest bus stop. Since she was warned to be cautious, the bus would be public enough for Samantha to stop asking any more questions compared to the deceptive privacy of a taxi. Besides, he had a limited budget, had paid for the taxi out of his own pocket since he did not want to alert anyone to his "extracurricular activities," as they surely would be interpreted.

Chapter Twelve

A fine thread connected the Dublin bombings in 1972 that killed Stokes' wife and daughter and the bombings two weeks ago. The dossier on Suleiman bin Daoud was in the copies of Israeli files about the 1972 bombings that Samantha had shown him. For whatever disorder there was in those boxes, the connections were there. They may have been overlooked by the agents as they had moved the files from place to place, disrupted by the recent events and the loss of one of their own. Stokes would not be surprised if all those files disappeared in the next twenty-four hours, shipped to Israel or another location with a load of steaks and ground beef. He wondered if his missing corpse had been transported like a carcass as well. He was absolutely sure that it was no longer on Irish soil and had been buried according to Jewish law with full military honors, however discreetly that might be done in the Israeli Secret Service. He couldn't help smiling at the pun: a secret service in the Secret Service.

The Littlejohns, the brothers who had robbed the Allied Irish Bank in October of 1972 were linked to but never implicated in the November 1972 bombings. They claimed they were double agents for MI6, the British Overseas Secret Service, and the IRA. Had they done the bombing on the orders of one or the other? If it was MI6, it would make sense they needed to undermine the IRA by bombing Dublin and convince the *Dail* (Irish Parliament) to pass the proposed stronger laws against terrorist groups. If it was the IRA, it would strengthen the extremists who saw the Irish government as a threat to their fight for unification because it would encourage more security cooperation on the Border with the Unionists. Either way, Suleiman bin Daoud or Solomon ben David, was involved and he may have been aware of who the real masterminds were in both bombings. Why had he been on Talbot Street that day? Who had killed him? Who had ordered his death? Did the Israelis know? Did G2, the Irish Secret Service, know?

Stokes was silent on the ride back to the office, deep in thought. He had to be reminded by Samantha that they had reached their stop. While he was trying to think things through, Samantha's mind was racing over all the possibilities and was arriving at the same questions that needed to be answered, but she was not thinking of 1972. Her mind was fixed on the moment and her experiences of the past few weeks.

Stokes nodded to his secretary as he passed through to his office without saying a word, which indicated he did not want to be disturbed. He entered his office with Samantha following. He motioned her to close the door behind her and sat down at the desk and picked up the phone. He paused for a moment and then put it down again. He looked at Samantha and shook his head.

"I am not ready to call Lanigan," he said. "We need to act quickly. The Israelis are not done here. I think they are not ready to leave until they get all their intelligence and exact their revenge. On whom, I do not know yet."

"Can we trust Lanigan?" Samantha asked.

"He is a pretty straight shooter, but he has a big mouth and a bigger ego. We need to use that to our advantage."

"How?"

"You know we are being followed, don't you?" Stokes asked.

"No, really?" Samantha asked, looking surprised and slightly frightened at his assertion.

"Of course. How else could you have gotten into that warehouse so easily? They wanted someone to check those files because they knew they had information that others don't want them to have. They saw you at my house and they saw you with me at the kosher abattoir, but they did not see us as a threat, but bait. They want us to tell their suspects so they can catch them in the act of trying to remove the incriminating evidence. Then they can find their leaders and those who have been collaborating with the PLO and get the cell that has been dealing with the IRA. We are pawns, so we are safe from them, but you must be cautious. If you have any thoughts of going back to that warehouse, forget them. Understood?"

"Yes, Professor," she answered, frightened by his expression that she had not seen before. She felt like kicking herself that she had missed this whole process. "But when did you notice?"

"The night we left your flat. There was a car following us in the distance. It was easy to spot since there were so few cars on the road. Pretty obvious, but whoever was following us wanted it that way. We were the designated "gofers," as the Americans would say. I went along with it because I want to know who has been involved as much as they do. The Gardai and especially Special Branch have been pretty casual about whom they hold responsible for these atrocities. They don't want us to know the full picture. Too embarrassing," he said.

"So, what are we to do now?"

"Did I not just tell you to stay out of it? *We* will not do anything. *We* will just sit back and watch what happens. *You* are on a need-to-know basis and will let Lanigan know if there is anything suspicious that happens to me."

He picked up the phone, glowering at her, let her observe, but his face reiterated silence. He dialed the number from memory.

"This is Professor Stokes, the State Pathologist, may I speak to Detective Lanigan?"

"He is out on a case at the moment," the secretary replied. "May I leave a message?"

"When do you expect him back?"

"I don't know, but he said he would ring in this afternoon. Is it an emergency?"

"It is urgent. He needs to get a search warrant and it needs to be soon," Stokes replied.

"Can someone else handle this?" asked the secretary.

"I would prefer this be managed between him and me since there is some sensitivity to the case."

"I will have him call you back as soon as possible."

"All right then, thanks," Stokes replied and hung up. He was still upset. Samantha held her tongue.

"Timing is everything. If we wait too long, the Israelis will act on their own. Of course, they let you go because they want to catch the bigger fish. But it was not the Israelis who were following us. Lanigan is unlikely to do any more than he has to on his own initiative. He doesn't want to step on any toes. It is probably Curran; he has not called me or asked for any more information in days. Either he has other leads, or he knows more than we do. This will be cat and mouse. Best to stay out of it. We have work to do," he said, looking at the pile of paperwork on his desk. "I will speak to you later," he said, dismissing Samantha.

Chapter Thirteen

Lanigan dropped back late in the day, just in time to rouse Stokes before he sat back in his chair to rest his eyes after plodding through the stacks of papers.

"How are things going with you, Professor?" Lanigan asked, bursting through the door without knocking.

"We need a search warrant," Stokes replied, surprised by the prompt visit, unlike the lackadaisical Lanigan he had experienced before.

"What do you mean, *we*, Professor?"

"For a warehouse full of incriminating files that I fear will disappear if we tarry too long," he said.

"And how did you discover this warehouse, Professor?"

"Never mind how, but you need to be able to confiscate these files before this evidence is compromised."

"And I assume you want to come along?"

"I do, but you need to bring a gun. There may be some dangerous people about. How quickly can you get the warrant?"

"It is almost teatime. The Judge does not like to have his tea delayed or interrupted. Not in a good mood then."

"How quickly?"

"Do you need a bloody SWAT team to get in there now?"

"We need to get the information that is in there as soon as possible with the least amount of trouble. I don't know who else knows about this, but we are not dealing with just a bunch of crooks 'out for a jar,' these may be terrorists," Stokes said.

"Well, why don't you just call Curran?"

"I don't trust him,"

"And you trust me? I'm flattered," Lanigan smiled. "Well, it's just half four now. I might be able to catch his honor. Can I have your phone?"

Stokes pushed the phone over to Lanigan, hoping that this confidence was not misplaced. He watched as Lanigan pulled out his little address book and searched for the number, surprised Lanigan would take such an initiative on his own and not cover himself by asking his superiors to clear it before he called. In this case, despite the sarcasm, he believed Stokes.

"Is this the Judge himself? Yes, your honor, this is Detective Seamus Lanigan. We need a search warrant to examine suspicious premises in Terenure. No, as soon as possible since we are afraid the evidence may be removed. Oh, the State Pathologist. He is right here. Would you like to speak to him?" Lanigan handed the phone over to Stokes.

"Yes, your honor. It is related to the case of the missing casualty. There are files there that may lead to the identification of the man and who may have removed the body. I can't reveal my sources since they may be in danger if I do. It needs to be done with the utmost urgency. I am afraid the evidence may be removed at any time. This evening? I'll come over with Detective Lanigan right now. Many thanks," Stokes said, hanging up.

"We need to get over to the Four Courts right now," said Stokes, putting on his jacket and grabbing his hat. He knocked on Samantha's door. She stood up quickly.

"We are going over to the Four Courts for a search warrant. Do you remember the address of the warehouse?" he asked. Samantha wrote down the address quickly.

"So, she was the little snooper, was she?" Lanigan asked, smiling. "Do you know breaking and entering is a criminal offense, young lady?"

"She is under my supervision, so I take any and all responsibility," Stokes said.

"Fair enough, chief, I never saw or heard this, unless I am asked directly in court," Lanigan said to Stokes.

He turned to Samantha, still smiling. "Nevertheless, better keep your nose clean, young Doc. You don't want to be the next body on the slab."

"Stay here," Stokes told Samantha and hurried out the door with Lanigan.

"How long will it take to get the warrant and round up some Gardai?" Stokes asked as they walked to the car. With Lanigan driving, it might be quicker than walking so Stokes screwed his courage and jumped into the car and Lanigan started the siren as soon as they were in.

"I'll round up some fellas as soon as we have the paper in hand," Lanigan answered, eager for some excitement, even if it was only for an excuse to use his siren and drive at high speeds in Centre City. They sped past cars and pedestrians on the narrow and curving streets. What should have taken at least fifteen minutes took five.

Judge Stephens was already waiting at his desk when they were ushered in. He was a big man with a ruddy face that may have been weathered by his long golf and fishing outings or his love of Porter. Stokes had never met him but knew of his bad temper and scrupulous appreciation for the law.

"It is not often I am issuing search warrants on short notice. Have you cleared this with your Superintendent?" the judge asked.

"No, sir, he is gone for the day, your honor," Lanigan said.

"Detective Lanigan, you should know better. What is the nature of this emergency? *I* should be gone for the day," Stephens protested. "If this order is compromised, so is the evidence. I will issue the order for tomorrow, pending your Superintendent's written request. You are wasting my time," Stephens said, dropping his pen and standing up.

"Your honor," Stokes interrupted. "I realize that this is an unusual request and beyond the regulations that normally determine your judgment, but I take full responsibility for this and will discuss this fully with Detective Lanigan's Superintendent. Remember, I am a functionary of the justice system as well. The information I think that is there may help us apprehend not only the body snatchers, but possibly the bombers and the people who may have helped them both now and in 1972. This evidence may be instrumental. The search falls within the Offences Against the State Act of 1939."

"How can you be so sure? Have you seen it? How were you able to see it? Have you committed the crime of breaking and entering? Your knowledge of it may be illegal, so why should I issue a search warrant?" the Judge said, still standing.

"The act of the search may be enough to attract the attention of the culprits, which I am hoping. That is why I need the Detective and the Gardai to accompany me."

"I will not endanger anyone, you or the Gardai or even Detective Lanigan without a Superintendent's knowledge. The Superintendent can call me in the morning. Good evening," said the Judge and walked past them and out the door.

"Shite and onions," Lanigan said. "Your man is a bit of a hardarse, he is. Better cool your heels and wait until tomorrow, Professor."

"I don't think we can afford to. The evidence may be gone by then," replied Stokes.

Lanigan and Stokes stood outside the courthouse for a moment, both stumped as to what to do. They turned and walked back to Lanigan's car.

"Well, we aren't getting anywhere here, are we?" Lanigan asked. "What are we going to do?"

"You risk reprimand, demotion, or worse if you don't follow protocol," Stokes cautioned, "so *we* are not going to do anything. We need to wait."

"Sure, there is no harm in surveillance, is there, Professor?"

"Who is going to do that day and night? I have a full-time job and the Gardai are not going to be very eager for a stakeout without knowing why; there is the risk of other people finding out."

"Let's see what I can do. You want to catch the bastards who killed those people and stole the body and so do I. Leave it to me, Prof, I come from a family of devious Irishmen. It takes a deviant to catch a deviant."

Stokes just smiled. 'Deviant' was good enough for Lanigan to get his point across.

"All right, then, I will leave you to it, but be cautious—I don't know who knows what. I suspect there has been a lot covered up and reputations and aspirations are at stake that may be worth their weight in gold and power."

"It's nearly time for tea. I could use a pint before I get home. The missus has been on a tear about me neglecting my home duties with the tumult and coming home late too many nights," Lanigan complained.

"Then it might do you well to forgo the pint and get home early. You never know what pleasantries you might encounter," Stokes said, smiling.

"Right you are, Professor. You are a man of wisdom as well as learning. I will give that a go, but the offer of the pint is still up any time," said Lanigan, smiling despite having been so easily diverted. "I'll drive you down to Terenure and I can swing by that warehouse just for the craic of it on the way home to Ranelagh since it's not that far."

"That would be helpful considering it is rush hour but do be cautious in your drive-by. I don't want you to stir the hornet's nest. No sirens, please," Stokes added as he got in the car, hoping that Lanigan would observe the traffic laws.

"You're no fun, Professor," Lanigan responded as he started the car, but did not leave in a lurch. The traffic was especially bad that evening and Lanigan cursed at everyone who passed him on the road, but he did not speed or use his siren. Stokes ignored him and thought of what he could do with such little time.

"How easy will it be to get the approval of the search warrant from the Superintendent?" asked Stokes.

"If it has anything to do with the Offences Against the State, he should be right on board," Lanigan said.

"If you knew that, why didn't you just go to him first?" asked Stokes.

"Well, I thought I would go direct to the organ grinder instead of the monkey,"

"Well, you didn't bring any bananas, did you?"

"Good one, Prof," Lanigan laughed.

They arrived at Stokes' house and Stokes glanced across the street. The white van was still there and there was no activity at the house. That was momentarily reassuring.

"Contact the Superintendent first thing, won't you?"

"If you need me there, just call. I will be at the office. Don't let anyone else know, especially Curran."

"No fear. But what should I tell the Chief if he asks about Curran?"

"Just tell him that this is only related to the investigation of the theft of the body. He does not need to know about the nature of the files, only that there may be information in them to help identify the thieves."

"Fair enough, stolen body, information about who stole it and where it might be, right?"

"Good man. Have a good night and please be discreet," Stokes said again. He was far out of his comfort zone.

"Right you are, have a good evening, Prof. Now home to the old ball and chain—she'll be shocked!" he grimaced and sped off, faster than was legally allowed.

Chapter Fourteen

Mrs. Kelly already had the tea set out, the knives and forks and spoons on their lace doilies, the water glass on the right that Stokes always moved out of his way to the left. He had arrived home before the Angelus, but the dinner plate was already sitting warm in the oven, guaranteeing the meal would still be hot despite his schedule. She did not ask him about his work, and he did not offer. She was accustomed to his silence and respected it, not really interested in his ghoulish profession. He spared her any details except for occasional complaints about the general bureaucracy. She had all the information she needed. She was always aware of his comings and goings and the windows saw the world.

"I couldn't help but notice, Professor. You got driven home. Was that the loud man Lanigan you complained about? I could hear him from outside," she asked.

"Yes, it was. We are working on a case together," he replied, looking down at his plate, cutting his food, clearly implying his interest was in his meal. "This is quite nice."

"'Tis. I got it from the kosher butcher. He has had some nice lamb chops lately. He said you dropped by the other day. He's not involved in anything is he?"

"No, I was just following some leads."

"I hope that crew across the street is not involved. Always peculiar comings and goings at all hours, day and night."

"Excuse me," she interrupted herself. The Angelus sounded on the radio which was on in the sitting room. It was a compromise the Professor had with Mrs. Kelly that she could have the radio on until the Irish news was over and then there could be quiet. It was not her fault that he had come home a bit early. The Irish news report distracted her enough so that the interrogation was interrupted. Thankfully, her respect for patient confidentiality and legal cases was such that her inquiries were not an issue, he thought to himself.

He finished his meal in peace and quiet since Mrs. Kelly was bustling around the kitchen cleaning up and making ready to leave for the evening. She was a help and a welcome, friendly voice, despite her chattering, in the silence of his otherwise empty house. He had thought of selling and moving to a flat, but he could not bring himself to do it yet. Although there were always reminders of his loss at the turn of every corner of the place, his home was still a comfortable, quiet familiarity. Stokes sat in his old chair in the living room and listened to a recording of Beethoven's 6th Symphony conducted by Arturo Toscanini. The music was soothing. He closed his eyes to savor it.

Chapter Fifteen

He woke with a start at 10 PM, irritated by his fatigue since the long nap would severely disturb his night's sleep and would get him into a nasty cycle of not being very energetic the next day. He toyed with the idea of drinking a small glass of sherry and went to the liquor cabinet that was next to the front window. As he glanced out, he saw there was more activity across the street and that the white van was being loaded with more boxes. Could these be the files that were being transferred or some other documents? He closed the door of the cabinet and continued to watch. There were a lot of boxes and at least four men, including the man with the limp going in and out of the house to load up the van. This did not look like the usual deliveries he had seen before. He was afraid this was a permanent exodus. He wanted to call Lanigan but was worried that he would not come soon enough. Stokes decided to take it upon himself to follow them. He watched and waited until they were done. He expected that they would be on their way to the warehouse, so he called for a taxi, knowing it would take some time to get to his house. He would view the movement at the warehouse at a distance without their knowledge.

He opened the locked cabinet where he kept his service revolver. He had the good fortune of never having fired it in battle but was comfortable about his abilities. He hoped he would not have to use it now but needed the insurance. He pulled out his old binoculars. If nothing was moved, he would call Lanigan early the next morning to get that search warrant. If they started moving, he would call him the moment he saw an urgent need. He was not happy about taking the law into his own hands, but he needed to know. There was no one he could really trust, to find the truth or act on it.

The van pulled away after another few minutes. If they were not going to the warehouse, all was lost, but he waited for the taxi. It arrived five minutes later. He gave instructions as to where to go and asked him to drop him on the corner before the lane so he could peer down undetected.

"Are you sure this is where you want to get out?" questioned the driver, looking around at the deserted streets with poor lighting, seemingly worried about his passenger's safety. There were no homes, just warehouses, mostly closed for the night.

"Yes, I am sure. I need to meet someone here who promised to show me a vintage MG car that was being repaired. I couldn't come earlier because I had to work late."

"All right then, but be careful, it is dark out here," the driver said and drove off after Stokes gave him a handsome tip.

Through his binoculars, Stokes saw the van parked down the lane through the evening fog and the orange streetlights bouncing off the mist. He could make out no movement. A light came on in the warehouse that broke through the slats in the bars. The motor on the van was off, a sign they were not in a hurry to unload or load anything. He focused his binoculars on the doors to the warehouse and then to the window. There was no movement. What were they doing in there? He hoped they would stay for a while, so all the worrying would not be in vain, and the truth would not vanish.

He noticed a phone box down the street and rushed to it. He rummaged through his pockets for some coins and fished out Lanigan's number scribbled on a scrap of paper. He could barely see it in the phone box light and pulled out his torch to make sure and called. The phone rang far too long. Finally, Lanigan answered.

"Lanigan here, who the feck is this?" he said.

"It's Professor Stokes. Sorry to call so late. I am down the street from the warehouse, and I think they will be removing the files tonight—there was a lot of activity. Can you get here soon?"

"Give me the street number and cross-street," said Lanigan who had his head on straighter than Stokes. Stokes thought for a moment and then gave him the number.

"Not too far. It will take me a while. I will want to get some

Gardai. All on the up and up, ya know, so don't be going off and doing any acts of bravery!"

"I'll be outside of the warehouse, standing by a nearby garage doorway down the lane." Stokes answered and hung up. He walked quickly back down the lane and could see the lights were still on.

He gripped his revolver, making sure it was easy to get out. He had not used it in the Royal Navy but practiced at the police shooting range every few months. Once he had brought it into the office when there was a particularly unsavory death of a mobster and there were threats against him and his staff. Nothing came of it. It was reassuring then that he could defend himself, but he was not sure he had that kind of courage now.

He got closer and heard loud talking. Not English, perhaps Hebrew or Arabic. Were these the terrorists he was looking for? Could it be Germans from the Baader-Meinhof Gang? Could it be Irish? All kinds of conspiracies and new threats came to mind.

He went up against the door of the warehouse and listened. They were shouting now, someone was speaking English, softly, sometimes crying, sometimes mumbling. It was an interrogation, he was sure. Whoever they were, they needed information and their prisoner was not giving them what they wanted. He tried to peer through the slats in the window but could see nothing. The conversation was still mostly foreign, but it did sound like Hebrew. The prisoner was mumbling "I don't know" again and again.

He heard a female voice, pleading to let them go. He did not want to believe it, but it was clear enough that it was Samantha. What in God's name was she doing there?

He pulled out his gun and leaned closer on the door and felt it give and swing open. As it did, he lost his balance. In a second, he was on the floor and in another there were two bearded men on top of him, quickly disarming him. They bolted the door—they had enough visitors.

"Who are you? What are you doing here?" they demanded in decent but heavily accented English.

Stokes ignored them despite their restraints. He glanced across the dimly lit room and saw Samantha, slightly disheveled, sitting tied in a chair, looking afraid.

"Are you all right?" Stokes asked Samantha.

"Yes, they haven't been rough with me. I was here before they came. When Curran followed me in, I hid in a corner. I saw them grab him when they came in. A rat startled me. I yelped and they caught me," she said.

Curran was tied to a chair. He had some bruises on his face and his lip was bleeding, but Stokes had caught his eye. Curran looked embarrassed.

"Now that we have that done, we assure you that you are not the enemy, but help us know who is. Do you know this man?" asked a tall, handsome, bearded man brandishing a Jewish ritual slaughter knife, long and very sharp with no tip.

"I do. You already know who he is," Stokes said.

"Don't be smart with us. We know you and your little assistant have been here already, and we know who you are. Not very good detectives, but you were good bait for this fish," he said, looking down at Curran.

"What do you propose to do with him?" Stokes asked.

"He is not a very good talker. Maybe if you ask, he will tell you what he knows. We have been following him and following you for a while. We think he is a killer and a traitor to his country. Should we kill him now or leave him to you?" asked the man with the knife.

"So, the dead man was one of yours," Stokes said, trying to ignore the knife, which could cut efficiently in one direction and then kill definitively in the other. It was designed, they said, to be merciful. Curran was looking down at it, placed close to his neck.

"He was a patriot and tried to save lives and died for his country, and for yours," the tall man said.

"He was a spy in this country and deserved what he got," Curran said.

"Did you kill him?" the man with the limp said quietly with a steady coldness and no hint of anger in his voice. "Give me the knife, Rami, I have the courage to do it," he said to the man holding the knife.

"No," Rami said, still holding the killing blade firmly, pressing it against Curran's neck, enough to break the skin. A trickle of blood leaked down his neck.

"The man you are looking for is from the PLO," said Curran, hoarse with apprehension, eyes widening.

"How do you know this?" Rami asked.

"I saw him," Curran said.

"You were there?"

"Yes."

"On Talbot Street?" Stokes joined in.

"Yes, he was on the roof down the street when he saw your man waving to his girlfriend, seconds before the bomb went off," Curran said.

"So, you knew the bombs were going to go off?" Stokes asked.

"Yes, we had an idea," Curran said, bowing his head.

"You had an idea? You had an idea?" said Stokes, outraged, barely restrained by his captors.

"Did you not see the body parts and the bloody prams and the dead among the burning twisted cars and shattered glass? How could you just have an idea?" Stokes cried out.

One of the men sat Stokes down in the chair, afraid he himself would use the sacred knife on Curran.

"And what about the Film Centre Cinema, did you know about that too?" Stokes demanded.

"We did, but that was the Littlejohn's crew working for MI6. We tried to stop them, but that bombing was necessary. We were strengthened by it. We did not expect anyone to be hurt—it was unlucky timing," Curran said.

"Who are *we*?" Stokes asked, pushing his agenda, surprised by Curran's confession. Perhaps Curran was appealing for leniency from a fellow Irishman since the Israelis were not so inclined, he thought. The blade was still at his throat.

"If I tell you, you won't believe me, and I will be a dead man," Curran said.

"You are a dead man if you don't talk," said Rami. "Go on."

"It was O'Neill. He has been doing gun-running and the counterespionage. He left me as the stooge when that PLO terrorist, he calls himself the Jackal, went off on his killing spree. He had been watching your Jewish friend, bin Daoud, or ben David, whatever you want to call him. He suspected he was a double agent. When bin Daoud found out about the planned bombing, he tried to warn his girlfriend. I was supposed to stop him, not kill him, but the Jackal had other ideas. O'Neill said he would protect me. So here I am," said Curran.

"So, *you* doctored the files—to make sure that no one knew about bin Daoud and connect him to the IRA. You were protecting yourself and O'Neill. And you lot," Stokes said to the Israelis, "removed the body to bury him under Jewish law and protect your undercover surveillance of the Jackal and his IRA friends. So, you can let us go now," he said to Rami.

"Not until we are gone. The files are yours. This IRA trash is yours. We still don't have the Jackal, but he knows we are looking," Rami said, motioning the other two to release Stokes. He went to Samantha, kneeling to release her bonds, smiled, looked up at her and said "Sorry."

Samantha did not have a chance to respond. There was a knock at the door with police lights suddenly flashing outside.

"Open up, this is the Gardai," said Lanigan loudly.

The Israelis had seen the lights before Lanigan spoke. They opened a trapdoor and disappeared quickly into it, but not before the man with the limp had picked up the dropped ritual knife and quickly made one slash on Curran's neck.

"This is for you to remember us if you survive. That was for my brother," he yelled, jumped into the trapdoor, and disappeared.

Stokes jumped over and pressed his hand against the jugular vein that was nicked. The wound was superficial but looked awful with the blood oozing down Curran's neck and the skin gaping wide open.

"Get me that rag," Stokes commanded. Samantha was already up with some old, discarded clothes and pressed them against the neck wound.

Curran was blubbering: "Am I going to die?"

"Not yet," Stokes said, not feeling very reassuring. Curran was still tied to the chair. Stokes did not untie him.

The police battering ram knocked open the steel door and Lanigan and the Gardai came streaming through. At the bloody sight, one of the Gardai fainted and another pulled him up.

"Get up, you eejit, sure it's only a flesh wound," the Garda said.

"Where are they?" Lanigan asked Stokes, ignoring the blood.

"Down the rabbit hole," Stokes nodded to the trapdoor.

"What are you looking at? Get down there." Lanigan yelled at the other two Gardai. He had come well reinforced, but too late.

"Will your man live?" Lanigan asked.

"Yes, he will, but he will have a lot to account for. Do you have a first aid kit in your car?" Stokes asked.

"Oh, yeah, sure. O'Reilly, get the kit and be quick about it. Do you not see your man is bleeding all over the Professor's suit?" said Lanigan.

Stokes looked down at himself as he continued to keep the pressure on. His hands and trousers were covered in blood. Samantha spoke to Curran to assess his level of consciousness and felt his radial artery. He was responsive but his pulse was rapid, not thready, more from fear than loss of blood, Samanth thought.

"What else do you know about the Cinema bombing," Stokes asked Curran, hoping to get to more truth, as far as one could get it from a scared and wounded man.

"No more than I just said to you and the Israelis. The Littlejohns masterminded it, and O'Neill knew about it. All I know is that O'Neill promised no one would be hurt, just like IRA bombs where there are warnings so 'civilians' do not get hurt."

"My wife and daughter were 'civilians', you bastard," Stokes hissed, tempted to release the pressure on the wound so he would bleed to death.

"Now, now, Professor, let's not let your emotions threaten the witness. We'll need him for later," said Lanigan, who was listening to every word.

"Does O'Neill know you're here?" asked Stokes.

"No, he keeps me at arm's length, as he does the others. Squeaky clean, the bastard is. You'll get nothing on him," Curran said weakly, knowing O'Neill could invoke plausible deniability that would keep him out of an investigation and Curran in jail or worse. Curran had nothing to hide.

The Garda finally brought in the rudimentary first aid kit that at least had proper gauze and surgical bandages and some antiseptic. Stokes released his pressure a bit to check the wound which was now just oozing slightly. It would be an easy fix since the cut was as clean as a surgeon's knife, he judged. He nodded to Samantha to apply the dressing as he released his pressure for a moment.

"Why are you stopping the pressure?" asked Curran, afraid he had given just enough information so that he was of no more use to them.

"Stop your whining," said Lanigan, "even I can see that the bleeding is slowing down. We'll have you down to the Casualty soon enough."

"What else do you know of the bombing in 1972?" Stokes persisted, his hand still pressing harder on Curran's neck than was necessary as Samantha finished the bandaging.

"Just that it wasn't the Littlejohns —they were already in Mountjoy jail. Then they broke out in March. The Brits may have had something to do with that. I think they are somewhere in England. I don't know much. I wasn't part of that," he said.

"Have you found the Jews?" Lanigan yelled at one of the Garda who had walked in the door.

"No, sir, not a sign. We went down the length of the tunnel and it leads out to an alley and down the road. They could be anywhere, sneaky bastards," he said.

Stokes ignored them and pressed on Curran's neck.

"Not part of what, agent Curran? Not part of the bombing or helping the Littlejohn's escape? What part are you involved with? You certainly stood by and let one man be shot a few weeks ago and let the bombers commit their barbarous mayhem. You did know their plans, didn't you? You did not speak out, did you? You let innocents die. You are a despicable piece of trash,"

"Now, now, Professor. He will get his time in court, and he will spill all his 'official secrets,' I promise you," Lanigan said, as soothingly as he could muster. "There is no point in going on now is there?"

Stokes let go of Curran's neck, realizing that Lanigan was right, and that Samantha's bandaging would hold. A wave of fatigue ran over him. It was the middle of the night. He looked over at Samantha who was also covered in blood.

"I guess we're done here," Stokes said. "Get all the files and keep them under strict surveillance. I think the Israelis completed their mission here now, but they will continue to chase the Jackal, or whatever he is called. You will not find them. Don't bother questioning Wolfe the butcher. You can check their offices across the street from my house, but you will probably find nothing there either," said Stokes.

"You're right, Professor," said Lanigan. "You're done too by the looks of you, a bit like Count Dracula." He smiled like he couldn't avoid his own macabre sense of humor. Stokes smiled wanly, trying to ignore the jibe, but looked down at his bloodied coat and hands, surprising himself at the gore.

"I'll have one of the Garda cars take you and your assistant to your house to get cleaned up. We know where to find you if we need you. We'll take this Gobshite to the Casualty to have him cleaned up a bit and then the station to have another go," Lanigan said.

"How are you going to keep this from O'Neill?" Stokes asked.

"I think we have enough information to give his bosses and my Superintendent reason to believe he is more than just a patriot. Let's see if he can squirm out of this," Lanigan said, pleased he had made an arrest that could lead to promotion out of homicides.

"Good luck with that," Stokes said as he and Samantha walked out the door, escorted by a Garda who opened the back door and spread out some plastic sheets on the back of the squad car. They were saved especially for the bleeding and the bloody. Stokes and Samantha sat down in the squad car. The sheets made a crinkling, squirting sound with the wetness of the blood. Stokes looked at his watch as they arrived at his house. It was already 1 AM. He had not realized they had been at the warehouse for so long.

"Are you all right?" Stokes asked Samantha who had been speechless during all of this.

"Grand, but I look a right mess," she smiled weakly as she got out of the car and went up the steps of Stokes' house.

"Well, Aisling had a whole wardrobe of clothes. I'm sure something will fit you, so be my guest and you can shower," he said, pointing up the steps to his daughter's room. It had not been touched or gone into by him since she died. Stokes saw Samantha standing at the door and again thought of Aisling. He held back a tear and cleared his throat. "Choose what you like," he yelled from the bottom of the steps "and I'll make some tea after you shower. I need to wash up as well, so I will be out of the downstairs bath by the time you are out. There is the bathroom," he pointed to the door opposite Aisling's room. "See you soon," he said.

Having washed up in the powder room and changed his clothes, he went to the kitchen and there was Samantha already putting out the cups and putting the tea leaves in the teapot after heating it with the boiled water.

"Mrs. Kelly had offered a cup of tea for me on the last visit, so it was easy enough to get the things together. She is quick on the trigger for a cup of tea," she said, amused at Mrs. Kelly's efficiency. "After the shower, I don't feel tired," she said, smiling.

"Neither do I. Still running on the adrenaline from the excitement," he said.

"You have a beautiful home," Samantha commented, hoping to decompress with small talk. It was the first time they had been at his home together. Stokes was happy to not talk about what had just happened or give Samantha another 'what were you thinking lecture.' He was at home.

"Thank you. My father was one of the first surgeons to live and practice out here. There is a downstairs entrance he used for his patients so he could conveniently commute from breakfast upstairs and work downstairs, which was fine in general unless we children were too noisy. He could be quite cross when there was too much of a disturbance, so we learned to play quietly," Stokes said.

"What kind of surgery did he do?"

"General surgery until he decided his hands were too unsteady for delicate work. Then he settled down to a General Practice which he did until he was ninety, God rest his soul."

"How many brothers and sisters do you have?" Samantha asked, feeling easy enough with him to inquire.

"There were five of us. I was the eldest and then my younger brother, Edward, who died of the measles at two and two sisters, Emily and Mary, who both live in England and the youngest, my brother Robert, who joined the British army and now lives in South Africa. We don't see much of each other. So here I am, the last Irishman in the family," he said wistfully. "And you?

"I am the only child. Mum couldn't have any more children after me."

"And what does your father do?"

"Dunno," she said, breaking into a Dublin accent. "He left when I was two and Mum doesn't talk much about him. He says he couldn't find a good job because he had joined the British navy during the war and some people never forgave him for that. My mother said he drank too much."

"It must have been hard for her, then, raising you on her own," he said, recalling how many were shunned in Ireland after leaving to go off to war for the English. The worst of the pariahs were those who had been in the Irish Armed Forces and deserted to join the British. They were cursed never to have a job in Ireland again. Stokes did not try to explain that to Samantha since he thought it would have made the discomfort of speaking of her father much worse.

"It was, but she has had a good job as an administrator at Trinity. She is Protestant so she was able to get a job from people she knew. She had an MA long before most women, before my father left. He was jealous of her, I think, since he was just an electrician. Gran and Grampa had some money, so she struggled through, and they took care of me when she was working, so it all worked out."

"Your mother must be proud of you."

"She is, but she mustn't know what happened tonight. She would be terribly cross," she said, thinking of the risks she had taken.

"I am sorry you are just realizing that now. I hope this won't happen again."

"No, I won't try that again, but I needed to help, to know the truth."

"The truth can hurt. It can be deadly," he paused, closing his eyes for a moment. "Now I'm feeling tired again. I will call a taxi and get you home," Stokes said, getting up. "Get some rest and I'll see you tomorrow. I am sure we will be testifying more than once about this."

The cab driver rang the bell in just a few minutes and Samantha left, wearing a borrowed casual dark blue blouse and skirt that Aisling especially liked because it brought out her colors well. Just as it did with Samantha, Stokes observed, not without a pang of sorrow at the image that was too alike, but not quite.

"Be careful," he warned again, more afraid of loss than danger. "I will see you tomorrow whenever you come in," he said, closing the door. He went to the window. The white van was no longer across the street, an absence he had never appreciated before. The taxi had taken off. He went up to bed and fell asleep.

Chapter Sixteen

The sound of the door closing downstairs surprised Stokes, waking him from a deep sleep. He heard Mrs. Kelly's footsteps moving to the kitchen. He was still tired but did not think he would go back to sleep, so he went to the bathroom and shaved and showered. By the time he was done he was wide awake and hungry. Mrs. Kelly had obligingly made him his scheduled breakfast. She had no idea he had been up much of the night.

"You look tired," she said, serving him his toast and eggs.

"I did not sleep well. It was the Jewish chaps across the street. They were moving a lot of boxes in the middle of the night and were not quiet about it. By the time I got back to sleep, it was already close to morning."

"They are a peculiar lot, up at all hours with a lot of comings and goings. This import/export business is quite an enterprise," she said, shaking her head. "You would think there would be someone looking into it with all the commotion, but someone is probably getting an extra leg of lamb or two." She was aware of any conspiracies on the street and knew all the neighbors, but Stokes overlooked her observations on most days. She could go on for too long about all the goings-on, trivial to important.

"Have they been moving much before this last night?" Stokes asked.

"A fair bit. I don't know if they are moving to a new headquarters or closing up, but there were a lot of office things moved, desks and such in the past two weeks. I wonder if the bombs have scared off their business."

"Perhaps. They would be sensitive to that kind of thing since one of their own was killed."

"A crying shame, the French girl, is that right? There will be fewer tourists coming here for a while I would say."

"Most likely. And many people won't venture to City Centre if they can avoid it. Most unfortunate…" Stokes said. He was tired and descending into small talk, but Mrs. Kelly at least confirmed the activity he already knew about.

"Well, I'd best be off to work. There are a lot of loose ends that have to be tied up and lots of paperwork to complete," Stokes said. "Oh, by the way, thanks for helping my assistant Samantha borrow one of Aisling's gowns for the College reception. She dropped by for a late cup of tea last night."

Mrs. Kelly looked at him and raised an eyebrow. It was the first time in at least a year that he had mentioned his daughter's name. Mrs. Kelly had been meticulously maintaining her room and wardrobe without a word to him.

By the time Stokes got to the office, Lanigan had already arrived. He was sitting in his office on the chair opposite his desk, looking as bad as on any morning when he had been out drinking far too late the night before, which was surprisingly less recently. The increased stress of work had forced him into sobriety. Last night had certainly not given him a chance to go for a leisurely pint or two.

Lanigan held a file in his lap, protecting it from Stokes' desk crowded with forms and reports.

"Good morning, Professor, if you want to call it that," said Lanigan.

"Good morning, Detective. Did you get any sleep?" Stokes asked out of politeness, clearly aware of the answer.

"Well, let's say I was too busy rooting around for more information. The files were a bloody treasure trove. I got one that might be of some interest to you," he said, waving the file at him.

Rather than sit down and peer at Lanigan over the pile of papers, Stokes stood up and accepted the folder and opened it. It was a dossier of a Provisional IRA member who had been captured in 1973 by the Gardai on the border for suspicious activities and movements between the North and South. There were transcripts of the interrogation, and although it seemed his questioners suspected him of activities in the South, especially around the time of the first bombing in Dublin in November of 1972, his claims of being elsewhere were pending confirmation. He was released after a few days for lack of evidence of any recent crimes he could be connected to, but he was, according to the files, put on the official watch list. The interrogation had been conducted by Detective Curran.

"Do you have any more of this?" Stokes asked.

"No, not yet. I'm having some of the Gardai sift through and organize the papers we found, and they have strict orders not to discuss this with anyone but me. They are not very happy doing this kind of work. It was a bit of luck that I even saw this file since it was sitting on the side of the boxes, as if someone had picked it out to save."

"I would say your man Curran was looking to clean up after himself when he found out about the copies of the files. The Israelis had caught him in the act, as was their plan. It is quite unusual for a G2 man to do the interrogations on an IRA suspect, is it not?"

"He might if it was over the border, but usually it was a local Detective would be conducting the interview. So, yeah, it was unusual, but it may have been kicked upstairs."

"How high upstairs?"

"Your guess is as good as mine, but the G2 people like to keep their cards to their chest, full of themselves they are, security be damned."

"Since Agent Curran is a bit more sensitive now, maybe you can pay a visit and see if he is willing to sing a little to save his hide."

"Well, he is heavily guarded, but only by some Gardai, so it shouldn't be too hard to visit a wounded colleague. But mind, I would suspect they'll be eager to spring that bird."

"He might be eager for some protective custody I'd venture to say."

"You might be right on that, Prof. He knows too much. I could offer him a safe place for more information."

"You would best be off, then. That wound won't keep him in

hospital for very long. Deep cut, but clean and easy to repair and should heal well unless the wound gets infected."

"Right, then, I'll see you later, but I'll take the file since this place is not as secure as I would like, no offense," said Lanigan.

"No offense taken," Stokes replied as Lanigan left the office.

Chapter Seventeen

"I'm a dead man," Curran croaked to Lanigan as he sat up on his bed, the bandages still tight around the throat so he sounded hoarser and more muffled than he really needed to be. He was feeling sorry for himself and Lanigan nearly sympathized but recalled what an arrogant bastard he was.

"No need for the theatrics," Lanigan said. "I saved your bloody life. What are you afraid of? The Israelis scarpered."

"It's not the Jews I'm afraid of, it's the Provos. Those IRA renegades have been after me since I stopped them freeing MacStiofain at the Mater during his hunger strike. All I got for being wounded then was promotion to Detective Sergeant and a lot more enemies."

"But you're still in G2 aren't you? Your mates there should be able to protect you."

"Mates? Not bloody likely. They would as soon hang me out to dry."

"Who is they?" asked Lanigan, not sure of who he was talking about and unaware of a conspiracy until now.

Curran did not answer, realizing he had said too much on the morphine he had been given for his pain. He turned over to look away, but his neck still hurt, worse when he leaned on his right side.

"If you come clean with me, I might be able to protect you from your 'friends.' The Gardai out there are under my orders, understand?"

Curran still did not answer. He looked very afraid.

"They will be moving you to jail pretty soon. You know how the fellas love cops in there. I can help with your staying here for another few days and arrange for some kind of deal," Lanigan said.

He had no power at all to make any deals and as soon as his superiors and their politician bosses got wind of who Curran was working with, they would all be jockeying for position as to who was the patriot who would uncover the terrorist conspiracy—a lot of loose ends could be tied up that way, true or not. Curran was under no illusions who the scapegoat would be.

"Save your breath," Curran hissed and said nothing more, still trying to look away, even if it hurt.

"Fair enough," said Lanigan and left the room. The two Gardai nodded. He looked back at them for a moment. "No one but essential hospital staff is to come in here, understood?" Lanigan said.

"Yes, sir," the senior officer answered quickly, acknowledging his mission. The other, just a rookie, looked on, bored at the duty and counting the minutes when he was to be getting off. His senior stared at him.

"Yes, sir," the rookie finally responded, a little too late.

"You'll never get another stripe with that kind of attitude," Lanigan scowled.

"Carry on," he said as he walked down to the nurses' station. He could see was inconveniently at the other end, separated by two open wards. There were only two private rooms, opposite each other, one with Curran and the Gardai and the other with an old woman who looked comatose from the distance. There was an emergency exit to a stairway on that end, also inconvenient and potentially dangerous, Lanigan thought. A fire alarm was next to it and an ax and fire extinguisher hung on the wall.

"Make sure that anyone assigned to that room is where they are supposed to be or I'll have the Matron keep you on bedpan duty for a month," Lanigan warned the three nursing sisters who had been watching the drama.

"Yes, Detective. No fear," the oldest of the three responded.

Lanigan left, hoping that was true.

Change of shift for the nurses and the Gardai was at 8 PM. While the nurses were busy signing out to their replacements, so were the Gardai, although the information that the Gardai had to exchange were simple pleasantries and warnings about Lanigan showing up at any time.

The two new Gardai checked in on Curran who was sleeping on his right side and didn't respond, or at least had his eyes closed.

"Bejaysus, he's a lazy sod ain't he?" Flanagan, the younger one, whispered to his superior, Magee, as they assumed their positions at the door. "Not much to do here, I suppose. They wouldn't even allow him a bottle of porter to speed his recovery."

"Not much of a recovery he is going to have. He will be in Mountjoy prison soon enough and then there will be a trial which could take a long time," Magee said.

"What did he do?" Flanagan asked.

"He knows too much about the bombing and they want to know more, much more, I think."

"There's many who would as soon kill him in his bed."

"Our job is to keep him safe here, not to be judges or executioners. Sure there will be time enough for that."

The nurses had finished their reports. The nurse assigned to Curran came down the hall to check him first. She would work her way back through the open wards which would be the bulk of her job for the night. Flanagan went in with her, just to be safe.

The nurse casually apologized to Curran for waking him to get his vital signs, but that was her job. There was no response. She went over to his right side and planned to nudge him lightly but was surprised by the blood through the bandages, onto the pillows, and bed. She did not scream but looked up at Flanagan in horror.

"Call the desk nurse and have her call for a code," she said to him.

Having heard the commotion, Magee came right in. He checked Curran's pulse even if the startled nurse had forgotten. There was no pulse. Curran was cold.

"Don't bother. Call the priest, but don't hurry. He has been dead for a while," Magee said. He looked over the body quickly and the only wound was the one on the neck with no sign of a struggle. He did not touch the body and ordered the nurse to remove herself from the room. "Call Lanigan. We will have a lot of explaining to do and it won't be a pretty sight."

While Flanagan walked down the hall, Magee looked around the room and checked the windows and the toilet and saw nothing out of place. There were no tracks of blood or footprints and no loose instruments or bottles. It was too neat.

As soon as Flanagan was on the phone, Magee could hear the protesting and hesitation and generally dismayed utterances from Flanagan. It was part of the toughening process he needed, Magee Garda thought to himself. It would take some of the pressure off so he would not have to withstand the worst of Lanigan's verbal onslaught.

Lanigan tramped down the hall, stared at all the staff he passed as if they were as guilty as the murderer. He did not ask questions now. The details would be repeated countless times in multiple venues. Instead, he put his gloves on and checked the wound and the body first. The original wound was covered in blood but there was a fresh incision that extended wider and deeper, probably with an instrument that was not intended for repair and healing but lethal destruction. It was, of course, not to be seen. Nothing indicated how the killer got in. The room was clean. Nothing indicated a struggle.

"Could you bring the staff sister who was responsible for the evening shift, please," Lanigan asked Magee.

She was lead in, distressed, but eager to help.

"Was there any unusual commotion here tonight?" Lanigan asked her.

"No more than the usual patient demanding help to the loo or pain medication. They are all mostly easy to deal with."

"Think again. Were there any new patients admitted tonight?"

"We had three, two of them old and frail and barely able to get up on their own power. And another who was queer enough. He would not say a word. They said he was found on the street, all wet and cold. He looked strong enough that he should not have needed the help to get in and out of bed, but he fell down twice and needed one of the Garda to help him up. He was too big for the nurses."

"Did he need one or two Garda to help?" Lanigan asked.

"The first fall only one, but the second time he wandered out on his own, all confused-like. He would not listen to the one nurse, so she called for the other Garda to help and pick him up after he fell again."

"Where did he fall?"

"He got as far as the nurses' station on the second try, so we put him in restraints after that."

"Where is he?" asked Lanigan, moving to the next ward.

"There, there, he was in the first ward," she said leading him to the open door.

"He's gone," she said, pointing to an empty bed.

"I can see that." Lanigan looked down the hall again, at the staircase door with the exit sign over it. It was ajar with the fire extinguisher sitting on the floor, propping the door slightly open.

"Would you ever check the stairwell," Lanigan said to Flanagan, knowing full well there was no hope of finding anything or anyone there. The Garda quickly ran down and then up the steps to the next floor.

"There is no sign of anyone, sir," he said, breathless.

"Is that door always open?" Lanigan asked the nurse.

"No, it's supposed to be closed. It should trip off the fire alarm. The sign says do not open."

"Does the alarm always go off if the door opens?"

"It was all right a few days ago. They just fixed it again yesterday; it started going off a few times. We thought one of the older patients got confused and pushed it open."

"Who admitted the stumbling wet tramp?" Lanigan asked.

"I am not sure, he just appeared on the ward, and we were told to find a room, so we did."

"Who told you?"

"One of the porters. Not very pleasant and very pushy. He said he was a replacement for the night because the usual man was out sick. I had never seen him before."

"You'll never see him again," said Lanigan. "Did he have an Ulster accent?"

"Yes, he did, now that I recall. How did you know that?"

"Lucky guess. Make yourself available for more inquiries," Lanigan ordered and walked over to the two Gardai.

"You two have made a right bollocks of it haven't you?" Lanigan said, not expecting an answer. "Stay here and wait until the coroner's people get here and call me as soon as they arrive. I need to make a few calls." Lanigan disappeared into the Matron's office and closed the door. Everyone could hear the yelling, mostly foul words.

Before the Coroner's men got there, the lab technician and the staff photographer from the detective's office arrived. They did not touch anything without their gloves on. The photographer snapped everything with the Polaroid.

Lanigan burst out of the office and, still irritated, yelled at the photographer: "Why don't you take a portrait of Tweedle Dum and Tweedle Dee here?" pointing at the two Gardai. "They can hang it on the wall in their office in Knock where they will be guarding the pilgrims and the souvenir shops for the rest of their days?"

He walked past the two and into the room again. He watched as the technician continued his dusting for prints and any other signs of the killer's traces and then stared at Curran's body, his position and his arms hung over the side of the bed which would have been painful if he had been awake at the time of the killing. He walked past the two Gardai and to the nurses' station again. The nurses were flustered but trying to work around the commotion, trying to calm the patients upset at the goings on. The Matron was there, almost as irritable as Lanigan at the upset to her evening and the disruption of the patients' care.

Lanigan ignored her and spoke to the night nurse, sister Morrison: "Did the victim get any sedation tonight?"

The nurse checked the records, flipping through the notes.

"Yes, he did, at 6 PM."

"Awfully early for sedation."

"Yes, it is."

"Who gave it to him?"

"It says I did, but I was on dinner break," she said, looking again at the entry and the signature, which was somewhat like hers, but not quite. "This is not my writing," she said.

"Was there anyone else there at the time?" asked Lanigan, looking at the other nurses who had been asked to stay for questioning. They were terrified of being accused and more terrified by Lanigan.

"Yes, I was here, but there was a substitute nurse who I never saw before who appeared as soon as Nurse Morrison had left. She said she would only be here for a short time since it was not her usual floor, but she insisted on distributing the medications although it was not the time for some of them," one of the junior nurses said, now suspecting that there was more she could have done if she had given it some thought. "I'm sorry, I just didn't know. I shouldn't have let her, should I?" she said, turning tearfully to the Matron who had been listening to the whole interrogation.

"No, you shouldn't have," Matron said.

"Well, do you recall what she looked like?" Lanigan asked the nurse, steering the interrogation back. This was no time for the blame game, he thought, but he didn't need to say it.

"She was tall and blonde, maybe a wig, too much makeup. She was a little unsure of herself, but I thought that was due to her being on a strange ward."

"Did she give medication to any other patients?"

"No, she didn't. She went straight down to the prisoner's room, returned in a few minutes and wrote in the book, looked at her watch and then said she had to be back to the other ward. I should have thought that was strange. I was too busy to notice. We were short-staffed. We were happy to see an extra hand. I thought you had sent us the extra help," she said to the Matron.

"Besides tall and blonde with too much makeup, was there anything else you noticed about her?" Lanigan asked.

"She had a slight northern accent. She didn't talk much," the nurse said.

"Right then, we'll put out a bulletin and see what we can get. I doubt she is blonde and is probably not even in town anymore," Lanigan said.

He watched as the forensics crew cleaned up the rest of their gear. He took one more look at Curran's body and shook his head.

"Poor bastard," he muttered, walked out of the room, and turned to the lab crew. "Make sure you get prints on the fire extinguisher and doorknob and the medicine cart and tray. Any bit might help." He turned to the Gardai who were still standing dumbly at the door. "See if you can guard the body a bit better than you did the prisoner. Call me when the coroner's people take him." He left the ward, muttering to himself.

Chapter Eighteen

Curran's body arrived safely at the morgue and Stokes did the autopsy first thing the next morning with Samantha at his side. He asked her to uncover the wound carefully and start probing how deep it was but in the middle of the measurement, she broke into tears. He had noted her upset at the College reception and thought that it was merely due to the sudden unwarranted attack by the grieving woman that had startled her. He realized that the stress of the recent weeks had mounted and that she was finally succumbing.

He was well aware of his profession's empathy syndrome, having experienced it several times. The first changed the course of his professional life. That was when he was in the Royal Navy, a General Duties Officer, the equivalent of a house physician, on a support ship. They were evacuating those they could after the invasion of Normandy. He was doing mostly triage and first aid rather than surgery. He did whatever he was told without much sleep and, when he could, found a place alone where he could cry over the overwhelming endless death and destruction. It was then he had decided that he could not be a physician to the living, talking to them as their lives disappeared before his eyes, feeling their pain so intensely that it hurt as much for him, and maybe more—he could not take morphine or Phenobarbital as they did to go to sleep. He could only watch them and go through the motions of helping, especially those he knew had no chance.

Then, at the beginning of his pathology career, he had to do a post-mortem on a child that had been beaten to death. There was another incident where he had to work on a young girl whose face had been impaled on a fence when she jumped out of a window. It had only taken a month to recover from those nightmares since they were cadavers, not warm human beings.

When he imagined the autopsies of his wife and daughter, it had taken a full year and a half to stop waking up in sweats imagining what his loved ones looked like. He had avoided their postmortems. They were buried in closed caskets, something he regretted; his imagination had made it more gruesome, but who could tell or would want to? He avoided reading the autopsy reports or attending the coroner's inquest. There had been no closure. There had been no trial with no suspects arrested or accused.

He had not shed any tears after his wife and daughter died, but weeks after, on a beautiful sunny Saturday afternoon, he had heard a Puccini aria from La Boheme on the radio, which he and his wife had enjoyed together in the past, and he had begun to weep. He cried for days. He remained alone, disconsolate, angry, called in sick and told Mrs. Kelly not to come. He was silent for days on end, staring from his armchair without much more to eat or drink than a piece of toast or fruit or, when he was feeling better, a soft-boiled egg or beans on toast. Whatever was left in the fridge, he finally ate until there was nothing left and there were no tears left, so he abruptly returned to work.

Most of his "patients," if one could use the term, carried no personal baggage for him. He was able to treat them as subjects to be studied. He could remain at a clinical distance and do his job without an accumulation of grief, or so he thought.

Yet here was his assistant, bawling her eyes out, releasing all her pent-up emotions and it was as if she were more the man that he was, not letting his feelings get in the way of his job and, sometimes, his life. He let her cry for a while, since there was no good reason not to.

He almost felt as guilty about Curran as Samantha did, seeing him alive and knowing that she had empathy for him, but he had felt none before. Curran was a liar and a traitor.

Stokes let her cry for a while longer. The sobs decreased and the tears subsided. He said nothing and did nothing, just sat beside her on an exam stool. There was no one else in the room when the sobs echoed against the tiles and stainless steel.

"It is right to feel sympathy for your patients," he said, touching her shoulder gently.

"You have been through a lot in the past few weeks. I am surprised you did not want to take a leave of absence. This has certainly been a most intense experience. I have not been through anything like this since the war when I was as young as you, so I know what you are going through." He paused to make sure she understood that he was not judging her but trying to console her. As a mentor, he could not avoid saying it.

"Empathy is not a safe feeling for us. It is usually easier since we have not been acquainted with these people until they have arrived here and that is a good thing; so, I am not surprised that you reacted this way seeing Detective Sergeant Curran, poor soul," he said, reflexively, out of respect for the dead. He avoided the familiarity of using his Christian name. He waited for her to respond.

"I want so to be good at this job and it has been very hard with all these terrible things happening. I know why you didn't want me to handle the pregnant woman or the baby since I dreaded the idea and avoided looking at the pictures in the paper and reports here and I was thankful for that, but it has still been hard. I thought doing the work would get me through, to help find the truth, but I have not been sleeping well and have had nightmares," she confessed.

"That is normal for any human being. I do not blame you for your tears. You have done a very good job. I may not have been able to bear it as well at your age. It is not unusual that after the adrenaline of the emergency wears off that you feel that way all the more. But be strong, we need to get our job done and record what we see and report it to those who would look for justice, wherever it ends," he said, standing up from the stool and returning to the examination table.

"This is Dr. Harold Stokes on the postmortem examination of Detective Sergeant Special Branch Niall Curran at 09:24, 1st of June 1974," he began to dictate into the microphone above him with a clear and distinct voice. It was not mechanical, but formal and practiced, honed by the experience of many years and second nature, almost like a prayer for the dead by a priest. He carefully removed the temporary bandages hardened by the clotted blood and cleaned the area with water from the handheld flexible spray nozzle directing it gently against the edges of the wound and the deeper tissues so he could see the line of the incision better, the disintegrating clotted blood falling into the draining valley below the table.

It was, as he had thought, that the assassin had used the line of the initial cut as a guide to cut much deeper and forward than the external jugular vein and passed it into the carotid artery with one quick stroke. The assailant knew his or her anatomy, or at least had practiced the fatal stroke. The knife used was as sharp as the butcher's knife that he had seen at the abattoirs, so the line was not jagged. There was no curve, the line was straight. It might have been a quick death. There had not been any signs of guarding. Stokes suspected that the victim was heavily sedated. Poison might have been easier. He reminded himself to get the toxicology reports, but he was pretty sure that the cut throat was intentionally dramatic for anyone who needed a "message."

Samantha watched, now dulled to the emotion she had felt earlier and concentrated on the drone of the description of the process, like a worshipper following a prayer and immersing herself in the sound and meaning of the liturgy. It was strangely soothing.

It did not take long to complete the autopsy. There was little else of note except that the liver seemed to be a bit worse for wear with suggestions of scarring due to early cirrhosis, probably alcoholic. Toxicology reports and antemortem blood tests he had in the hospital might help to confirm that.

"Be sure to get those blood test results from the hospital as well as the toxicology reports from our lab," he reminded Samantha, who awoke from her trance as soon as he had spoken to her. He had said nothing to her during the conduct of the autopsy. He imagined she was fine with that since it would have been more difficult for her to be subjected to a Socratic session on this case. She had learned enough watching.

"Yes, Professor," she responded. They did not speak another word together that day.

Chapter Nineteen

Lanigan came to the morgue the next day, having busied himself with tracking down more clues as to the identity of the culprits who killed Curran. It was a fruitless task. If they were not paying close attention because it was not significant to them at the time, the witnesses' recall of the events would be inaccurate and, worse if they felt ashamed or guilty for not noticing, they fabricated to match their impression of that momentary reality. The evidence he had gotten last night was probably the most important. It showed that the killers were probably well acquainted with the Mater hospital and no strangers to the protocol for watching of prisoners in that wing. They also were well aware of the weaknesses of the protocols and may even have learned it from other attempts to free or get to prisoners, like the attack of the IRA to free MacStiofain during his hunger strike two years before. Ironically, that was the same event where Curran had been wounded when he had been fighting off the attackers. Was this revenge for that or to keep him from talking anymore about what he knew now? Just speculation. Lanigan was not interested in speculation. It always hurt his head. He liked facts.

"Well, what did you find out, Professor?" asked Lanigan.

"It was simply a deeper and more extended cut of the wound on the neck that severed the carotid artery. He bled to death in minutes. There were no signs of guarding or struggle, so he was probably unconscious at the time. I am still waiting for the toxicology report which should be available later. We did it in-house rather than through the hospital," replied Stokes.

"There were no prints anywhere except for those from the Gardai and the floor nurses. People wearing gloves would not have been much noticed, it being a hospital," Lanigan added. "Still, there must have been some inside help and it was well planned."

"I have no problem releasing the body to the family, unless you think there would be any need pending the coroner's inquest."

"No, let the poor sod be buried, probably will be military with honors since he was a veteran of the Irish Defence Forces and An Gardai Siochana, no questions asked," he sniffed.

"I suppose so."

"I'll be back if I have any more questions, but it looks like this investigation is at a dead-end, eh?" asked Lanigan.

"You might be right, but I will call if I have any more information," Stokes said.

There was nothing more left to do. He completed a load of paperwork that morning and glanced over at the pile that he would relish the least—the French documents. He would skim through to get the gist of what it wanted and write a response in English since he wasn't going to give them the satisfaction of having to resort to their language.

Both the French and the British had the same attitude towards each other's lack of facility in the others' language as a pure ignorance, a sign of decreased intelligence and lack of culture. Since the feeling was mutual, there had been wars and now there was detente, for lack of a better English word. Still, Stokes would have to muddle through and get the report sent over. The death of that poor French woman was related to the death of his missing corpse and the Israelis were part of it. He was hoping he could get some more information from French authorities. How much did they know about the Israelis or the PLO, or for that matter, their own dead French citizen? He looked over the papers again and looked for some name attached to the documents that he could contact. There was none. He called the French Embassy, despite it already being afternoon, hoping for an answer.

"Hello, this is Professor Harold Stokes, the Dublin State Pathologist. Is there anyone there I might speak to relating to the death of the young French lady in the bombings in May?" he asked.

There was a pause since the receptionist had to think for a moment. "Yes, how tragic. I am sorry. I will transfer you to the Ambassador's secretary. Perhaps he can direct you better," she said quickly and there was a click and a silence, which, fortunately, was only momentary.

Stokes had to repeat his title and the nature of his inquiry to the secretary who also expressed his condolences.

"I have some forms that have to be completed for the French Ministry of Justice, but I wanted to make sure that they understood the details of my report. I have some questions about the dead woman's identity and connections. Is there anyone I might speak to at the Embassy about this?" Stokes asked.

"This would be a police matter, would it not?" the secretary asked.

"Yes. I am working with the police on this. I am not sure if they have gotten to this point in their investigations or contacted you." Stokes hoped that there had not been anyone asking the questions that he needed to be clarified since there might quickly have been a cover-up.

There was some hesitation before the secretary answered. "He is out at this time, so give me your number and I will have our security officer call you back."

Stokes was afraid he would lose the initiative if he hung up since the security officer might call to clear this with his superiors or even with the Gardai or G2. That would be like broadcasting his suspicions, suspecting leaks in the chain of command.

"May I come over with the documents. I don't want to delay this any further," he pressed.

"He may be available soon, but I can't promise anything. I would hate to waste your time since it is late in the day," the secretary said.

"I need help with the forms in any event and I'm sure one of your employees might be able to help me complete them, so I assure you it wouldn't be a waste of time."

"Very well. We will be expecting you," the secretary said.

Stokes grabbed the papers and his own files and the files he had confiscated from the warehouse and shoved them into his briefcase and dashed out of the office, quickly informing his secretary that he would be out on business for the rest of the day. After a short taxi ride to the French Embassy, the receptionist told him that the officer, Pierre Cloudot, (too close to Peter Seller's Inspector Clouseau for Stokes not to smile) was still unavailable, calling in daily only since he was on a special confidential assignment and had been for the past month. She listened to Stokes' complaints politely but refused to accept his papers until Inspector Cloudot returned her call. She did not give him any specific time but hinted it would unlikely be today since he usually only called once a day and had already called that day. Stokes demanded to see the Ambassador and she responded by telling him he was out of the office as well. He looked at the clock on the wall, an ornate gold copy of something out of Louis XIV Paris, which only showed 3:30. The sign on the wall in French and English announced the closing time for the Embassy was 4 PM.

"Call him again and I will wait for the response and tell them this is official urgent Irish business involving a French citizen, then," Stokes insisted, taking a seat on a worn wooden seat against the front door. No Louis IV chairs, he thought.

The receptionist raised an eyebrow and said, "Please yourself," not giving any more hope to a meeting, and added, "The office closes at four." She called and left a message and then continued with her duties on the phone and occasionally got up to file copies of documents. Precisely at four pm she stood up and announced, "The office is closed," staring at Stokes coldly as if she were at the gates of heaven and his entry had been irrevocably denied.

"I am an official of the Irish government. This is an outrage. I will be complaining to your ambassador," Stokes said.

"You are on the property of the French government, and I must ask you to leave. You can file your protest through the proper channels, Bon Soir," she said, pointing to the door.

Stokes remained a gentleman and left the office as she closed the door behind him. As he was walking down the stairs, he was greeted by a short dark man who did not look very French, like someone from the Middle East. He suspected he might be of some Algerian lineage but was too polite to inquire.

"You are Professor Stokes? I am Pierre Cloudot, I got the call that you were here to see me. My apologies. The receptionist is not a very pleasant woman. She hates the Irish and hates being in Ireland, and she makes everyone pay the price. How can I help?"

"Well, I need these papers completed for the French police so the body can be transferred back to Paris. My French is awful, and it looks like these need official stamps as well. Can you help me with this?"

The man was friendly enough and shook his head sympathetically.

"As you can see, the Embassy is closed. Allow me to escort you to a pub that at least serves decent Irish beer, not that any pub could not be convenient enough," he smiled.

They walked down the block and went into the closest pub, obviously familiar to Inspector Cloudot. Stokes ordered a Harp Lager and Cloudot ordered a Guinness.

"Have you acquired the taste, or had you been a fan for years?" Stokes asked, nodding at the glass, making small talk.

"I have only been here for a month or so. It is an acquired taste, but addicting," Cloudot smiled back, had a sip, and made a face that strangely did not show pleasure, but tolerance like a child eating Brussel Sprouts.

"When in Rome," Cloudot smiled, and got to the point: "We think the woman who was killed was a Mossad agent. She had been followed from her home in Paris ever since she arrived in Dublin. She had lived in Israel as well and had been in the army, we suspect, intelligence. We were not sure why she had been transferred here, but we suspect she was tracking the association of the IRA with PLO factions and we were most interested in how much she knew about this terrorist who is known as Abn Awaa, Arabic for the Jackal. All these terrorists want to be known as the Jackal after that silly movie, the Day of the Jackal. It makes my job harder because it makes these people look like heroes. It used to be that police were the good guys. And even harder for me since my mother was Algerian," he explained, shrugging his shoulders.

"We knew Abn Awan had been in England but did not know if he had been to Ireland. It was unfortunate that she was killed since she was scheduled to return to France the next day and we were going to question her. The Mossad are very reluctant to share any of their information with anyone unless they are absolutely sure something will be done," he said. He reviewed the rest of the files that Stokes had shown him, looking more than once at the picture and the dossier on Suleiman bin Daoud.

"We think this one could have been her boyfriend, but we're not sure since they only met twice at the place she was staying in Dublin, and only briefly. Why was a PLO agent speaking to an Israeli agent unless he was Mossad too and working undercover? We are more concerned about the PLO in France than the Irish here would be. We think he was trying to find the association between the PLO and the IRA. We know he disappeared as did Abn Awaa after the bombing, but we don't know why, do you?"

Stokes was not sure how much he should tell him, but the files were already on the table, and he was concerned that if he went to the Gardai with this information, it would soon get to the culprits, and Stokes might be the next victim. Of course, Lanigan and Samantha knew, but they were not collaborators as far as he was concerned. Lanigan had saved his life and Samantha had already foolishly risked hers. He knew he would not be getting any more help from his Israeli "friends"—they had vanished. There was no point in telling Cloudot about them, unless he already knew. What he was sure Cloudot didn't know was that Curran was killed yesterday and he suspected he knew nothing about Curran's activities.

"I know that the agent you were looking for disappeared, and I know why," Stokes confided. "Suleiman bin Daoud was Solomon ben David, and he was an Israeli undercover agent in the IRA. His comrades removed his body from my morgue to protect his identity. It may have been because they wanted him to have a proper Jewish burial with military honors, but I think they wanted to remove any evidence of their involvement. I think he was killed by your Abn Awaa and I think he is still here. That's why I came here today. If you can capture him, he may be able to tell you who in the Irish government, if anyone, was involved in ben David's murder and the identity of the other IRA bombers. I need the proof and the closure. My wife and daughter were killed in the bombing in 1972," Stokes confessed.

"I am very sorry to hear that. It has been difficult for you Irish during these 'Troubles'. It has been hard with all the extremists in France as well. Nowhere is safe. Bombs and assassinations and kidnappings, all in the cause of liberty, equality, and fraternity. Nothing changes. My ancestors, petit bourgeoisie, were killed in the French Revolution. Why? Because they had more money than their neighbors. And you Irish, you are killing your own countrymen for the same principles and the same lust for the same power. We are all the same human beings and do the same things to each other. But I go on too long. . ." he paused, and Stokes took a deep breath, not sure if he wanted to hear any more history.

"Why do you think Abn Awaa is still here?" Cloudot abruptly returned to the inquiry.

"I think he killed one of the conspirators to shut him up," Stokes said.

"Who was this? I did not read anything in the papers," Cloudot asked.

"He was an agent in G2, Irish Special Branch," Stokes said.

"They allowed a Special Branch agent to be killed?" Cloudot asked, astonished.

"I think it was a setup. The Gardai had no idea and there were people inside who did it, I am sure of it. That's why I need your help. I can't trust Special Branch. Surely you must have some agents here?"

"We are not here to interfere with Irish politics or Irish sovereignty. We are only observers. We will go through diplomatic channels to obtain information, but we will ask about anyone knowing the whereabouts of Abn Awaa, the Jackal, as an alert. Sometimes these rats come out of the, how you say, the woodwork, when they smell the smoke," Cloudot winked.

"I would appreciate any help you can give me. But, of course, this is confidential," Stokes concluded. He hoped he had not confused the investigation, but he was pretty confident that the French would only be looking out for their interests and not the Irish and, certainly, not the British, although he was surprised that Cloudot was interested in any information about the Mossad.

"Thanks for handling this report. I will give you my certified pathology findings which are straightforward —her cause of death was due to the car bomb, and you can attach it to the form. It would help greatly since you know what they want and I would probably be in a bureaucratic mess otherwise, thanks."

"Of course, of course, Professor. It is a service the Embassy should provide since she was a citizen, and we assist our citizens. But one more thing. Could I hold onto the Ben David dossier for now? I would like to check with our security department and see if they can confirm your suspicions. I will get back to you as soon as I get some information. In the meantime, if you have any clues about the location of Abn Awaa, please call the receptionist at the embassy. She will contact me by pager, and I will call back," Cloudot said, showing him the little black box with a thin green screen, a new electronic marvel.

"The receptionist is aware I am on an assignment so secret that I will not be in the Embassy during this time and has been directed to tell people that I am 'out,' to leave a message and I will call back. No one else knows of this assignment at the Embassy to reduce the possibility of leaks. The PLO has spies everywhere," he whispered.

Stokes was intrigued by the pager and was envious that there was a way he could be reached without being interrupted. He accepted the explanation of secrecy since Cloudot seemed to be aware of enough confidential information that it probably was true. Stokes reciprocated with his limited technology and handed him his personal card and wrote his home telephone on the back. He thought it was strange that Cloudot did not have an official card to give him.

Stokes left the autopsy report for Cloudot to handle, but he did not give the papers about Ben David. As he walked out of the pub, he had reservations about what he had done. He had consulted a foreign power about Irish affairs. Was this a state secret? He was not sure there was anything classified he had. But these were copies of documents that were not generally circulated. Even the press knew nothing of all of this, though they had their own suspicions. He was only going on a hunch himself since Curran was dead and would never testify to the collusion in high places with the IRA. Stokes would not tell anyone about the visit. It would be best to protect Samantha and even Lanigan. Stokes needed a plan now.

He had no doubt that he would be followed and that he and Samantha were at risk. He did not know who he was at risk from. He suspected that the Jackal would be after him because Curran seemed more fearful of him than his IRA cohorts. His reputation of being a bloodthirsty fanatic was all over Europe and, although he had not been spotted in Ireland, he had been in and out of England leaving bombs and co-conspirators there and throughout the continent. Stokes had toyed with the idea of going directly to the Israelis, but they would probably deny any knowledge of their agents being in Ireland for their own protection —they had been too exposed in Dublin already. He would just have to lie low, hoping that there would be some sorting out. Curran was already a liability, and his story would have to be buried quickly. If O'Neill was behind this, the ex-Minister would make sure that his connections would disappear.

Chapter Twenty

Stokes went directly home. It was too late to get back to the office and do anything meaningful. He would call Lanigan in the morning and tell him he was off the case but would be pleased to be informed of any further developments. He was trying to forget this all as he walked into his house and was greeted by Mrs. Kelly.

"You got a letter in the mail. Quite mysterious—do you know anyone in Israel?" she asked. "Come to think of it, I noticed the delivery van has not been across the street in weeks. Did you know them?"

"In a way, I did, just casually. By the way, Mrs. Kelly, don't be alarmed, but please be cautious about opening any unmarked letters or packages. If they look suspicious, just leave them on the console table. I will deal with them," he said as matter-of-factly as he could.

Mrs. Kelly was still holding the mysterious letter and dropped it onto the console table as if it was a hot poker. "If you put it that way, you won't have me touching your mail at all. I will just leave it at the door, and you can deal with it any way you want. I think you have made far too many *friends*."

"It is just a precaution. I don't expect any unusual mail, Mrs. Kelly," Stokes said, picking up the Israeli letter and holding it up to the light, then opening it. Mrs. Kelly grimaced and crossed herself.

"No need for all that," he said, waving the letter after he opened it.

He scanned the letter. It was from one of the Mossad agents, the one who called himself Rami, thanking him for the help. He was warning him about Abn Awaa but cautioning him not to look any further for more clues. As far as Rami and his superiors were concerned, Stokes' involvement in the case would be closed. Rami apologized for the inconvenience and would not be troubled again.

"It is just from an acquaintance who has been traveling to the Holy Land. He wanted to let me know they arrived safely. Very pleasant fellow. I served with him in the Navy and after the war, he got religion and became a vicar in Shropshire. He was a wild fellow during the War." Stokes smiled and put the letter in his pocket. He would keep it there until he could burn it, unobserved, in the fire.

Whether Mrs. Kelly believed the story or not, it was no longer a subject of discussion, as were so many other sensitive topics. She was disturbed, however, by the suggestion of threats of a letter bomb and other dangerous packages coming to the house. She was upset enough by Professor Stokes' grisly profession and his cool disregard of its associations. Only once had she ever seen any emotion —when he was so devastated by his wife and daughter's death that he would not come out of his bedroom for a week and left barely eaten scraps of food at the door. That was another subject that was not discussed. She was careful not to suggest he find a new companion, which she just once was reminded, was none of her business. Men were all the same, she concluded, hard to talk to and hard to change. She served his dinner, as always, promptly after the Angelus. Stokes was surprised he did not salivate to the sound of the bells by now.

He knew the letter was a warning, a friendly caution to back off and leave things as they were. He was hoping he could do that but expected that there were new players on the scene that would pursue the murderers and their collaborators. The more the merrier, he thought. He decided to pursue other interests and just do his work. He finished his dinner, bid Mrs. Kelly a good night, read a bit more of a journal in Irish of a squire before the famine, and went to bed.

Samantha, on the other hand, could not get enough of the excitement. Like some of her colleagues in the Casualty Department, she had been primed by the bombings, waiting for the next catastrophe, to feel the adrenaline that the panic and chaos compelled her to control. Stokes had warned her off, so she would have to be secretive. She had done some detective work on her own, driven by the need to search for truth and justice that Stokes had shown her. She sensed, in Stokes estimation, she was too young for that, unfettered by mature judgment or fear.

She had been scared by the Israelis. She truly thought that they were going to kill Curran, especially the one with the limp. The tall dark one they called Rami was attractive and strangely tender to her, even though he had trussed her up like a Christmas goose, but she did not feel he was going to hurt her. He was the leader and seemed in control, emotionally and physically. She could see that the others accepted this. She had not told Stokes. He would think that she had Stockholm syndrome or was infatuated with his good looks. It was more than that. She was intrigued with spy craft. She did not expect to see these agents again, however. She resumed her work at the morgue, waited for the next interesting case that would show some unexpected pathology or some unexplained death.

She got a similar letter at home the same afternoon that Stokes got his. Instead of telling her the case was closed and thanking her for her help, Rami asked her to meet him in London. He said he needed to ask her more questions and help with the capture of the Jackal. She read the letter several times. He suggested they meet at Trafalgar Square at the base of Nelson's column at 2 PM in two days, a Saturday. The letter did not imply any obligation. It requested she take the ferry and rail to London. There was a check enclosed, enough to cover a return trip and a hotel room. The spy trade must have a limited budget, she smiled. It made sense a plane ticket would be more likely to be detected; there would be more questions at airport Customs and Immigration than on the ferry. This letter was an invitation to adventure. She did not even have to take a day off, but she would have to cancel dinner with her mother. That would need a bit of explaining. She could easily get around that. She looked at the letter again. There was no return address, and there were no explanations as to how Rami could be contacted. It was simply show up or not.

The next morning, she did not say a word about the letter to Professor Stokes. He did not mention his letter to her either. They went through their routine for the day, and he commended her for being able to get through the mountain of paperwork that the bombings had generated. As he had predicted before, there was a lull in the homicides and deaths right after the bombings and they were enjoying the slow period although the paperwork was not nearly as interesting. By the end of the morning, Stokes was relaxed enough to consider going out to lunch rather than have the dry ham sandwich Mrs. Kelly packed for him. There was a pub that had decent lunches and it was a wonderful spring day.

"Care to go the pub for lunch today? No pressure," he said.

"Of course, tired of all this paper. We haven't even had an interesting murder in the past two weeks."

"Yes, thank God. We've had enough work to last a year."

They left the offices and strolled down the sunny streets to the pub on the corner. It was not crowded. People were rattled by the tragedy. Fewer people were shopping or doing anything casual that would require them to be in the City Centre. The pub owner was happy to greet them. Business was off and they were quasi-regulars. They both ordered meat pie and chips, which were decent. Stokes had a half-pint of Guinness and Samantha had a Shandy.

"Any plans for the weekend?" he asked.

"I am going to see a friend in London. It would be all right to leave a little early Friday, wouldn't it?"

"Of course. There is no pressure at this point to complete any extra work. A bit short for such a long trip, isn't it?" he asked, not relishing the idea of such a long journey himself. For him, a jaunt to the Wicklows, the mountains outside of Dublin, was a long trip. He did enjoy the walks when he took them.

"Well, she is a close friend, and I haven't had a chance to get over to London since I graduated school. It will be a quick adventure. There are so many things to see."

"Yes, it is hard when you are a student to enjoy anything—no money to be extravagant. I suppose you should take the opportunity now. When I was in London during the war, I had some money, but there were curfews and blackouts, so I missed things when they shipped us out."

"My father enlisted in the army," Samantha said. "There were no jobs to be had in Ireland during the Emergency, as I think they called it. What a bloody understatement. It was a bloody World War. He was wounded in North Africa and there was no work or help for him when he returned home. Mum had a hard time until he left, working and taking care of me."

"It was a hard time here and a hard time there in England as well. I was lucky to get back to a post as a surgical registrar with my war experience, but after all the deaths I saw, I didn't want to be contributing to anymore, and was drawn to pathology."

Samantha was glad he did not discuss her visiting London any further. She was afraid something secret might slip. After finishing their lunch, it was time to return to work, so nothing more was said.

Chapter Twenty-One

The ferry from Dublin to Holyhead took no more than three hours and the train to London was only about another 4 hours, so Samantha arrived at Euston Station in the evening. It was nice passing through the English countryside before the sunset and, with the late setting, she saw the massiveness of the sprawling metropolis before all the evening lights came on. It reminded her how small the city of Dublin was and how quaint everything seemed there. The small bed-and-breakfast Rami had recommended was pleasant and reasonably priced. She had a decent sleep and leisurely breakfast since her appointment was later in the afternoon.

Samantha was not intimidated by the city, but she was disoriented. She consulted her tourist map to see a bit of London before her assigned meeting. The National Gallery was along the way. She walked the half hour with good directions from the proprietor of the Bed and Breakfast who was more than eager to direct his guests to anything nearby. She was not sure he was Jewish, but she would not have been surprised.

She spent some time in the galleries and was captivated by the richness of the art, filled with Dutch Masters and French impressionists and antiquities and Turners. She was struck by Rembrandt's Belshazzar's Feast; the Hebrew writing was on the wall where God said the king was wanting. She could have spent all day but looked at her watch and realized it was time for her meeting. Until she remembered what she had come for, she had not been anxious.

She hurried out into the light, bright after being in the Museum, even with the gray clouds over the city. Standing by the base of Nelson's Column, she watched people rush by as others sat at the edge and fed the pigeons. Rami was there right on time, only momentarily delayed because he had not specified which corner of the tower to meet. He was not in his black Orthodox clothes and his face was shaved. He was not even wearing a skullcap. She was shocked at how much more attractive he looked in just plain street clothes and a smile. The last time they had met, she was afraid she was going to be killed, but his gentle demeanor with her and his reassurance showed he was on a mission and no threat to her.

"Did you have any difficulty getting here?" he asked.

"No, no hassles with the trip at all and the bed-and-breakfast you recommended was pleasant and very close by," she responded, unable to keep her eyes off him and his smile.

"Have you eaten yet?"

"I had a nice breakfast, but I am a bit peckish now."

"Peckish, what is that?"

"Hungry," she said. "Sorry, I forgot you haven't been in Ireland for that long that you picked up all the slang words."

"Well, there is a little Israeli café close by. We can sit down there and talk. The lunch crowd has probably left by now." They walked towards one of the side streets off the square. It was crowded in the middle of the day with tourists. She could hear the many languages that were being spoken. Although there were strip clubs, jazz bars, sleazy souvenir shops, and what looked like prostitutes and weird classes of people standing around, she felt safe with him. They arrived at the café, which was just a takeaway counter with some chairs inside. She looked at the menu and did not know what all the things listed were. She watched a huge slab of meat slowly turn, roasting on a spit. There was constant chatter in Hebrew from behind the counter.

"Have you ever eaten this kind of food before?" he asked.

"No, I haven't. Maybe you should order for me."

"Do you want some of the meat or would you like a vegetarian specialty that is just fried chickpea balls that has a lot of flavor and my favorite."

"That sounds nice, yes please," she smiled.

He ordered two falafel rolls and warned her to peel the wrapper down and watch for the sauce dripping at the bottom. She was intrigued by all the flavors and spices. She coughed at least once on the pepper but was amused by the experience. He said he was pleased she was pleased. They washed it down with some orange Fanta which was also unusual for her. When they finished, his smile had gone. He seemed more like the serious and determined person she had seen in Dublin what seemed to her ages ago.

"We needed to meet here because I cannot go back to Dublin. It would be too dangerous now. I need your help to be our eyes and ears. Our work was interrupted. We have not been able to catch the killers of my colleague and his girlfriend or those who were behind it."

"But I have no connections with those people. They are part of the police and the Special Branch and the army intelligence. Besides, you are asking me to spy on my countrymen. How do I know if you have evil plans for Ireland?"

"You won't be spying, just give us information on people who are as much enemies of your country as mine. Abn Awaa, a Palestinian terrorist some call the Jackal, is wanted by many countries. We want to break the chain he has created so your country and ours will be safer." He pulled out some pictures and placed them on the table. "These are of some men we have been following and are probably involved with arms shipments. They are all, how you say, shady," he smiled.

He pointed to the first picture. The image was grainy, and it looked like it had been taken from a distance. The man was probably in his 50s, dressed up in a blue suit and a yellow straw fedora and he was in a crowd of spectators at a racetrack. She looked at it for a while but did not recognize him. Rami saw the quizzical look on her face.

"This is Major John Gray. He says he was a major in the British army, but he lives in Dublin and has no obvious occupation. He is a gambler and a drunk and is friends with O'Neill, the former Agriculture Minister and before that Minister of the Department of Justice and Equality. They often gamble and drink together, either at the track or at a local club where they play poker. O'Neill has run up some debt with his gambling, yet he continues to do very well, even owning a nice farm and some racehorses. We think that Gray knows where the money is coming from. He may be supplying it to him."

"Isn't this something that you should be telling the newspapers or the police?"

"The newspapers have a rough idea, but they have not been able to prove anything. The police don't want to know, half of them owing something to O'Neill or sympathizing with him."

He pointed to a newspaper clipping of an older man with the caption: "Maurice Dussault, Belgian refugee seeks Irish asylum." The article explained he was a collaborator with the Nazis during the war and had fled to Ireland to avoid further investigation and prosecution. Rami nodded at the photo and said, "He will sell guns to anyone who will pay."

Rami pointed to another photo. "This is the three of them together, O'Neill, Gray, and Dussault, walking out of the Shelbourne Hotel in Dublin, smiling at each other. They are all dressed in dinner suits and seem to have been enjoying themselves at the art auction benefiting the victims of the Troubles on the border. All of them have money to burn. They are very open about where they go and who they meet. No one seems to care," Rami said, a bit angry.

"What would I have to do with them?" Samantha asked. "I am just a poor doctor and way out of their class."

"You are a very attractive and intelligent young lady and that goes far in any class," Rami said, matter-of-factly, but looking straight at her.

Samantha blushed. From him, his hazel eyes staring at her as he paid her the compliment, his pale face already starting to tan from being out during the days instead of the nights as he had in Dublin, shook her. She could not avoid looking back. He was handsome, but he was also very confident. That made him all the more attractive to her. She had been socializing mostly with her classmates, most immature even when they had graduated Medical School, since Irish students started as young as 16, as she had. There was some maturing during the training. The clinical years sobered them quite a bit when exposed to real people and all their sufferings, which they were required to respond to and tend to, in their own ways. Samantha had been trying to avoid all the personal dramas because she felt so inadequate, so she had leaned towards pathology because of the science and the personal isolation. She was shocked that she had fallen instead into the midst of catastrophic tragedies and was still recovering from her overwhelmed state. Yet, here was a person looking at her who said she should be more social because she was beautiful and smart and seemed to mean it.

She caught herself. He was here because he wanted her to do a job she was not trained for or mentally or emotionally prepared to do. He wanted her to be a spy. She looked down at those pictures sitting on the cheap metal cafe table. He wanted her to make them tell their terrible secrets. He was the same person who had bound and gagged her and scared her half to death on that dark night in a dank warehouse in Dublin. This noisy little café that smelled of chips and roasting meat and spices was more exotic, but no less unusual for her. What am I doing here? she asked herself. She did not have to answer—she came on her own. She looked back at Rami's handsome smiling face and knew that brief rush of adrenalin from the excitement of breaking into the warehouse and even of being detected was something she had never experienced in her good, predictable, safe life. It was as if she had been awakened. She wanted more.

"What do you want me to do?" she asked.

"Keep your eyes open and listen well. That's all. You will report to me, and we will do the rest. You will be helping your country by ridding it of some bad people. You will be helping the world to make it safer. We think these three are part of an arms supply ring that is giving the Provisional IRA guns and bombs funded by Qadaffi who is also helping to arm and train the PLO who are killing people in Israel. Now, these terrorists are working together. They need to be stopped. You will help. They are gamblers and drunks. They like pretty women, so it will be easy for you to gain their attention." He pointed to Gray. "He has a facility for finding more money and people of power. He is an old school friend of O'Neill. Even though he claims he was in the British army during the war, O'Neill still keeps up with him as a drinking companion. Gray connected him with Dussault, the Belgian, the arms supplier. We know he has had dealings with Qadaffi. We think he also has had contact with a PLO operative who has been working with the IRA, who is known as Abn Awaa. We have no pictures of him but think he has been to Dublin and Belfast several times. We think he killed Solli, Solomon Ben

David, the man whose body we recovered from your morgue. We will get revenge, but this is more important, we need to break this arms exchange. Qadaffi will continue to supply guns and money as long as he is safe from any obvious connections. If we can break the chain, the arms will go away. O'Neill will pay for his collusion. We will expose him for the terrorist he is. The other two, we don't care what happens to them, but they are the way to get to Abn Awaa. You will watch their meetings and when we see the chance, we will strike. We need to know what they do, their habits, their weaknesses. They will suspect any Israeli, but they will not suspect you. You probably don't drink or gamble. That is not necessary. Just be around them. Tell us their comings and goings. Can you do this?" he asked, staring at her intently. She shifted in her seat, straightening herself, like a self-conscious schoolgirl caught daydreaming by the teacher.

Samantha had been listening to his plans. She was transfixed and could not analyze the danger. She was rationalizing the argument that all she had to do was observe, encouraged by the peculiar excitement of the deception, like the taste of a new spice. She wanted to do something to avenge the dead she had seen and stop the perpetrators. She would be in a new adventure, among a class of people who she hardly would ever have mixed with—it might even be interesting. She dare not tell Professor Stokes, but he had, in his own way, led her down this path. He had been spying on the Israelis and Special Branch himself.

"I'm not sure I can do this," she said, not able to stop herself. It was her mature side talking. All she had ever wanted to do was be a doctor, but when the science part of her met the human part that would empathize too much with poor sick patients, she felt unprepared and overwhelmed. She had opted for pathology, the quiet, analytic, retrospective view of helping. Yet, she had jumped at the chance of determining causes of gruesome deaths, listening to their histories like cheap mystery thrillers she had devoured in her teenage years. Of course, she could do this.

"Let's go for a stroll. This is a wonderful city to walk through. It has so much history and life. Like a big Dublin," Rami smiled. She liked his smile. She liked everything about him, his tall dark handsomeness, his self-assurance, his unspoken secrets.

He paid the bill and led her through the busy streets full of all kinds of people from hawkers to tourists to reserved but quick residents who only used the narrow streets as a shortcut to somewhere more important.

"Where are we going?" she asked.

"Over to the water. We can walk through St. James Park and then on to Big Ben. Have you ever seen Parliament? We can watch the boats go by and the people. I like to watch them and imagine their lives from their faces and clothes," he said, obviously knowing London much better than she could recall since her last trip before Medical School. Her mother had taken her as a reward for high marks in her exams and her acceptance to the Medical College. It had been a short trip, but she was thrilled by the sights and the sounds and enjoyed everything about it, even if her mother had taken her and escorted her past anything that looked unacceptable. They had gone to the theater that evening and seen a wonderful production of the Pirates of Penzance.

She was easily distracted by the sights and sounds and had completely forgotten why she had gone to London. She easily engaged in the game that Rami offered to play, tried to describe people's histories from their clothes and demeanor. It was easy to spot the kids who were groovy in their bell-bottoms and miniskirts who had probably left their suburban houses with their mothers yelling at them about dressing in those clothes. Just as easy to spot the businessmen still wearing their dark pin-striped suits on a Saturday afternoon, probably finishing up last minute accounts from their banking offices in the City, she thought.

"Those look like businessmen," she observed. "They are still carrying their attaché cases and must be finishing their banking for the day."

"No, they are from Whitehall, the government offices nearby. They probably were coming out of some important meeting. Be aware of the locations you see these people. No banker would walk here from the City, but the place is crawling with bureaucrats. Take a deep breath. You can smell the ink, paper, and stamps," Rami laughed.

They continued to walk towards the Thames in the afternoon's setting sun. The clouds had dissipated for the time being and the prettiness of St. James Park along the street they were walking made it a pleasant stroll. Samantha enjoyed Rami's company. She wasn't thinking about Dublin and work.

"Tell me about Israel," she asked.

"It is an old country and a young country. My family survived the Holocaust in Poland. They could not go back to the old days of the 'shtetls', the little villages where there was little money and less hope. They became citizens of a new land that was filled with many kinds of people and hope and a history as old as the Bible. We will fight for our country, as your countrymen have fought for theirs. There are prices to pay for that freedom and independence. I am willing to pay that price." His jaw clenched.

"That must have been hard for them, losing everything. Why are you bothering spending all your time chasing some bastards who don't harm you there? After all, Dublin is so far away. Surely, if you ignore them, others in their own countries will eventually catch them and put them where they belong," Samantha asked.

"The world is all connected. They do bad things in many places and spread their hate and fear all over and contact more like them who are willing to risk themselves for whatever they believe is right, like the IRA. The PLO, Libya, even the extreme left Germans, talk to each other and exchange money and guns and hate. I do not want to stand by and see other innocent people hurt. You have seen their work on your morgue tables. You can't ignore them any more than I can," he said, stopping at the Thames embankment, looking out at the Parliament and across to Westminster Bridge. They were there already. Some barges passed under the bridge, tour boats with tourists almost hanging over the sides to get the perfect photo of Parliament and Big Ben as they passed. Seagulls swooped low to capture any errant scraps of food left by careless strollers. It was all postcard perfect.

"This is just a one-off, isn't it?" Samantha asked.

Rami looked at her quizzically.

She was not sure if he understood the question or was pondering the answer.

"You know. Are you going to use me just this once and then the problem solved, I am back to being a civilian?" she explained.

"I'm sorry. I didn't know what you meant by 'one-off'. English is not my first language. Yes, I suppose this will be just a one-off," he paused, staring at the water, cars, and buses passing by along the road above. He was glad she had not meant a personal relationship.

"Well, then, what else are we going to see in London?" Samantha asked.

"The Museums are closing soon. It is too early for dinner. You said you like opera. We could walk to Covent Garden and see if there are any standing room tickets left at the Royal Opera House. I don't know what is playing, but it is a beautiful building, and it is not far from here."

"I didn't know you liked opera," she said.

"My parents listened to it on the radio when I was young. I didn't like it then but got used to it. Now it reminds me of my childhood and my parents," he said.

"All right then. We can give it a try. I like walking and this is a nice tour," she said.

They doubled back past Trafalgar Square and walked on to Covent Garden. There were some standing room spots left for Der Rosenkavalier and so they hoped to be lucky enough to find some left seats and get to sit down. All the walking had made them both hungry by the time they had finished. They found a café to have a light meal. Rami insisted on paying and invoked his expense account. This was the last they talked about him and his mission. They spoke of their childhoods. She emphasized how happy she had been with her mother despite her father having left. Rami spoke of his parents and their struggle to stay happy despite the memories of the Holocaust. He was envious of other children who could visit their grandparents and extended families, but it was just his parents who had survived. He had been born in Israel, the only country he ever knew and loved.

"What made you join the Special Branch?" she asked.

"You mean the Mossad?" he asked.

"Sorry, yes, the Mossad. What does that mean anyway?" she asked.

"It is short for the very pretentious 'Institute for Intelligence and Special Operations' and so we just call it the Institute, or Mossad."

"Very academic. So why did you join?"

"I was in the Six-Day War in 1967. I was young and saw my friends die. I did my service, but I couldn't help feeling that the victory would not be enough. I didn't find anything I wanted to do after I finished my service, so I stayed. Then I was promoted and because I was good at languages, they taught me more about how to use the languages in interrogation and getting and remembering information, so they said I needed to be in the Mossad. Here I am," he smiled. The story was simple. Samantha thought it was too simple, but she saw him more hesitant and not making eye contact. She did not try anymore.

"And you? Why did you choose to cut up dead people?" he asked, still smiling, but she was not sure if he was joking or just defensive.

"I like the science and the quiet and the puzzle. We both like questions answered, don't we?"

"I'm sorry. I didn't mean for it to come out that way. It is just that death is hard for me to take, so many people I knew, I mean."

"I know what you mean. It has been hard for me this past month. I don't want to see any more people dying and their families suffering in that awful way."

"Then you can help us prevent this. We say, 'If you save one life, you save the world.' I hope you can do this."

"I still have to think about it. We better go. The performance starts soon," Samantha said pointing at her watch.

They paid the bill and hurried to the theater. They were escorted to the standing room area, but one of the older ushers pointed to some empty back orchestra seats.

"They probably won't be coming. Once the lights are lowered, go for them. Cheers," he smiled.

Sure enough, the couple did not show, and Samantha and Rami went for the seats quickly as the lights dimmed. They watched the performance in silence but smiled at each other, watching Der Rosenkavalier, a comedy of false identity that ended happily.

It was raining when they came out, the drops hitting loudly on the pavement in the warm night. Rami called a taxi, and they climbed in.

"Shall we stop somewhere near your Bed and Breakfast for a drink?" he offered.

"Sure," said Samantha, not wanting the night to end. He had not offered a drink in his rooms, which was reassuring. She was not ready to go so far. Either he was too smart for that or not aggressive or just not interested. She did not question it. She liked him.

They stopped just before the B&B at a pub down the corner. It was Saturday night; the noise had gotten louder with the well-lubricated customers feeling their drinks. The denizens were not rambunctious yet, so they found a booth in the back and ordered half pints, she a shandy and he a Guinness.

"Have you been converted?" she asked, nodding at the glass of stout.

"I got used to it. They say it has lots of vitamins," he smiled, amused at the Irish rationale for the drink.

"It's true," she said. "It has B vitamins and Iron. They still leave a bottle at each hospital bed for those they think it might help," she confirmed.

"Well, to life, L'Chayim," he said lifting his glass.

"To health, Slainte," she said clinking his glass.

They sat quietly as they watched the activities of the drunk, and not so, engaging in the perennial socialization of either flirting, looking for partners for the night, or commiserating about lost football games or loves. The music was loud. People got louder. They couldn't hear themselves talk, so they left. It had stopped raining. He walked her to the door of the Bed and Breakfast.

"I will meet you tomorrow for breakfast."

"That's a plan," she agreed, disappointed that he did not propose any more. Was it her or him or just that this was a pure business arrangement, and she should not be a bloody fool? she thought to herself. He held out his hand. She pulled him in and kissed him. He kissed her back. They both looked at each other and knew that this should end but would not.

"You can come to my room, and we will just talk," he offered.

"OK," she said.

The night was cooler after the rain. The moisture hung in the air, making it feel colder than it was. They walked closely together. It was a short walk to his flat, which did not surprise her. She suspected this was part of her surveillance, to keep her observed, but not suspicious. Still, he was a gentleman, or cautious, or both.

It was a small flat, not a poor bedsitter like hers. It had its own small bedroom and bathroom and kitchen alcove. There were not many decorations. It did not look cluttered or much lived in.

"Do you live here?" she asked, surprised by its neatness, unlike the chaotic hovels of old student boyfriends.

"Not very much. We all use it at some times. We try to keep it clean since we share."

"How many of you are there?"

"You don't need to know."

"Sorry, just curious."

"Yes, you are. And smart and beautiful," he said, brushing her hair back so he could see her face shine in the dim light. He kissed her again. She kissed him back. They collapsed on the small sofa behind them and made love.

Chapter Twenty-Two

They both awakened in the first light of morning. She looked at him and smiled at his handsome, dark face. He touched her pretty pale skin. Neither regretted the night.

"We can't spend any more time here," he cautioned. "We both have busy days."

Part of her wanted to chide him for being so businesslike and the other part warned her that this was all just business. She was living in Dublin, she reminded herself, and asked what kind of future they might have together. She decided she was not interested in the future at that moment.

"There is a café just down the street," he said. "You can have a shower here and then we can have breakfast."

It felt awkward to be there, but she took the offer of the hot shower and the clean towel. She had thoughts as she cleaned herself that she was being conned into being a traitor to her country of sorts since the IRA, no matter how outrageous their offenses, with many innocents killed and maimed, were fighting for all the people of Ireland. But she recalled the bodies and the indiscriminate carnage that may have been the result of that patriotism and rejected the idea that she was a traitor to a greater cause. She was angry and wanted the evildoers to be brought to justice and the Troubles to end. She resolved to do it, no matter the danger to herself. Had she not already put herself in danger and survived, with the help of these Jews who had no dog in the fight, but wanted their own revenge and to prevent further death and destruction?

She dried herself off and combed her long red hair until it shined. She put on her modest dress and prepared herself to say yes to the Jew, like Molly Bloom in the Alameda Garden, but it was no Garden, just a gray old flat in the heart of London. Her train would leave at 1 PM. She didn't want to be late and get into Dublin on a Sunday night when people would be pouring out of the cinemas and clogging the streets and transports. Despite the many people who stayed home now to watch television and avoid any more risk of bombs, there were still a good number who would go out on dates to see the latest films rather than the leftover programs that were years old from England or America. Ireland always got the leftovers.

After a weekend in swinging London, she was almost tempted to not go home to the work and dreariness. But Rami had not offered more than this weekend. She knew he would not. This was still a mission for him. And was she just another job? She walked over to the café with him, more so she could be with him longer rather than to have breakfast. A bowl of cornflakes would do for her most days, although her mother chided her for being such a 'Yank' when a bowl of porridge would last her longer. The café was nearly empty, a couple of older men in the corner arguing with each other about last night's football game. Rami ordered a cup of coffee.

"The coffee is weak, but the place is close. What will you have?" he asked, looking at the menu himself.

"Just some toast and tea. I'm not a big breakfast eater."

"Well, I could use some eggs if you don't mind watching me eat."

"Not at all."

He ordered two soft boiled eggs and toast and tea this time. The waitress asked if he wanted some chips or sausages or bacon. He declined, making a little grimace. Samantha realized he had just avoided eating pork without revealing any dietary restrictions.

"How do you manage to not eat all the pork in Ireland and England? They put it in everything?" she asked.

"It is just a conscious observation. I am not that religious, but my mother still keeps kosher, so it is just an easy habit most of the time."

"Have you ever eaten pork?"

"Yes, but not intentionally, or if I did, I was undercover, and it was for my country," he smiled.

"I would eat bangers and mash for my country. It is my duty. Sure, what would the pig farmers do without us filling our gobs with the stuff?" she smiled.

"Well, are you willing to do more than that for peace in your country?"

"Aren't you all business this morning?"

"We don't have much time. You have to decide."

"What will I need to do?"

"Remember the photos of the people I showed you?"

"Yes, I do, and their names, O'Neill, of course, Gray, and Dussault," she said without hesitation.

"Excellent, Dr. Monaghan. They will all be at a reception at the Shelbourne Hotel again. I want you to be there. It is in honor of another of the gun-running crowd, Mullaney, who is retiring from politics, or so he says. He was also acquitted with O'Neill in that last arms trial trying to smuggle guns from Libya. He figures he can do it again, especially since they think that the Dublin bombing is going to bring reprisals from the IRA in the North and that they will need more guns for defense," said Rami, up to date with all that was going on.

"And I am supposed to ingratiate myself and get all this information from them and give it to you?"

"Small steps. Since you will be there amongst them, they can get to know you. You will be going to other affairs, pubs, or clubs or races, whatever is needed, to let us know who else they meet. I expect Gray will be the easiest to get information from since he is a drunk and can't keep secrets very well. He goes everywhere, but between the drink and the gambling, he will say something somewhere. Although he likes boys, he is an attraction to pretty girls. He is not a threat to them and is amusing. That keeps him socially useful. He is a weak link and will do some boasting, if given the chance."

"How will I get into the Shelbourne?"

"Here is the invitation," he said, handing her a fancy engraved envelope. "You will be the guest of the former Mayor Briscoe's aide, Howard Bernstein. He has been a friend of Israel for years and plans to retire there. He keeps on promising. Right now, he knows everybody and anybody in Dublin politics. He also knows how to keep his mouth shut. All you need to do is listen and smile. Let the men do the talking. They love to hear themselves, especially if you nod and smile." Rami smiled.

"How am I to tell you of what I find out?"

"Very easy. You will send letters to this PO Box in London." He wrote the PO Box number on a napkin as well as a telephone number. "If it is an emergency, this is the telephone number to call in Dublin. You will have to call from a phone box, leave a message that you are calling, and we will call you back at the box. Understood?"

"What if there is trouble?"

"Get out of wherever you are and call that number. No heroics and, if it looks like trouble, it is."

"When will I know I'm done?"

"All we want is the time and place of the shipment. We will handle the rest. If we can get to that, maybe we can also catch the PLO leaders in the act."

"How is that going to find the bombers?"

"If we get their friends, we can get them as well."

"Before I forget, here is the money to pay for your room and travel expenses," he said, sliding a few pounds to her. "You are not a paid agent and will not be. You will be doing this of your own free will and you will have my and my country's gratitude. I hope your country will appreciate it one day, as you will when this is over."

"When will we meet again?" she asked, trying not to seem too eager.

"This may take months, but I want to see you back again in London soon," he answered, still smiling, looking at her like he meant it.

He had not eaten half his eggs, but finished the toast and tea, she noticed, and had even spread some marmalade on the toast—a bit of a sweet tooth, she thought to herself, and smiled.

"I guess I have to go now. I don't want to miss my train," she said, putting the envelope and money and the invitation to the reception in her purse.

Rami paid the bill and left a tip on the table. He looked at her as if he wanted to say more, but did not, and just smiled. They did not kiss. He shook her hand.

"Good luck," he said, standing up, motioning her to stay.

"You too," she smiled, sipping the last few drops of tea, overlooking the leaves at the bottom that had not been strained very well. She watched as he walked out the door, discreetly checking the street in both directions.

She made her way back to the bed-and-breakfast, gathered her bag and left for the train. The trip back to Dublin was uneventful. She got home in the late afternoon, enough time to make herself a light supper, finish reading the cheap romance paperback she had picked up at the train station, and then went to bed.

What have I done? she asked herself before she fell asleep, exhausted from the weekend and the trip back.

Chapter Twenty-Three

Stokes was busy that weekend as well. Cloudot had given him information about the Jackal. He was a Palestinian who had grown up as a young boy in a prominent family in Jaffa and had been in exile since Israeli independence in 1948. He had joined the French Foreign Legion, was trained as a sharpshooter, and then joined forces with Algerians fighting French colonialism. He was more than just a sharpshooter. He made good money in arms smuggling throughout Europe and had worked with Qadaffi in concert with the PLO. The French were aware he had strong connections with Libya and Libya with the IRA. So that is what brought Cloudot to Dublin, Stokes thought. He would be a useful ally. Stokes was less suspicious since Cloudot had been willing to share this information. He hoped he had not overstepped his sharing.

Stokes did not think that Abn Awaa, the Jackal, had killed Curran. His MO seemed more to bombs and assassinations with high powered rifles. Curran had been under surveillance, but the people who killed him knew Dublin well enough. Stokes appreciated their determination that he should not talk. They must have been aware the Mossad had captured and questioned him. They were not aware of what he had told them, but his silence had been their most important concern.

How did Curran know the bombs would go off? Stokes asked himself. How was Curran there before all the other police and rescuers began gathering up bodies and debris and evidence? Where were the bullets that went through that Mossad agent? For that matter, where was the rifle?

Stokes went back to basics: he reviewed the surgery reports of that dead agent and his own preliminary autopsy reports and stared at the Polaroid photographs. If it was a high-powered rifle, why did it not do more damage? Was it too far away? Or did the surgeon concentrate on the entry wound which was narrow and looked reparable until the body, too late in the chaos, was turned over and the gaping hole in the back showed the massive damage that a bullet from a high-velocity rifle had made as it tumbled through the body. He had never had the chance to open the body, but looking at the Polaroid, it was altogether possible a surgeon could have misinterpreted the entry and exit wounds, the larger posterior wound thought to be a flying car fragment entering rather than a bullet exiting. Stokes was sure this was an assassination.. He made a note to call Lanigan on Monday morning to locate the rifle. He recalled the photo on the wall of Curran's office, a picture easy to retrieve as evidence. He hoped the rifle would be in Curran's house or somewhere nearby. If not, there was more covering up to discover.

Stokes reviewed the police report leading up to Curran's murder. Based on his autopsy, his death was due to the one knife wound that had extended the original incision he had witnessed in the warehouse. How did the murderer know where to cut? Had he reviewed the hospital records? That meant he or his accomplices had time to check, and they had hatched the plan at least a day before. No one else knew about Curran's injury and hospitalization except the police, who were with Lanigan and the hospital staff. The hospital staff on duty could be identified. He would ask Lanigan to question them again. The investigation had been stalled in bureaucracy or by someone higher up at the hospital or the Gardai who did not want any more questions asked. Still, he would have Lanigan get to Curran's office and check through Curran's possessions if they were still available or requisition them from the evidence room.

Curran did not have any immediate relatives. He and his wife had long been separated and they had no children. His funeral was quiet and poorly attended, despite the obligatory military honors with 10 military policemen, his immediate supervisor and colleagues, a few drinking friends, and Stokes, Samantha, and Lanigan. His coffin was draped with the Irish flag, but there had been no gun carriage and the military salute was only performed by three riflemen, as if he were not as important to the state as other agents. Or was it because too much notoriety would provoke too many questions and associations? The Minister for Defence and Justice was not present, nor was O'Neill, the ex-Minister for Defence and Justice he had served under. Why did they not want to be involved?

It was rainy and everyone was eager to get in out of the wet, so they all adjourned to the nearest pub for the courtesy of a drink rather than a proper wake beforehand. Stokes did not recognize any of the faces in the crowd; neither did Lanigan, but both made a point of trying to meet anyone who was there to observe his loss and discuss his quirks. They sat down with one of his closest mates, George Murray who identified himself as one of his closest mates who was eager to reminisce.

"He was a great one for the conspiracy theories, had all the books about Kennedy and the assassination plots, even bought that Mannlicher-Carcano rifle, as the Yanks called it, when it was just an old Italian Carcano rifle if you read the books, as he did and made sure to correct anyone if they called it by the Warren Commission name. He practiced with it on the range. People would do a competition with him if they were foolish enough, betting he could not fire off three rounds in seven seconds, which he could, which proved his point that there was no conspiracy, though he wished there were. Still, he was all Secret Service with his aviator sunglasses and tan trench coat, just like the Americans, even on the warmest, sunniest days here when there seemed no chance of rain. A queer fella, he was, but a patriot. He was willing to give his life for the struggle," George Murray said.

"He was from the North, wasn't he?" Lanigan asked.

"Near enough. He had many cousins, aunts, and uncles over the border. There was more than once that he promised he would go over with that Carcano and kill the RUC bastards who threatened his family, but he never said he did, or didn't tell anyone about it. If he had anything to do with the Provos, he didn't utter a word. He may have helped try to smuggle those guns in with O'Neill in 1970, but he was never even questioned at the trial. He moved up in the ranks of the Special Detective Unit without any complaints or whispers.

"Where is that gun now? It might bring a pretty penny to a collector," asked Stokes, probing off-handedly.

The question startled Lanigan, but he did not let on.

"Good question. Curran complained that someone nicked it a few weeks ago after he had been doing some target practice," George replied. "He was bloody more than upset and vowed to shoot the bastard who stole it with the very same gun, but he did not have a clue who took it."

"Did he inform the Garda?" Lanigan asked.

"No. He knew that would only bring more questions as to how he got it in the first place. He was a bit mysterious about it, if you get my meaning."

"Where did he do his target practice?" Lanigan asked.

"Over at the Dublin gun club. I went with him a few times, but didn't much care for the hoity-toity company, if you know what I mean. Too rich for my blood. There were a few ministers who would go around there and show off their talents. There was some betting going on, too. Also, too rich for my blood."

"So, Curran hung around with some influential people?" Stokes asked.

"Yeah, and it was kind of strange-like, since he didn't have that kind of money himself. But they bought him drinks, and he joked with them enough, having common backgrounds from the North and thereabouts," George said. His Dublin accent was so thick no one would make a mistake that he was a Culchie, a country boy, like Curran, Lanigan thought.

"There were usually two other strange blokes there, one with some French kind of accent and another English, and they would get together thick as thieves with your man O'Neill and Curran. They gambled and drank a lot after target practice. I don't know where he got the money. I wouldn't stay too long then. Too rich for my blood, you know."

Samantha had not said a word, but she recalled the photos Rami had shown her. She felt she could see them around that table, scheming and drinking and laughing. Yet they were nowhere to be seen in that pub now and they had not been at the funeral. Strange for such a close drinking mate not to be remembered now, she thought. She just smiled and watched as others came and went and then left as it was getting close to afternoon closing time. Stokes looked at Lanigan and they nodded at

George, who would have been happy to go on for a while, but he had also heard the Holy Hour "time now, lady and gents" and finished his pint.

"Well, it was nice to talk with you fellas. I hope you find out what happened to him. Even his workmates are not sure how he died. Some state secret, I suppose. He should have had a better funeral for a former soldier and G2 Special Branch and all that. No one stuck up for him, I suppose. Queer man," George said, shaking his head.

"We're looking into it from my end," Lanigan reassured him. "Let us know if you hear what happened to that rifle. I would buy it myself, if I could afford it," Lanigan winked. Stokes nodded and shook his hand and expressed his condolences, as did Samantha. They left the pub to get back to work but did not get as much information as they had hoped. They all seemed disappointed that they did not see any hint of perpetrators or collaborators.

Chapter Twenty-Four

Stokes went back to his office. His secretary informed him that he had a call from the French Embassy, an Inspector Cloudot. He quickly looked over his mail and messages and since there was no other immediate work, he called the Embassy again to see if he could get any more information from Cloudot. When he finally got through to the receptionist, who did not recall who he was and was going to refer him to another bureaucrat, he again mentioned Inspector Cloudot and this was a police matter. This time she recalled him. She said Cloudot was out of the office, but she would notify him, and he would contact Stokes on his return. Stokes did not bother asking when. He did some paperwork while he waited and finally got a return call.

"We have information on Abn Awaa," Cloudot announced. "He was sighted in London yesterday, speaking to a Libyan diplomat who we have been following. But before we could alert the British, he had disappeared again. I don't know if he will be coming back to Dublin, but we will keep you informed, as I hope you will us as well," he said.

"What about that that Belgian Nazi, Dussault, from the arms trial a few years ago, have you been following him as well?" Stokes asked.

"We are not sure if he has been working with Abn Awaa, but we know he has been meeting with O'Neill —he calls himself a patriotic Irishman now," he sneered.

"He calls himself a businessman. He runs a hotel and restaurant outside of Dublin. He has a lot of friends high up so no one asks any questions. The Belgians should have shot him when they had a chance," Stokes sniffed.

"We also have information that Mossad is following Abn Awaa. I am sure they are more interested in him than the others, but we don't know where he is. And the, how you say, the elephant in the room: the

IRA has dropped out of the picture for now, so Abn Awaa may be on his own. We won't know until something happens. We are only able to give you information when they decide to do something. Let us hope that it is not after the fact."

"You said that the French girl may have been Mossad. How do you know?" asked Stokes.

"She had a boyfriend who may have been a Mossad agent, but he has disappeared and for all we know, he could be dead as well."

Stokes did not say anything. The French seemed to know less than he did. Cloudot was not aware of Curran's involvement and his murder. It was best, Stokes thought, not to muddy the waters. He was not sure if it was Abn Awaa or another IRA faction that had killed Curran. It was obvious that no one was going to give him any clues. He had reached a dead end.

"I suppose that closes things for now, don't you think?" Stokes asked.

"For now, yes, but one can never tell, n'est-ce pas?"

"One last thing," Stokes asked. "We are done with the young lady's investigation, is that right?" he asked.

"Yes. She was another unfortunate victim. I do not think we need any more information to complete our reports. I assure you, your report will be translated properly and filed so you need not bother yourself about this tragic case. I hope to meet you soon again," Cloudot said, hanging up.

Stokes did not know what he was going to do with that information that he got from Cloudot. It could be that having completed his mission, whatever it was, in Dublin, that the Jackal move on to other ventures in Europe. But who killed Curran and why? Curran knew he was a marked man, and it was more likely that the IRA had commissioned his killer rather than anyone else. He knew too much, so it was most likely part of a cover-up. That got back to O'Neill who was still "clean," looking for more power and more money. Were they going to try another arms shipment? Was there collusion between the IRA and the UVF in the bombings to forward their own agendas of constant warfare, chaos, and struggle for power? Why else call in a professional terrorist and killer? Stokes was not convinced that this was the end of it. He was sure that the Jackal would return. All the possibilities overwhelmed Harold Stokes. Despite the time he had wasted, he planned to complete the remains of his days' work, peaceful and straightforward by comparison.

Chapter Twenty-Five

Lanigan decided to visit the Gun Club that Curran's mate had mentioned. Perhaps he could get a lead on where the Carcano had disappeared. Whoever removed it knew it was the perfect weapon to implicate Curran in the killing of the disappeared corpse. It would have been in Curran's best interest to remove the bullets from the scene of the crime so that no one would pin it on him and, for now, he was in the clear, although it really didn't matter to a dead man.

Being a weekday, the range was not as busy. Most of the members were weekend warriors. All sorts of weaponry were on display, rifles and hunting guns and pistols. The users were more than willing to display their toys. Lanigan really didn't like guns. He knew they were a necessary evil in his profession, and he dutifully practiced at the police range to pass his proficiency exams, but not out of pleasure. He was disturbed by the concept of having to shoot or be shot and since most of the citizens of Dublin were not armed, he saw no need to use them himself.

He sat down with the manager of the club, Mr. O'Rourke, a jovial fellow who was always interested in promoting the club and cooperating with the police, he asserted.

"We are investigating the theft of a gun of one of the members of the club, Detective Sergeant Curran," Lanigan told him.

"No wonder we haven't seen him for a while. He would talk about that gun like it was his baby. He kept it clean, and he was very proficient in its use. All to prove his argument that there was no conspiracy, and that Lee Harvey Oswald did it. He was always ready to show his speed shooting the gun and in general, was pretty accurate. It was his little passion and we put up with it. Sure, he would talk of nothing else while he was here, but I suppose we all have our own special hobbies.

Are you a gun fancier, Detective Lanigan?" he asked.

"No. I learned how to use the gun like a carpenter uses a hammer, part of the business," he said noncommittally, not wanting to encourage his enthusiastic host.

"When did he first complain about the rifle being stolen?" asked Lanigan.

"About three weeks ago, just before the bombing. He was very upset. He kept it under lock and key, very meticulous he was with it."

"So, he never loaned it to anyone here or gave it out to others."

"No. It was too valuable to him. And that would be illegal, wouldn't it?"

"Did he ever bring anyone with him to the club?" Lanigan asked.

"No, not that I know of, although I was not always here. My partner might have seen someone while I was away on holidays last month, but he has not been here for a while since he has been on holidays himself. He fancied a trip to the south of France, but he settled for a trip to the beach at Lahinch."

"When will he be back?" asked Lanigan.

"Another few days." He looked like he was getting tired of the questioning. It was clear to Lanigan that he was no fan of the police, and this inquisition made him suspicious.

"What's this all about, anyways?" he asked.

"Police business. Ongoing investigation. How can I get a hold of your partner?" Lanigan asked, irritated, not willing to give out any more information than he needed to, including Curran's murder. Apparently, O'Rourke had not heard yet or did not let on that he did.

"You can't. He's in a caravan with all the mod cons and a bunch of children. No phone nearby. Sort of peace and quiet," he chuckled.

"Well, let me know if you know of anyone who might have seen Curran with anyone while he was here, especially any dark-looking fellas," Lanigan said, giving him his card with his name and number.

Lanigan was not sure if he had gotten all the information that O'Rourke knew, but it was hard to extract information from an old Dubliner like him, especially one who liked to play with guns. His ancestors, distant and near, had developed a habit of not talking to officials, whether they were English or Castle Irish or even Gardai, for self-preservation. He might know nothing or everything and Lanigan concluded that he was not worth wasting time over. But he had planted the information that they were looking for the carbine, which might or might not produce results.

Samantha went through the day half-heartedly. With no new autopsies to perform, she was stuck with finishing the paperwork for the others she had done as well as any other official papers that needed completion that she had been delegated to do by Professor Stokes. Her mind wandered to the more exciting thoughts about her recent adventure in London and her first foray into espionage. She had put the invitation to the reception in a safe place in her drawer and had marked the date on her calendar at home. She was wondering how she would get out of work early that day since she had just been away for the weekend. She did not want to gain a reputation as a slacker. She took a deep breath and dug into the work at hand and tried to focus on it rather than any other extra-curricular activities. The day passed quickly when she got into it. Stokes wasn't there to give her another job to do on top of everything else. He was a decent boss, but being a workaholic, he expected everyone else to do the same. Where was he anyway? It was unlike him to be out of the office for more than a few hours. This whole case had enthralled him as much as her, but she did not want to question him any further. She did not want to arouse his ire or suspicion. The reception was tomorrow, so if she could complete the work she needed to do, she could just show him her tasks completed and ask for an early evening.

How would she approach O'Neill? she thought. She would try speaking to Gray first. He would be the most approachable since he would speak with anyone and everyone about anything. He had no obvious job but was rumored to be fixed for life because of an inheritance, although he was quick to look for any business or social opportunities that could further his interests. He was a bit eccentric and there was an infamous story of him having hired a taxi to drive him to the North to an RUC base where the driver had to wait for him while he had a meeting and then threatened the man to never reveal the trip because he was a "double agent." The driver was scared enough to begin with but later discounted the story completely. He told everyone he knew later Gray was so drunk the porter had to help him up to his rooms in the Shelbourne. Whether he was just a loquacious drunk or a chancer or both, Samanth would have to be careful to make the first encounter casual.

She recalled the photo Rami had shown her where they had left an art auction. She would engage him in a discussion of the art of Jack Yeats, the only artist she knew much about since she had done a paper about him in secondary school. She had been so excited about the research, she wanted to go on to study fine arts and history, but her mother insisted she continue with the sciences and medicine since they were more practical. She was still fascinated by the reviews of art that related to medicine on the front page of JAMA and read every one of them. There was the latest copy on her desk with an illustration by Andrew Wyeth, but she avoided the distraction of reading a review now and set to complete her days' work.

Stokes came in late that afternoon, having run his errands of inquiry and come up with very little. He chided himself again for spending his time being distracted from his real work, but he could not help himself. He might save some lives, bring the guilty to justice, and bring his own closure. He could not stop. He paused at the door of his office, though, as disinterested in completing his paperwork as Samantha and, he had to admit, as excited about the hunt as she was. He strode in, nodded hello to his secretary who was busy with transcriptions, her earphones plugged into her ears. Stokes stood at the desk to review his mail and messages. There was yet another invitation for another reception in aid of the children of the North. He tossed it aside, disgusted at the excuses for raising money that went to activities that were distinctly not for the benefit of any children, but for politicians, gullible rich, and opportunists. Besides, the reception was tomorrow. He was not really interested in another late night.

He sat down at his desk and was ready to heave a pile of papers in front of him when he got a call from Lanigan.

"What do you have?" Stokes asked, direct and irritated that this was going to be yet another wasteful wild goose chase.

"Another body for you, but you're going to have to make a house call on this one, Professor."

"Why is that?"

"His evidence is splattered all over the footpath and we will need help collecting it. The coroner specifically said he wants you to do the honors."

"Who is this?"

"He had friends in high places. He called himself Major Gray, but he looks like Major Gray Chutney right now," Lanigan smiled over the phone, amused by his own wit.

"Where are you?" Stokes asked, picking up a pencil and poised to write down the address in case he needed it.

"Not far—the Shelbourne hotel, one of his regular haunts. The shot missed Minister O'Neill by just a few feet. Lucky for him. That's why the place is crawling with Gardai and G2-men. Like I said, friends in high places."

"I will be there soon. Anything else?"

"No. Sorry to spoil your evening. Oh, the reporters are already crawling all over this even with the wide police tape cordons, so be prepared to make a lot of no comments. I've sent over a Garda to pick you up. He should be there shortly," Lanigan said, hanging up.

Stokes walked over to Samantha's office where she was still hunched over the papers she was eager to finish. She had gotten into the rhythm of scanning over each document and writing pertinent comments and then filing them into a neat pile until she could see her progress with the "in" pile appreciably smaller than the "out." She looked forward to relaxing that evening and the mindless work distracted her from the adventure she was anticipating the next day. Stokes startled her when he knocked on the frame of her open door. She nearly jumped from her seat.

"Come on. This will be a learning moment. We have a fresh corpse at the Shelbourne Hotel who will need significant examination and an extra set of eyes will help," Stokes said, motioning her to hurry.

She grabbed her umbrella and raincoat since it had started to pour as she looked out the window. Stokes already was prepared with his Mac on and cursed to himself for the bad luck that the rain would wash away clues as they looked around at the scene.

"Lanigan has sent a Garda in a squad car to pick us up," he said. "This is going to be a special assignment, so keep your eyes open."

"Who is it?" Samantha asked as they walked to the lobby.

"Major Gray. An eccentric fellow, I have heard. An acquaintance of O'Neill. A drunk and a gambler. This does not sound like an unpaid gambling debt, but that is for Lanigan to find out." The Garda car pulled up, the rain letting up a bit as they stepped into it.

Samantha did not utter a word. Her mind was racing. This was the man she was designated to meet tomorrow at the reception. She could not acknowledge this to Stokes. She was wondering how Rami would find out about this. She accepted this sudden cancellation of her adventure with relief and then fear. She shivered once as she followed Stokes out the door. He did not notice.

It was a short ride to the hotel and just as well since traffic had been diverted around the entrance facing Stephen's Green and even pedestrians were inconvenienced by all the police tape and the press and other curious onlookers peering over, even in the rain, to get a look at the body.

Stokes and Samantha were led over to the scene which was now covered with raised tarpaulins to help preserve the evidence as much as possible. Stokes could see half the skull blown off, laying a few inches away from the head which was barely recognizable for all the blood. It looked like one clear shot. The angle looked somewhere from above, Stokes reckoned. He bent over to see the point of entry. It was small, suggesting a high-powered rifle since the exit wound or, one should say, exit fragments of skull were shattered like glass on the pavement and the contents of brain and blood oozed onto the street, mixing with the rainwater.

"So, what do you think, Professor," asked Lanigan appearing out of the crowd, bending over to get under the tarpaulin and hear his answer over the chattering crowd of spectators, reporters, and other police. Special Branch agents were standing over the scene as well, easily identifiable in their black suits and grim expressions, still looking around for any suspicious activity.

"High powered rifle from some distance I would say, probably a rooftop or high window," Stokes said. "Did you find any spent bullets?"

"So far, just the one, near the head." Lanigan nodded to the small, marked metal object at the base of the skull, easy to mistake for a pebble to the casual eye. "But there were two shots fired and one missed O'Neill who was nearly next to him, so we are still looking."

"Good shot. If only Lee Harvey Oswald was here. . ." Stokes paused. "Once you've gathered all the information, send me copies of all the photos. Let me know when you will transfer the body," Stokes said, eager to leave. He had seen enough for the day, and he was sure nothing would happen until late into the evening. The coroner would be on him to get the job done quickly, late-night quickly. Samantha was thinking the same thing and looked over the crime scene but was distracted by the thought she might have been closer to that last bullet than she would have liked.

"Do you think it was the same gun?" Lanigan asked, stopping Stokes before he left.

"Maybe the same kind. We never got the bullets that killed the disappeared corpse. Curran may have known where they went to, but we have no Curran to ask," Stokes said. Lanigan did not give him any more answers, since he had none. It occurred to Lanigan it might be worthwhile to find those spent bullets and check Curran's flat again.

"I'll leave you both to get home for tea." Lanigan motioned for the Garda who ferried them here to come over.

"Would you ever take these two important people back to their homes and be ready to pick them up and take them back to the morgue when needed," Lanigan ordered. The Garda made a face, slightly turned away so Lanigan barely noticed, but he noticed. "That should keep youse out of trouble," he smiled, "and dry," he added, indicating the favor he had bestowed on him.

Stokes got home, dried off and sat down to his tea, Mrs. Kelly refrained from asking a lot of questions that evening, immediately seeing he was in a pensive mood and knew he was on a case. She was discreet. Stokes appreciated the silence. Fortunately, the news was over and there were no favorite programs that evening so the radio and TV were silenced as well. Despite this, Stokes ate quickly in anticipation of the phone call which came just as he had absent mindedly looked at the dregs of his teacup and avoided the last bitter sip. He would remind Mrs. Kelly to get a new strainer, if he could remember.

It was Lanigan, telling him that Gray's body had been delivered to the morgue and, as had been discussed, that the coroner wanted the report promptly. He said, true to his word, that he was sending the squad car over and, if he wanted, could pick up Dr. Monaghan as well. Stokes agreed and warned him to call her to be ready. He regretted having to drag her in, but she might as well get used to the idea that, despite the impression that it was a 9 to 5 job, that it wasn't always going to be so.

The rain had decreased. It was muggier and warmer as they were ferried to the morgue. Mr. Johnston, faithful assistant that he was, had already set up the body, the lights, and the instruments. All Stokes and Samantha had to do was put their gowns on. Stokes gloved up and checked to see that the dictation tape was in, and the machine switched on. He did the preliminaries of sampling some blood for toxicology. Samantha took some more Polaroids before the procedure.

"This is Professor Harold Stokes, Dublin State Medical Examiner, witnessed by my assistant, Dr. Samantha Monaghan, dictating an autopsy report on Major George Gray, a 54year old Caucasian male who was found dead by the Gardai after a witnessed gunshot wound to the head on Tuesday, July 16, 1974, at 4:45 PM. The time is now 7:51 PM on the same date," he began.

"He is 170 cm, 81 kg, obese, well-nourished, anicteric, with no obvious rashes or stigmata other than the head wound and lividity. Facial rigor mortis is evident but minimal, consistent with the time of death and my examination. His clothes had been removed by Mr. Johnston, the diener, after they had been photographed and sampled by the Gardai. There were no markings on the garments evident of any other bullet wounds or bleeding other than from the aforementioned head wound which splattered the back of his neck, collar, and shoulders of the suit coat."

"There is a 10x5 mm wound at the superior border of the left frontal bone along the hairline and a 10 x 13 cm wound at the right lower occipital bone where there are shattered fragments of bone and a deficiency consistent with the fragment of bone found on the pavement where the body was found."

Stokes paused at this point and looked at Samantha who had been observing the body and listening to the dictation, making sure she picked up every detail. He would be asking her questions. She was ready.

"Based on my description, where was the entry wound and where was the exit wound?" he asked her.

"The smaller frontal wound must be the entry and the larger occipital wound the exit since the bullet wobbled on its way through the brain and out the back of the skull, which would make the trajectory somewhere down from high up and to the left of the victim," she concluded.

"Precisely, and since the assassination was witnessed, we know that it was not fired from his rear since it would have had to pass through several people who were behind him, including the former minister O'Neill, who was not seen with a high-powered rifle. Please get the X-ray machine so we can check for any bullet fragments in the brain before we do the craniotomy," he ordered. "Be sure to get the lead aprons. With that old machine, we need as much shielding as possible," he warned.

She wheeled in the portable X-ray machine which was a jury-rigged device scavenged from the radiology department of the hospital. It did the job but was woefully ancient.

She wheeled the machine back to its place in the corner of the autopsy room and Mr. Johnston was called to develop the films while they completed the external examination. There was little to see other than the obvious head wound, but the meticulous process of observation and description had to be completed. Stokes quickly completed his dictation of the external examination, making sure he noted that there were no powder marks that would indicate the gun was fired at close range.

"We don't see many assassinations in this town, thank God. This looks much like the wounds from the gun that was used to kill our missing John Doe, but our assassin had a much cleaner shot since he was moving much slower," Stokes surmised.

"That same missing gun?" Samantha asked.

"I think so and that same unknown assassin, wherever he is."

"Are those films ready yet, Johnston?" yelled Stokes, not willing to wait any longer.

"Yes, sir, here they are," Johnston said, handing the X-ray films over.

The small pinpoint fracture to the frontal bone was obvious as the entry and the comminuted bits of the occipital bone were obvious as the exit wound. There was a small fragment of metal just at the orifice of the exit wound which was consistent with the bullet found. At least he knew where he had to look. He carefully removed the skin of the scalp and looked at the surface of the skull and saw no other marks suggestive of blunt trauma or another bullet. He opened the skull with the saw and saw blood ooze from the meninges, the membrane surrounding the brain, especially at the entry of the wound, and noticed small particles of bone in the frontal cortex of the cerebrum, the gray matter behind the forehead. There was no evidence of fragments of the bullet there, so he washed the area around there and completed the removal of the brain, taking care to leave the parts of the back of the skull that had been fractured into pieces intact so that it could be carefully shown that these were due to the exit wound. He removed the brain. As he placed it in the pan, he heard a slight click against the metal and there was a small fragment of the bullet, which was consistent with the X-ray. No surprises there. The brain weighed 1.48 kg and was only distinguished by the friability of the tissue that corresponded to the exit wound in the skull. He sectioned the brain to follow the track of the destruction and again, the areas where the bullet had passed were friable, almost liquefied. He described this in his report. There was only one track that he found, and it was consistent with the one bullet traveling in the trajectory on the left to right from front to back. A good shot, perhaps a lucky shot, or just the mark of an expert. He would ask Lanigan and also Cloudot to investigate as to whether the Jackal was that good a shot since it was that remarkable.

He carefully observed the body for any other unusual signs before he made his vertical incision in the midline of the chest wall and then the two diagonal lateral incisions below the ribs to access the abdominal organs. He sawed through the sternum to remove the heart and lungs and weighed them. He commented on the heart which had wads of fat on several parts of the muscle and felt the thickened, hardened arteries that suggested his likely heart disease. His lungs were the usual mottled gray of a smoker and there was a calcified nodule at the right apex of the lung that suggested healed TB, also not unusual. His liver was fatty and enlarged and there were fibrous areas with some nodules suggestive of early cirrhosis consistent with his history of his having been a heavy drinker. The large pannus of fat below the skin along his lower abdomen indicated an overindulgent life unmitigated by exercise. All in all, a great candidate for an otherwise early death, the head wound notwithstanding.

He dictated the report with the ease of a seasoned practitioner but was careful not to make the report so rote that he would miss an important detail that needed mention. Fortunately, there was nothing more suspicious during the autopsy than the head wound which was obvious. It was not for him to decide any more than the cause of death, but it was certainly very worrying that it seemed to be like the same gun and shooter that had done the job, a single shot from above. It was obvious that if Curran was involved in the original shooting of the John Doe, he was only an accomplice. Stokes made a mental note to remind Lanigan to look for the bullet at Curran's flat and check the roofs near the Shelbourne for the spent shell. He was sure that Lanigan was still looking for the fabled rifle.

"Do you have anything to add to this autopsy, Dr. Monaghan?" Stokes asked.

"No, Professor, but we certainly would be interested in the weapon, let alone the killer," she said.

"Not our job, Doctor. You can sew up. Be sure to be careful about any signs that might be helpful in evidence, even if there was only one bullet and one obvious wound. Check on toxicology to see if there are any other signs of foul play besides the alcohol which was chronic but not an acute cause of his death."

Stokes took his gloves off and washed his hands. Finding the killer was enticing, but he felt that there were more people in the city who were in danger and that the Gardai had to step up and complete the job. He was very concerned that Samantha was too involved in these cases.

"We can finish the paperwork tomorrow. It is late and no one is going to be very quick to snooping for likely subjects or knocking on doors for evidence tonight if they haven't already done so," he said.

Samantha nodded and continued her cleanup of the autopsy. She saw his point but was disappointed in his caution and in her missing the opportunity of being part of the solution by interrogating the same man she was sewing up. She resigned herself to not going to the reception the next day.

They left the office together and shared the taxi to their homes. He wanted to make sure she was safe and felt he needed to be more protective of her, but there was no immediate danger he could reasonably expect. He was just shaken by the number of violent deaths recently and, perhaps, cumulatively. He was tired and did not talk much. She dared not. He was more irritable than she expected.

He watched as she was dropped off at her flat and opened, then closed the door behind her. Further on to his house, he said nothing to the cab driver who was fine with not having a conversation. As he got out of the cab, Stokes looked across the street and noted the absence of the van and felt relieved. He was hoping for no more adventures. He opened the door of his empty house and relished the quiet and looked forward to a good night's sleep. As he loosened his tie and put his jacket up, the phone rang. It was Lanigan.

"Any more on the autopsy?" he asked.

"Not really. One gunshot, one shattered skull, and brain. Anything on the bullet fragment?"

"Probably the same carbine, but how would we know since we haven't found the first bullet. I have a warrant to search Curran's flat, so I'll do it in the light of day tomorrow, but I don't expect any surprises," he said.

Chapter Twenty-Six

When Samantha opened her door, she noticed an envelope had been slipped under. She looked around. There was no one there. She was surprised that anyone could have gotten in since the main door to the flats was locked when she came in. She opened the envelope; it was a simple message: "Go to the reception tomorrow. Howard will introduce you to O'Neill. Use your charm, we will do the rest. Love, Rami."

She ran to the window to look out on the street, but there was no one there. She sat on her bed, excited at the idea that she would still be a spy for a good cause, but also hoped to see Rami again. But as her excitement abated, her rational mind took over. She was still worried about the risk. Two deaths into this investigation, she knew she was in danger. Stokes thought they were at risk. Had he not called a cab to get them both home safely? Had he not warned her not to look any further into this? Was this curiosity worth it? She was a pathologist. Any answers that needed solutions would be on the person she was examining. Wasn't that enough? She already knew that answer. She could not ignore what was going on outside the autopsy room. More bodies would be showing up, more innocent victims of these "Troubles." If she was really to help, she had no choice—she would have to take the risks. Rami was as much a professional as Professor Stokes, so there would be some support, at least she hoped there would be. She looked at the clock and realized it was later than would be "healthy" for her, as her mother would nag. She washed up and went to bed.

By the next morning, Lanigan had already set out to visit the gun club again and resolved not be as easy on the proprietor as he had the last time. He wanted to find that gun and its new owner. The hours of the club were later during the weekdays with fewer members, so he would catch him earlier and be more intimidating. He knew his chances were slim, but he had detected a reluctance from O'Higgins to be completely forthcoming on that first interview. Some people who used guns were more interested in things other than sport, although the proprietor would argue otherwise.

When Lanigan pulled up to the entrance, a light was on inside, but the closed sign was up. Just perfect for what he needed, he thought. He knocked on the door and Seamus O'Higgins came quickly to the door showing an irritated face as he peered out the window of the office.

"It's Detective Lanigan, Mr. O'Higgins. We need to talk again," he shouted to the door. He was used to talking through doors.

O'Higgins opened the door and let him in, motioning him to sit down on the chair next to his desk.

"You probably heard about the killing at the Shelbourne yesterday, didn't you?"

"Who wouldn't have? 'Tis news like that that spoils it for all of us. One shot, though, wasn't it?" he asked.

"No, it was two shots. The other missed the ex-Minister by a hair. Everyone else was pretty rattled, to be sure. We think it was from that Carcano I asked about. Can you recall anyone else had a rifle like that or anyone else who has been with Curran in the past month or two? Lives depend on it, maybe even yours."

"What do you bloody mean, mine?" O'Higgins said, now moved, shifting in his chair.

"I mean that this yabo has been going around killing people who had anything to do with Curran, including himself. There are some secrets going on and someone doesn't want them to come out," Lanigan said in an almost whisper, waiting to hear his response.

"All right. Curran did bring in someone else with him and the carbine, about a month ago. He was tall and looked military without the uniform, if you know what I mean. He had a Northern accent. They didn't stay long, but he was good with the gun—like he had years of practice. They didn't stay long, and they didn't talk much. Like this was a short training session," he said.

"You have a ledger where you have people sign in and out, have you?" Lanigan asked.

"Of course. Those are the rules. No one ever comes to look, but I would hate to pay the fines if it wasn't quite square," he said, getting up to get the book. It was nothing unusual, like a guest book at a hotel with a date, time in and out, name and address, and signature. Lanigan flipped through it to find Curran's name and anyone who might have come in with him. Curran came in about every two weeks. Lanigan scanned the lines and noticed that about six weeks before he died, Curran had been in. Below his name was that of Major George Gray.

"Did you see a picture of the man who was shot yesterday?" Lanigan asked.

"No, I didn't," replied O'Higgins.

"Do you recall seeing this man?" asked Lanigan, showing a photo clipped from today's paper. He avoided the one from the tabloids since they were more interested in displaying the head wound than the face. There was no shame in the press, Lanigan thought to himself.

"No, don't know him, but was that the man who was killed?" he asked.

"It was—a fat, soused British ponce, by all accounts," Lanigan answered.

"That wasn't the man who came with Curran that time. Like I said, tall, military-like, Ulster accent," O'Higgins repeated.

"How do you know he was military?" asked Lanigan.

"He looked like he was wearing a uniform, standing straight and all. He treated the gun with respect. Definitely not that man," he nodded to the picture.

"Give me a ring if you see him here or if your members can recall talking to him. He might be our man, so be careful," Lanigan warned, hoping that the proprietor might do the legwork of asking the other club members since he didn't want to have to go through the whole list, although there were a lot of "regulars" on the ledger.

"Do you have the names, addresses, and phone numbers of all the members of the club?" asked Lanigan, wanting to make sure of getting any leads he could if O'Higgins was not more cooperative.

"I do, but I would have to do it by hand. I don't have a Xerox machine here. I'm not doing that well," he said, waving his arm around the shoddy office that had never seen better times and was unlikely to in the future.

"Well, then, give me the ledgers and the lists and I will have the Gardai office do it for us, since I am pressed for time now," Lanigan offered, sounding like more of an order than a request.

"What will I do for the ledgers? They are not cheap and then the Gardai could write me up for not keeping proper records," O'Higgins protested.

"You still have pens and paper. I will get you a bloody dispensation if the Gardai bother you," Lanigan said.

"All right then, here you are," handing his papers and books to him. "Mind, I need it all back soon. It will soon be the end of the month and I will have to do some reckoning on the memberships."

"Not to worry. I'll have them back in two shakes of a lamb's tail," Lanigan reassured him, walking out the door with the pile in his hands and an uncomfortable stare from O'Higgins. Lanigan threw the whole pile in the back of his car and drove back to the office. He had gotten enough to have a lead and needed to look at Curran's office as well for any more clues that had been overlooked.

As he got to the office, he was warned by the sour face of his clerk that there was trouble brewing. They were not the best of friends nor the worst, but having worked together long enough, they had learned to communicate by various scowls and quick looks that would warn them of impending trouble, usually by "higher-ups," and most likely from the Superintendent. He was in Lanigan's office when he came in with the jumble of "borrowed" gun club files and ledgers.

"When are you going to report to me about your findings in the Curran case? Special Branch is not excited about your handling this at all. It was just that you were johnny-on-the spot for that one as well as on the disappearing body. They are thinking of investigating *you*, so you better be after producing some paperwork soon, Boyo," said the Superintendent in his Dublin accent that had not changed much in his movement up the ranks. He had a tolerance for Lanigan and had overlooked his lackadaisical attitude to rules and regulations because of their common background, but the pressure was on to make all the recent drama go away. It was bad enough that the investigation on the bombing was going nowhere and that there were some who would want to make the events history and less embarrassing than they already were. Curran's death and Major Gray's assassination only made things more complicated and the Superintendent's position more difficult. Neither Curran nor Gray was a favorite of the Special Branch, exemplifying their inability to keep their show together. It was no mistake that the turnout for Curran's funeral was so sparse. No one wanted to be associated with him. For whatever the truth of it, he was considered an informer, and even if the Special Branch was not full of IRA sympathizers or members, that's how Curran had been seen.

"I'll just have to tie up some loose ends, boss. I have a foot in the door. Whoever has the rifle now had something to do with Curran as well. After all, it was his rifle, according to ballistics, that killed Gray," Lanigan pointed out.

"I'll make this simple. You have till the end of the week to wrap this up. They are pushing me to give it to Special Branch and if they do that, they will close the investigation whether you have a bloody foot in the door or not, and your toes and mine be damned," the Superintendent said, walking out the door of the office without closing it.

Lanigan muttered under his breath as he left his office and tramped up the stairs to Special Branch. He was headed to Curran's office to hunt for any more clues before the office was cleaned out and occupied by another agent. He glanced around the small office The old certificates, diplomas, and photos were still on the wall. He looked at the photo of Curran holding the Carcano, a la Oswald, and the photo of him in a group of agents standing next to O'Neill.

Lanigan had brought a briefcase with him, just in case there were some bits and pieces of "evidence" that he might be able to put together for the discovery of Curran's killer or the killer of the disappeared unknown body, or both. The pictures were still hanging on the walls of the office. They were too familiar to those who saw them every day. They could be interrogation aids or, if there were any relatives, just mementos when Lanigan saw fit to release them. All the papers on and in the desk had been removed to the appropriate police files if they were relevant and had official stamps or were official-looking forms, but all the "personal" papers were still on a box on the desk. They had been sorted by some lowly clerk who didn't know or care that this was the detritus of a life, important or not. Lanigan threw the pictures in the box and quickly carried them out of the office. He was proceeding down the hall when one of the detectives stopped him.

"Oy, who gave you permission to remove these?" he demanded, glancing at his ID badge, but not really noticing or caring who he was.

"I'm in charge of the investigation of Curran's death," Lanigan slowly explained, holding the heavy box uncomfortably under his arms.

"By what authority? He was Special Branch, for what that was worth," he sneered.

"By my detective Superintendent. This was a homicide. I'm on the homicide squad, if you hadn't noticed the badge," Lanigan said nodding to the badge dangling into the box.

"Those are his private possessions," the detective said.

"They are, but right now they're evidence, and they will be released to his next of kin when we're done."

"Good luck with that. He had no family and no friends," the detective sneered, again.

"Well then, you'll have to do some detective work on your own and find some. Right now, I'll be off," Lanigan proceeded down the hall.

"Lanigan, is that right?" shouted the detective as Lanigan proceeded down the hall.

"That's right, he said, turning slightly, shifting his box as he proceeded down the stairs.

Chapter Twenty-Seven

Samantha got ready for the reception by completing the work for the day and sneaking out early. She knew she wouldn't have time to get her hair done, but she did her best to make herself attractive to her target. She was not shocked that the fundraising event had not been canceled even though O'Neill had been a near-miss in Major Gray's death. It was politically expedient to show his bravery under fire to encourage donors to the Ulster Rescue Fund to contribute more than they had planned. Security would be tight, so she was at least guaranteed some safety. Her only orders were to be there and make an initial contact, nothing more for now, which was fine with her. O'Neill would be more cautious about making advances in a more vigilant public venue. Still, it had been more than once that day that she had been ready to call Howard Bernstein and call the whole thing off. Fortunately, the Professor was out of the office again and she did not have to hide how anxious or inefficient she was.

Bernstein arranged for a taxi to pick her up at half six. She was ready at six. She sat reading newspaper interviews of O'Neill that had been dropped by the day before in an official-looking brown paper envelope by one of Bernstein's aides. They were still sealed when her landlady handed them to her and commented about official secret papers and how important they must have been. To her credit this time, the landlady had been more discreet than usual. There was not much she did not know about her tenants. The lace curtains of her window were worn from their constant opening and closing night and day.

Most of the interviews were puff pieces about O'Neill's various interests in horses and his farm and only tangentially of his political aspirations and his Ulster Republican pedigree. His father had fought in the war for independence and was one of the founders of Fianna Fail. O'Neill still had family on the other side of the border and lamented their sad and restricted lives under Loyalist rule. There was no mention of the arms smuggling trial, still a sore point, despite his exoneration. But there was the self-promotion of his leadership in the Ulster Rescue Fund more than once in many of the articles, making sure that his time was not wasted talking to these social columnists.

Bernstein met her at the lobby of the Shelbourne Hotel and escorted her into the reception room where the charity was being held. She was not noticed, but Bernstein made sure to introduce her to all the "right" people, those who knew or wanted to know O'Neill and had the money to show it. Bernstein stood by, making sure that he was giving his approval of her presence and engaging in the small talk that a politico of his experience would make about families and holidays and other pleasantries like the latest play at the Abbey or concerts in town. He was cautious to avoid the reason for the gathering since it was too obvious and sensitive and, after all, they would be reminded by O'Neill and the other speakers. Samantha was overwhelmed by the intricacy of the social discourse. She was near to an anxiety attack that she might be asked anything. They had not taught her anything like this in Medical School. Her social circle was still limited to her old classmates. She was eyeing the champagne as it was passed around and debating whether that would calm her down or just dull her concentration. She grabbed a glass as it was passed but paused to sip rather than swallow it down. That was the right thing to do, she reassured herself and when the question came around from one of the kindly matrons as to what she did to pass the time, she admitted that she did not have much spare time, that she worked as a pathologist with the Medical Examiner. The Matron momentarily raised her eyebrow and then congratulated her on being a working woman. She did not ask for more details, but smiled and then excused herself, to Samantha's relief.

Bernstein spotted O'Neill who was floating through the crowd, nodding to some, grasping another by the shoulder, and shaking this hand and that with the ease of a professional. All whom he addressed either smiled or made a joke and they laughed together. Bernstein nudged Samantha forward towards O'Neill and she took the hint to introduce herself again to him. Not averse to a pretty face, O'Neill turned to say hello. She re-introduced herself as Professor Stokes' assistant. He extended a hand and nodded to Bernstein, someone he tolerated as a Fianna Fail party member, but did not trust since his former boss, Robert Briscoe, had openly expressed his disdain for O'Neill at the last party meeting.

"Oh, yes, Professor Stokes has had his hands full lately, hasn't he? I am keenly interested in the inquiry into my friend's death. How is the course of the investigation of Major Gray's death coming?" he asked, getting right to the point.

He expected it would be easier to pry some details out of this naive girl than press his contacts in the police since they would report any questions to their superiors. He had not been asked any questions yet by the detectives but expected to be questioned soon enough.

"Have you gotten any clues as to this assailant?" he asked.

"I only know what we have found, that he was killed by one shot to the head. The Gardai don't share any more information with us than they need to, especially in an open investigation," she answered cautiously.

"You are learning your craft well," he smiled weakly. "Perhaps we can speak more later since I have work to do here," he said, excusing himself, looking around at other members of the crowd who were eager to attract his attention.

"Good girl," Bernstein congratulated Samantha. "You have gotten his attention. He will be back to you since he thinks you know more than you do. I will hang around, but at a distance. Have a drink or two and the canapés are tasty," he smiled, grabbing one as the tray passed by. She was too nervous to eat and too wary to drink any more than the glass of champagne she was holding. She smiled at the crowd and was about to wade into a circle and introduce herself when she was struck with horror; across the room, just coming in from the entrance, was her mother. Her mother, the recluse and anti-socialite, was in a gown, accompanied by her boss. She had not seen her, and Samantha quickly dodged behind a column.

Holy shite and onions, she exclaimed to herself. I am sunk if she discovers me. She will be asking me all these questions and totally distract me, and O'Neill will forget me completely. Pull yourself together, she said to herself. All you need to do is go over to her and do some banter and explain why you are here. Better yet, ask her what she is doing here. She will be put on the defensive and try to avoid any explanation. Samantha had a suspicion that she and her boss, the head of the Trinity Library, had been spending extended work hours above and beyond the call of duty. She knew he was recently widowed. He was attractive enough and just her age. Samantha could ask her mother some questions and make it more uncomfortable so they would just flee in embarrassment, and she could get on with her job.

"Mam," said Samantha in her best colloquial Dublinese, disconcerting to her proper mother at the best of times. She had been a stickler for proper English and the avoidance of slang all Samantha's life. "What brings you out here?" She nodded to her boss, Professor Lilly, and smiled. "How are you Professor Lilly?" she said quickly, not missing a beat and anticipating her mother's response, who would have admonished her for not greeting him first.

"We are fine. The Professor invited me. He needed some moral support. He detests these gatherings but felt obligated because his superior 'recommended' he attend," she said, smiling at Professor Lily.

Professor Lilly tried to defend himself further: "Conor O'Brien hates anything to do with O'Neill—they detest each other but he is the chancellor, so every faculty member has to walk a fine political line. I think it is politically prudent for Irish Protestants to attend this and support the Catholic minority in the North—solidarity in the Irish Republic," he said.

"Why are you here?" Samantha's mother asked her.

"I was asked by Professor Stokes to be here since he was busy on a case and I was escorted by Mr. Howard Bernstein, the aide to former Mayor Briscoe. He is somewhere around, mingling," she said, looking about, smiling.

"Well, I better be off and mingle too. Have a good time Mother, and you too, Professor," Samantha said cheerily, dashing off to speak to Bernstein.

"Mind the champagne," her mother said a bit too loudly, watching her disappear.

Samantha found Bernstein and warned him. "My mother is here. She will be watching me like a hawk. If you can divert her, I can speak to O'Neill and get together with him later. He wants to know everything about the murder of Major Gray. I will tell him what I know."

"Good. You do that and I will see to your mother," assured Bernstein, moving towards her.

There was no need for diversionary tactics since O'Neill got up on the podium and asked for attention. He gave a speech about the little children and the mothers in danger and impoverished at the hands of the Loyalists. He urged all the participants to open their hearts and their wallets to help in the humanitarian struggle and reminded them that if there was strength in their support for the poor people in the North, that there was always a good chance that Ireland would be united again. Someone started singing unashamedly "A Nation Once Again" and many joined in, making it clear that this was not just a fund-raiser for refugees and unfortunate victims.

After the stirring reminder, open pledges were made. Few did not offer something, especially under the watchful eyes of their neighbors. O'Neill just beamed and applauded with each pledge. When the "offerings" were completed, he encouraged them to enjoy the buffet and the music from a traditional Irish band who were happy to belt out rousing Republican tunes. The party lasted for a few hours and, it being the middle of the week, ended promptly at 11 pm.

Samantha made a beeline for O'Neill and congratulated him on his rousing speech and the successful fundraiser. Having reminded him of her presence, he thanked her for coming and encouraged her to give him a call as soon as she heard any more "developments." She looked around and did not see her mother, whom she assumed had already gone home. She expected to be ambushed soon enough by her in the next few days.

Bernstein approached Samantha and winked.

"Well done," he encouraged in a whisper which she could barely hear in the crowd. "Let me know if there is any progress. I know Rami will be watching."

Samantha was encouraged, even more so when Mr. Bernstein promised that Rami would hear about it. She looked forward to another meeting, even if it might be clandestine. The evening sky was clear, and it was still warm as they walked out of the hotel, down the same steps that had been a crime scene just days before, the blood having been scrupulously cleaned. Bernstein had a doorman hail a cab and directed Samantha to enjoy the night, giving her enough money to cover the ride and a decent tip, and turned back to greet some more of the party members who closely watched that there was no more than escorting arranged.

Chapter Twenty-Eight

Stokes had been alerted to another case that had been brought in the night before, what Johnston characterized as another "bloody eejit." The Gardai had discovered a body of a man who had fallen and been impaled by spikes on the top of a wall. He had successfully broken into an upscale home in Ballsbridge, not far from the French Embassy, and on his way down the outside plumbing that had recently been renovated, had given way and he was thrown down onto the wall and killed. If he had survived, he might have wanted to sue the contractors for shoddy workmanship and poor anchoring of the pipes, but the only issue relevant to the homeowner was the cost of the repairs and his lucky retrieval of the sack of money and jewelry which had fallen inside the wall. By coincidence, the house was the temporary residence of the French Ambassador who was back in Paris to attend a family gathering. Stokes was sure he would get a call from his Surete contact to get any details that might be significant for him to report to the French authorities.

On examination, the man looked like a workman with thick calloused palms and right-handed, the heavily muscled forearms more developed right than left. He had a thick bull neck and looked shorter than he could have been if he had had better nutrition in his childhood. He had a number of tattoos, including a rope and anchor and another with Eireann Go Bragh. He had probably been a sailor in the Navy or, at the least, in the merchant marine. Although relatively young, he had a large gut and probably had drunk as much as he worked.

His X-rays showed left cervical fractures on C5-6 as well as a fractured left humerus and fractured ribs posteriorly. Stokes had glanced at the bruising on his left side which was consistent with the injuries. He expected injuries to the lung and spleen and kidney but opening him up would probably show more extensive internal damage and bleeding. The puncture wounds had gone through his side as well. He had extensive subcutaneous bleeding that tracked along his trunk. He hoped that the cervical fractures had been quick, so he did not suffer long. He would have to check the spinal cord to know that. His toxicology report would take some time to get back, but he probably had been drunk. His permanent look of annoyance and surprise and no grimacing indicated he had been awake when he landed but probably died instantly on impact, a comfort to the next of kin, if Stokes could find them.

This was a perfect teaching case, but he had excused Samantha today because she had asked for a day off to deal with some personal business. He did not deny her the personal time. She had been working flat out for the past few weeks except for her brief trip to London. Still, he envied her youthful energy. His energy was more generated by duty and less invigorating.

He dissected the neck and found that the spinal cord had indeed been cut. If he had survived, he would have been paralyzed on his upper and lower limbs, but above that crucial C6, he could not have survived for long without immediate help. There was so much swelling around the neck as well with the bleeding from the blunt trauma. As he opened the chest wall there was a flow of old blood near the heart and in the lungs. He noticed an angled rib puncturing into the back of the lung. He documented all of this and moved on to his abdomen and, again, there was a lot of free blood concealing a mashed spleen. It is likely with the force that he saw in these injuries that the plumbing had catapulted him onto the wall and into the spikes, which coincidentally punctured his diaphragm and kidney. Stokes completed the rest of the autopsy but was careful to check the brain for blunt trauma and the rest of the body for bullets or knife wounds or any other signs that the injuries were not related to his death by any other misadventure than his own. Johnson had called it—he was a "bloody eejit."

The autopsy had not taken very long. It gave him time enough to have a break with a Nescafe and milk that he preferred to make himself, pouring the warmed milk into a cup filled with the instant coffee. It was like an adult's version of hot cocoa, without the cocoa. He just sat at his desk and did not bother doing anything. He needed a moment without distractions that allowed no thought, like meditating, but not. He was just staring, holding the warm cup and enjoying freedom from involvement. He had been so involved in the past few weeks that it sapped the free energy from his normally compulsive activity and reduced him to just wanting to sit with his eyes opened, not seeing. He looked down at his cup and realized it was already empty, like an hourglass with the sand falling upward, telling him it was time to get back to work. He took pleasure at the "wasted" time and stared at the bottom of the cup, then a thought crept in: he needed to contact the French Embassy and speak to his police contact, just to let him know, as a courtesy, that nothing had been found. Unfortunately, he still had to get past that haughty receptionist. He did not speak to Cloudot directly and just left a message.

When Cloudot finally called him back he wanted to be quick, but had to remark, jokingly, "Are you ever in your office? I just wanted to let you know that I found nothing suspicious on the autopsy of the dead burglar. He fell on the wall and broke his neck and punctured his lungs. No marks or signs that anyone else was involved," Stokes remarked.

Cloudot hesitated before he responded, as if he had not heard of the news of the burglar breaking into his ambassador's home. "I appreciate the call," he responded casually, uninterested, even though Stokes thought Cloudot would have had more questions for a follow-up. "It will probably take weeks before the official police report confirms the details, if the Irish police are anything like the French," he said, smiling.

"You are welcome. Any more about Abn Awaa?" Stokes asked, just in the off chance that there were any new developments.

"No. We have lost sight of him again. He has not been seen in London or Dublin. He might have gone back to Libya or even Belfast, but I will keep you posted, merci, au revoir," he said politely, hanging up.

Stokes was surprised at the abruptness of the call. Cloudot had been happy to engage in long conversations previously, willing to share as much information as he could. There was still a lot of uncertainty as to the activity of the Jackal and who else he was involved with in Ireland.

Had he been told to back off by the French government or had the Jackal truly disappeared and left Ireland? Or, worse, had his plot been accelerated and another bombing or murder was anticipated and Cloudot wanted to keep Stokes out of danger, or at the least, out of the loop so there were no leaks? The conversation raised his suspicions. Come to think of it, he had not heard from Lanigan in the past day. From being content this morning with his usual job that had to be done, Stokes was now unsettled and perversely, missed the excitement. He tried to concentrate on the rest of the paperwork that was on his desk, but he couldn't help feeling uneasy.

There was something else gnawing at him. He had never really come to terms with his family's death. The recent bombings had opened up that wound again. He had been content in his job for years. Now he was discontented with everything. It was not so much a mid-life crisis as it was a crisis. He felt his eyes fill with tears. No, it wasn't an irritation from formalin. He had gotten used to that temporary discomfort —the new fans and vents in the autopsy room had helped. He was crying because he felt sad. In the quiet of his office with the door closed, his secretary oblivious to any sounds with the headphones in her ears as she transcribed the latest dictation, he simply blubbered. It was not long, and it was not loud. He had not done anything like that in years, not since his mother died; that was understandable. This was not. He had cried the day he buried his wife and daughter, but that was two years ago. His sadness now was worse because it was inexplicable and despairing. He had faced death every day, objectified it, dissected it and analyzed it, but this despair was different. It was the tiredness of it all, that all this work was pointless and all the enthusiasm he had had was down the drain like the static fluids that were released from the bodies when they were opened. He cried again. What was the point? He did not care if he was "caught." He cried some more until he stopped. It could not have been too long. His secretary was still typing. He wiped his eyes and noticed the papers on the desk. They were the last death certificates that had to be signed off for the past few days, including Major Gray. He signed them and opened the door to the outer office.

"These need to be delivered to the coroner. I am going out for a quick stroll to clear my head. I have some thinking I need to do. If there are any calls, leave the messages on my desk," he ordered the secretary. She was new. Millicent was her name, he had to remind himself and she was older and very efficient, he had noticed. His previous secretary, Maeve, had quit, overwhelmed by the bombing despite her fifteen years at the job without a complaint. She would have noticed this unusual behavior, but to Millicent, this was the prerogative of the boss, and she accepted it.

"It's a lovely day for a walk," she agreed amiably. "I will get these over to the coroner's office as soon as I am done with your dictation."

"That's fine. See you later," Stokes said, stepping out into the warm Dublin sun, which lifted his mood for the moment.

Chapter Twenty-Nine

Lanigan removed the picture from the frame, careful not to damage the glass or the edges. He placed it in a folder with some other pictures of possible suspects that he would show to the gun club owner. Perhaps this would jog his memory. He did not have much time, as the Chief Superintendent had reminded him. He drove down to the Dublin Gun Club, which was opened for business, but it was not crowded since most of the enthusiasts were weekend warriors. O'Higgins, the proprietor, recognized Lanigan immediately and looked around to make sure there weren't any customers who needed help, or at least, that's what he seemed to be doing. No one was moving and the pop, pop of the guns was distant enough outside that Lanigan would not have to raise his voice to be heard.

Lanigan opened the file with the pictures and flashed the unframed photo at O'Higgins.

"Do any of these people look familiar to you?" he asked, without any introduction. He had dispensed with a hello when he walked in the door. It was a group shot of a troop of sharpshooters proudly displaying their medals and Curran was in the center, smiling broadly.

"Well, I see Curran there. He must have won the top prize, being in the center and all. I'm not sure of the others," he said.

"Look again. Were any of these men guests of Curran at the gun club recently," Lanigan asked.

O'Higgins paused and looked at the picture.

"Your man to the right of Curran. That was Major Gray, or so he said when he came here. Looks nothing like the bloke in the papers. You know, the man who was shot."

"Are you sure?" Lanigan asked again.

"Pretty sure. I thought he was military, his walk, and how he handled the gun. Good shot, too."

"Any of the others look familiar to you?"

"No. Just the two of them. They seemed like old pals, been in a war or two I'd say, very comrades like."

"Thanks. That was a great help. Stay around, we'll need to hear from you again," Lanigan nodded and left.

He drove quickly to Harcourt Street and barged into the Chief Superintendent's office, waving the photo.

"I've got your man," he announced, slapping the photo on the desk over some papers that the Chief had been reviewing.

"Whose man?" demanded the Chief, irritated by the interruption and the excitement. He was not a fan of enthusiastic conclusions.

"The sharpshooter who killed the disappeared John Doe and Major Chutney, I mean Major Gray."

"This is a group photo. Who picked him out?" the Chief asked, not yet excited, but still irritated.

"The owner of the gun club—spotted him with Curran two months ago. They were both playing with the missing Carcano. Both pretty good shots by his account. This has got to be the guy. He called himself Major Gray on the ledger," Lanigan said slowly, to be sure the Chief got the significance of the relationship.

"Do we have an identification of him? He looks vaguely familiar," the Chief said.

"I am going upstairs to Special Branch. The photo has been hanging in Curran's office for a long time. Someone must have known him from the military," said Lanigan.

"Hold your bloody horses, pardner," the Chief said in an American cowboy twang. "How do you know he wasn't working with one of them? We think Curran was a bad apple—that's why someone killed him because they thought he was a tout," the Chief said. He was keenly aware of the Provisional IRAs propensity for punishing informers, "touts," with more bodies found just south of the Northern Irish border in the latest escalation of the Troubles.

"Well, this would be the way to smoke these people out and clean this mess up."

"You might be the one to get "smoked" Boyo," the Chief said softly. He was well aware of the latest misgivings that his superiors had about the reliability and allegiances of some members of the Gardai. There were too many near captures and near misses of Provo terrorists on both sides of the border for it to be a coincidence that just when they should be more alert, his force had been more lax. Of course, he was undermanned, but he was under pressure to perform better, escalation of activities or not. His job was to uphold the peace in the Republic.

He stared at the picture again of the man standing next to Curran. They were both in Irish Army uniforms and although the picture was probably about ten years old, he could see the badges on their chests and the two diamonds on their shoulders. They were both lieutenants and in the infantry. He flipped the picture over and there in small letters was the date and the caption—UN Irish Defence Forces, Congo, 1964. They had probably both served together in that difficult part of the world and their views of the world outside of Ireland had been shaped by it. Now the Chief recalled who the man standing next to Curran was. It was the same Captain Brennan, as a younger lieutenant, who had been in the papers and implicated in the 1970 arms trade and had been let off, like O'Neill because of "insufficient evidence." He had been forced to resign from the Irish Army, but O'Neill had appointed Brennan as one of his aides in the Ministry of Agriculture when he was minister. No one had thought at all about him since the trial. O'Neill had lost his position and since most of these "aide" jobs only lasted as long as the party in power, no one gave Brennan a thought afterward. Yet, there were the two of them, smiling proudly.

"That's your man," the Chief said. "He needs to be found, and quickly. Who knows how many other victims he has in mind? Get as many men as you can to hunt him down, but no bulletins. He needs to be able to move freely because if he gets wind, he will scarper, and then we're lost," the Chief said.

"On it, Boss," Lanigan said, letting his affection for American gangster stories slip out.

"Chief Superintendent to you, Detective Lanigan," the Chief said.

"Right, Chief Superintendent," Lanigan saluted and ran out the door to his office and to his clerk.

"Do we have any photos of Captain John Brennan, your man who was in the Arms Trial?" he said, pointing to the photo of Brennan.

"I suppose we do, somewhere in the files," the clerk said, slowly getting up and walking towards the file room.

"Make at least ten copies of the latest photos and tell Hayes and Cunningham to meet me in the lobby as soon as they can come in and be sure to give them copies of the photos," Lanigan ordered, moving from side to side, impatient, but remembering to put the photo back in the drawer and locking it.

When the two other detectives met him in the lobby, he explained to them as he walked, to look for Brennan at his last known home and that he would go to the last place he had worked, the Ministry of Agricultural Affairs. He knew there was no time to lose. They signed out guns and he warned them that Brennan was probably armed and dangerous. When the two Gardai he had called in arrived, he told them the same and showed a copy of the photo, just to be sure who they were looking for and told them to come with him.

To be sure, he told them they did not need a search warrant under the Offences Against the State Act. He was well aware that Special Branch was looking for the assassin of Major Gray as well, but he ignored their investigation and did not inform them of his hunt. He was not comfortable with G2, fearing at least another IRA informer in their midst.

But instead of going to the Ministry first, he went back to Curran's flat. The yellow police tape was still on it. He cut it and pulled out his gun and kicked in the door. The place was still empty, but he was looking for something else—the carbine ammunition. He found an empty box in the dustbin. The caliber of the bullets fit the Carcano but he was careful to glove and place the box in a bag he would pass on as evidence. He was pretty sure there would be Brennan's prints on there as well as Curran's.

"Bloody hell," he muttered. No one had bothered to look under the bed. There was a packed suitcase, complete with an Irish passport with a fresh visa to Australia. Curran had been feeling the heat and had planned to disappear, a long way away. Lanigan blamed himself for not looking before, since all he wanted to do was find the gun at the time. When he found the case was empty, he knew the whole story made sense and that he had missed the whole point of Curran's murder: Curran was running from Brennan.

Lanigan sped to the other side of town where the Ministry of Agriculture was housed. Agriculture House was a nondescript gray government building on Kildare Street. Lanigan parked right at the front door and put his police business sign on the windscreen of the car, hoping he wouldn't be harassed by the receptionist. He asked her if anyone had been using Brennan's office recently and she looked at him blankly. "He was O'Neill's aide when he was Minister of Agriculture," he explained, trying to suppress his annoyance.

"Oh, yeah," she said, "the military guy who wouldn't be able to tell a bull calf from a heifer," she smiled. "Down the hall to the left, right next to the Minister's Office. They are out, don't you know?" she said.

"Can you get someone to open the door? This is urgent police business," he insisted.

"Cattle rustler, pardner?" she twanged, smirking.

"Would you ever just call the porter, or I'll bloody bang down the door," he demanded.

"Hold your hosses, pardner" she twanged again as she waited for the porter to pick up.

Lanigan did felt ridiculous. It certainly was amusing for a Dublin policeman to be standing in the middle of the Ministry that represented the most rural parts of Ireland. I hate *Culchies* (country Irish), he thought to himself. He waited for the porter and the receptionist just smiled at him, amused. She obviously did not get frequent visits from detectives. She was young and attractive enough that she could get away with her insolence frequently, at least Lanigan thought so, since he himself was allowing her the joke.

The porter arrived, a bit more respectful, and led him to the office that Brennan formerly occupied. "This is his stuff," the porter pointed to a pile of boxes. Brennan had never picked them up when his position was unceremoniously vacated during the last election. It was a matter the porter saw so frequently that it was as casual as a death at a funeral home. "We were going to toss them in another week if he didn't show up since we sent him a letter last month," the porter sniffed, indicating his dislike for the man.

"Did you know him?" Lanigan asked.

"Only to say good morning or good evening, though he wasn't the most friendly or courteous of sorts, not like the other politicians who made sure they were everybody's friend, part of the job, don't you know," he said.

"How did he get on with O'Neill, the Minister?" asked Lanigan.

"Fairly well at the beginning, it seemed, with him going down with your man to his mansion in the country pretty often, and he even bragged that he stayed in his guest cottage, but they seemed to have a falling out recently. It may have been because of O'Neill losing his post. They had some arguments at the end. I think he walked out before it was all over," the porter noted.

"Does Brennan still live in town?" Lanigan asked. "We need to find him." Lanigan looked through the boxes to see if there were any letters with home addresses. He did not see much of importance.

"Did you say he was at O'Neill's guest cottage?" Lanigan asked.

"As much as he said it, Brennan went down with him and came back up to work pretty regular. O'Neill saw him more often than he saw his wife, she always traveling on grand holidays without him."

"Any other places he stayed, as far as you know?"

"Well, he went up to the North quite a bit, had family near Derry on the other side of the border," the porter answered. He was a fountain of knowledge, an example of the servant class who knew how to keep his eyes and ears open and his mouth shut.

"Thanks. I'll give him the word that he should pick up his things if I find him," Lanigan went for the door, considering if he should bother going to Brennan's flat or just head for O'Neill's estate.

"All the best," the Porter answered as he locked the door.

Lanigan rushed down the hall and asked the receptionist to use her phone. She didn't protest and propped the phone on top of the desk. Lanigan called to his clerk and told him to call his assistants to follow him to O'Neill's mansion out of town. He jumped in his car to get his start in the evening rush out to the north Dublin suburbs.

Chapter Thirty

Stokes strode out the door of his office to the beautiful sunny mid-afternoon street. He had no particular direction, but knew he just wanted to walk. He turned the corner and there he was on Talbot Street, one of the bombed streets, still with a few remaining boarded-up fronts of stores that needed new windows and some shattered brick facades that needed new plaster and paint. The blood and debris of bodies had eventually ended up in his morgue and they had been cataloged and buried. The mangled cars and other flying objects had been gathered up and removed to the scrapyard or the municipal tip. It jogged his unconscious that this devastation was what he was so tearful about a few minutes ago, among so many other things that had briefly overwhelmed his logic. He had lost sight of the football in the melee. He, as an agent of justice, needed to find and bring to light those perpetrators of the atrocities, make them aware of their sins, and prevent others from repeating the same crime. He did not want to be an avenging angel, just an enforcer.

He thought about these latest cases again and knew that the conspiracy was all around him. It was driven by that need to right old injustices with new ones. Curran and Gray were the most recent casualties in a calculated web of silences that would put more people down to protect the power at the center. But what didn't make sense was Gray being shot. He was part of that group that O'Neill had kept close to him to facilitate connections with the people with money who could pay for more arms for the North. Did someone miss his target? Had the deal gone wrong? Had this Jackal stolen the Carcano and used it when he sensed he might be discovered? Or had he been betrayed and sought revenge and missed his target? He noticed a phone box and went in and fumbled for some coins. He rifled through the phone book to find the number of the French Embassy which he had left in his office. He called. His least favored receptionist answered. She knew it was him—contempt breeds familiarity. She again said Cloudot was out but would contact him to call back. He gave her the number of a coffee shop down the street and went in and ordered a coffee and waited for the callback, mindlessly watching passers-by through the new window and customers coming and going, until the call finally came through. The proprietor was prepared and had put his phone up on the counter since Stokes regularly used the shop as an extension of his office when he needed a break.

Stokes was still nursing his coffee when Cloudot called.

"Any more on the whereabouts of the Jackal?" Stokes asked.

"You mean Abn Awaa? No, Professor, we have no idea. I thought you were going to end this hunt. I certainly have. He is probably in England, or worse, Libya, where we can't touch him. Our sources say the Irish arms deal is dead for now since Gray was killed. I will be on my way back to Paris soon since my assignment is done."

"He may still be around. I think he is after O'Neill. Can you come with me to warn him? O'Neill is less likely to listen to me than you and you have a car and a gun and have an idea of what the Jackal, sorry, Abn Awaa, might look like," Stokes said.

"Where are you now?" Cloudot asked.

"Just off Talbot Street. I will meet you at the coffee shop on the corner of Talbot and Mountjoy."

"I am on my way," Cloudot said, hanging up the phone.

Stokes had almost finished his coffee when Cloudot found him still sitting at the counter next to the phone. He had spread out a map marking the O'Neill estate with a line along the main road to the small town nearby.

"How long will this take?" Cloudot asked.

"Only about a half-hour, but there will be a bit of traffic now, Friday rush hour with everyone scattering for the weekend."

"This is still a small town and even though the Irish are as crazy as the Parisians when they are driving, I think I can get there soon,"

"Well, let's be off then," Stokes said, having the last gulp of his coffee.

Chapter Thirty-One

Samantha had been invited to O'Neill's house for the weekend. Never in a million years would she have thought to have accepted if she did not think she could accomplish what she hoped—catch him in his lies and bring him to justice. She was aware of the risks, but she was hoping that Rami would be watching nearby. She told Bernstein she got the invitation at the reception. He congratulated her but warned her to stay sharp. She had packed a small weekend bag and took the train up and was picked up by one of O'Neill's men who treated her respectfully. He made sure she understood that the former Minister was a generous and gracious gentleman.

"Will there be other people this weekend?" she asked.

"Yes, they plan a little reception for those larger contributors to the Northern Irish Rescue Fund and one of his good old friends, Maurice Dussault, the Belgian hotel owner, who is overseeing the fund to make sure the right things get to the right places. He has become a true Irish patriot. It is complicated, this transfer of funds. You would think giving away money is easy, but when there is money to be had, one has to be careful."

"I wonder why he invited me. I have no money."

"Mr. O'Neill finds that intelligent young ladies like yourself always add to the mix in a party. He may be looking for some friends in the coroner's office, though I don't think he plans on visiting you soon," he chuckled. She didn't bother correcting him that she worked with the Medical Examiner.

After a short ride from the station, she was taken to the front of the house down the long gravel driveway flanked by hedges on either side that narrowed almost to a point and made it look longer. The Mansion overlooked the sea on a cliff. There was more greenery with a driveway that wrapped around the back to the front, flanked by trees and stables on one side with a wide-open area for the horses to roam. Samantha felt totally out of place and said nothing when she was helped out the door but smiled.

"'Tis a fine place. Don't let your jaw hang too low, but I think you will enjoy yourself. The Minister is at a meeting, but I'm sure he will meet you personally when you are settled in your room. Maria will lead the way," he nodded as a maid opened the door and greeted her, her accent clearly not Irish, perhaps French or even German. She was young and attractive, only slightly older than Samantha. She was short, thin, but fit with strong arms used to work and stood military straight. She took Samantha's bag and led her past the wide chandeliered lobby and broad staircase to a smaller hallway and then through a door that led down some stairs that led to a tunnel.

"Don't be disturbed by the tunnel," she said, flicking a switch on to light the darkened passageway. "It leads to the Guest House. It surprises everyone who stays when we lead them through," Maria commented, less amused than factual, somehow deliberate, like a warning. Samantha took note of her tone and memorized the configuration as she would have the course of an artery through a vital organ. The tunnel ended at another set of steps past another door which was bolted closed that Maria said opened to the back garden of the house. Samantha was led up to the other door and, opened, she saw another hallway leading to a cozy lit sitting room facing the ocean. Samantha was speechless. Maria pointed out the position of the rooms of her suite, complete with her own bathroom.

"If you get lost, just follow through the tunnel to the door. It opens next to the big stairway on your left and leads to the Great Room. Mr. O'Neill will meet you there," she advised Samantha mechanically and left abruptly. It was as if Maria had been uneasy with her presence, or perhaps uneasy about something else and preoccupied. Samantha was left in the opulent guest room and felt out of place, her little suitcase looking more like a shopping bag someone would be carrying for a meager purchase of groceries. She was well aware of O'Neill's appetite for young ladies and his casual arrangement with his wife who was away on yet another trip. She had been warned by Bernstein to be careful, so it would be a cat and mouse game, she giving him some information so she could get some, avoiding tipping her agenda. His agenda was more obvious.

Samantha freshened her makeup and hung up her clothes and then left through the Guest House door that opened to the grounds rather than walking through the creepy tunnel again. She was not wearing her gown. She was saving that for the evening but was wearing the dress she had worn all day and traveled in so as not to make herself so obviously enticing as to reinforce his impression of her and his expectations. She shivered at the idea but made herself smile as she walked through the open door to the Great Room. O'Neill was discussing the evening plans with the same servant who had driven her to the estate. As she entered, O'Neill, noticing her, dismissed him.

"How are you, Dr. Monaghan," he smiled, extending his hand. "I hope you did not have any difficulty getting here?" he asked.

"No, it was quite simple and thanks for having your assistant pick me up," she answered, shaking his hand.

"I am glad and hope you enjoy the weekend, but I am anxious to hear from you about my dear friend, Major Gray. Let's go to my study," he said pointing to another door off the Great Room. She passed the tables and chairs that were still being set up for the evening by the servants who were quietly arranging what was needed. Although the Republic had decreased some of the layers of the ruling class by removing the British, entrenched class structure and wealth still dominated here.

He brought her into his study, a room lined with books and paintings and photos commemorating his accomplishments. He sat down in his big chair behind a clean mahogany desk and motioned her to sit in a large chair next to it.

"What have you found out about this terrible murder?" he asked directly.

"I'm just a pathologist. All I know is what I saw at the autopsy. Pretty obvious, really—he died of a massive bullet wound to the brain," she answered, matter-of-factly. She would try to keep the information at a minimum, she resolved. She didn't add – you were standing there you bloody eejit, but she certainly thought it at the moment.

O'Neill paused for a moment and held back his irritation. He was not interested in the pathology report, of course, but whether she knew any more than the obvious.

"Have the Gardai any idea of who this madman is?" he asked.

"All we could give them was the corroboration of the evidence they collected—that the bullet fragment we found in the brain and that was found on the steps of the Shelbourne were consistent with a shot from a high-powered rifle that the killer was an excellent shot, and that you were very lucky."

"I know, I felt that second shot whizz by me just as I ducked. If I hadn't moved aside, I would have been a martyr for the cause. But I am not sure if it was meant for me, was it?"

"Well, if it had been the first shot, I would have thought so, but witnesses said it was the second shot that missed you, and ballistics said it was most likely in the same direction for Gray."

"That is helpful, thanks. You are a very valuable asset to me. I am glad I invited you," he said, smiling, attempting to inflate her ego a bit, always a useful tool in interrogations and politics. "Do they have any idea of what kind of gun it was?"

"It may have been the same gun that was stolen from Detective Sergeant Curran," but we can't be sure," she advised. She now realized that he did not have a clue and was probably not behind Curran's death.

"Is this some kind of conspiracy, do you think? Curran was an undercover agent in the IRA for G2. Reports circulated through the Dail, strictly confidential, you know, but I have my sources," O'Neill confided in a lower voice, dramatically looking about.

"I wouldn't know about that, Sir," Samantha admitted to him, but had her own suspicions and one of them was that O'Neill knew that all along and more, but she was sure he wouldn't admit any more unless she swore the IRA oath, which she did not expect he would ask her to do, at least not yet.

"This is a matter of utmost importance. Fianna Fail expects to regain power soon. It could mean something to you if you could be a source of information for us. It would certainly affirm your patriotic duty to help us."

"I am a civil servant, sir, so I am bound to help whichever party is in power."

"Yes, yes, I realize that, and I in no way am asking you to compromise your position, but only help us to get to the truth," he smiled.

Samantha did not know how much she could push him on the issue, but she took a stab at it anyway: "Do you think this conspiracy is against you or your supporters? Is it the IRA or the UVF?" she asked.

"I have enemies in the IRA and certainly the UVF are no friends of anyone here in the South. I am not even sure if this last bombing was an atrocity by a radical faction of the IRA or the UVF and/or the British. Maybe they were all working together. I just don't know. But let me tell you this, I will get to the bottom of this, and you will be instrumental to me if you can keep your eyes and ears open, especially in that office. I don't think your Professor Stokes is a friend of mine."

"I think the Professor is a loyal and honest man and is interested in finding the truth, whatever it is," Samantha said defensively, quickly.

"I'm sorry to have mentioned it, but I must say, he is not a strong supporter of anything but a peaceful resolution of the Troubles—he did sign the petition to work for a peaceful resolution after Bloody Sunday. That was a mistake. His own wife and daughter were killed in more violence, not a good argument for peace and reconciliation," he sneered.

Samantha could see he was getting fired up and knew that she should keep her mouth shut. She could also see that his paranoia, real or imagined, was part of his nature and just heightened by the bullet that whizzed by him the other day.

"I will do my best to help you," Samantha swallowed, "but I will not spy on Professor Stokes," she said.

"My dear, all anyone wants is the truth. I'm sorry if I misspoke. Your help is appreciated. I hope you can enjoy the gathering tonight, which reminds me, I must excuse myself. I must see to some of the details," he said, standing abruptly, walking to the door, ending the conversation.

Samantha just sat there for a moment, hoping that she had not upset everything. He was not a very likable person, she thought, but she was not there for his company, nor he for hers, she thanked herself. She stood up and looked out through the window and onto the sea. Strange, she thought, that his desk would face away from the beautiful vista, but this whole place was for show. He was showing rather than looking. She walked back to her room, this time through the tunnel, noting the partially opened door to the back that had been bolted before. She hurried through the tunnel to get ready for the ball, like bloody Cinderella, she smiled to herself.

Chapter Thirty-Two

Lanigan pulled up just short of the O'Neill estate and looked around for the best vantage point to observe the goings-on inside. He chose a small stand of trees just outside with a clear view of the mansion entrance down the road. He radioed his men to meet him close to there, nearer the village that abutted the estate, describing his position and warning them not to come with their squad cars, but park them near the local pub and then walk to the meeting spot. He expected that Brennan would show up some time that evening to finish the job he set out to do. He did not think that Gray had been his intended victim and, he thought, neither did O'Neill.

Slippery fella, this O'Neill, he thought to himself. He probably thought that he could hide in his estate and wait for the Gardai to find the killer. Rather than hire a private bodyguard, he arranged to have an armed police escort from the security division to watch his every move. He had them stay discreetly on the grounds outside and gave them strict orders to not interfere or frighten his guests. O'Neill wanted to avoid observation as much as the "criminals" who were after him. Lanigan had brought his binoculars and had his gun ready. He waited for his men.

"We're here Detective Lanigan," Cunningham said, nodding to Hayes who was quiet, either to contain his excitement or fear. Neither of them was ever recruited for "undercover" work before and were not sure what to do.

"You two are backup for me. It may come to nothing, but I think Brennan will show up here. I would like to catch him without a shot. He has a lot of explaining to do, understand?" Lanigan said, very business-like in a whispered voice. He hadn't the slightest idea of how he was going to do this but was hoping that patience would win out. It was now late afternoon. The sun would be down soon. This would be when

Brennan would make his play. There were no high buildings nearby, so Brennan would not shoot in broad daylight. There were stables further down where O'Neill kept his horses and that certainly could be a good hiding place. As well, there was a Guest House on the other side. It might be occupied by Brennan, waiting for his moment. Lanigan had a good view where he was. He watched for people coming and going in plain sight or someone not taking the right route to the right place, which now would be those arriving for the party.

"Remember, patience lads," he warned. "You, Cunningham, go over to the stables and just quietly wait there. If anyone asks who you are, just tell them you are a Garda with Special Assignment to watch O'Neill and flash your badge. And you, Hayes, take the other flank to the hedges leading down the gravel path near the Guest House and use the same story. If there are any questions, tell them to call Harcourt Street headquarters. No one will call your bluff but tell them not to say a word to anyone since you are undercover," he warned. Lanigan hoped no one would question that or be rash enough to tell O'Neill. Undercover was the operational word. He expected that most of the staff were spooked by the shooting and would believe the story.

It might have been an easy ride over to the estate for Stokes and Cloudot, but there was more traffic than usual because of the warm and sunny forecast. More people were on the road to go to cottages or beaches for the weekend. They were creeping along when an articulated lorry, going much too fast for its lane turned sharply and sideswiped a car some distance in front of them. The car swerved and then hit a guardrail and other cars piled into it. Cloudot sped up and wanted to drive on the shoulder past the terrible mess, but Stokes, ever the physician, yelled at Cloudot to stop. Cloudot looked at him hard for a moment and had a crazed, angry, look in his eye that startled Stokes, but suddenly took a deep breath and pulled over to the shoulder and stopped.

Stokes jumped out and ran to the wrecked car to check if anyone was injured. It was a little old Morris Minor with two adults in the front and three children in the back and none of them had been in seat belts. They were lucky they were not traveling very fast, but the driver had hit the windscreen and was semi-conscious and the children had been tossed about. The mother in the passenger seat was awake and screaming for help. Stokes ran up after Cloudot, his breathlessness reminding him that he was out of shape. He saw Cloudot speaking to the woman and trying to calm her down. He focused on the driver.

"Are you all right?" Stokes asked, not so much asking the obvious as assessing his ability to respond.

"Grand," the man groaned, responding mechanically.

"Can you open your eyes?" Stokes asked, assessing motor function and comprehension. The man did. His eyes were bloodshot with a small area of blood at the lower border of the eyes, a small blood vessel broken in the superficial layer of the eye with an adjacent swelling and bruising of the skin and bones around the eye and lids.

"Can you follow this finger?" Stokes asked and moved it from side to side. The eye movements were normal, he observed, but he was moving his neck stiffly.

"My neck," he complained, "It hurts."

"Don't move it," Stokes ordered and took his tie off and rolled it up and placed it around his neck as a soft splint. "This will keep it steady. Can you feel your arms and legs?" he asked. The man began to reflexively move them.

"No, don't move them," Stokes ordered.

"Is he all right? Are you a doctor?" His wife asked, having been calmed down by Cloudot and reassured that the children were all right, but were still crying.

"Yes, I am," he answered. He did not bother to say he specialized in dead bodies. "I think he will be all right," Stokes said, "as long as he sits still," he warned the man who seemed to understand by nodding slightly, his neck bundled enough that he did not move much.

"Are you all right?" Stokes asked his wife through the driver-side window and when he saw her grimacing, came around the front of the car to the passenger side. The door was pushed in. Cloudot had tried to open it, but it was deformed by another car that had hit it.

"Some pain in my rib and some difficulty with taking deep breaths," she answered, now realizing she had been hurt as well. She tried to turn to see the children and groaned when she tried to make a move. The children were now quiet in the back, stunned by the event but not injured and curious as to what was happening to their parents.

"Where is the pain?" asked Stokes. "On the left side," she answered, which was just about where the dent was. Stokes did not have a stethoscope with him, but worried that she might have a broken rib that punctured a lung.

"I am going to press your side to see if there is any serious damage, so it may hurt a bit," he warned and then slid his hand inside the open window and down past the door. He felt her side but did not feel any suggestion of air bubbles under the skin which might indicate the lung had been punctured. He didn't press hard. She was exquisitely tender and yelped to confirm it. This frightened the children who started crying again. Stokes tried to calm them down again by explaining what he was doing, and they paid attention which distracted them, and he reassured them that their mother was going to be all right. Cloudot was directing traffic, bravely standing in the middle of the road, pointing and waving for people to move on.

"They seem to be well enough for the time being," Stokes yelled at Cloudot.

"Let's hope that the police can get through this mess. They are watching my directions and moving on. I used to be a traffic cop when I started, so they understand authority," he smiled, still directing the cars to move along and winding his arms for them to move along.

The Gardai arrived quickly, barreling down the shoulder of the road until Cloudot waved them over to the car. There were a few other cars behind, just battered on the side of the road or in the middle. The police moved them along so they could have some space to work and leave room for an ambulance. One of the Garda ran over, and Stokes identified himself.

"Are they hurt bad?" the policeman asked.

"Enough. They need to get to hospital by ambulance, but they should be all right. I will wait until it gets here, though," he said glancing at the man and woman, to make sure they were awake and breathing.

"Fair enough, Doctor. It should not be long. Your man is doing a crack job of moving the cars along," he smiled.

"Former traffic cop. French. He's with me," Stokes smiled, then glanced at the car again. "I'll give you a full report later," Stokes said, handing him a card, "but we need to be somewhere soon. It is urgent."

"In that case, I will call the station to get things moving," he said, pointing to his squad car.

Before he even took a few steps, the ambulance sirens could be heard blaring and he stopped and turned. "As soon as they are loaded in, take the shoulder past this mess and you should be on your way. All the best, Doc," he said, tipping his cap as he got out in the middle of the road to help move cars along. Another police car had already arrived and acted as a barrier so that cars were driving around at a safe space. Cloudot stopped waving and ran over to Stokes, who was telling the family to stay calm since help was almost here.

"We better be on our way," Cloudot yelled at Stokes, motioning him to get in the car. He seemed more concerned about getting to the Estate than helping the victims of the accident.

Cloudot opened the door and started the engine but watched carefully for movement around him. He motioned Stokes to get in, but Stokes just stood there, waiting for the ambulance to finally stop. He spoke to the driver, directing him and his assistant on what to do. Once the man and woman were safely on stretchers, he ran to the car, and they took off.

Chapter Thirty-Three

Lanigan had been waiting a few hours for any sign of Brennan. He was starting to get hungry. The sun had finally set, and he checked the inside of the mansion with his binoculars. He had watched as multiple cars had delivered the guests, none looking suspicious, as far as he could tell. Now those guests were milling around the lobby and the Great Room that he could see through the large windows. Two big Special Gardai were standing outside the doors, probably hand-picked by O'Neill. One looked like someone he had seen before and maybe had had a run-in with. He was sure of it when the door was opened and there was more light on them. His name was Rory O'Connor, an Ulster man as well—could even be a relative of O'Neill's, for all he knew. More trust if he was part of the clan. He was a nasty big brute and quick to anger, he recalled, almost getting hit by him in a bar fight when he missed a swing on a pal. At the time, Lanigan had flashed his badge and had calmed him down. Good thing too since his fists were like Sunday hams.

Inside he could see the guests were having cocktails and canapés. This would not be the time that Brennan would take his shot—too many people to waste his bullets on. Lanigan figured Brennan would try a closer shot. This might happen if O'Neill went out to the lawn to get a smoke or some air. He was in the habit of going outside to speak in private with people whose attention he needed. That, unfortunately, could be any time. Lanigan's stomach growled. He had to pee as well. He did not have a walkie-talkie and would not have broken silence anyway, so he merely sauntered down the road, along the bushes, counting on his assistants to keep watch so he could get to a chip shop he had seen down the way. Some would call him a chancer, but he was hoping the odds were in his favor, so he ran once he was out of view of the mansion grounds.

The shop was a small hole in the wall, as were most, just a window to the rest of the world where a hamburger and a bag of chips could be gotten quickly. He ordered a hamburger and chips but nothing to drink, reminding himself that he would need to be watching again, this time without a break if his bladder was less demanding. He was told that the food would be ready in a minute. He paid his money and told the girl at the window that he would be right back.

He had noticed there was a narrow dark alley around the corner, so he had a quick piss which was a great relief, then hurried back to the window. She handed him the hamburger and chips and he ran back to his place in the bushes and put the food down so he could get a glimpse of what was happening in the mansion. People were still milling around. He could see his two men still at their posts, one at the stable and the other near the guest house, only visible because he knew where they were and slightly illuminated by the lights in the house. The two uniformed and armed special Gardai were still standing near the front of the doors of the mansion at alert, which gave more than one of the guests reassurance. There had been a few abrupt cancellations shortly after the assassination since more than one of his friends and associates had thought that Gray's assassin had simply missed O'Neill.

The crowd on the inside was still chatting and milling around, enjoying the poshness of the affair and their own participatory importance. Since dinner had been scheduled for half eight, they were getting their last drinks in, almost like pub closing time. O'Neill saw the opportunity and went over to Dussault, the Belgian, and asked him to come out to the front grounds with him. On their way, they interrupted Samantha who had been unable to escape a pompous middle-aged man from chatting her up. O'Neill invited her to join them. She excused herself and went out into the warm evening air with the two gladly, although she hadn't a clue as to why she was part of the separate meeting. She noticed the two Gardai who stood at the front door and was reminded that this place and this minister was not completely safe.

"I wanted to get out into the open to be able to discuss something with you and M. Dussault," O'Neill explained as he turned to Samantha. "I realize that you of all people are aware of the recent killing, but you may not be aware of who the killer might be or why," he paused.

"I think it is someone who wants to compromise my activities in the North. Have you ever heard of someone called the Jackal? He is a PLO terrorist backed by Qadaffi and he thinks I have been working with the government to help capture him. One of the leaders of the Provos contacted me and M. Dussault about getting a shipment of arms to them and to help them broker the deal with the Jackal. They are under the impression that because of the false charges against me and him in the arms trials a few years ago, that we would be their men. Nothing could be further from the truth," he said. "Nevertheless, this Jackal thinks I informed against him since not only the Irish police but the British and French have been looking for him here. He wants revenge on us and eliminate the middlemen so he can deal directly with the Provos," he explained.

"He got rid of Gray, I suppose, because he thought he was giving up too much information too easily, according to my contacts with the Provos, who have warned me of the danger. That is why you see the Gardai here," he turned to smile at them, and they nodded back.

"You are here because you might be able to help. We think your professor, an old Royal Navy man, has been working with the British. Perhaps you can be our eyes and ears."

Samantha could not believe this story. She certainly would not reveal what she knew, but she was not going to spy on Professor Stokes.

"I'm sorry, but even if what you say were true, I could not do anything against Professor Stokes and I have never seen him speak to anyone British."

"But you know they are searching for the man who used the stolen weapon on poor Major Gray, n'est-ce pas?" Dussault asked.

As far as she knew, no one else knew that there was a stolen weapon and the shooter had not been identified in any of the reports she had seen. How did he know about the rifle? There was a leak somewhere from the Gardai. She did not know what to say.

"If you can't spy on Stokes, and I admire your loyalty, can you at least help us find this terrorist? If you hear anything from the Gardai, let us know. It might protect us and remove this dangerous person. I have friends who can help," O'Neill urged, not saying who his friends were. It might be another faction of the IRA, some who might be more supportive of his goals, or at the least, she thought, his power. She was not convinced he was just doing it for his country.

Samantha was impressed by the amount of intelligence she was thought to have and how useful she was thought to be, all from cutting up dead bodies! She was now being recruited to be a double agent. They had no clue that Mossad had already recruited her.

"I will have to think about this, excuse me," she said, and she turned to go back to the party, to which she would have preferred to never have been invited.

"Of course, of course, enjoy yourself," O'Neill said, watching her go to the Mansion.

A shot rang out, barely missing her and hitting O'Neill as he turned. Dussault ran for the door and Garda O'Connor pushed O'Neill down while the other Garda ran towards the noise, his gun drawn, and torch pointed to the bushes near the front gate. Cunningham jumped from his hiding place and ran in the direction of the shot. Lanigan frantically tried to adjust his binoculars to see where the shot was coming from. The Garda turned to Cunningham, who yelled, "Don't shoot, I'm a detective," flashing his badge at the Garda. "He is headed for the gates," Cunningham pointed with his torch and ran with the Garda towards the bushes where the first shot had come, their guns blazing in the general direction.

Three shots came from the opposite side of the Garden, in or near the Guest House. Cunningham mistook the shot as another echoing from in front instead of behind him and kept running with the Garda in the direction of the front gate.

O'Neill and his bodyguard, O'Connor, were still on the ground but Dussault had stumbled on the steps outside the door, flinging it open, the sight of his bloodied white shirt repelling the frightened guests who ran for shelter. Samantha crouched behind a hedge.

Another shot was fired from the bushes near the front gate towards the Garda and Cunningham, but it hit wide past, and they hesitated. Another shot, from near the stable, flew at the shooter in the hedge. It almost hit Hayes, who was running from the stables, but hit the limping shadow in the bushes at the gate. Cunningham and the other Garda fired at the hedge, while O'Connor left his post guarding O'Neill, turned, and reflexively shot at a motorcycle rapidly moving from near the stable through the trees lining the back driveway. Another shot, from the now fallen shadow near the gate, whizzed past Cunningham and hit O'Neill again, who was already down from the first shot. This killer was determined to get O'Neill.

Lanigan was close enough to the gate to run over and pull his gun, ready to shoot. As he approached, he could see the man was down, bleeding from a wound in his thigh, but holding his stomach, his rifle near him, the Carcano. He flashed his torch at his face. It was Brennan.

"The jig is up, Brennan," Lanigan said, fulfilling his American cops and robber's movie dream.

Cunningham, who was closer to the gate, ran quickly and saw that the man down was covered by Lanigan, and pointed his torch that way.

"Put it down, you bloody fool," Lanigan yelled, "we still have a shooter who is out there somewhere. You want to light us up?" Lanigan figured that the shooter from the Guest House was not finished.

But there were no more shots from there. Garda O'Connor turned to see if O'Neill was safe. He saw him nod and wave his hand. He turned and saw Dussault's body on the steps blocking the open door. He joined Hayes at the Guest House front.

Cunningham, realizing the shot that brought down Brennan came from the stables, ran back to check if the motorcyclist had an accomplice, but there was no one there. He ran back to the front gate to help Lanigan. Samantha emerged from the bushes nearby, her hands up in her soiled evening gown, worried she would be mistaken for the gunman.

"There is a tunnel in the Guest House," she yelled to Garda O'Connor and Detective Hayes, enough for them to figure out going through the door was safe to pursue the stranger. Now that the shooting seemed over, Samantha checked Dussault and saw he was dead, his blood spreading on the polished parquet wood floor. She ran over to

O'Neill to do some first aid. He was propped against the ornamental lion that probably saved his life.

"Where were you hit?" she asked.

"My leg and my shoulder. I can move them," he answered.

Samantha checked the wounds —they were not bleeding heavily. Probably no major arteries hit, she thought, pulling up his pants leg to feel his dorsal pulse and check for warmth in the calf. They were fine.

"Can you move your hand?" she asked, to make sure the brachial plexus, the bunch of nerves that emerged from the shoulder, was not damaged. He did but tried to move his arm as well and yelped in pain. "I just said your hand," she snapped, and O'Neill tried to pay more attention. She checked the pulse to his hand, and it was intact, and the hand was warm. "Lucky bastard," she muttered to herself, not caring if he heard.

The party inside had not noticed the shots initially and had continued to drink and speak loudly with music playing in the background. But after the second few shots, and Dussault falling in the door, they had all stopped and were heading for the back of the hall or to other rooms to look for shelter, other exits. No one had enough time to respond to their panic. The guests were yelling and crying.

Hayes and O'Connor ignored the noise and ran through the Guest House and down into the tunnel, their guns drawn and alert to any movement. There was none. The tunnel from the Guest House had two other doors and one led to the mansion, the other out to the back of the house, which was wide open.

"He must have gone this way," Hayes whispered to O'Connor, his gun and torch pointed to the door. They slowly approached the open door and Hayes put out his torch and peered out. The shouting of the people inside the mansion was muffled by the thick walls of the tunnel and the waves hitting the cliff that overlooked the Irish sea, obscuring any other sound. Some of the lights through the mansion windows illuminated the back gardens but cast more shadows. There was no movement. A little service road ran behind the grounds and there was a car parked there. Hayes and O'Connor saw some movement and pointed their torches, holding their guns ready.

"Halt, we are the Gardai," Hayes warned.

The two shadows stopped and lit their torches.

"We are with you. I'm Professor Stokes and this is Inspector Cloudot of the French police," Stokes said with his hands raised. Cloudot raised his hands as well to avoid any confusion.

Stokes explained what they knew. They had arrived just before the shooting started and Cloudot had jumped out of the car and grabbed a rifle from the boot, which had surprised Stokes. He had ordered Stokes to stay where he was and immediately ran to the stables near the mansion, mumbling something about needing to get some cover. He was gone before Stokes had a chance to stop him. He assumed that he knew something that Stokes didn't. It was like he had been there in the past and had been ready for this moment. When the firing started, Stokes stayed in the car and was in the dark, save the light from the windows inside the mansion. He had heard the multiple shots and saw someone leave the Guest House through the tunnel and then saw a motorcycle roar past him. Cloudot appeared right after, cool and calm, explaining that he had missed the shooter, but seemed unperturbed.

"Did you see anyone leave the mansion?" Hayes asked, still approaching cautiously.

"No, other than the man on the motorbike," said Stokes. "Was anyone hurt?"

"The Belgian, dead, O'Neill, wounded. That lucky bastard was probably the target, but we got the shooter, and he is still alive. Lanigan is with him," Hayes said. "Any idea who the other shooter was?"

"It could be the man I have been chasing in three countries," Cloudot answered.

"Well, I suppose he is well gone. I will alert the local Gardai to put a bulletin on him," Hayes said and picked up his walkie-talkie. "Heading north you say?" he asked, and Stokes nodded. He broadcast the alert, his voice crackling over the radio.

The crowd emerged from their hiding places and the staff ran to help O'Neill, carrying him in and laying him on a sofa in a small anteroom off the main hall. The police pushed them all back to the main hall from the lobby and closed the door so that they did not have to see the dead man. Hayes had returned to the building and told them they would be called as witnesses, but they would have to sit tight for the moment.

"But we didn't see anything," one of the ladies protested.

"Perhaps you didn't, but there is a dead man lying across the doorway and none of you would like to step over him, would you?" Hayes asked.

They all backed off and went into other rooms to wait, some nervously nibbling at food on the buffet table or having another drink, or two.

Stokes had walked into the building and had left Cloudot sitting discreetly in his car. He saw Samantha still standing over Dussault's body.

"What are you doing here?" he demanded, confused and angry. He had tried to protect her from any more dangerous misadventures and there she was standing over yet another dead body.

"I was invited to the party, but I didn't know I was going to be the death of the party," she smiled. "The Gardai called the Crime Scene Investigators, so they should be here soon," she said, dutifully reporting the status of their new case to her boss. Stokes looked at her in his daughter's green dress and all he could think of was all the blood on it. He felt weak and nauseous for a moment but controlled himself.

"I guess you will have to change," he said as casually as he could, trying not to convey any upset.

"I will, yes," Samantha said, looking down at herself, still considering this was a borrowed gown. "I'm sorry," she stammered.

"No fear," Stokes said, waving his hand. "We'll leave after the photographers have done their job. At least we know what we are going to be doing Monday," he looked again at Dussault's body, taking note of the position and the distribution of the blood, in case the photographers or the detectives failed to note something critical. The Garda who had been with Lanigan told them to hurry to the front gate since the shooter was still alive but wounded.

Lanigan had a chance to speak to Brennan, looking down at him as they waited for an ambulance, not realizing that Stokes and Monaghan were nearby. He was planning on taking Brennan to a secured bed at the

Mater. He would give orders clearly that this culprit would need at least four guards watching at all times and that the room would be isolated. The administrators at the Mater had changed the prisoner protocols after Curran's death and knew they would not be able to explain any more "oversights."

"You are a bloody failure, aren't you?" Lanigan said, making sure that he could rub this little bit of salt into Brennan's wounds.

Brennan said nothing, which Lanigan expected from his taunt.

"Who was the other shooter?" Lanigan asked.

"Don't know," Brennan muttered angrily.

"No friend of yours, I'd say," Lanigan smiled.

"Would you have any enemies besides O'Neill?" Lanigan asked.

Brennan said nothing.

"You are pretty good with that fancy Italian rifle, yours?"

"When is the ambulance going to be here?" Brennan asked, slurring his speech and looking dazed.

"Soon enough. Don't go out on us, you hear?" Lanigan said, shaking him. "You won't die on us like Curran."

"Curran needed dying. I don't care."

"Ready to die for the Cause, are you?"

"All of us should be," he said, spitting it out, with disdain.

"So, we are the traitors, are we? We and O'Neill. He betrayed you, didn't he?" Lanigan pressed again, hoping the loss of blood would impair his judgment.

"He did, and he will die for it."

Lanigan was glad the ambulance was slow in coming. It was giving him time to plumb Brennan's anger.

"Are there others?" Lanigan asked.

"There will be," Brennan warned, confirming, as far as Lanigan was concerned, that he was acting alone, for now.

"Well, then, who shot you?"

"Dunno," Brennan answered, more dazed and confused now.

"If you can tell us some more, we can get the bastard."

"The UVF or the British," Brennan said, pausing with his sluggish thoughts. "It must be the British. The UVF don't have the brains.

They're working with O'Neill."

Was this a concoction of Brennan's conspiratorial imagination, his brain bleeding out, or some secret knowledge that he had as a former G2 agent? thought Lanigan. Where was he going with this anyway? he asked himself again, as he waited for more "intelligence," doubting his own common sense.

"Who shot you?" Lanigan asked again, trying to get back to the subject, to have another chance at Brennan's motives and actions, watching him fade and thinking that he would need to call a priest if the ambulance did not arrive soon. He gave up, knowing that would require more thought than Brennan was up to—he probably didn't know who shot him, so he tried to ask another, easier, question before he faded completely.

"Did you kill Curran?"

"Yes, I did," he paused, more labored. "He was a tout," Brennan mumbled, thinking the same thing that Lanigan was thinking, only more slowly.

"Did you kill the John Doe on Talbot Street?" Lanigan pushed, bending over to ask again when he did not hear or perhaps comprehend the question the first time.

Cunningham looked at Lanigan, uncomfortable for so many reasons. "Shall we call a priest?" he asked, reminding Lanigan of his responsibilities.

"Did you kill the John Doe?" Lanigan asked again, louder, ignoring Cunningham like an annoying fly.

"I did. He was a traitor," Brennan relinquished, in pain and with his last bit of consciousness.

"Call a priest. We're done here," Lanigan snapped at Cunningham.

The sounds of the ambulance were getting louder. Cunningham went for the priest he had seen at the mansion and passed Stokes and Monaghan running towards Lanigan.

"He's still alive," he said to them.

The priest came right after them and administered last rites as Stokes and Monaghan were giving first aid to Brennan. He had massive bleeding to his abdomen and the leg wound had punctured his femoral artery. Despite the tourniquet applied, despite CPR, by the time the ambulance squad arrived, he was dead.

Chapter Thirty-Four

The party was over. O'Neill was taken by police escort to the nearest hospital for emergency surgery. Brennan and Dussault were taken to the morgue. The guests, all important people, were questioned perfunctorily by Hayes and Cunningham and were warned they might need to be contacted for further inquiries. Stokes escorted Samantha around the back to the car and introduced her to Cloudot as a friend. He offered to drive them both back to town.

"I need to change," Samantha said, looking at her dress matted with blood and made a mental note that O'Neill had at least been right about the French snooping around.

"I can wait," Cloudot gallantly offered. He said he had not seen the gunfight. He did not tell Samantha who he was and why he was here. The Gardai largely ignored him. He seemed to have arrived with Stokes. They were more concerned about all the protesting guests who were "inconvenienced." Lanigan, Hayes, and Cunningham were more concerned about securing the scene.

"Thanks, I won't be long, I have a change of clothes," she smiled and went into her room in the Guest House which had already been checked by one of the Gardạ. She had a quick shower and dried off with one of the luxurious towels that had been provided. Pity, she said to herself, this might have been a nice party. She opened her purse to grab some lipstick and saw a scribbled note: "Your job is done. I will contact you, Love, Rami."

She could not believe it. She thought she was supposed to trap O'Neill and Dussault in a conspiracy and Rami was going to get the Jackal in the bargain. She looked at the paper again and tore it into little pieces and flushed it down the toilet, twice. Who, if anybody, had Rami shot? There were shots from the other side of the garden and who was

218

the shooter there? She was dizzy and tired from the cocktails and the lack of food. Her wristwatch, after all was said and done, read nearly midnight. She gathered her things and ran out the door to meet Stokes and Cloudot, who were waiting. Stokes and Samantha sat down in the back seat and Cloudot started the drive.

"Whatever were you doing here?" Stokes demanded once they were settled, his usual calm dissipated after the immediacy of the duties he completed on the garden "battlefield."

Samantha was taken aback. She had not expected him to act like her boss when, just a few minutes before, he was her colleague and friend. Cloudot did not say a thing, as discreet as a taxi driver.

"I was invited to the party by Mr. O'Neill and thought it an opportunity to meet all the people he knew," she lied. She dare not tell Stokes about Rami. She detested O'Neill and all he stood for. She did not tell Stokes this either, even though it would have put her in his camp. Perhaps that is why he asked. Or was it this fatherly, protective, thing she sensed? Or was it just the boss who had ordered her to stay out of politics and danger?

"A bad decision. Leave the politicking to those who need it. The less bias you show in your position, the more likely you are to survive," he admonished.

Father? Boss? She thought again. She did not have to make the distinction in her response.

"Sorry, Professor," she replied.

There was silence the rest of the drive. Cloudot was happy to stay out of this, but he was also curious as to why she had been at the party. He did not ask her, but knew he had to stay in Dublin for another few days.

Stokes directed Cloudot to a few more turns and they arrived at Samantha's flat.

"I will see you tomorrow morning at ten at the morgue for the autopsies," he said perfunctorily as he turned to her. "Get some rest."

"Goodnight, Professor," Samantha said, getting out and taking her bag from the boot.

"Thank you for the lift, M. Cloudot," she said.

"My pleasure, mademoiselle doctor," he smiled.

They saw her fumble for her keys, open her door, enter and close it. They still waited to see her bedroom light go on.

During the wait, Cloudot saw this as a tacit opportunity to break silence.

"She is very courageous, your assistant," he turned to smile at Stokes.

"Too courageous," Stokes replied, still disapproving.

"I think Abn Awan is gone," Cloudot said, returning to the subject. "Even if O'Neill was a target, this party was a good excuse for a planned meeting with him and Dussault. We will never know. He is probably on a plane or boat to England."

"And the man on the motorcycle?" Stokes asked.

"Who knows? Abn Awaa?" Cloudot suggested.

"Perhaps. Anyone would have been scared off by the police and shooting," said Stokes

"*Quelle dommage*, a pity, if O'Neill, Dussault, and Abn Awaa were working together for another arms shipment. We were hoping to catch both of them, how you say, red-handed," he explained.

"And the dead French woman, will you investigate her death?" Stokes asked.

"No. She was just an unfortunate coincidence. I have been here for weeks," he said with a pause, eager to change the subject. "You will let me know the autopsy report on Dussault and, if you please, forward a copy to the Surete to my attention. It was a relief to know this man was finally punished for all his war crimes. He was smart to have become an Irish citizen, since Ireland was a neutral country during the war. He had betrayed French, Belgian, and Dutch partisans, Communists, and Jews and made some money in the process as well. Perhaps we will find the identity of the killer from the bullets he used. If it was not Abn Awan, we can offer him a medal. I will drive you home. It is not far, I believe."

"Thank you," Stokes replied. "I will have to tip you for the ride."

"The only tip I will need is what you come up with at the autopsy," Cloudot winked, sped Stokes home, and then took off into the night.

Chapter Thirty-Five

Saturday morning was unusual for an autopsy, but Dussault's body lay prepped and ready for dissection on the autopsy table. Johnston had arrived just before Dussault's autopsy but was miffed that he had been left out of the initial excitement. He never hesitated to come in at any time he was needed. He heard on the news that there had been some murders at O'Neill's estate and wanted to be in the thick of things. He felt his job as a Diener was an obligation and his worth was measured by his dutifulness.

"You should have called, Professor. You had a long night by the sounds of it and you and the little doctor could have used my help sooner," he scolded as Stokes entered the autopsy room.

"Thanks, Mr. Johnston, but I didn't want to disturb you, it being a Saturday."

"It's my duty," Johnston reminded him, quickly moving Brennan's body from the case to the table, demonstrating his strength and agility so his age should never be an issue.

"I appreciate that, Mr. Johnston. You have it all set up I see. Well done."

Samantha was gowned and standing ready, but Stokes nodded at her perfunctorily.

"Thank you, Professor," I will be in the office if you need me," Johnston said, leaving quickly, sensing the tension.

"Good morning, Dr. Monaghan," he said in a flat tone, attempting to be polite.

"Good morning, Professor," she responded despite the cool greeting. "I have taken the X-rays with the help of Mr. Johnston," she informed him in a soft business tone, then cleared her throat. She was still tired from last night, but it was clear Stokes and the coroner would be pressured to get some answers quickly. She had taken the initiative to be there earlier than him but realized this was not enough penance.

"Any retained bullet fragments?" he asked, again, in a business monotone.

"None that we could see on the X-ray," she said, nodding to the films which were hanging on the viewer.

Stokes was impressed by her efficiency. He pulled the films off to hold them up to the light at another angle, seeing nothing as well.

"I assume we have the photos taken by the coroner's office?

She held up the photos that were on the work desk.

"Did they find any of the cartridges or bullets?" he asked, pressuring her knowledge, as she anticipated.

"They could have come from a Browning, ballistics thinks."

Full marks, Stokes thought, but did not say—she would have to work harder to deserve a compliment. He nodded and stepped over to examine the photos and then looked at the body.

"Three penetration wounds, one to the right thorax, another to the left thorax, and the last to the heart, all entry wounds. Shot in the front at close range," Stokes emphasized. He had not put his gown on as yet. He stood there for a moment and then looked at Samantha. She quizzically returned his gaze. The holes at the front were obvious exit wounds.

"Conduct the autopsy, Dr. Monaghan, after all, you were there," he gestured with an open extended hand.

Samantha got on the examining stool so she could lean over the body. She positioned the microphone and the "on" pedal so it would be comfortable and began her description of the body, measured the wounds in the front, and then paused and reviewed the photos, then the X-ray. She did not want to make one cut before everything had been properly measured. She then made her incisions, carefully avoiding the wounds, and reviewed the wounds layer by layer in the lungs and the heart. Professor Stokes assisted her in turning the body on its side so it was propped by blocks, and she could run the probes through to measure the angle of entry and exit. Stokes did not say a word but allowed her to continue.

She was more nervous than she had ever been in anatomy class, or assisting in surgery, or even at her first autopsy. His silence hung heavy on her, worse than a resounding "no" or "stop" or "pause, please." Was he going to allow her to mess this all up on her own so she would be fired? She paused at the examination before she removed the heart.

"Aren't you going to say anything?" she stammered.

"Are you?" he asked.

"What do you mean?" she asked, more nervous now, almost tearful.

"He died within a few feet of you, in a place where you should not have been. What was going on?" he asked calmly.

She put her dissecting scissors and tweezers down. She couldn't hold back the tears, but she did not bawl, but sniffled and breathed deeply.

"I was recruited as an agent for the Mossad," she blurted out, still crying softly.

"What?" he exclaimed, shocked and confused. He knew her behavior had been unusual for a while. She had been off work too many days with too many flimsy excuses, but this? What was a nice Irish girl doing with the Mossad?

"I was spying on O'Neill because he was planning another arms deal with the Jackal, the PLO terrorist. The Mossad said they wanted to stop him or kill him. I was used. They wanted to kill him," she said nodding down at the body whose heart was open to her.

"Have you told this to anybody?" Stokes asked.

"No, just you, but Howard Bernstein, Mayor Briscoe's old aide, knew," she said.

"You haven't told him anything, have you?" Stokes asked, quietly, less shock in his voice.

"Then you must let him know you are out of this," Stokes insisted.

"I don't have to. I was notified my services are no longer needed. That's when I realized I had been used to help kill Dussault. The Jackal is still out there, isn't he?" she asked.

"I suppose he is," Stokes mused, thinking of Cloudot, but not revealing his arrangement with him.

"Complete the autopsy. You are doing fine," he reassured her, not absolving her of her recklessness or deception, but only to get her focused on finishing the autopsy.

She completed the examination. All that was found was the obvious cause of death—three bullets to the heart and lungs, point of entry through the back at relatively close range with the likely weapon a handgun.

"I would like you to state in this preliminary report that the points of entry were from the front, not back. I am not correcting you, but I need to review this case and will amend it when I sign off on the final report," Stokes said without explanation.

Samantha was surprised but would dictate the report as he directed. She would argue with him later since that was not what she had seen during the autopsy or recalled at the scene. Dussault was shot in the back and, most likely, by Rami. But she dare not say this out loud. She nodded and said, "Yes, Professor," and began her dictation.

Stokes abruptly left her and went out to the secretary to check on her progress.

"I want this typed out and delivered to my desk today. You can stipulate this as a preliminary report since I will sign off on it when we have the rest of the information from ballistics. I will be performing the autopsy on Brennan now and am pleased at your speed on Dr. Monaghan's dictation and expect the same on mine. I will be busy and want no interruptions, even from the coroner or Lanigan. You will say nothing to them or anyone else," Stokes added, surprised he had not had any calls from the press as yet.

It was unusual for the coroner or Lanigan to be at their offices on a Saturday morning, but this was an unusual case. In light of the recent killings and after the bombings still, so that the whole of An Garda Siochana, police, detectives, and security forces were mobilized by their superiors to find out what happened and determine who was responsible and bring them to justice. Nothing was routine. That a former Minister of the opposition party was nearly assassinated twice made the whole affair more than just an issue of national security, it had become political. More than one TD of the opposition demanded the resignation of the Taoiseach as well as every official remotely related to the events.

Stokes was not surprised when Lanigan picked up his phone at the first ring. He had expected him to be at the autopsy this morning, but he deduced that Lanigan had probably slept at his desk the whole night until the phone awakened him.

"Lanigan," Lanigan answered sleepily.

"Did you get any sleep last night?" Stokes asked.

"Not to worry, Doc, I am going home to get a few hours' sleep, so you can reach me there if you need to," he advised.

"Put a rush on ballistics and I can release the body by Monday."

"Everyone is on alert here, so I wouldn't be surprised if they give you some answers in a few hours."

"Thanks. I'll give ballistics a call in a few hours. Get some rest," Stokes said and hung up. He paced over to the secretary who had been called in to help with the dictation and the paperwork. She was busy typing when he attracted her attention from her headphones by suddenly standing over her, looking down.

"I'm almost done Professor," she informed him, not startled at all. She had the benefit of sleep and the calm of someone whose job was not at stake as long as she did her work.

"Thanks, I'll be on the phone again," he advised her, pacing away again. He was anxious that this all be done quickly since he knew others would want it even more rapidly than humanly possible. Bureaucrats never saw any emergencies unless they created them, he observed. He noticed a small irregularity on his nail that protruded out irritatingly, an errant fragment that he had been unconsciously fingering while he was watching Samantha and had been fingering as well speaking to Lanigan. He took the nail clippers out of the drawer and clipped it before he called the coroner, the momentary delay decreasing the distaste of the next conversation.

The coroner also answered the phone himself. He was responding to calls from many "concerned" parties. He would have walked into Stokes' office himself but for the fact he could not get off the phone. The longer he spoke, the more he was protected from yet another phone call, so he was taking his time.

"The phone has been ringing off the hook all morning," the coroner complained. "I hope you have some answers."

"The shots that killed Dussault, the Belgian, were not from Brennan's rifle," Stokes replied. "They were from a handgun at short range and may have been fired into him from the front, not the back. As Lanigan probably told you, he thought there was another shooter," Stokes said, hoping this falsehood would be accepted and percolate up to the right ears.

"Then who shot Brennan?" the coroner demanded.

"We don't know that either, but ballistics is looking at that as well. At least we were able to get the slugs from the wounds last night, or so Lanigan told me."

"I don't have to tell you what a balls-up this is, do I?" the coroner asked.

"No. You don't. All I can give you is what I know," Stokes said, not wanting to take part in this finger-pointing.

"Well, let's give them what they need, and soon."

"Of course. That's why I am here on a Saturday morning. I will let you know when I know," Stokes hung up the phone, generally more irritated at the arrogance of this ignorant apparatchik who survived on his charms and affiliations. Stokes was not charmed. He walked over to the secretary and paused a moment before he got into her line of sight. She was still typing. She saw him and stopped.

"Almost finished, Professor," she said, almost cheerily.

"Thanks, carry on," he said, smiling back at her. There was no point in his getting upset with her when it was the whole Irish bureaucracy and body politic he was upset with. He paused at that and took a deep breath and thought of Osler's essay "Aequinimitas," the physician urging his students to have "imperturbability" and "equanimity." All this turmoil had disturbed that. He asked himself when he had last had a vacation and his answer was the sad memory of him and his wife and daughter in Dingle, riding a donkey cart, of all things. They were laughing like children when they were caught in a sudden rain and could only escape as quickly as the donkey could carry them and laughed and laughed about that. He smiled to himself, walked back to the autopsy rooms and saw Samantha cleaning up with Johnston's help.

"Please stay and observe Brennan's autopsy. I am sorry. We have all been stressed and we need to get back our bearings. Let's finish this. We need some rest for the weekend, but no country estate visits," he smiled.

Samantha was so relieved at the comment that she wanted to hug him and say thank you but reminding herself she was gowned and ready for business, she just smiled back.

"We were there, and we saw his demise, but he had at least two wounds with at least three assailants, by all accounts, so we have to take care the wounds and the bullets match with our impressions," he observed, just walking around the naked body and viewing it at different angles and from different heights.

"The leg wound was from a large caliber pistol and from a distance, most likely one of the Garda. Do we have an X-ray of that?"

Johnston held it up against the viewing box and Stokes could see the fragment of the femur that had been shattered with the bullet lodged there.

"That's one. Let's take care not to lose it down the sink," he urged, having had to take the plumbing apart more than once to capture small particles of vital evidence that escaped through the grates.

He looked at the abdominal wound and it was much larger, more consistent with a high-powered rifle from the large exit wound posteriorly. It was remarkably like the wound that John Doe had sustained in the same area. Was it coincidence or did this marksman also have a liking for the abdominal aorta? he thought.

"Did you notice any other wounds, Dr. Monaghan?" he said, turning to Samantha.

"There was another gunshot on the right arm, also small arms fire, I think."

"That was probably why he did not get a good second shot at O'Neill," Stokes thought out loud. He looked at the X-rays on the examining box this time, more carefully and with a magnifying lens as well. There were no other bullet fragments or bone breaks that he could see. He hoped that Lanigan and his crew had combed the area for the spent bullet from the rifle. It might shed some light as to whether it was a similar or the same gun that killed John Doe. He still had the bullet in his locked drawer, saving it for the comparison of the rifle when it was obtained. It was assumed that Brennan had shot John Doe. Now he was not so sure.

"Let's dig in," Stokes said, putting his gown and gloves on and quickly made the chest, then the abdominal incisions. He ignored the brain, since it was not likely to reveal any new information, and for expediency. Everyone was under pressure to get the basic facts—he could always return if there was more information needed.

He was impressed by the size of the liver and its fatty degeneration, so often seen in early alcoholic cirrhosis. He dissected the stomach and found multiple small erosions throughout the lining, also suggestive of alcoholic gastritis, both suggestive of someone who was drinking heavily first over a long time, then increasing over a short period.

"This man might have died of acute alcohol poisoning if it had not been for the acute lead poisoning. His anger was the death of him," Stokes commented after pausing during the dictation. "He seemed under a lot of stress, and it would be interesting to know if he had a history of alcohol abuse now or in the past. Let's see if we can obtain any medical records and service records," he said to Samantha.

He then examined the abdomen and, yes, there was a nick to the aorta, just enough for him to bleed slowly into the abdomen but there was extensive tissue damage surrounding, consistent with a high-powered rifle injury. The one shot was effective enough. Whoever the marksman was, he had done his job. He debated whether to call Cloudot now or wait until he was finished. Since Cloudot said he would be around, he decided to continue the task at hand and make his calls later, in private, after he had dismissed everyone, especially Samantha since she had demonstrated poor judgment and put herself in danger too often. The less she knew, the better. He thought As was expected, the bullet that lodged in his femur had also nicked the femoral artery and he had been bleeding there as well. Stokes got a substantial fragment of the bullet, and it looked like the standard caliber from a Garda pistol. He would get confirmation from ballistics soon enough. The other wound in the forearm was superficial, so there was no slug to be found and he expected the forensic team would find it close to where he had lain. There was nothing more to do, so he instructed Samantha to clean up, reminding her to make note of any other irregularities she might see as she did, and then to go home and get some rest. She nodded dutifully and did not ask any more questions, seeing he was again in no mood for answering or speculating.

By the time all the niceties were done, it was already half two and he hadn't had lunch. He was tired from last night as well and really didn't want to make any more calls, but he knew he would only be harassed by the coroner if he didn't call him. He picked up the phone and dialed his direct number. He answered immediately.

"He died as a result of two wounds, one from a rifle and the other probably from a lucky shot from a Garda handgun. I'm afraid you still have a shooter on the loose and you should alert all the police of this danger. I don't know who else he is out to get, but he is a good shot and warn them all to be careful," he reported. This would be enough for now; he had done his duty. He would call Lanigan and meet him at the local pub.

Chapter Thirty-Six

The pub was crowded since there was always a contingent who wanted an early start for the night and others who just wanted to watch football on the television. So, it was loud, but Stokes saw Lanigan at the bar and pointed to the quieter lounge where men and women could quietly enjoy a drink. He ordered some food and offered to buy Lanigan something, but he was not very hungry, just tired, and wanted to get home and get some sleep.

"I have a feeling that there is going to be a lot of trouble about this," Lanigan said.

"You don't know the half of it," said Stokes. "That shot that got Brennan in the stomach, I think it was another Carcano—even the placement of the bullet was in nearly the same position as the one that got John Doe. I think the Jackal was involved in both shootings and he is still at large," Stokes revealed.

"Shite and onions," Lanigan whispered.

"You know that Frenchman I came with to O'Neill's? He is from the French police, antiterrorist division, and he has been hunting for the Jackal for years. He also had hoped to lure Dussault out of Ireland and arrest him for his Nazi collaboration, but Dussault has already paid for that," said Stokes.

"I don't think we'll be chasing anyone else very soon," Lanigan said. "The muckety-mucks have been meeting today. Time for some head rolling. I would expect we will hear on Monday," Lanigan shook his head, sipping his beer to just wet his dry mouth, since he was too nervous and didn't have the heart to enjoy his drink.

"We can stall them for a little while, but you know as well as I do that as soon as they release O'Neill, he will have as much sympathy as he needs to take over and they will bury the truth," Stokes said.

"Well, there's nothing more to do, is there?" Lanigan answered, having another swig and then getting up. "I'm going home. You can ring me if you have any better ideas, but I'm going to sleep all weekend and the rest be damned," he said, waving his arms, nodding to Stokes, and putting on his hat as he went out the door.

Stokes did not sit any longer than to finish his fish and chips and beer. He was not any more heartened by this turn of events than Lanigan. O'Neill had escaped assassination and his cohorts could not be questioned—they were all dead. Only this Jackal remained, and he may well have left the country by now. He reminded himself that the cigarette smoke irritated him and though the lounge was relatively quiet, the noise of the football spectators did not allow him to think. Perhaps he would do just nothing and try to forget the sordid events. Perhaps he would take a vacation himself. He paid the bill and decided to take a walk home. It was a beautiful sunny summer day, and he expected the stroll would help clear his mind.

When he arrived home, no sooner had he sat down than he got a call. It was from an old comrade-in-arms from the Royal Navy, Commodore Anthony Smyth-Jones. He had retired and joined one of the ministries at Whitehall, but Stokes was not sure what his job was. He had been evasive about his position, claiming some security issues and the Foreign Service. He wanted to get together since he was in Dublin for a few days on business. It was unusual, Stokes thought, since it was a bit late for their early June reunion which they had kept for the past 30 years. Stokes wondered about that since Smyth-Jones was quite the precise fellow. He did not push the point since Smyth-Jones still felt indebted to Stokes for saving his life during the D-Day invasion, which Stokes will acknowledge reluctantly.

Stokes had been a junior officer on the hospital ship. In the melee, his old friend, then quite young, had sustained a nasty wound to the leg. Stokes had been assigned to do the amputation since that was the most expedient course of treatment and would probably save his life. Stokes had ignored the order and did some skillful vascular surgery after he had stopped the bleeding and Tony, as he liked to be called, was eternally grateful. He visited Dublin at least once a year since Stokes was not keen on going to London.

They decided to meet at the Gresham for dinner since that was where he was staying. It was a grand hotel in the heart of the city, right on O'Connell Street but it had seen better days and business had dropped since the bombing. Even the Gresham had been evacuated at least twice due to bomb scares.

Stokes was amused by his intrepid friend. He had gone through a lot since the war. Smyth-Jones had regaled him with stories about traveling the world in war and peace. He hoped his business was just business since there seemed to be no peace from Stokes' perspective. He hoped he was not in uniform because a British accent itself could start a fight in these tense times, let alone a uniform.

Tony, wearing a three-piece pin-stripe suit, was already in the hotel lounge when Stokes arrived, having dressed more casually in tweed jacket and slacks. They sat in the lounge and chatted as their table was not quite ready. Saturday evening was still busy. Stokes rarely visited the Gresham, but this was a special occasion, and he appreciated the plush sofas and the excellent Irish whiskey that Tony had insisted on ordering.

"What brings you here?" asked Stokes.

"A terrorist, if you must know," he said bluntly.

"Isn't that for the Irish to deal with?" Stokes replied, surprised at the openness of the discussion.

"He is not in the IRA, but he is generally an enemy of the Western World," Tony answered tendentiously.

"It is not the Jackal, is it?" said Stokes, afraid of where this was going.

"How ever did you know?"

"Join the posse, pardner," Stokes replied in a cowboy drawl.

"I read that you had some run-ins with some of his victims."

"I'm afraid so. Too many, and these few months have been so chock full of victims and perpetrators, it is so confusing that I do not know who not to suspect."

"I have to admit I am after some of the same suspects. I am here on Her Majesty's service to ferret out the whereabouts of the Jackal and his Irish accomplices. In the course of my intelligence briefings, I got some news that struck home. I would have hoped to have told you this sooner and in a less business-related way, but I now know who killed your wife and daughter," Tony said, sitting forward in his chair. Stokes leaned forward as well.

"They were three IRA operatives from the North. Two were killed in the North and the other, though questioned by the police in the South, was released for 'lack of evidence." This last suspect is on the run now, but we have some intelligence he had been acting on O'Neill's orders as well as working with him on some arms trades. That's why I am here. I'm sorry I couldn't reveal my sources and let you know the truth before this. I have been ever so sorry for the reticence, but it comes with the job, and it took almost two years to find this out. Take heart, justice will be done, but I will need your help." He paused, letting Stokes take the information in.

Stokes did not know who he should be angrier with, Tony or O'Neill. He had been struggling for answers and closure for two years and there was his "old chum" finally telling him the truth over a drink before a casual dinner. Bloody English and their bloody understatement, he thought to himself. Stokes paused for a moment and just stared at his old comrade. Anthony Smyth-Jones stared back, well aware of the effect he had on his old friend.

"I always suspected O'Neill had something to do with it, as so many others did, but we couldn't get anything on him, the slimy bastard," Stokes said, still choking with rage, but redirecting his anger at the message, not the messenger. He took a deep breath and calmly asked, "How can I help?"

"We know O'Neill is trying to arrange another arms shipment soon. I'm sure this weekend's fireworks have not helped the plan. We were going to allow his henchmen Dussault and Gray to complete the process, but they now will need to move others forward. This improvisation is their weakness. We think this Jackal fellow is still at large here in Dublin and may have to step out from the shadows to help complete the deal, but we dare not try to do anything here south of the border."

"I would think not."

"Where do you plan on staging the capture, then?"

"Antwerp. We have been working with the French and the Belgians."

"Have you heard of Inspector Cloudot?" Stokes asked.

"No, who is he?"

"He is from the French Embassy, their police attaché, or so he calls himself. I am surprised he has not been able to coordinate his plans with you since he has been on the trail of Dussault and the Jackal as well."

"And you have been working with him?"

"Yes, I have," Stokes admitted. "He is the one who told me about the proposed arms deal."

"Well, then, this certainly is a big posse," Tony smiled. "Still, best not to show our hand here in Dublin. Don't let this Cloudot know we met. All I need from you is where O'Neill is and will be. Try to identify who else he will be working with in this new Plan B."

"Well, we plan on making him more suspicious of his own men, since I have leaked a report that one of his Gardai henchmen may have killed Dussault. I do agree with your observation O'Neill will have to take some of the responsibility of the trade on himself."

"That would be splendid, the more active he is, the more exposed. That is all we need," Tony said.

The waiter approached to let them know their table was ready.

"Enough of this, then. Let's enjoy a decent meal. I'll never forget the steaks and chops we were dying for in England that we got here when we were on leave during the war. Sometimes it pays to be neutral, eh," he smiled, getting up only slightly unsteady on his bad leg. Stokes was glad to have helped him continue his life in relative fitness for all his activities. He was uncomfortable that his British friend had casually and insensitively revealed one of the most painful mysteries in Stokes' life. He wondered but for this spy-hunt Smyth-Jones was on, if he would have ever been told. He was grateful enough for the whiskey that he was able to restrain himself from any more upset and went on to the dining room where they sat down for dinner.

He reluctantly looked at the menu. How could he eat? he thought to himself. He had found the killers. Two had been brought to justice, but that did not make it any less painful for him. He had no appetite, but accepted the steak Tony ordered for him, as he had done so often before. He did not concentrate on Tony's conversation, but that was not unusual since Tony would regale him with old stories he had heard many times before. Tony was content to recite them again, despite Stokes' near vacant stare.

"Is your steak all right?" asked Tony. Even he had noticed the large piece of meat still on Stokes' plate after Tony had consumed, despite all the talk, most of his.

"I had a late lunch," Stokes excused himself.

"And a sad dinner, I would say, by the look on your face. I'm sorry I gave you that painful intelligence and spoiled your appetite. I thought it might encourage you to know O'Neill and his friends will soon be on the run. I hope we can get some cooperation from the Irish police, but that, especially now, is like walking on eggshells. Tell me more about this Frenchman. Cloudot is it?"

Stokes did not want to be a source of his intelligence. It was hard enough just sitting there, making stabs at his steak from time to time, sipping the wine to calm himself.

"Well, we got together because he was gathering the information for one of the bombing victims, a French citizen. He helped me get through the paperwork the French requested, worse than the Irish, and in French, no less," Stokes replied as casually as he could muster.

"So, he enlisted you in the search for the Jackal, did he?"

"He did. The Jackal has probably been involved in some of the murders, but one can't be sure since no one has seen him. He seems to be involved in this arms plot, though, and if we can catch him with O'Neill, that would be the end of O'Neill, to hell with the Jackal."

"You have become quite the detective, haven't you?" said Tony, smiling.

"More or less. Dragooned into the service, you might say."

"Well, keep me posted. I will be here at the Gresham for at least a few days, unless they blow up the place," he said distractedly.

"Listen, I really must go. I have not been feeling myself. I had a long day and since you will be around, at least we can get together again. I will let you know anything I know," Stokes said, not being able to tolerate any more of this espionage.

"I understand, old chap. Get some rest, you do look exhausted," Tony said, grabbing his hand as Stokes got up.

Stokes did not look back when he left the dining room but expected Tony would be having a port and a cigar, enjoying his time off. Stokes, without hesitation, accepted the cab the doorman had hailed and went home to bed.

Chapter Thirty-Seven

Sunday was a beautiful day. Stokes had planned a trip to the Wicklow mountains so he could view the city and the Irish sea all in one vista and breathe the fresh, clean air and clear his mind and lungs with a brisk walk. That was the plan, but the phone rang just as he was setting out. It was from Lanigan. He complained to Stokes he had not slept very well the night before and he was frustrated that even with his heroic exploits he was going to be punished rather than rewarded by his superiors. It upset Lanigan no end. There were still too many loose ends: Who killed Dussault? Who killed Brennan and was this truly over? O'Neill was at the top of the heap and the Jackal was running free and, who was he, anyway? He went on with the pressure of speech of a man obsessed.

Stokes tried to calm him down, but there was no reasoning with him. He was a bulldog and he had latched on and would not let go, no matter what.

"What if we hatch a plot to end this all?" Stokes proposed.

"Catch them all in one go?"

"Precisely. We know O'Neill and his friends were trying to get some arms in and must have been frustrated by all this interference by their enemies, including us. What if we were to make it easy for him to complete his plans with the help of some new friends?"

"Now who would that be?"

"Do you recall that French policeman who had accompanied me to the Estate?" Stokes asked.

"I don't. I was too busy at the time."

"Well, neither did O'Neill. The inspector stayed in the background. I think he would be interested in playing a part in flushing the Jackal out. As far as we know, O'Neill has not seen the Jackal and avoided direct contact. He manipulated affairs at a distance, so he would not be implicated, unlike his unfortunate agent Brennan. I don't think O'Neill can afford to wait. The Frenchman says he knows the arms are waiting in Antwerp but without Dussault's henchman to deliver the money, they won't complete the deal and the Jackal won't get his share.

"So, what do you propose?" Lanigan asked.

"Our French agent, posing as Abn Awaa, you call him the Jackal, meets with O'Neill and proposes to go to Antwerp himself, but asks him for the money up front. Then we catch him, red-handed," Stokes proposed.

Lanigan was all for it, so Stokes paged Cloudot. He responded quickly. The inspector had planned on bad coffee and croissants at the only "French" patisserie in Dublin.

"I know the place. We will meet you in an hour," Stokes proposed.

"We?" asked Cloudot.

"Detective Lanigan. He is working on his own and will be discreet. He has been following this all along. He is afraid he won't have any cooperation from his superiors, so being a stubborn Irishman, he is ready to press on," Stokes said.

"Are you sure he is trustworthy?" Cloudot replied after a long pause.

"He is. This is totally unofficial. The Irish police will not know," assured Stokes.

There was another long pause.

"If you say so. We must be careful. I don't want this more complicated."

"Trust me. It should make it easier for you since we can get you past O'Neill's special Gardai. They are all Irish police," Stokes explained.

Another pause. "See you soon," Cloudot replied abruptly and hung up.

Chapter Thirty-Eight

"Mon ami, do you think that O'Neill is that stupid?" asked Cloudot sipping his coffee and eating the last morsel of the croissant.

"He is greedy and ambitious," replied Stokes, not finishing his coffee, which as Cloudot had judged correctly, was not that good.

"He will not stop at any length to make more money, and the arms deal will help fund his mansion and political aspirations. He plans on becoming Taoiseach. He has his supporters. He needs to get that money and Dussault was going to make it happen. Now he's dead, so he must have another plan," Stokes reasoned.

"We must be his other plan. I have been working with another agent in Antwerp who was tracking Dussault's shipment which started out in Czechoslovakia labeled as farm equipment. He knows it is in a shipping container and is ready to be sent to Cork, but he does not know when. Dussault was supposed to have given the word. But where is the money? O'Neill must know. He has to give that money to Abn Awal, the Jackal, now that Dussault is gone. They must get together. I don't think he trusts the Jackal and he may think that he killed Dussault and Gray, but he has no choice. I will play the Jackal and make a deal, splitting the money with him. Our man in Antwerp will call him, claim to be working with Dussault, complaining he can't delay the shipment any longer since he thinks the Belgian authorities are suspicious. That will put the pressure on him. Then I will meet him and voila!" Cloudot exclaimed.

"What if the real Jackal shows up? He might come out shooting," Stokes asked.

"That is a chance we will have to take. If he does, I have some men who you have never seen who will also be watching," Cloudot smiled.

"A real international dragnet you have. You have approval for this?" Lanigan asked suspiciously, quiet since they sat down, wary of this new player.

"Mais oui, but of course," Cloudot smiled again, but still not sure how much he could trust Lanigan.

"How am I in this?" Lanigan asked, still looking skeptical of the whole plan.

"You must have your trusted men lying in wait at the meeting place. I think O'Neill will have his own men watching, to protect him and the money, since he must be tres uncomfortable now," Cloudot answered.

"There are a lot of moving parts here," Stokes observed. "I hope you will not create more work for me."

"Neither do I. I do not think O'Neill will want any fireworks if he is caught," Cloudot speculated. "There have been enough dead men around him," he said.

"I think I can smoke him out, get him more paranoid and panicked. I am going to give a preliminary report that the shots that killed Dussault came not from the Guest House behind him, but from the front near the door, from a gun of the caliber of the Gardai. That will put the Gardai who were watching him under his suspicion, especially if he has any access to leaks from the coroner's department. I will stipulate that is mere speculation until the final report is completed," said Stokes. This was not ethical, he realized, and Stokes had stepped over the line with the truth, but this man was not ethical, had tampered with the truth, endangered many lives, and caused some deaths, his family included. They agreed to be in contact by phone, but each privately to the other. No other word would be spoken until O'Neill's plot could be determined.

Stokes took the bus directly from City Centre to the Wicklows. He wasn't going to let the day be spoiled completely. It was still sunny when he got to Mount Pelier, the site of the old Hellfire's Club. It had been a house where the young rich gentry of the 18th century had gotten together in exclusive debauchery until it finally burned down. It was a great vantage point to see the city and the bay. It must have been a vision with all the lights glimmering at night and nothing but the evening boats moving in and out of port. The legends of lascivious and blasphemous behavior lived on long after the ruins. He speculated whether some of his ancestors might have been a part of the goings-on, the British overlords enjoying their money and power, but he had no pretensions and felt little guilt about his heritage. He had worked for his status and enjoyed the comfort and shunned any notoriety, what was left of it. He ignored the sordid history and enjoyed the pleasant vista.

There was a car park near the promontory. Many a family man was sitting in their car, windows rolled up, muffling the noise of his children running around outside, reading their newspaper, likely the only peace he had in the whole week. Like them, but outside in the fresh air, it was the only peace that Stokes had had in months.

Chapter Thirty-Nine

Stokes went to his office Monday morning, expecting the events of the last week would coalesce into some giant wave of repercussions. He was not mistaken. When he walked in the door his secretary handed him messages to call Lanigan, the Coroner, and the Detective Chief Superintendent. He took a deep breath, sat down at his desk, and called Lanigan first who might give him the lay of the land. The other two would only be the purveyors of bad news and their implications.

"How are you Seamus?" Stokes asked, using his Christian rather than official name, hoping being more personal would calm the onslaught of fears, complaints, and self-recriminations.

"How can I bloody be? I've been taken off the case, put on bloody desk duty, and been told I was lucky not to be taken off the force."

"What is the rationale for that behavior?" Stokes asked, as if he didn't know, but wanted to confirm what he suspected.

"O'Neill is complaining we failed to protect him and his companions and wants us all to be replaced, says the Detective Chief Superintendent. The Chief is afraid he will be fired, so he did me the favor of throwing me under the bus."

As Stokes suspected, O'Neill was making his play, taking over the narrative so he could get what he wanted, making his enemies look weak and allies stronger, he the good guy surrounded by incompetents. He planned to confound his opponents by attacking them for their weakness and diverting the suspicion of his misdeeds.

"That means he is going to act soon. Look at it as your lucky day. It is good you are out of the picture, so you don't have any distractions by having to investigate other cases. How are your men in this?" Stokes asked.

"They're fine, but they took O'Neill's bodyguard, Garda

O'Connor, in on suspicion of murder of the Belgian. It was the same caliber gun that killed him and based on what was said in Monaghan's preliminary autopsy report. Ballistics has been working all weekend, but they haven't matched the bullets yet," Lanigan reported.

That confirmed Stoke's suspicion there was a big leak somewhere and too many people knew about the autopsy reports which should have been confidential until he had signed them, he thought.

"Are you going to be ready with your men? I hope you will have O'Neill followed every step today," Stokes warned.

"I hope you are figuring all this right. My job is on the line. Now you want me to rope my boys into unauthorized shenanigans."

"Oh, I'm right. This rogue needs to be prosecuted and jailed," said Stokes. "I will be calling the Chief Superintendent myself now, so stay calm."

"I'll concentrate on the paperwork on my desk, some distraction," he muttered and hung up.

Stokes immediately rang the Detective Chief Superintendent. He was busy on the phone, his secretary claimed, and said he would call right back. No doubt he was doing some damage control as well. It had not been going well for him or his boss and there were charges of incompetence up to the Deputy Commissioner and even the suspicion of intentional negligence by the Justice Minister. The whole Fianna Gael government could fall, ripe for O'Neill and his Fianna Fail party to take over, even as O'Neill was getting his sympathy press 'recuperating' in the hospital while coordinating his coup. He, unfortunately, had not been shot in the mouth, thought Stokes.

He was about to call the coroner, his least favorite colleague, when he got the call from the Detective Chief Superintendent. They had not had many conversations in the past, but he respected him as a no-nonsense and non-partisan official who did his job and was committed to getting at the truth and doing what was right.

"Hello Professor," he said without any further introduction. "I hear you think Dussault was a victim of one of my men. Are you sure about that?"

"No, just a conjecture. I did not do the autopsy myself; that was my junior pathologist, Dr. Monaghan, but I will review the case then give a final disposition when all the information has been gathered. I merely expressed the preliminary findings for expediency. I had no intention of implicating anyone without all the data. I think it was premature to arrest Garda O'Connor," said Stokes.

"Bad news travels fast. No doubt you have spoken to Lanigan. I put him on desk duty for his own protection. He has been sticking his nose where it doesn't belong once too often and there are a lot of blame-seekers lurking. Believe me, he will thank me in the end," he said.

"I'm sure you have the best of intentions, but what can I do for you?" Stokes asked, accepting the Chief Inspector's explanation, seeing no reason to make an appeal for Lanigan.

"Get that final report in as soon as possible. It is bad for morale to have a Garda on suspicion of murder, especially in these difficult times."

"I will have it finished soon. No report is final or definitive until I sign off on it," Stokes replied. He hated to implicate Monaghan in an error that could mean someone's being wrongly accused, but this was the perfect way to follow the trail of intelligence and separate the friends from the foes. He would put the Chief Inspector in the friendly camp. It also meant O'Connor, a nasty character in any case, would be neutralized so he could not protect O'Neill from any conspiracies against him.

He called Dermot Murphy, the Coroner, back. Stokes knew it would be Murphy's intent to protect his own skin at all costs. He would be happy to offer up Stokes as a sacrifice, if that's what it took. Besides, he was a staunch Fianna Fail party man and it would not go well for him if he went up against O'Neill, even if he didn't like him very much. In fact, there were a good number of party members who didn't like O'Neill very much, but O'Neill had a large inventory of favors to bestow or threats to use against any one of them. He'd been gathering them for years.

"Are you sure O'Connor shot your man?" Murphy asked.

"No. As I said, Dr. Monaghan did the autopsy and I signed off on the preliminary to expedite matters. I will review the case today."

"I have had enough of these conspiracies. Let's get to the bottom of this quickly. O'Neill is pressuring all of us. He has been shot at twice and has the whole Justice Ministry to blame, so you better pull your finger out."

"Would you like to come over and do this yourself?" Stokes challenged. He knew that despite his title, Murphy was the most squeamish of characters—even in medical school he fainted at the sight of blood. How he got through. Stokes never knew. But that was the past and now he was Stokes' superior, so it was 'yes sir' and 'no sir', within limits. He had just pushed that limit, but the silence on the other end of the phone gave him his answer.

"As I said, I should be able to give you an answer later today."

"Fair enough. I will be in the office all day," he replied and hung up.

Stokes decided he would warn Monaghan he had pointed her in the wrong direction when he asked her to dictate her inaccurate findings. He would wait, however, until the end of the day since he needed this to play out and see if any of the other characters would show their hands. He did not want her to get more upset than she was. She had been reprimanded, but he was afraid her confession did not mean her Mossad handlers had left her off the hook.

Chapter Forty

"O'Neill has signed himself out of the hospital against doctors' orders," Lanigan reported to Stokes not much later that day. Lanigan had his Garda connections who had let him know as soon as it happened.

"Well, we know he will be recuperating at home, good enough excuse for him to be in his element without prying eyes. I would alert your men to take their posts at sunset since the place will be crawling with reporters for the rest of the day until they have to post their stories for the evening papers," Stokes directed.

"What is your man, 'The Pink Panther,' going to do?" Lanigan asked.

"Cloudot, you mean? Keep to the plan we discussed. I would say it is best not to know more than you need. That goes for your men as well. Just have them keep an eye out. No heroics."

He did not mention Smyth-Jones and his men, but he had no clue about what he would be doing either. He guessed Tony was poised to move when the exchange had occurred, and he could safely capture the Jackal without any detection by or discussion with the Irish government.

Stokes told Lanigan to convince any of the additional Gardai who were assigned as O'Neill's guard, to mistrust the man whom they were protecting (that would not be a hard job—most of them loathed O'Neill as much as Lanigan) but not to let them know any more than things could be suddenly unpredictable. Lanigan understood and accepted.

"I will have some reinforcements for you, but I can't tell you how or when, but I will be supporting you."

"Right, then. I will be watching and warn my men to take care. We've had enough of feeding you customers."

"Good luck, Seamus," Stokes said and hung up.

Stokes edited his dictation on the Brennan autopsy. He would leave it up to ballistics to append their report when it was ready. For the moment, he left Samantha's autopsy report on Dussault unchanged.

"You can send out the Brennan autopsy report to the coroner. I have not signed off on Dr. Monaghan's report on Dussault for now. It needs some changes," Stokes directed his secretary.

Stokes considered what to do next. He did truly want to participate in the capture of O'Neill in the midst of an incriminating act, but he was worried about the risk his presence would do to alert O'Neill that he was part of a plot. He would have to stay away and use Lanigan as his surrogate, the same strategy O'Neill had used for years to appear innocent despite all his associates and cohorts succumbing to capture, prosecution or, at the least, accusation and disgrace. Lanigan was taking a chance as well, but he was willing and accepted the possible cost. He had already suffered innocent ignominy.

Stokes called the French Embassy again and spoke to the receptionist. She at last recognized his voice and was tolerant rather than annoyed. He was wondering if roses might help, but discounted the idea, hoping that soon he would not have to talk to her at all. It was a cumbersome arrangement, but at least he got relatively prompt call-backs from Cloudot if he called before the hour.

"He needs to call back as soon as possible since we need to act on an issue this evening," Stokes emphasized.

"I will let him know. You will be at your office?" she asked. She did not need his number since it had been promoted to her shortlist of frequent callers.

"Yes," he answered. Stokes looked at his clock. It was just before 11 AM, so he expected he would be called back on the hour or so. She promptly bid au revoir and hung up. What, he wondered, was Cloudot doing besides handling this hunt for the Jackal and why was he really never in the office? Surely, he must have other duties, Stokes thought, but he did not have time to speculate. He just hoped he had a real plan and would follow through on their plot.

Cloudot did call back promptly after eleven. He said he was rounding up some operatives who would be available after 6 PM.

"Who are these people?" Stokes asked.

"It is best you do not know —the less any one part of the operation knows, the safer it will be," Cloudot responded.

"Can I tell Lanigan?" Stokes pressed.

"No," answered Cloudot. "He will be back-up. We may not even need him if my plan works," Cloudot insisted, soundings irritated.

"Is there anything I can do?"

"No. I will let you know when the plan is completed. You must be patient."

Stokes had gone all this way with the cloak and dagger enterprise and now he felt left out. Leave it to the professionals, he advised himself. After all, you would leave your surgery to a surgeon, wouldn't you? he reasoned, mumbling to himself. Still, he was surprised the logistics of this plan had not been fully plotted out and Lanigan and Cloudot had not discussed this fully. How would Lanigan know? How would Cloudot know?

"Well. Let's meet again. I want to make sure everything is covered," Stokes insisted. "Let's meet at Toner's in an hour. I have some more information for you I don't want to discuss on the phone," Stokes said.

There was a pause from Cloudot. Stokes was suspicious of his hesitancy. Perhaps it was just spy craft, being cautious, Stokes thought, giving Cloudot the benefit of the doubt.

"All right then, but this is a very delicate operation. The fewer people know, the better. Au Revoir," Cloudot said and hung up.

Stokes called Lanigan again.

"My boys are ready; all I have to do is give them a call to meet me at the Estate," Lanigan said. "I'm going to take a 'lunch break' so we can meet."

"Cloudot seems reluctant. He has told me it is a 'secret mission,' and he can't be seen at the office. He calls to check on his messages and arranges meetings outside. I suppose he is afraid of a mole or an informer," Stokes speculated, "but I still think we need to get together."

"Have you ever seen him in his office?" Lanigan asked simply, unlike his usual circumlocutions.

"No, just outside," Stokes replied after a pause.

"So, we're meeting him outside of the Embassy?" Lanigan asked.

"Yes, Toner's, since he knows the place," Stokes said.

"Grand, I know it well," said Lanigan. "I'll call you when I get there."

Stokes dealt with some administrative details so that if he left abruptly, they would not be left until tomorrow. He did not want someone catching him out as derelict in his duties. He was specifically thinking of the coroner, who would be happy to play the blame game if anything were amiss. Well, there was nothing amiss, but he decided to at least have Samantha cover for him. He went to her office where she was busy doing her pile of paperwork, larger in volume but lesser on a scale of importance and more tedious, which was the unenviable burden of her position.

"I will be going out this afternoon, probably sooner rather than later, and will not return through the evening, so cover for me since I know there still will be numerous inquiries. Just tell them what we know so far, the less the better. I will rely on your ignorance to convey the truth," he smiled.

"Have you signed off on Dussault's autopsy report yet?" she asked, still bothered by its inaccuracy.

"Not as yet. There are some crucial points that need revision, but I will speak about that with you tomorrow. That is all you need to know."

"Very well, then," she smiled. Perhaps I will be able to earn his confidence again, she thought, then reminded herself he just had delegated her to be spokesperson, which must mean something, even if she was to bear the brunt of any and all inquiries.

Chapter Forty-One

Stokes got the call from Lanigan—he was on his way to Toner's. It was just past lunch and there would be the anonymity of a crowded place to mask their conversation, although it might be hard to hear each other above the din. Stokes took a bus that dropped him nearby, just off the Green and the Shelbourne. He walked the rest of the way down Baggot Street and met Lanigan at the door. Stokes saw Cloudot on a bench in the snug, less noisy than the lounge, and good enough for the meeting. Cloudot was visibly surprised to see Stokes enter with Lanigan but smiled after his momentary discomfiture and waved them over.

"Detective Lanigan thought he might be helpful to you," Stokes explained, and Lanigan nodded in agreement, shaking Cloudot's moist warm hand.

"Stokes and I have followed this thing all the way through, after all," Lanigan explained.

"There is some element of danger to this," Cloudot warned.

"I am prepared," Stokes nodded.

"Well, this is my plan. I will contact O'Neill later this afternoon posing as the Jackal and arrange to meet him this evening. I expect he will be eager to transfer the money and get this shipment out of the way," Cloudot proposed.

"How are you going to get him to trust you?" Lanigan asked.

"I know who he needs to contact in Antwerp, and I will call them. They are part of Dussault's gang there. We have been watching them for some time —they know me as an associate," Cloudot explained.

"Lucky for you that you have played the long game, then; the other players dead leave you the cock of the roost," Lanigan noted, not flatteringly and not caring if this 'frog' didn't know what he was talking about.

Cloudot was cool enough to ignore the comment, out of ignorance or indifference. It was his plan, and he would follow through on it, as long as the Irish did not interfere. He did not care that he was operating as a foreign agent on their sovereign soil and even if Lanigan or Stokes were to say anything, it would look worse for them since they would be accusing a powerful former minister of misdeeds and spying on him without permission or support.

"We should be going," he said, not interested in any more small talk and irritated by the detective's tone.

"Hold on, what is your plan? I think we need to know a wee bit more," Lanigan pressed.

"You will guard the outside of the Mansion to make sure no one interferes with the transaction. Once I get the money, voila, on my signal, you will appear. I will leave with the bag; you can do what you want with O'Neill but give me time enough to leave. Convince O'Neill to cooperate—offer full immunity and anonymity. He will call the real Jackal's accomplices to tell them there has been a change of plan. With Dussault dead, O'Neill will say he had to give the money to me, his agent. The Jackal must be told he has no choice but to meet me as O'Neill's courier in Antwerp or the deal and the money are gone. O'Neill will call his IRA colleagues in Antwerp to confirm the plans have changed and he is sending me to take the money there. The Jackal's people in Antwerp, whom we know from our spies, will confirm the money transfer and release the arms to the IRA, expecting the Jackal to meet them. We will capture the Jackal and his colleagues and the IRA smugglers. Is that a plan?" Cloudot offered.

"How do you know O'Neill will go along with this?" asked Stokes.

"If you are there, how can he refuse?" Cloudot responded, looking at Lanigan whose face showed no enthusiasm. Cloudot thought he might want to play poker with this policeman sometime—it would be easy to win.

"With all this money around, he might want to protect it with some guns and friends," Lanigan warned.

"That is the risk we must take, mon ami," he smiled.

Lanigan swallowed down his pint. "Our risk, your glory," he pointed out.

"Surely you will be back in the good light with such a capture," Cloudot encouraged.

"Or in jail or shot for attempted extortion of a politician. I am not authorized to do any more than sit at my desk right now," Lanigan said.

"Espionage is always at the frontier of the law, mon ami," Cloudot said.

"Right. What time are the fireworks?" Lanigan asked.

"Be there before sundown to check the neighborhood, plant your men and watch for danger. I will light a cigarette at the window when the deal is done," Cloudot answered, finished his own Guinness with the same face of what Stokes could not mistake for distaste. "Bon chance and Au revoir," said Cloudot and stood up and left the pub.

Lanigan ran to the window, stumbling between some chairs in his haste and getting some jeers at his clumsiness, but got there in time to watch Cloudot get in his car and drive off, noting the make, model, and license plate of the car. He stood there for a moment before turning back to Stokes.

"Do you still want to be part of this adventure?" he asked Stokes.

"What did you just see?" Stokes asked, unsure of the reason for Lanigan's frenetic observation.

"He has Belfast plates. Why would he have Belfast plates?" Lanigan asked himself out loud. He went over to the phone, made a phone call and repeated the license plate he saw, then waited. "Yes," he said, "that's right. When you find out, meet me at the chip shop near the road to Kinsealy in an hour. No, I won't be at the station any more today. Me ma is sick. Bring guns and don't forget mine," he said, and hung up.

"What is going on?" Stokes asked again.

"This all stinks," he observed nervously. "This frog and his story stinks. We don't have much choice but to find out for ourselves, do we?" Lanigan paused. "One more chance, Professor, are you with me?"

"In for a penny, in for a pound," Stokes answered.

Stokes and Lanigan got into his car and Lanigan drove in the direction of the estate.

"Would you mind explaining yourself?" Stokes demanded,

"He is no cop. Did he ever show you his badge? What did your man in the sombrero say in the "Treasure of the Sierra Madre?": "We don't need no stinkin' bloody badges," he said. And how many times did he see you in his office in the French Embassy? Bloody zero? He is trying to pull a fast one on O'Neill and us and get away with all the money," Lanigan said.

"If this is true, how do you plan on stopping him?" asked Stokes.

"We will follow his plan and be there to help, but not," Lanigan said.

"You will need more backup than your two men," Stokes pointed out.

"They will be enough. You don't expect O'Neill is going to let Cloudot walk off with the money without batting an eye, do you now?" Lanigan asked.

"So, you will recruit O'Neill's men?" Stokes asked.

"No, O'Neill will give his orders and we will help along as official Gardai with your help," Lanigan answered.

"There will have to be a lot of fast talking," Stokes observed.

"That's where you will come in. He is more likely to believe you than me. You can't arrest him, and you won't have a gun. No threat. It won't be hard. He wants his money and reputation—the rest be damned," Lanigan pointed out.

"Surely, you must be joking. On what pretext will I be there? I am no policeman."

"You can say you are there to complete the deal. He will listen to you, trust me—he loves deals. He is a politician."

Stokes paused for a moment to consider the situation. "Right, then. I will boldly walk in and work this out," Stokes said, already thinking about how he would avoid being shot by anyone, including Cloudot or whoever he was and how preposterous this plan was. "Are you serious?"

"I think your pal Cloudot is not who he says he is, and we will need you to make it look like he is still fooling you so you can help him complete the job," Lanigan said. "It will slow him down enough so we can find out if he is the real thing or not."

"You're still putting me between the crossfire if things go wrong."

"Relax, there will be five of us, my men and the assigned Gardai who I am sure I can convince, and either Cloudot or O'Neill against us. Whoever is the bigger liar and thief, we will know soon enough," Lanigan said.

"What about the men Cloudot claims to have?"

"He's bluffing, but we'll keep a watch out."

"I hope you are right," Stokes said, as the car stopped.

Chapter Forty-Two

They had arrived near the chip shop and parked on the corner, waiting in the car for Lanigan's men. The weather had changed, and it was darker and blustery. Not a good evening for hiding out, Lanigan thought, but he had been caught in worse weather. He thought of Cloudot's plan and expected he would leave as soon as he had given the signal for them to show up, so he would wait outside the window instead and have his men guard the doors. He was worried O'Neill would have men guarding the grounds as well, so they would have to be careful to have them "convinced" before the arranged meeting time, the earlier the better. He was expecting Cloudot would be alone and armed.

There was not much Stokes or Lanigan wanted to talk about, sitting in the car. They watched as children went in and out of the chip shop to spoil their tea with ice cream, candy, and chips. That was how kids were. That's how Lanigan was, and his kids were, if they had an extra penny or two, if they ever did. His children were grown and gone to England or America. He never had the strength or opportunity to leave and was comfortable enough where he was, thanks, he thought.

"Are you comfortable using a gun?" Lanigan asked Stokes, breaking the silence as they waited for his men.

"I would rather not."

"Fair enough," Lanigan said, expecting the answer. Wouldn't it be just grand to just finish this without firing a shot? he thought to himself again.

"We have a spare if you need it. I would advise you to carry it, just as a precaution. I don't expect O'Neill to do anything fancy, but his men, if they are there, might think otherwise," Lanigan said.

"I will keep that in mind, thanks," Stokes replied.

Hayes and Cunningham pulled up behind their car. Hayes got out of the passenger seat, looked at the chip shop, pointed as he walked to Lanigan's side and leaned into the window.

"Do you fancy any chips, boss? It might be a long wait, don't you know," Hayes said, smiling.

"Forget the shagging chips. We have a job to do. Get Cunningham over here," Lanigan said. "Hayes always has this nervous hunger coming over him before an operation," Lanigan explained to Stokes. Hayes motioned for Cunningham to come over and Lanigan opened his window wider.

"Get my gun and get the spare for the Professor, just in case. Then we will wait in the cars to view the Mansion gate until there is some activity. Hayes, watch the Mansion from the trees near the stable for anyone else camping outside or near and report back to us. No contact. We don't want to alert the bastards that we are here. If you see the blue Cortina with the Belfast plates, come anywhere in but the front drive, get back here pronto. Otherwise, stay put, keep an eye out for visitors," he ordered. "We go in when he goes in, as long as it is clear, understood?"

They both nodded. Hayes walked past the chip shop with a sidelong glance but kept on moving down an alley that ran along the trees of the estate and some houses that bordered it. Cunningham went back to the car and moved it to an alley opposite for a good view of the entrance road to the Mansion. Lanigan did the same in another alley.

Cloudot arrived not long after. Lanigan wondered why the delay; it did not take more than a half hour to get there from the pub in Dublin to the Mansion. The gates were open, prepared for any visitors. There was no one else in the car with him and no other cars arrived. He could see as he got out of the car to talk to the two special Gardai who were at the front door with automatic weapons at the ready that he had changed his clothes, however.

Lanigan suspected Cloudot had gathered up what he needed for a quick getaway. He had the urge to confront him right there and search him for a new passport and tickets to somewhere, but he controlled himself. Cloudot was greeted at the door by O'Neill himself, who must have reassured the Gardai there was no danger. After a brief conversation, Cloudot got back in the car and drove it around the driveway at the side of the house near the Guest House.

Meanwhile, O'Neill returned to the study and went to the drawer next to a large painting and pulled out a gun. He checked the magazine. There were three bullets missing. He hurriedly placed three more bullets in, not caring who had discharged the gun. He swung open the painting with the safe behind it, placed the gun in a bag in the safe and closed it before Cloudot was called in.

"Time to get out —he has parked himself," Lanigan told Stokes. Stokes just nodded. He had kept his eye on the moving car as it made its way slowly along the gravel road and was hidden behind the mansion.

"Time to move in," Lanigan said, handing Stokes a gun and putting his own in his pocket. He left the car where it was and motioned Stokes to follow. They moved quickly towards the side of the Estate near the Guest House and Cunningham, seeing them, got out of his car and walked to the opposite side near the stables. It was getting darker. They did not see anyone besides the Gardai but were not seen by them. They were attending to their posts, more alert with the arrival of Cloudot.

As soon as Cloudot was escorted through the front door by O'Neill and the door was closed, Lanigan and Stokes strode up the path to the front door. Lanigan flashed his detective badge and explained who Stokes was and pointed out Hayes and Cunningham on either side. The Gardai nodded. They were probably not O'Neill's special men, since they accepted Lanigan's explanation without question. Lanigan suspected there were others who might arrive who would not be so easy to convince.

"Be on the lookout for suspicious characters," Lanigan warned the Gardai, pointing to Hayes and Cunningham in strategic positions in the bushes. He told them he and Stokes would wait behind the house, out of sight and O'Neill needn't be informed since this was for his own protection. The Gardai shot glances at each other, but neither made any protest, so Lanigan and Stokes made their way around to the back of the house, making sure they were not seen through any windows. From a distance through the window, with his binoculars, Lanigan saw O'Neill and Cloudot standing in the study in front of a large painting depicting Brian Boru at the Battle of Clontarf. Stokes recognized the painting as a probable copy of the original and smiled at the irony that Boru was an enemy of the ancient O'Neills. Neither of them could hear what O'Neill and Cloudot were saying. They waited for the cigarette to be lit as their sign to move, but the talking went on, like a negotiation.

"They are taking too much time at this," Stokes whispered.

"I don't think Cloudot is telling him what we discussed. He may be warning him," Lanigan responded, ready to pounce if he needed, but waited.

O'Neill walked to his desk and picked up the phone and dialed. Cloudot looked on. It was a short conversation. O'Neill hung up and looked at Cloudot and swung the painting aside on its hinge to reveal the wall safe and opened it. He pulled out the large duffel bag with his left hand his right arm still in a sling. He put the bag on the desk.

"O'Neill made a call, but Cloudot has not given us a signal. What is he up to?" Lanigan asked Stokes, more to himself, but out loud.

"O'Neill has shown Cloudot the bag of money. Cloudot knows we are watching. Perhaps he is making a deal with O'Neill," Stokes said, still hoping Cloudot was a policeman.

"If he is, then Cloudot needs to call Antwerp to arrest O'Neill's contacts and we need to be there to witness this," Lanigan said. They watched. There was no movement from Cloudot to use the phone. He did not light a cigarette as planned.

O'Neill was still standing at the duffel bag and clumsily opened it. He pulled the gun out of the bag with his left hand. Cloudot grabbed it out of his hand and grabbed the bag with one quick motion. O'Neill gave a yelp as he fell on his right shoulder. Lanigan moved towards the French doors, followed by Stokes.

They were suddenly in the dark. O'Neill got up quickly, cursing and yelling for help as he put the lights back on.

"He's in the tunnel," yelled O'Neill, pointing to the open secret door in his study.

As quickly as he had burst through the French doors, Lanigan turned around and ran along the back, towards the side of the Guest House to where Cloudot's car was parked, hoping to cut him off. He yelled for Hayes who appeared from out of the bushes and rapidly moved along the side of the house, his gun drawn. Cunningham and the Gardai were running on the opposite side of the house to block the exit on the other side of the circular driveway. Lanigan and Hayes approached it, torches on, guns drawn. The car was empty. Cloudot was gone.

"He must be on foot. Surround the Estate exits," Lanigan ordered as he opened the boot of the car. All that was there was a suitcase and a Carcano rifle. Stokes had joined him, waving a torch into the bushes.

"He couldn't have gotten far," Stokes said, walking gingerly to the hedges that lined the back of the house and the cliffs to the sea beyond.

O'Neill had walked to the back and watched the waves in the distance, shaking visibly, more with anger than with cold. "There are steps down to the beach. That's where he has gone, you fools" he bellowed. Lanigan, Stokes, and Hayes ran along the walk to the steps and heard the sound of a motorboat as it moved rapidly in the dark out into the Irish sea.

"I will alert the Water Unit," Hayes said, running back to the house.

"You can bloody well call the Navy and the Air Corps as well," O'Neill yelled sarcastically over the sound of the waves.

"You had best come in to answer some questions," Lanigan said calmly to O'Neill. Hayes dialed the Gardai Water Unit and described the fugitive boat and passenger.

"You had best call your Chief Superintendent," O'Neill said.

"Listen, your lordship, you were caught holding a duffel bag full of cash. At the least you were robbed of your own money, but considering you personally opened the door to this Frenchman with witnesses watching, this looks like a deal gone bad about a bunch of money that you extorted from patriotic Irishmen to *help* their families in the North," Lanigan said.

"You have no right to enter my home without a search warrant. I will not say any more without my solicitor," he said, folding his arm over his bad one, glowering.

"I have every right under the Offenses Against the State Act. I have good information this money was to be used for arms for the IRA, just like you tried before."

"You will have to prove that in a court of law. In the meantime, I will have you suspended by the Chief Superintendent for unauthorized policing and surveillance. As for you, Professor," he said, nodding at Stokes, "you will be sued for trespassing on my property since you are no policeman."

Stokes did not say a word, but smiled grimly at this pompous, arrogant politician whom he loathed intensely.

"That is quite enough," Lanigan said, not willing to lose his temper over any more of O'Neill's protestations. "You are coming down to Harcourt Street to sort this out. Be sure to bring that gun as evidence. We can check if it is registered," he said to Hayes and Cunningham.

O'Neill's staff watched as he was escorted out the door by the detectives and Gardai, who were no longer needed at his Estate. There were neither cheers nor jeers, just knowing nods and slight sighs of relief they were not going to have to accompany their employer just now.

O'Neill did not stay at Harcourt Street for long. One of his solicitors promptly presented themselves at An Garda Siochana Headquarters and demanded O'Neill's release on his own recognizance. The Chief Superintendent himself suggested that O'Neill might need to stay under protective custody, but O'Neill declined the offer. The Chief advised he would not be able to provide any protection if he left, but O'Neill just bellowed he would get his own bloody bodyguards since a fat lot of protection the Gardai had provided. The Superintendent did not apologize for the arrest. O'Neill was advised he would be called again to aid with inquiries.

"Our money was stolen, and you are threatening me?" O'Neill shouted at the Chief. "I will have your job and you will be 'inquiring' under stones in Connemara!" he railed; his solicitor barely able to restrain him.

"You will have your day in court," the Chief responded calmly and walked away, not wanting to jeopardize his own position with an equal and similar outburst.

Lanigan watched the spectacle with amusement but kept the triumphant smirk off his face. He finally knew when to shut up.

Chapter Forty-Three

Stokes had left for home. He expected his job was done for now. He felt very tired, washed out, unable to concentrate on anything, and relished the remainder of an evening of a modest quiet meal, a boiled egg and toast perhaps, a good read, and a decent night's sleep. *The Third Policeman* by Flann O'Brien had been sitting on his bookshelf and he had meant to pick it up so often. He even contemplated a sabbatical or, at the least, a holiday in Galway or Dingle. That is how tired he was. He fell asleep easily, eschewing a glass of sherry since he was drowsy enough and did not want to oversleep. He set his alarm for fear of not waking in time for work, unusual for him since his circadian rhythm was quite set, but just as a precaution.

He needn't have feared—he rose at his usual hour and made ready for work. Mrs. Kelly had quietly let herself in and prepared breakfast. He had left the message not to come in the night before, so she indulged herself by going to a film that evening in the middle of the week. She saw the "Black Windmill," a spy thriller and was very pleased the cinema was not very crowded. She was so relaxed in the morning that she was chattier than usual and recommended the film to him, describing the plot and the stars, but was discreet enough not to reveal the ending.

"You should be going out more, Professor. It would do you good. Just the cinema or theater, leave your troubles at the door," she smiled encouragingly, placing the rack of buttered toast and the tea in front of him. Stokes put his paper down for a second, just to acknowledge her suggestion, and smiled pleasantly back at her.

"Thanks, I just might do that," he replied and went back to scanning the paper for any news of last night's adventure. Too early yet, he thought, which was fair enough since there would be more than one periodical that would magnify and expand the incident for days or even months to come. He flipped over the page to the latest films playing, then perused the directory of plays and concerts being performed. The latest Peter Sellers comedy had just come out in Dublin, "Soft Beds, Hard Battles," a farce about the absurdity of war. He decided he would see that. He had enough of thrillers for a while, life being thrilling enough. He felt some of the weight off already. He would be able to handle the office a bit better today, now that the culprits were under close surveillance or out of his sphere. He did not feel guilty on that last part— he was not a policeman and hated politics. He enjoyed the logic of science and puzzles of medicine. He would get through the day with the thought this was all behind him, back to the usual, dependably satisfying work.

He walked into the office and expected routine. Instead, he got two messages, one from the French Embassy and the other from Murphy, the Coroner. The Embassy was inquiring about the completion of the autopsy report of the French woman who had died in the bombing. The coroner wanted to see him in his offices. He asked his secretary if anything was pressing, he needed to handle while he was in. She said it was quiet today.

"Do you have a copy of the autopsy report of the French woman?" he asked. She popped up and pulled it from the file.

"Please be so kind as to make a Xerox of it. I'm sorry, but I will have to deliver it to the French Embassy myself. It was lost in translation, no pun intended," he smiled. She made the copies, and he went back to his desk and called the Embassy himself, wanting to make sure he could certify the authenticity of the communication. He was surprised by the quick answer after only two rings. It must be a slow day, he thought. The voice of the receptionist on the other end was already too familiar and she responded with a smile of recognition in her voice.

"I would like to finish this as expeditiously as possible and bring the document over myself, so could you make the police liaison available, please?" he asked.

"You mean Inspector Cloudot? He is not available. He did not call in today," she responded.

"So, who would be responsible in his stead?" asked Stokes.

"That would be the military attaché, Capt. LaFarge," she said. "He is quite upset by the extra work he has been having to do with Inspector Cloudot on his special assignment," she said, sounding as irritated, in support of the Captain.

"Is he there?"

"Yes, he is."

"I would like to come right over, if that is all right with him."

"I will transfer your call to his office. Hold on, please," she said with a click.

Stokes hoped the click did not mean the usual disconnection that would prompt another set of conversations, but he was able to speak to the captain after a brief interlude that allowed him to formulate some questions.

"I submitted all the forms for Inspector Cloudot to forward. Where are they?" Stokes asked.

"What forms?" the captain asked.

"Copies of the autopsy report and the parts of the details that were requested on the French documents I could not decipher. Inspector Cloudot kindly offered to fill out the rest for me," Stokes answered.

"You have seen him? He has been on his 'special assignment' for at least three weeks. It has been difficult for me to do his job and mine as well," the captain protested.

"I can well understand. Did you actually speak to him in the past three weeks?" Stokes asked.

"No, only our receptionist, playing with the pager whenever he was needed," the captain complained.

"I will be down there promptly. By the way, do you have any photos of Inspector Cloudot?" Stokes asked.

"I will check. There should be at least one in his personnel file. I was never very close with him. The Surete did not give me much help when I complained of his absence and my having to do his duties. Do you have any information that can explain this?" he asked.

"Perhaps I can. I will be right over," Stokes told his secretary. He would be out on business and would call the coroner back when he returned, making a perceptibly irritated face as he left.

The receptionist at the Embassy picked up the phone and called the captain as soon as Stokes arrived. The captain, in uniform and epaulets and name tag with his picture dangling from a lanyard seemed the real thing. He escorted Stokes up the wide and winding marble steps to his office with his name stenciled on the opaque glass door. Why Stokes had not previously noticed all the irregularities during the meetings with Cloudot, or whoever he was, in the ~~past,~~ it was clear to Stokes that he had made a lot of mistakes. The Captain picked up the copy of the requested report, sat down, and ~~scanned~~ looked at it.

"Is it usual for a death of a French citizen abroad to be reported to the French police?" Stokes asked.

"No," Captain LaFarge answered, "that would go directly to the Embassy's staff then details would be sent to the police in Paris. If the death was suspicious, then the authorities in the country would be asked to submit the forwarded forms and we would leave it to them to do the police work."

"So normally, you would not have your police do an investigation?"

"No. That would be your police people's job. Only if there were questions would it be reviewed and our police involved." Lafarge paused a moment. "Was Cloudot on this case?"

"That was what he said, although I am not sure he was Cloudot. Do you have his photo?"

"Here it is, from the personnel file," LaFarge passed the photo over to Stokes. The picture he was looking at looked nothing like the person he had had dealings with. This man was thin with a very pale face and bald, somewhere in his fifties, not olive complexioned, in his late thirties, with short dark curly hair like his 'Cloudot.'

"Who investigates terrorists?" Stokes asked.

"Do you think Cloudot is a terrorist?" the captain asked, surprised at the question.

"I think the man who posed as Cloudot is a terrorist. Who should I report this to?" Stokes asked.

"That would be me, for now. I will call the Surete to let them know Cloudot is missing. Why didn't you let us know sooner?" the captain asked, irritated.

"I didn't know until yesterday," surprised at the question since he could also ask why no one had noticed Cloudot's strangely absent behavior for the past month, but, diplomatically, he did not. "Do you know of the Jackal?" Stokes asked.

"We have been searching for him for years."

"He may be headed for Antwerp, perhaps by boat or via England by plane," Stokes replied. He wasn't planning on doing any trips or pursuing any terrorists and was just conveying information.

"Here is the autopsy report of the French woman who was killed here in the bombing. I have completed my job. Good luck on your finding Cloudot, the real one, I mean. You can reach me at my offices if you need any more help," Stokes offered, hoping not to be taken up on it.

Stokes hurried for the door, to avoid any more extracurricular activities. He steeled himself for an encounter with the coroner, who would yell and scream and whine and threaten, he was sure, then ask for his help so he would not be implicated in any wrongdoing.

He stopped by the office again to make sure there weren't any other messages before he took the walk next door to the office of the coroner. It was yet another call—this was from Smyth-Jones. He wanted to meet him for drinks at the Gresham. At least it wasn't dinner, he thought to himself, recalling the awful meal he had not eaten. Perhaps this was good news since drinks would imply a shorter meeting. He would wait to call Mrs. Kelly later to cancel tea and take his chances for a short meeting. He walked over to Samantha's office and peered in. She was busy with her notes but looked up and smiled. He smiled back.

"I'm over to the coroner to have a little friendly discussion. I will keep you out of it, then we will have to do a review of our last few days since this mess will require more testimony and a coherent story in the near future, I would expect. No other pressing business?"

"No, Professor. We're good here. Good luck," Samantha smiled.

"See you later, then," he smiled back.

The coroner was on the phone when Stokes entered his office and pointed for him to sit as he nodded and said 'yes, minister' many times and nodded more, unseen by the minister who was providing a continuous barrage of what seemed to Stokes, uncomfortable information or opinion. Stokes waited patiently, expecting to receive the same discussion in person.

The coroner finally hung up, stroked his furrowed brow, and looked at Stokes, not in anger, but supplication.

"I'm bloody fucked," he said to Stokes and took a deep breath.

"I have no choice but to resign. It will all go on me, from the Minister and the Chief Superintendent. The wind will be blowing through the offices and only the most ignorant or the most loyal will be left. As far as I can tell, Stokes, you are the acting Coroner," he blurted.

"I don't want the job. I am happy with my position. Calm down, you have done nothing wrong, Dermot," said Stokes, one of the few times he addressed Murphy by his Christian name. At that moment, he was attempting to be collegial since it was obvious he was a person in need of friends even if Stokes did not really consider him one and vice versa.

"O'Neill got his "get out of jail free" card, but that won't last, and his former friends are disappearing into the woodwork. Any member of Fianna Fail needs to watch their back and I'm certainly on that list, civil bloody servant or not," he despaired.

"Well, I will do my best to support you. You weren't part of this mess. You were just doing your job. O'Neill was caught as he should have been and all you need to do is hold fast as the good Civil Servant you are. Don't quit. I don't want your job," Stokes reiterated.

"Don't patronize me," Murphy snapped. You may lose *your* job with the body and the evidence disappearing and you and your assistant showing up in all those places where more people got killed, so it may not come down on me at all. You certainly have made an enemy of O'Neill and you have dragged me into it, your superior. There are a lot of people out there wanting to 'clean up the mess,' as they say, and they will be making you and me the mess," he said, sitting down in the chair, stroking his brow again.

Stokes had seen this passive-aggressive behavior in Murphy before. He felt cornered and was lashing out again, blaming Stokes for everything that was going on. He took a deep breath so he would not say anything he would regret later.

"Sit tight, there is nothing more you need to do. I have all the reports and I am ready to present them. They will see this was a major conspiracy with O'Neill at the soft and rotten center. The truth will come out, trust me," Stokes said as confidently as he could muster.

"Be warned, you may yet become the coroner, even just acting, but I will watch and wait. Get that report to me by tomorrow. We need to wrap this up," the coroner said, resuming his business approach, with his usual impatience and failure to understand proof is slower than speculation.

"I will do my best," Stokes promised, not committing to anything more, and left. He walked back to the office and called the ballistics lab.

"Have you got any more on the bullets from the Carcano?" he asked the lab technician, a very precise and rigid fellow who was easily irritated and overwhelmed if pressed.

"Not quite yet, but the bullets from the gun that shot the Belgian are not the bullets from the Garda's gun, same caliber and probably same make pistol, a Browning, but not the same gun," he said firmly.

"Are you sure?" Stokes asked, which he realized was a mistake as soon as he asked it.

"Are you questioning my competence?" the technician bristled.

"No, no, of course not, merely confused—then we have another culprit who has escaped. We don't have the gun. Have you run through the guns and bullets from the other Garda?" Stokes asked, knowing that would be another irritating question.

"Of course not. Why don't we just disarm the whole lot and put them all in jail for questioning? I have more work to do. Have your detectives finish the job of detecting," he said, hanging up.

Stokes did not bother calling back to berate the technician for his insolence, since he was an implacable civil servant. He would let it rest and give him time. Stokes could submit his reports and let the investigators follow up on the ballistics He would settle for the best possible outcome under the circumstances: at least O'Neill was implicated.

Stokes went into Samantha's office where she was intent on completing her reports.

"I have given some thought to the autopsy on Dussault. I reviewed your notes and the photos and what I recalled, and I think he was shot in the back and not the front, but as close an eyewitness as you were, did you recall any Garda behind you in the melee?" he asked her.

"No. I'm sure they were all in front of me or at least to the sides and not behind," she responded, hoping not to have to answer the question he was formulating.

"Did you see anyone in the Guest House? That is the most likely direction the shots came from with the distance and the damage done. Could that be the only point that made sense?" he asked and answered himself.

"No, there was no one in the Guest House I saw," she said, which was true. She did not mention the note, but thought it had to be Rami who shot Dussault as soon as she saw his note in her handbag. She did not say anything since Stokes was upset enough with her "secret agenting." Besides, the note did not say he did it, just that she had completed her mission.

"Very well, then. I will have the secretary type the corrected report and you can sign it and I will co-sign it and we will send it off and leave it to others to make what they need of it, understood?" he said, emphasizing-any further investigation or speculation was neither his nor her job.

"Yes, Professor, I will get on it now," she said, shuffling around her desk for the original report she had dictated, which was perfect as far as she was concerned. She was glad she had not torn it up, which was her first impulse when he had ordered her to "correct" her dictation.

Stokes did not linger. He was intent on straightening out his part of the process so no further questions could be made of his integrity and the appropriateness of his recent activities, though he, if he were his own superior, would have fired himself outright for deviation from his prescribed duties. He was also given a 'get out of jail free card' since the coroner was in no position to make such charges, being under the gun himself. He expected Lanigan was in a similar position, but his Chief was more likely to get the ax than him. It might happen after all the evidence was discovered but would take some time. Still, getting his house in order now would be better than later.

Having done all his messages, Stokes thought of poor Lanigan and his precarious position. There was not much he could do to help, but since he knew exactly where he was, he called to reassure him that he would do what he could.

"How are you getting on with the turmoil?" Stokes asked.

"Grand, if you like sitting at a desk waiting for the hangman to call your turn," Lanigan answered.

"There are far more important people than you who may be dangling in the breeze soon enough. I will give you all the support I can. There are still a number of questions that have not been answered and with O'Neill the most conspicuous offender, you won't be the first to go. Besides, ballistics has not even started on the second Carcano. I think it was Cloudot or the Jackal, whatever you would like to call him, who shot Brennan and I think he also shot Gray. If the bullets match, we have part of the puzzle," Stokes observed.

"Brennan admitted he shot your Israeli man because he thought he was a tout, working for another faction of the IRA. Curran knew about Brennan and was ready to talk, so that was why Brennan killed him," Lanigan said.

"Brennan was working with those who wanted the bomb to go off to preempt the Sunningdale agreement and accelerate the battle," Stokes proposed.

"Could be. There were Provos mad enough to work with the UVF," Lanigan agreed.

"But we don't know if he killed Gray and who killed Dussault. All we know is a Carcano killed Gray and a Browning killed Dussault." A thought occurred to Stokes. "What kind of gun does O'Neill have?" he asked Lanigan.

"I think it was a Browning as well. We didn't check it since we didn't know he had it until later when he fumbled it to the floor, real or not. He wasn't quick to offer it to us either. We need to get it. The investigation is still on in Dussault's killing and I think they put Corrigan on it. You know, 'Wrong Way'," he said, alluding to the pilot who flew the wrong way and crossed the Atlantic instead of the US. "He gets ragged enough for the name, but he is a good man and will listen to reason. I will give him a call to get the gun into evidence. Ballistics will look at it to make sure. We have plenty of bullets to work with, sure we do," Lanigan said, heartened by the search for answers, at least by proxy.

"Well, we still don't know where the real Cloudot is. I might find him on my table, sooner or later," Stokes said. "Any word on the fugitive Jackal?"

"No, not from our side, although who knows anything around here that you can trust," Lanigan replied.

"Well, I will let you know if I hear anything," Stokes promised. "Good luck," he said.

"You as well, Professor," Lanigan said and hung up.

If Cloudot and Brennan and O'Connor didn't shoot Dussault, who did? Lanigan asked himself. It could have been anyone at the party who knew how to get to the Guest House without being seen, that is, anyone who knew the way through the tunnel. He didn't even think of the staff and should have thought of that first. He picked up the phone and called Corrigan, explained the situation and urged him to question O'Neill's staff as well as reading the guests' statements to make sure they rang true. He offered to read through them to help since he was on desk duty anyway.

Stokes couldn't help but think of the same questions but hoped his involvement would just be in testimony at the inquests and trials, if any. He still had to get over to the Gresham to discuss whatever important issues Smyth-Jones had to discuss. He was still disturbed by the last meeting with him, getting the most significant and troubling mysteries in his life answered as a cold matter of fact. Was it his military reserve, his British reticence, or Her Majesty's Secret Service he resented the most? Nonetheless, he would meet him and receive whatever other bits of information he could use for closure, both for his past and this strange set of cases. Before he left, however, he decided to interrogate Samantha again. Perhaps she might have a clue as to what had happened at O'Neill's.

Samantha was still toiling away at papers while she had the chance since there had not been any new autopsies to perform. As in the weeks immediately after the bombing, Dublin was unusually quiet and all the homicides were laying low, waiting until it was safe to come out. She looked up and was surprised by Stokes who had quietly walked in unannounced.

"Oh, you startled me, Professor," she said, the blood rising in her face. He had absent-mindedly forgotten his manners.

"Sorry, Dr. Monaghan," he responded respectfully, addressing her in a manner she associated with a professional discussion.

"I have a few questions for you about the Dussault murder. I am not quite sure how we should keep the report in perspective since I am sure that as a witness and as an Expert Witness at the same time, you may be asked to consider the circumstances of the killing," he said.

Samantha had dreaded this moment since she did not have any more of an idea of what had happened than he did, save for the cryptic letter from Rami, which she did not want to discuss. She was still recovering from the Professor's strong disapproval of her spying adventures, especially after the warehouse incident which nearly cost both their lives.

"Did you see anyone in the Guest House when you ran out the door to see what was happening?" he asked.

"No. There was no one there but me."

"Did you notice any lights on besides those in your rooms?"

"The lights to the tunnel were off when I came out and they were on when I went back in, but I don't know if they were turned on before or after the shooting since I was outside."

"How many of the house staff had access to the Guest House?"

"I don't know. I know I was given keys so I could have access to the front door and the tunnel. I locked my door, I can recall, when I left the room for the party, but I'm not sure if the tunnel door was locked when I went back in," she answered, her eyes closed to better recall.

"So, someone may have gone through the tunnel and out the front Guest House door?"

"Yes, it is possible, and I would not have seen them, hiding in the bushes after I heard the first shots."

"And the first shots you heard were not near you?"

"No, they were from the distance near the gates. It was only after I heard the shots behind me that got Dussault."

"That's why your autopsy report concluded he was shot in the back."

"Yes, it did," she said, this time, looking directly at him, waiting for an answer as to why he had asked her to change the report and then change it back again.

"I apologize for using you, or I should say, your erroneous report as a decoy, but I set up a false trail for the guilty parties to follow and it worked. I suspected there were many leaks in this department that led right up to the former Minister and had him believing one of his henchmen had been the killer. This was enough for him to mistrust him to carry out the transfer of the money to our false Cloudot, the Jackal, and have to do it himself. The Jackal, on the other hand, had misled us into thinking he was one of, as the Americans like to say, "the good guys," so he could keep an eye on all the police goings-on without suspicion.

This whole thing was part of a broader plan to subvert the government and get Mr. O'Neill to power so he could give strength to the IRA both in and out of the government and reunite the whole of Ireland by any means he thought necessary. He failed since the Jackal was obviously seeking the money for the arms for his own reasons. I think the Jackal killed Gray because he was a talkative, indiscreet gadabout and shot Brennan as the homicidal maniac he was. Brennan probably did kill Solomon ben David.

I have discussed this with Detective Lanigan, and he considers this to be the case as well, but we still don't know who killed Dussault. O'Neill is still free, and the Jackal is at large. I say this as a warning since there are many enemies, known and unknown, among us and you must keep this in strictest confidence since all has not been uncovered. You understand, don't you?" Stokes asked. He wanted to make sure she understood she was in danger, which he thought she failed to appreciate previously.

"Of course, I do," she answered, "and I appreciate your fears, but I am out of this spy business," she said with conviction, but she was still wondering about Dussault's killing and Rami's cryptic letter, which she did not discuss with the Professor. She was afraid he might link Rami and Dussault's killing.

"Fine, then. If we are clear, let's work on the backlog of paperwork while we have the chance. I will prepare for testimony at the inquests," he said, making sure she knew the regular work could not be delayed any longer.

Working through the rest of the afternoon, he prepared his notes carefully with conclusions based on the facts. He did not intimate any conspiracies. He kept to his Pathology work, leaving spaces to be completed when final toxicology and ballistics reports were received. He looked at his clock and realized he needed to meet Smyth-Jones. He peeked into Samantha's office, saw her busy at work, did not bother to say good night, but bid his secretary a good evening.

It was a short walk to the Gresham, and it was a fair day with the late twilight of summer still some time away. He didn't mind the bustle of the traffic or the people crowding the streets since it was always good to get out of the office for a breath of air. He expected he would be getting some report about the Jackal that was only available to British intelligence. He was aware of the confidentiality required, but he resented the inability to share the knowledge with those who really needed to know since the British and Irish governments could not be seen cooperating in these tense times. But were they? He was too low on the totem to know, and it was just as well he didn't, he thought to himself.

He walked into the lounge of the Gresham and there was Smyth-Jones nursing a drink near the window, careless of the possibility he was being watched, more interested in watching. Smyth-Jones greeted Stokes warmly. The waiter promptly arrived.

"What are you having?" asked Stokes.

"Pimm's. Just in the mood for something light," he smiled.

"I'll have the same," Stokes said to the waiter, who nodded and walked off efficiently but courteously. Stokes hoped that "something light" was not in preparation for more bad news.

"Sorry about the other day, old boy. I left you in quite a state since I had assumed your police friends would have given you the tragic information earlier. But communication with the Irish government is pretty difficult these days, as you are well aware," he paused.

"I will be leaving this evening for London. We have been following the Jackal since his escape in the speedboat to get to the trail of the other smugglers. We plan on setting a trap in Antwerp and capture him and his ring. He may be there already for all we know, but by the time I arrive in London, it should all be over, and this terrible man and his accomplices will be rounded up and transferred to Brussels for trial."

"How can you be so sure?" Stokes asked.

"Between the intelligence we received from our people in Antwerp who have infiltrated the IRA, and help, after inquiries and negotiations, from your former minister O'Neill, we know the time and location of the cargo. I am letting you know so you can get some closure on this whole affair," he said quietly, then paused as the waiter placed Stokes' drink in front of him, the wedge of lime precariously dangling on the edge of the glass as it was placed down.

Stokes dropped the lime in the glass, unable to say a word. The bastard (he couldn't help to think the word for O'Neill) had made a deal, he thought to himself. Instead of being an accessory to the crime and possibly the murders, O'Neill had turned it around and would be a hero. Closure indeed. He took a deep drink and thought this drink was too sweet and too weak for what he had just heard.

"Are you sure you will have him?" Stokes asked.

"Nothing of this kind is ever certain, but it should stop Qadaffi in his tracks. He is unlikely to trade arms with the IRA for some time. O'Neill will behave himself, I would think, and we will have gotten one of the most elusive and dangerous terrorists in Europe, so I think this will go well, or else I would not be telling you," Smyth-Jones said, sipping another bit of his drink.

"Well, thanks for the intelligence. I guess I will have to tread carefully since O'Neill will be using this for anything he can," Stokes replied, not hiding his disappointment.

"Not to worry, as the Irish say. We, the Irish and the British governments, have enough on him that he will be forced to stay on his best behavior, at our discretion," he smiled.

"Well, I must go," Smyth-Jones said, standing abruptly, slightly unbalanced, but quickly recovering. "I will drop you a line, but you will probably read it in the papers before I send it. Sorry again, about the news and its delivery, now on two counts. You must come up to London some time or we could arrange a fishing trip soon, perhaps Scotland or in the South here," he said. He did not wait for an answer but just said goodbye, shaking his right hand and covering it with his left, warmly, firmly, looked him in the eye with what Stokes thought might actually be sincerity, then left.

Stokes sat at the booth and sipped his drink and watched as Smyth-Jones disappeared into the crowd so effortlessly and inconspicuously, despite his limp, that he could not help but admire his stealth. He knew he was more than just a functionary in the British Foreign Service and his casual demeanor belied more knowledge and power than he let on. He trusted Stokes' discretion enough to give him information that would not be easily obtained and would be readily denied were it not him being the recipient. He was grateful for the intelligence and forgave him his bluntness previously—there was no easy way to have recounted the circumstances. The Pimm's grew on him, and he looked up the street and recalled he was close enough to two cinemas to conveniently choose at least one. The Peter Sellers film was at the Ambassador, the converted auditorium of the Rotunda, the same obstetrics hospital he had clerked in as a student, so he made his way there. He needed the comedy, not the obstetrics.

Chapter Forty-Four

Samantha finished her paperwork, as much as she could tolerate, and went home. She was pleased with the explanation the Professor had given her and it made her feel less sensitive since the "correction" he had made on her report was totally of his making and not a criticism of her work. That he took the time to confide his plan with her made her think he had forgiven her confession. She hoped not to be part of any more extra-curricular adventures, but she was curious about Rami's letter and who killed Dussault. Someone had taken the opportunity for the assassination in all the confusion. It had to be someone close by that night, but she promised herself she would leave it to the professionals.

As she opened the door of the house, she noticed a motorbike parked in the alley. She did not recall any of the residents of the house or the neighbors rode a motorbike. Still, she went in without hesitation and opened her door and was startled to see Rami sitting in a chair, smiling.

"Didn't your mother teach you it is impolite to visit without notice?" she said, irritated. He had broken into her house, more effortlessly than any thief.

"My mother doesn't know I am here," he still smiled.

"Your mother probably doesn't know what you have been up to either," she paused. "Why are you here?" she asked.

"I am leaving, and I wanted to say goodbye. You got my note?" he asked.

"Yes, I did, and that didn't help at all. Did you kill Dussault?"

"No, I didn't. He was dead just before I got there. I heard the gunshots and thought you were in danger. When I got to the Guest House, I could see through the window that he was dead and you were hiding in the bushes, so I got on the motorbike and left. Just as well, since the police began shooting at me," he explained.

"Why were you there?" she asked.

"To save you. I was afraid the Jackal would kill you as well," he said.

"Why me?"

"Because you knew too much. He wanted to kill your professor as well but did not get the chance. I was going to stop him, but he was busy trying to kill Brennan to protect O'Neill and get his money. Then he had to leave since the police were getting too close. He fooled your professor and all the police and came back for the money. We knew he would, but we couldn't touch him because the British were watching him all the time. They didn't know we were here, and we couldn't expose ourselves."

Samantha wanted to believe him but could not accept how complicated all this was. She did not want any more of this. She was angry he had lured her into this web of deceit and danger, yet she was grateful he had been looking out for her.

"You are leaving?" she asked.

"Yes, I have another assignment. That is why I said your job was done. I don't want you to be in danger anymore," he said, cautiously approaching.

"Why should I believe you? You are a spy."

"Believe me. It helped that you helped. Us and your country. Thank you. I have to leave, but I wanted you to understand what happened and why. I will be back soon. I promise. I love you," he said, getting closer to her.

She did not move. He kissed her.

"Goodbye then, and take care," she said kissing him back.

No sooner had they finished a long embrace and kiss, than he had gone for the door and was out, without a look back. She stood there for a moment, was tempted to run out, but stopped, hearing his motorbike start and take off.

Chapter Forty-Five

As Stokes left the cinema, having thoroughly enjoyed the distraction, he was met by a woman in the lobby. He was not sure they had ever met, but she looked strangely familiar. She had no compunction in speaking to him and was quite animated, again in a strangely familiar way.

"Excuse me, Professor Stokes, but allow me to introduce myself," she said, almost blushing herself, unused to being so forward. "I am Judith Monaghan, Samantha's mother," she said, extending her hand.

"Oh, this is a pleasant surprise," he said, returning her smile. He looked again and the familiarity was now clear. "Your daughter is a fine doctor and an apt pupil, although I don't tell her often since she is already aware of my confidence in her. It is a pleasure meeting you. I hope you enjoyed the film. I thought it was quite amusing," he said, happy to speak about anything other than work, even if it was a comedy about World War II.

"Yes, it was quite amusing. Mr. Sellers is quite the talented fellow. I really had to say how sorry I was my daughter ruined your daughter's beautiful dress. It was quite kind of you to have loaned it to her, but she asked me to help after she described the awful circumstances. I tried but failed to remove the blood; we simply had to throw it away."

"It was certainly in the line of duty, and we can't dress for such emergencies, although she looked the elegant medic. Do not think a second thought of it, Mrs. Monaghan. I was happy she got some use out of it," he said graciously, not having thought of the dress since he gave it to Samantha.

"Well, I still feel guilty about it. I would love to have you over for dinner with Samantha, not just for that, but just to express my gratitude for how you have taken her under your wing," she smiled.

"Well, it would be a pleasure," he smiled, blushing slightly. It had been a long time since an attractive woman had invited him anywhere.

"I will let Samantha know. I'm sure she will be embarrassed I asked, but she will get over it and it would be my pleasure to say thank you in some real way," she said.

"Well, I must be off," Stokes said, still pleasantly surprised and suddenly self-conscious. He really had nowhere else to go but home, but did not want to be forward, although he was pleased with the encounter and the invitation.

"Of course, of course, and forgive me for accosting you, but I couldn't miss the opportunity. I've seen you in the Trinity Library, but you are so focused on your studies, Irish medical history, I did not want to disturb you."

"The history of Ireland is one of my hobbies. I wasn't aware you had noticed. Looking through old musty books is such a solitary endeavor. I would appreciate a quiet chat as a break."

"I will say hello the next time you pop in. Again, thank you for your help," she said, extending her hand.

"My pleasure," he said with a handshake.

"Goodbye, then," and she smiled and turned to the exit. It was a clear evening and still warm and she walked through the line of people waiting for the next performance. Stokes watched as she left, feeling good for once in the past few weeks.

Chapter Forty-Six

"You're not out of the woods yet, Boyo, but here is your badge and you can resume your investigations," the Chief Superintendent said to Lanigan. Lanigan understood the warning—there were still enough people around who did not like his skirting the periphery of other investigations. Being one of the Chief's favorites was not always the enviable position it seemed. There was still confusion about who killed Dussault. Lanigan would have to press ballistics again, always a tenuous task since the Chief technician was such a Prima Donna. He would also have to question O'Neill again, Stokes and Monaghan as well, as a formality, but in due time.

Since O'Neill had admitted he had planned on trading the sack of money for arms, he was on notice that his political power was at an end. There were enough people he influenced who were more than happy to keep their mouths shut and just do what they had to do to survive. All the threatened retaliations and usurpations O'Neill promised had vanished. Dermot Murphy, the coroner, relieved and continued his self-promoting behavior and Stokes just persevered, happy he had not been elevated as his acting replacement. Stokes sighed with relief as well when he heard it from the relieved Murphy, who again thanked him for his support. This all meant the inquests after the completion of the investigations would come soon. Stokes returned to completing his reports.

Samantha walked into the office the next morning and was not sure she wanted to tell the Professor about Rami's visit, having sworn not to be involved in spying anymore, but she wanted to let him know it was not him that killed Dussault, and he was gone, as far as she knew. Instead, Stokes walked into her office, smiling, and said he had met her mother last night. Samantha was shocked. It was not like her mother to go introducing herself to strangers, although she had mentioned him before, and she had seen his pictures in the paper and in interviews on the television when he was asked to comment on a notorious death.

"That was rather forward of her," she said.

"Not at all. She was very pleasant and wanted to thank me for overseeing your work and helping you, as well as giving you the dress, which she apologized for not having cleaned enough. She offered to repay me, but I never expected it back, you know, and, under the circumstances, it was perfectly understandable that it was ruined. You weren't exactly gowned for surgery, were you?" he smiled.

"So, what has she done?" Samantha asked.

"I have been invited to dinner, which I accepted."

"I will have a word with her."

"Yes, you will, so we can arrange the date and time," Stokes responded.

"Bollocks," Samantha said under her breath. "All right, then, I will let you know," Samantha responded, returning a smile, resigned to the event, pleased at least the Professor was not put out and might even be amenable. She did not tell the Professor about Rami.

"Splendid. We will need to polish those reports for the inquests. I will call Lanigan to see if he can help clarify some issues. I hope we don't have to give any more testimony," he said, leaving her office.

Samantha hoped she would not have to swear under oath since if they asked her any questions about Dussault, she might have to reveal more than she would like. But she was reminded that in a deposition or even an inquiry, all she needed to do was answer the questions and leave it up to Stokes to give expert opinion, or at least she hoped so. Besides, she didn't know who shot him either since Rami had sworn to her it wasn't him.

Chapter Forty-Seven

Stokes' phone rang just as he was coming in early to his office. "I'm back," Lanigan said, sounding like an inmate who had gotten a reprieve. "We need to sort out who killed Dussault."

Stokes noted the "we," but did not correct Lanigan.

"It might come to the ballistics."

"I suppose it will. We have the preliminaries, and it was a Browning, like the police model."

"Didn't you say O'Neill had a Browning?" asked Stokes.

"Yes, he did, and we have it in evidence, prints and all. O'Neill's prints were on the gun, besides those of Cloudot, but someone else had prints on the gun, on the butt and trigger. O'Neill wanted the gun back, made a big stink he needed to defend himself, fat lot of good it did him the last time he pulled it out," Lanigan sniffed. "We will have to drag him in again, but he will have his solicitor with him this time, I expect."

"Nevertheless, he has plenty of witnesses he was being shot at himself when Dussault was shot,"

"He did indeed. I hope I don't have to pull everyone from the bloody party again, but from the looks of it, that will be the job."

"Any of his staff have any access to the gun?"

"I suppose anyone could. We'll get the fingerprints of all the staff. Thanks, Professor, I'll get back to you on that."

Lanigan had Hayes promptly go down to the Mansion and fingerprint each one of the staff and warned them they might need to be brought in for further questioning. Maria, the new maid was not at the Estate, the chief butler told them.

"She took a few days off; she was so distressed by all the happenings. She said she was going to visit her family in Belgium," he said.

"And did you not think that was a wee bit unusual to do after we warned them all not to leave the area?" Hayes remarked.

"We all have been stressed with this matter. Sure, I'd like a break myself with all the goings-on, but O'Neill would fire me, I have no doubt," the butler said.

"Do you have the address of her family?" Hayes asked.

"Yes, I do. Just outside of Antwerp, I think," and he showed him the address from her employee file.

"Give it here," Hayes said.

"This is personal information."

"So is murder. It says she was just employed a month ago."

"Yes, that's right. She came with a lot of references and had been working for one of Dussault's associates in Belgium."

"Do you have a Xerox machine here?" Hayes asked.

"Yes, we do. It is in Minister O'Neill's study," the butler answered, implying its restricted nature, but pointing the way.

"Well, I'm sure he won't mind since this would be helping inquiries," Hayes said, opening the door to the study.

As Hayes walked to the Xerox machine, a large box that looked more like a small refrigerator incongruously placed in his 18th century "study" lined with leather-bound books and old paintings, he noticed the drawer next to the Brian Boru painting was slightly ajar. He opened it to see why it was stuck and there was a cloth that had been trapped at the opening, like a cover one would use to wrap a precious instrument, and next to it was an open box of cartridges of the caliber that would fit a Browning pistol.

"Did we give O'Neill's pistol back to him yet?" Hayes asked the butler.

"No, they said they were still examining it which has Minister O'Neill upset since he has nothing to defend himself but an old shotgun he uses for hunting," the butler said.

Hayes was well aware it was still in ballistics, but this confirmed the butler's knowledge of his artillery, not that he was a suspect he had been observed by eyewitnesses to be in the parlor at the time of the shooting.

"Do you recall where this Maria was during the shooting?" Hayes asked the butler.

"She was back and forth between the kitchen and the parlor most of the evening, serving the guests," the butler recalled. "She did a decent job, even if she seemed a bit bothered," he added.

"Bothered? How so?" Hayes asked.

"Well, she was not happy to have to serve Mr. Dussault. She may have had some recommendations from his associates, but she certainly did not like him and said as much to me and the other staff, called him a monster, she did," the butler said.

"But she got the recommendations from his associates in Belgium. That is strange, isn't it?" Hayes asked.

"Yes, it was, especially since she talked about Dussault as a great businessman and benefactor when she had the interview."

"Did you interview her for the job?"

"Me and the Minister, but he did not spend long speaking to her since he usually takes my word —I have to work with the staff and judge how they will fit in."

"Did you check on the references?" Hayes asked, waving the copies he had made on the Xerox.

"No, I didn't. I left that up to the Minister. He was busy at the time, and I assume he did check up on her after he hired her," he said.

"He hired her on the spot?" Hayes asked, surprised.

"She seemed good enough and she was pleasant enough, so why not?" the butler answered.

"Did she have access to the study?"

"Yes, she did, but she didn't have any keys for the locked drawers or any way to get into the safe."

"How about you?"

"Yes, but I kept them on meself and no one touched them."

"All right, then," Hayes answered, trying to calm him down. "I'm not accusing you; I just want to know about this disappeared Maria."

"I guess you do, especially if she doesn't come back like she said she would."

"Exactly. By the way, where are the servant's quarters? I'll give her room a look around," Hayes asked.

The butler led him down the hallway to another door behind the steps where there was a small passage that opened to a row of rooms, all locked. The butler opened the sleeping room that was dark but had a small window that looked onto the grounds near the stables. At least there was part of the day there might be light in here, thought Hayes, who was claustrophobic and uncomfortable here, but gritted his teeth and looked around carefully despite the distraction. A dresser, bed, and a small table with a washbasin on it barely fit in the room. There was a bar overhead across a small alcove, with empty hangers save for a maid's uniform on one. The staff shared the bathroom down the hall. Hayes opened the drawers and there was nothing in them but a receipt for a one-way ticket to London, not Antwerp.

"Didn't she say she was going to Antwerp?" Hayes asked.

"Yes, she did," the butler answered.

Hayes had looked at her references and saw none from London. Her family was listed as being from Antwerp.

"Did the first lot of detectives warn her not to leave the country?" Hayes asked.

"Yes, they did. They lined the whole staff up and made the announcement after they did their questioning. Everyone was upset then, feeling like they were going to be accused of something. I had to spend a while calming them down and pointing out none of them had been arrested. Maria did not seem worried, and I guessed she had nothing to hide, don't you know."

Hayes walked out of the room and took a deep breath, relieved at being in a more open space, even if it was a dark hallway. He still had seen enough and would report to Lanigan.

"Let me know if she does come back. Call me at this number," Hayes said, giving him his card and left.

"Scarpered, has she?" Lanigan asked Hayes, already knowing the answer. Now this Maria, or whoever she was, was the prime suspect for the murder of Dussault. It was all the more irritating since the chaos of the investigation had to deal with several deaths with different guns at the same time. Lanigan picked up the phone, annoyed it was ringing yet again, but pleased it was forensics.

"Did you get the ballistics on O'Neill's gun?" He waited for the negative since that's what he expected. "How about the Garda gun?" he asked. "Well, thanks for that little bit of help. I know I'm pressing you, but O'Neill's gun may have been used by Dussault's killer, yeah, the Belgian, and I think the maid is the prime suspect since she has disappeared. No, not O'Neill. You checked all the prints were taken before you tested O'Neill's gun, right? Good man, you are. All the best. Let me know as soon as you have the answers, thanks. I owe you a pint," smiled Lanigan as he hung up.

"See, all you have to do is be nice to the bastard," Lanigan smiled at Hayes. "So, London, you say? Well, that's a lost cause. Call her references right now and try her relatives too. I'll bet they never heard of her," Lanigan ordered Hayes.

"Good man you are for hunting this down," he congratulated Hayes. "I wish we had been quicker, but not to worry. We have enough on everyone else," Lanigan smiled.

Chapter Forty-Eight

The promise of the pint must have expedited the discovery, but the prints on O'Neill's gun identified one set as Cloudot, the other O'Neill's, and another set unknown. The teletype from France confirmed the "Cloudot" prints were those of Abn Awaa, the Jackal. Lanigan got his story from a Garda agent he could trust in G2.

What Lanigan didn't know was British SAS commandos were ready at the loading docks at Antwerp. MI6 had not bothered to discuss with Belgian or French police their intentions to kill or capture the Jackal. They were more interested in him than they were in the IRA men who would be receiving the arms. They were easily convinced to surrender with the promise they would be turned over to the Irish police. The British had tracked the smugglers as soon as their agent had given them the warning after the phone call at O'Neill's house. The Royal Navy had patiently tracked the Jackal's tedious passage from the little boat he escaped on at the Mansion to the rendezvous with the Irish trawler which was destined for Antwerp. The trawler had not deviated from its specified plan—there was a load of fresh cod to be left on the docks in exchange for the fresh guns.

The night was moonless. The commandos hid among the rows and rows of shipping containers with the security lights fixed on the entrances and the docks. The night watchmen were making their scheduled rounds, as fixed as the lights, not noticing the quiet movements of the commandos. The shipping container of Czech "farm equipment," the AK-47s and RPG-7s and various handguns and ammunition and explosives, destined for Cork was identified. The hired longshoremen waited along the dock. They were discreet, getting night shift pay and a "bonus" promised by the mix of surly and intimidating IRA and PLO men.

The trawler arrived on time and docked with ease, routinely and inconspicuously. The fish was unloaded by the same dockworkers who were to load the other cargo. The IRA and PLO observed, unarmed but cautious. The captain and his first mate discussed the cargo with customs who reviewed the papers and made a careful count of the crates. Nothing was unusual. The Jackal stood on the deck, watching the process, bored by procedure but calmed by the routine. He counted the number of men watching the process and recognized some of the PLO operatives but did not acknowledge them nor they him. Routine. The IRA men were a bit more nervous, stuck in a foreign port with little excuse for being there. They did not trust the PLO men or the longshoremen and felt naked without their guns. They huddled together and eyed the proceedings, ignorant of the process, so they were even more distrustful.

"I wish they would just get on with it," one blurted out, a tall, thin, fortyish man chain-smoking, his butts piled on the ground.

"Tell me about it," another shorter older man agreed, staring at the Palestinians, not liking their demeanor and swagger. He got the feeling they would just as soon strap a bomb on themselves and walk into a pub as shake your hand, he thought, but did not say. He stared at them, and they stared back.

After the cod had been unloaded and stacked on lorries for delivery to the fish market, the Jackal stepped off the boat, carrying a duffel bag. The PLO men moved towards him to discuss the logistics and occasionally glanced at the IRA men standing aside near the crates that held their "equipment." They had not lost sight of those crates since they had been delivered during the day. They were to board as soon as the crates were transferred on. The Jackal nodded to the Irishmen and motioned for them to begin the loading with the help of the longshoremen.

At that signal, the SAS emerged from their hiding places, surrounding the PLO and the IRA men. There was no place to go, and it was clear the SAS had more guns and men. The smugglers were ordered to put their hands up. They looked to the Jackal for guidance, but he simply nodded and put his hands up as well. The longshoremen put their hands up and immediately proclaimed their nationality and innocence in

Flemish, one so frightened he collapsed, crying for mercy. He was nearly shot by a hypervigilant member of the SAS squad, but the commander sensed it and ordered him to stand down. The Irishmen saw it as part of the game and surrendered without resistance, but one cursed at the Palestinians, "Bloody Arab scum can't be trusted," prepared to fight them with his bare hands.

"That will be enough of that," the Commander shouted. "You are all under arrest by authority of the British Crown. I can shoot you all now or you can all bloody well shut up," he ordered. No more noise was made. No one was hurt. The Commander ordered some of the team to go aboard and search for any more stragglers and hidden guns. The captain of the trawler and the crew were presented to the Belgian police who had arrived moments after the capture. There was no more to be said at the docks. It would be days before the newspapers would announce the capture of the Jackal, the IRA and the PLO smugglers, and the guns. There was £50,000 in the duffel bag, but the money was not discussed except at the trial and even then, it was not all accounted for from the Northern Aid money O'Neill claimed had been stolen.

Chapter Forty-Nine

The other set of prints on the gun could not be identified immediately. Lanigan had to ask forensics if they had any identification of the prints from other, non-criminal sources. That was asking a lot and he had nowhere to look, but the maid who had disappeared had to have a passport and a work visa and may have had fingerprints. A check with the immigration office indicated she was a Belgian. He called the Belgian embassy. They had no more information than the immigration office. They identified her stated address as a vacant storefront.

"By the way," Lanigan asked, "do you know Dussault?"

"Of course, we handled his case, and he was well known to the police as a collaborator with the Nazis. He was lucky to have escaped extradition, but he did not escape his death penalty," she added, unsympathetically, having read about his killing in the paper. "Do you think she did it?"

"Now that you're asking, would you be able to help me with some inquiries?"

"If I can. I will call our police attaché who deals with murders outside the country, and he might be able to speak with you. I know he would be interested in the circumstances and would cooperate. If she was the murderer, she is guilty of a crime as a Belgian citizen, even if it was morally justified," she said, following the rules and protocols as a dutiful representative of her country.

"I will call him to let him know who you are, so he does not ignore this. His name is George Martel, and he is the chief murder investigator in the foreign office." She gave Lanigan the number for future reference.

Lanigan got the call from Martel the next day. He confirmed the woman known as Maria was Esther Steinberg and she had traveled under a Belgian passport that was forged. It was of excellent quality and might have been issued by a government. She did not have a record of any crimes in Belgium and under her Jewish name, she had traveled and lived in Israel for at least ten years, working as a clerk. She had also served in the Israeli army. She had no other relatives who were living. That was all they knew.

Lanigan wondered if she knew the escaped butchers, but it would be hard to make the association without the help of the Israeli government. They were not likely to give up their secrets. Her parents were deceased, killed in the war.

"Killed in the war, you say?" Lanigan repeated.

"Yes, they were deported to a concentration camp. The daughter was hidden by some good Christians, brave souls," said Martel. The information was in her dossier. She claimed dual citizenship in Israel. "Who could blame her," Martel said sympathetically.

Chapter Fifty

Stokes received another letter from his "vicar friend" in Israel. It had the same address as previously and informed him his friend would be staying in Jerusalem for at least a year with a new post as a representative of the C of E, any communications to be addressed to his business address. It also had a telephone number where he could be reached if that extravagance was necessary. His friend said he was awaiting the permanent return of an assistant via London who had just been to Ireland. She had found her trip most fulfilling. She had renewed an old acquaintance and had closure on some old issues while there. He closed the correspondence by wishing Stokes well and hoped to see him again, perhaps during the holidays.

Stokes accepted the letter as confirmation that an Israeli had been responsible for Dussault's death, and it would be dealt with. He resolved to forget this whole affair and move on, leaving it up to the politicians and police to sort out any more details. He now knew who had killed his wife and daughter—two of them were dead and one was on the run. O'Neill the architect of these atrocities and probably many more, he concluded, would eventually stand trial and be disgraced, he hoped. He had a quiet tea and read a bit and went to bed.

Stokes went back to the office the next day with a clear head and lighter heart. He was glad there was a resolution and the relative calm of his job had returned. He walked into Samantha's office. She was busy plowing through the mounds of paperwork It looked like she had made a substantial dent.

"It looks like you have been slogging through, congratulations," he said smiling.

"Yes, Professor, I can see around the pile now and I hope not to have to stand up to see the door soon," she smiled back. "By the way, fair warning, you will be getting an invitation to dinner from my mother. You can always say you are busy or indisposed. I would be happy to back you up, if you so choose," she said, standing so she did not have to crane her neck or lean past the papers to speak to him.

"Not at all. It would be a pleasure. After all, she meant it as an expression of gratitude, and one should accept gratitude gracefully. Besides, she seems a delightful woman, like her daughter," he smiled again. Samantha blushed.

That evening, Samantha noticed the motorcycle in the alley again. She was not surprised to see Rami sitting on her chair in her bedsitter, smiling, as she opened the door.

"I hope you're not going to make a habit of this," slightly irritated her privacy had been invaded again, but then she smiled, since she understood he could not afford to be identified with her or her, perhaps, with him.

"No. I really did mean to go the last time, but there was a detail we had to handle. I will be returning to London tomorrow."

"Am I the detail?"

"No, but it gives me the chance to explain something."

"Go on."

"It is about this Dussault killing. It was not authorized by Mossad. If I had known, I would have stopped it, but it was too late by the time I arrived. At least I found you were safe," he paused. "This person who called herself Maria had made it her mission to avenge the death of her parents. If it had not been for Dussault, they might have survived the war—he turned them in and got a reward for each Jew who was rounded up. Many good Belgians hid Jews and saved their lives. This bastard would do anything for money and would collaborate with anyone who would pay. He deserved what he got, but it was not Mossad who told her to do this. She planned this on her own. We are not a terrorist organization; we just want to defend our country."

"Do you know where she is?"

"She was still here. We found her in a Mossad safe house. She surrendered without a fight. She will go on trial in Israel for murder. We have laws. She was a good agent, but she broke the law." He was silent and did not expect Samantha to say anything.

"You said you were leaving tomorrow," Samantha said.

"Only if you don't want me to stay," he said.

"Are you going to need a key or is this it?" she smiled.

"This is it for a while," he said, getting close to her.

He stayed the night.

Dinner with Mrs. Monaghan and Samantha went well, as far as Stokes was concerned. She was a kind and intelligent woman and despite some motherly chiding of Samantha on some of her more difficult traits, like her stubbornness, they hit it off well enough. Samantha ignored her mother's comments and was pleased to see the two of them got on well, though she did not hope for any more than a casual relationship for them. She also did not expect any favoritism. She would keep her mouth shut about what she knew and perhaps in time she might tell her mother about Rami, but she would keep her secrets from the Professor since they had only gotten her in trouble. Stokes did not tell her about the letters from the "vicar."

Epilogue

O'Neill's trial was brief but well reported. They could not convict him because he was portrayed as a victim of a robbery and assassination attempts. His connections to his dead acquaintances were never clarified since there was no one alive to testify. Anyone else associated was either wanted or unknown. No one questioned his income or finances or how he maintained his estate since it was not relevant to the trial. He was left powerless and on the backbench for a few years, but regained his influence, gradually with favors and secrets, and was elected as Taoiseach a few years after. He was gracious enough to not seek revenge against his opponents since he could afford to.

About the Author

Max Burger is a retired Family Physician, a graduate of the Royal College of Surgeons in Ireland. He has published personal interest stories in *Medical Economics, JAMA,* and *AMA News.* He has completed *My Father's Father, a Holocaust Family Saga,* the first chapter published in *Embark* magazine.

VISIT OUR WEBSITE
FOR THE FULL INVENTORY
OF QUALITY BOOKS:
http://www.roguephoenixpress.com

Rogue Phoenix Press

Representing Excellence in Publishing

Quality trade paperbacks and downloads

in multiple formats,

in genres ranging from historical to contemporary romance, mystery and science fiction.

Visit the website then bookmark it.

We add new titles each month!

www.ingramcontent.com/pod-product-compliance
Lightning Source LLC
Chambersburg PA
CBHW061941170626
46813CB00006B/2488